From being on their c
stooge back to base, they
sedately and at right an
bomber and—too late i...
incoming fire from an attacking British Spitfire. The
control yoke in Jane's hands jerked and twitched at the
same moment they both felt cannon shells striking the
tail of the Anson.

"Bloody hell!" they both cried at the same time,
with Penny making a wild grab at the yoke in an
attempt to help Jane control the damaged plane.

"Look out!" Jane cried, jerking the column to the
right, having spotted the bomber's upper gunner firing
back.

Whether he was aiming at the Spitfire or
deliberately at them didn't matter. What mattered was
that they were hit, this time by enemy fire. Some of the
gunner's fire went through the side of the cockpit, and
other bullets smashed into the instrument panel. At first,
it didn't appear to be as serious as what they'd already
suffered, but then Jane's attention was drawn to the
smoke beginning to pour from the left engine, and the
control yoke gave another, deeper, longer shudder.

"Buggeration! Penny!" Jane yelled. "Give me a
hand." When she got no immediate response, she
looked to her right, and her heart nearly stopped.

Penny was slumped over the control yoke, and Jane
was shocked to the core to see blood pouring from a
wound in her friend's upper arm.

Praise for M. W. Arnold
and the books of the Broken Wings series

"*WILD BLUE YONDER* is a delightful World War II story…a lovely cast of characters…importance of true friendship…very knowledgeable about the ATA, RAF, airplanes and women pilots, and I very much enjoyed finding out more about these special ladies."

~*Christina Courtenay, Best Selling Author*

~*~

"[*A WING AND A PRAYER*] reminded me of the work of prolific and successful author Elaine Everest. A flowing WWII mystery, filled with authentic detail." '

~*Sue Moorcroft, #1 Amazon Best Selling Author*

~*~

"You…feel like you're there. I…loved the friendship of the women…it has a mystery… a bit everything!"

~*Miranda Dickinson, Sunday Times Best Selling Author*

~*~

"Clearly…a lot of research into The Air Transport Auxiliary and this shines through in his writing and helps to make the story that bit more authentic."

~*Ginger Book Geek blog*

~*~

"This story has everything. There's friendship, history, intrigue and romance in an entertaining blend that I thoroughly enjoyed."

~*Linda's Book Bag*

~*~

"I'm delighted to see that this is the first in a series—I'm hooked and already looking forward to my return to …more time with the ladies of the ATA."

~*Being Anne book blog*

I'll Be Home for Christmas

by

M. W. Arnold

Broken Wings, Book 3

I'll Be Home for Christmas

Cover Art by *The Wild Rose Press, Inc.*

The Wild Rose Press, Inc.
PO Box 708
Adams Basin, NY 14410-0708
Visit us at www.thewildrosepress.com

Publishing History
First Edition, 2021
Trade Paperback ISBN 978-1-5092-3878-1
Digital ISBN 978-1-5092-3879-8

Broken Wings, Book 3
Published in the United States of America

Acknowledgements

Here we are with the third book in my Broken Wings series, and I can't believe the time has gone by so quickly since the first. *A Wing and a Prayer* came out in November of 2020!

Christmas in World War Two was a strange affair, somehow more so if you were a stranger to the shores of the United Kingdom. The byword was "austerity"—re-use, don't go overboard, et cetera, not that this was possible, for the most part. I've learned so much about that time of the war during my research for this book, though I don't think my suggestion we have a chicken-wire Christmas tree put up whilst I wrote this book, to create the correct atmosphere, went down too well.

As she did for books one and two, there's my wonderful editor, Nan, to thank. She puts me right when I get things wrong and is always there with words of encouragement. My wonderful covers are designed and brought to life by Wild Rose Press co-founder, vice president, and all around good egg, RJ. Thanks for finding ways to create such memorable covers, boss!

For answering and checking and double-checking everything police procedure wise, a big thank you to Kelvin of Hampshire Police. Keep safe, mate!

As always, the Maidenhead Heritage Center—https://maidenheadheritage.org.uk/—was a tremendous source of both inspiration and information. Take time, if you can, to learn there about some real heroes of the Air Transport Auxiliary. You won't believe some of the stories.

For everyone in the Romantic Novelists Association, you're the best bunch of friends and authors out there, bar none! I can't wait to see you all and say this to your faces.

Finally, to my Lady Wife, who's put up with my absently waving my hands about as I've tried to work out a plot point or the maneuvers of an imaginary plane. You're a constant source of strength to me, and I couldn't do this without you. Love you, Thumper!

Chapter One

November 24, 1943

Betty Palmer stared into the saucepan and frowned. She glanced over at the kitchen table and let out an exaggerated sigh. Doris sat there, leaning forward expectantly, her head propped upon her hands.

"Is it ready for a taste?" she asked, eyes widening in—not anticipation but something more akin to resignation.

Turning back to the stove, Betty leaned over the steaming mess—"mess" would be the word she'd choose to describe the concoction if she had to. Laying the wooden spoon against the rim, she wafted the steam upward and with hesitancy brought on by experience, breathed in. When she didn't immediately want to cough her lungs out, Betty took hold of all her courage and brought the spoon to her lips. Tentatively, she stuck her tongue out and dipped it quickly into the postbox-red mixture. Widening her eyes, she swirled her taster around her mouth and—winced! Her left eye snapped shut and her head tilted to the left, before she spun around, took up a glass of water she had ready on the table, and drank the whole lot down in one go.

Getting up from her seat, Doris Winter patted her friend and landlady upon the back until she managed to catch her breath. "No good, huh?"

Turning off the burner's flame, Betty picked up the saucepan and put it before Doris on the table. "If you feel brave enough, please, go ahead." She offered her the spoon.

"Third time bitten," Doris muttered. Without the same hesitation as her friend, the American dipped the spoon into the pan and, in one smooth movement, brought a large mass of the sauce to her lips. Briefly sniffing the aroma, she nodded to herself and tipped it into her mouth.

Somewhat to Betty's surprise, Doris didn't immediately collapse and demand a glass of water and a doctor, as she had done for her previous attempts. Despite matching Betty's own facial expressions, Doris seemed to be relaxing back into her seat, and her face was gradually returning to normal. Betty reached a hand across the table and placed it over her friend's left one, still finding the feel of the brand-new engagement ring upon it strange.

Doris was rich, having been paid off by her New York family who wanted nothing to do with her after she'd made what they considered an inappropriate marriage. Unfortunately, the union had been short-lived—he'd been killed whilst flying for the Republican cause in the Spanish Civil War. Since coming to the United Kingdom in 1942 and joining the Air Transport Auxiliary, Doris had become fast friends with her housemates and their landlady, Betty. Unexpectedly, the outgoing pilot had become close friends with a local newspaper reporter, and after a few months, they'd surprised everyone by getting engaged. The ring wasn't flashy—Doris even admitted it wasn't gold—but it served its purpose, and she was extremely proud of it, refusing to take it off even when flying.

"Doris," Betty ventured gently, "are you okay? I haven't finally killed you off, have I?"

As if hearing her friend through a haze, Doris slowly opened her eyes and allowed a smile to grace her lips. She gripped the hand laid over hers. "Far from it, Betty. You've nailed it!"

The look upon Betty's face said you could have knocked her over with a feather. Without thinking, she took the spoon from Doris, dipped it into the pan, and took as big a taste as the American had. Immediately, she had to stumble to her feet, fill her glass at the sink, and knock it back as quickly as ever. Gasping, she leant back against the table. "Seriously? You're telling me it's supposed to taste like that?"

Now it had cooled, Doris had begun to dip her finger into the pan. "Perfect cranberry sauce."

"Is it always so...sour?"

Surprisingly, Doris shook her head, then appeared to think about it, and nodded.

"You're not helping."

"Sorry," Doris told her. "Let's put it this way. Traditionally, over the other side of the Pond, we tend to like it much sweeter. Yours, however? I've never tasted the like."

"So why did you ask me to make it?" Betty demanded.

"Well, for a start, I can't cook."

"A fact we're well aware of," said a new voice.

Both their heads turned as the voice's owner, Penny Blake—everyone was still having a hard time thinking of her by her married name of Alsop—strolled in to join them.

3

"Anyone can burn toast!" Doris protested.

"True," Penny agreed. "Though not everyone can boil an egg until it's so hard we're still able to use it to play fetch with Bobby two weeks later!"

"Bobby's not complaining," Doris pointed out.

"I think Ruth's worried he may try and eat it and break a few teeth," Penny informed her, though her lips twitched as she struggled to keep a straight face.

Doris looked around for something she could throw at her friends without causing any real harm. Foiled, she fixed them both with a stare.

"Seriously," Betty asked again, "why did you want some?"

Unable to find the energy to keep up her stare attack, Doris flopped back into her seat and glanced around at her family. "I love you all, but there are some things I really miss about the US. Thanksgiving dinner is one of them."

Betty and Penny both nodded their understanding. Then, seeing Doris was still dipping her finger into the pot, Betty snatched it back. "If you keep eating it," she admonished, "there'll be none left for Thursday! And there's no sugar left to make any more, let alone cranberries."

"Just as well you got it exactly as I like it on the last attempt then, Betty," Doris declared, licking the vestiges of the sauce off her fingertip.

"Somebody had better get me a jar, then," Betty said, lightly smacking Doris's hand as it snaked toward the pan once more.

****

Mary Whitworth-Baines hopped from one foot to the other, unable to keep still. Waiting on a freezing cold train platform had never been something she was fond of. She imagined it could be considered, at a push, romantic, though only if it was at either a big city station or one which had one of those charming cottage-style canteens. Perhaps there was a good movie to be had there, but an open platform, on a dank and dark Tuesday night, wasn't even close. Pulling her woolen coat closer, she wrapped her arms around herself and stamped her feet hard on the cold concrete platform, trying to keep warm. She held up her wrist in an effort to use the moonlight to see the time and was in the process of squinting at her watch when someone tapped her on the shoulder.

"What the hell!" she shouted, nearly jumping out of her skin and turning to find standing behind her the owner of the local newspaper, the *Hamble Gazette*, Ruth Stone. It appeared Mary's reaction to her innocent greeting was enough to freeze Ruth's entire body in place, as her mouth was hanging open and she hadn't lowered her arm. "Um, Ruth?"

The blast of a train whistle startled them both. "Oh, Christ," Ruth began. "I'm so sorry, Mary. I didn't mean to scare you."

Mary linked her arm through one of Ruth's. "Apart from losing a life or two if I were a cat," she told the older woman, "I think I'll forgive you."

Ruth stood on tiptoes as a burst of steam could be seen from just beyond where the rail curved before straightening to come in to the platform. "Is that his train?"

A gust of cold air off the Solent blew in and tried its best to blow them both off their feet. Digging her free hand deeper into her pocket, Mary decided against trying to check the time again. "I really hope so," she said, for the umpteenth time cursing her bad judgment at not wearing her gloves. "Otherwise, I'll let him walk home on his own."

Ruth took Mary's freezing hands between her own two woolen-gloved ones and endeavored to rub some warmth into them. "You and me both, and I've only just got here."

Fortunately, the train that approached the station with its sole two passengers did turn out to be the one they were waiting for. Only one door opened, and through the opening, a single large duffel bag came flying, closely followed by a tall, sandy-haired man clutching a small brown suitcase, a hat in his other hand.

"Lawrence!" shouted Mary, waving a hand.

"Herbert!" Ruth yelled at the same time.

The women looked at each other and burst out laughing. The expression of confusion on the man's face was priceless. Still with their arms linked, they trotted down the platform to meet him.

"You're nothing if not persistent," he informed Ruth.

"Guilty as charged, Detective Inspector," she declared, holding out her arms as if they should be handcuffed, a huge grin upon her face.

"Aunties first," Mary told him, shooing Ruth forward into the man's waiting arms.

"How are you doing, Aunty?" Lawrence asked Ruth, as they wrapped their arms around each other.

"All the better for seeing you," she told him, before kissing her nephew on the cheek and letting him go. "Now, go and say hello to your girlfriend."

"I should say so too," Mary informed him before rushing into his arms. "Oh, so good," she murmured into his chest, crushing her cold face into his warm body.

Placing a hand each side of her face, Lawrence lifted her face toward his and lowered his lips to hers. Surrendering to the tingles she was feeling from the tips of her toes to the tops of her ears, Mary decided the saying "absence makes the heart grow fonder" was quite true.

When Ruth cleared her throat, she had to cough three times before the pair finally came up for air and parted. "As romantic as this is," she announced, "I suggest we get off home before we all freeze solid to this godforsaken platform. Agreed?"

By way of an answer, Lawrence, albeit reluctantly, let go his hold of his girlfriend and bent to pick up his duffel bag. Slinging it across his back and placing his hat on his head, he picked up his suitcase and held out a hand toward Mary. "Shall we?"

"Don't worry about your poor aunty. I'll trail behind the pair of you, all on my own."

Both turned to face her, mouths open to make their excuses, only to be met by the sight of her holding her sides in silent laughter.

"You should see your faces! They're a picture!"

"Someone's in a good mood," Lawrence stated with an expression of confusion upon his face.

"Ignore her," Mary urged, pulling him back toward the exit to the station. "She's been like this for a while."

Handing their tickets to the elderly gentleman on duty at the exit, the three of them began the short walk into town and thence to the riverbank where Ruth lived at Riverview Cottage.

"Anything in particular brought this mood on?" Lawrence asked.

Not until they were passing the Victory public house and he was wondering how long it would be until she replied, did he get his answer.

"If you're not going to tell him," Mary said, "I will."

Ruth took another few minutes, during which Mary pondered whether she'd have to be the one to tell her boyfriend. She didn't want to, mainly as she wasn't a hundred percent sure of her facts. Eventually, with an exaggerated sigh, Ruth leant against the wall surrounding the church.

"There's nothing much to tell."

Mary eased her hand out of Lawrence's and came to stand with Ruth who, contrary to normal, appeared unsure of herself. "If it helps, I won't tease you. It's up to you, Ruth."

Lawrence came and stood on her other side. "I have no idea what's going on, Aunty, but you don't have to tell me. Whatever it is, it sounds personal, so it's entirely up to you."

Before she could change her mind, Ruth began to talk. "She's making a mountain out of a molehill. I'm finally able to hold a little get-together to thank the local Home Guard for putting my little cottage back together."

"And?" Lawrence said, feeling very confused and scratching his head.

Before Ruth had the chance to say anything, Mary filled in the gaps it appeared she'd been champing at the bit to say. "What she's not telling you is that a certain Sergeant Matthew Green is coming."

Taking his aunt in his free hand, Lawrence pulled her off the wall, and the three of them started toward the river. "Come on, it's too cold to hang around. What's it matter if this chap's coming to the get-together anyway?"

Walking on his other side, Mary took his suitcase and transferred it to her other hand so she could take his with her free one. "Only this. The scuttlebutt around the village says Ruth and Matthew have been seeing each other."

"Mary!" Ruth said with carefully tendered outrage. "That's a bit much. We've only had a few drinks down the pub."

They turned the corner where one way led toward RAF Hamble, the other toward the river and their home. "Well, I think it's wonderful. Do whatever you want, so long as it makes you happy, Aunty."

Ruth leant her head upon her nephew's shoulder. As they walked, after a couple of minutes they came upon their friend Betty's place, the Old Lockkeepers Cottage. "Good boy. You can stay after all."

Lawrence chuckled. "Very glad to hear it." As they passed their neighbor's cottage, he came to a stop and glanced over his shoulder. "Do you think Betty's still awake?"

"What's the time?" Mary asked.

Lawrence brought his watch up, and Mary was a little envious of the luminous dial it had, making it much easier to read in the dark. "A little past half ten."

"I doubt it," Ruth decided. "Whatever it is will have to wait until tomorrow."

"Why do you need to see her?" Mary asked as they

came around the final corner before Ruth's place.

Lawrence opened the gate, immediately setting off Bobby, Ruth's black-and-white Cocker Spaniel. "I've something to tell her. I've found something out about the brass key she found in her sister's effects."

"Not another mystery?" Ruth asked as she put her key in the door.

"Sounds very much like it," Lawrence agreed.

Placing Lawrence's suitcase down in the hall, Mary stooped to fuss the excited dog behind the ears. "My girlfriends next door will be delighted. The Air Transport Auxiliary Mystery Club has another mystery!"

Chapter Two

"Smooth take-off," Second Officer Jamie Mansell commented, watching as the second Anson took off from its taxi run.

Jane Howell let her binoculars rest against her chest, a satisfied smile gracing her lips. "One of my best pilots, Third Officer Penny Alsop."

"She could give mine a refresher. Half the time, I think my taxi pilots are using kangaroo fuel, what with all the bouncing around they get up to."

Flight Captain Howell patted him consolingly on the shoulder. "Come on. I take it you've time for a cuppa before you have to be off."

Looking at his watch, Jamie happily agreed, and together the two of them strolled toward the mess.

"Two cups of tea, please, Mavis," Jane asked when they got to the head of the queue.

"Any milk, luv?" Mavis asked Jamie when she plonked a cup of steaming liquid in front of him.

"Yes, please."

Upon hearing him answer, the little elderly lady immediately reached across and drew his cup back toward her. "Lawd 'elp us. Not another bleedin' tea-hatin' Yank?"

Jamie reached across and gently pried her fingers from around his cup. "Not at all. I'm a tea-loving Canadian."

"Oh. Well, then, enjoy yer cuppa, me luv."

Jane took her own, asking the mess manager, "No sugar today, Mavis?"

"'Fraid not, sorry."

"Ah, well," Jane replied, "can't have everything. Heard from your son lately?"

At hearing the question, Mavis treated her boss to a wide gap-toothed smile. "Got a letter only yesterday. Says 'e's keepin' well, though 'e can't tell me where 'e is."

Jane returned a smile with slightly more teeth. "Wonderful. Please give him my best wishes when you write back."

"Will do, luv," Mavis happily agreed.

Turning back to her companion, Jane invited him, "Follow me, Jamie. There's something I want to show you."

As they strolled through the empty chairs, everyone being out on deliveries apart from a few bods taking a much deserved tea break, Jamie said, "I've got to ask, Jane. What's up with—Mavis, I think you called her? Tea-hating Yanks?"

Chuckling, Jane took his arm. "Ah, Mavis. She's like a breath of fresh air since she took over as mess manager. Can't make a cup of tea to save her life, but you can't help but love her."

Jamie nudged her gently in the ribs.

"Sorry, yes. Well, we've a single American on strength. She hates tea, and not only the stuff Mavis makes. She isn't shy about saying so, either. The two of them have a kind of love-hate relationship. If the truth was told, I think they both love the banter."

Jamie chuckled, shaking his head.

"Now," she said, drawing his attention to the collage spread against the back wall. "What do you think?"

"What do I think?" Jamie turned to face Jane and clapped his hands together. "What a terrific idea! Would you be terribly offended if I asked my boss if we could put up something similar?"

"I'd be delighted," Jane replied, holding out her fountain pen. "Well, don't you want to sign? We invite all visiting pilots to give us at least a name and maybe a few words. Just…try to keep it—clean."

Taking her pen, Jamie leaned down as Jane held the sheet tight. "I'll be delighted."

****

"So where do you know young Jamie from?" Thelma Aston asked her friend as they walked back to Jane's office toward the end of the day.

"I knew his father before the war kicked off."

Thelma raised an enquiring eyebrow, waiting for more information.

Jane promptly pinched her arm. "Cheeky monkey. His father ran the airfield I flew from. It nearly killed him when Jamie had his accident. I still believe learning to fly saved Jamie from the scrap heap. Thanks."

Following Jane through the door, First Officer Thelma took a seat before Jane's desk as the lady herself pulled out her own chair and sat down. "What accident?" she asked, with a most puzzled expression. "He looks fine."

Jane's deep frown indicated recollection of memories obviously long suppressed. Thelma didn't miss this. "It's all right. You don't have to explain."

Eventually, Jane recovered her composure and told

13

Thelma what had happened to Jamie. "It's a real shame. He was only a kid. I doubt if you ever did it, but back in the twenties, it was quite popular to do tours of the Great War's battlefields, and Jamie's family did such a tour. Well, there were still an awful lot of unexploded shells left, and he stepped on one. It took his left leg off below the knee, severely cut up his right—suffice to say, he went through an awful lot of operations and was lucky to live. He also lost his left eye. Yet somehow, he can still laugh."

"Jesus!" Thelma muttered, shaking her head. Enlightenment struck her. "Did you teach him to fly?"

Jane nodded. "One of my proudest achievements. He joined us a few months back, as the RAF wouldn't take him, and took one of his days off to come down and say hello."

"Very nice of him," Thelma mused.

Further conversation was interrupted by a knock at the door, swiftly followed by the entrance of Betty. Jane liked to run a somewhat relaxed base, circumstances allowing.

"Hi Jane, Thelma, sorry for the interruption. I wanted to check you're both still coming around on Thursday evening?"

"Definitely," Jane said, and Thelma nodded in agreement.

Betty perched herself between her friends on the edge of Jane's desk. "Excellent. You know it's not going to be a proper Thanksgiving meal, but we've still managed to get some treats in for Doris."

"Like what?' Thelma asked, leaning forward, a little saliva gathering at the corner of her mouth.

Betty held up a hand and ticked off on her fingers,

"Turkey, mashed potatoes, peas, carrots, and pickles. We've also got cranberry sauce, which Doris gave her approval of last night, and pumpkin pie for dessert."

The more Betty ticked off, the higher both Jane's and Thelma's eyebrows went, and when she finished, both women were staring wide-eyed at their friend. Betty merely returned their stares.

"You ask her," Jane said to Thelma.

Thelma shook her head. "You're the boss. You ask her!"

"Ask me what?" Betty wanted to know.

"You know, it's probably best we don't know," Jane mused, stroking her chin.

"So we don't get thrown into jail, you mean?" Thelma nodded her head.

Betty looked decidedly puzzled by now. "Why on earth would you be jailed?"

What Thelma said next was, considering the lady's own history with the wartime food black market, a little cheeky. "You're telling us none of the food you've just mentioned—which, I have to say, we haven't seen since 1939—is slightly…"

"Slightly what?" Betty demanded.

"Hard to obtain," Jane supplied diplomatically.

A little to their surprise, Betty let out a laugh, "Oh, please! Well, perhaps some of the sugar I may have bartered with some of the local farmers for," she told them. "Most of the rest of what we'll be eating came from either my own vegetable patch or Ruth's, or are on the ration."

"But the turkey? And where on earth did you get pumpkin pie from? I've never even seen a pumpkin growing in this country!" Thelma couldn't help but ask.

Betty's smile turned a little predatory. "Let's say I'm on very good terms with a certain adjutant over at RAF Polebrook. He was able to slip me a few things when I mentioned our Doris was feeling a little homesick."

"You mean he's still feeling guilty about accusing her of stealing, and you took advantage of him?" Jane returned her friend's grin.

"Something along those lines." Betty nodded.

"What does pumpkin pie taste like, anyway?" Thelma asked.

****

Betty, Penny, Mary, and Doris were all sitting around the kitchen table in the evening, the first three enjoying a real cup of tea, not like the muck Mavis made. Doris savoured what was likely to be one of her last cups of coffee. The stash she'd obtained when visiting RAF Marham a few months back was running out, and no matter who she'd asked, she had been unable to obtain any replacement. Even trying to hit up the adjutant at Polebrook had been a dead end. He'd claimed supplies were a problem, and he couldn't help.

"Will Walter be able to make the party?" Penny asked Doris.

Doris took out a small diary, opened it to the week of the party to check, ran her finger down the page, and then looked up. "Looks like it."

"Anyone here, apart from our dear Yank, ever had a Thanksgiving dinner before?" Mary wanted to know.

"What I want to know," Betty said, blowing on her cup, "is what's the deal with pumpkin pie?"

"It's tradition," Doris replied, obviously feeling nothing else needed to be said.

"And you like it?" Mary persisted. When Doris didn't answer right away, she gave her a nudge. "You do like it, don't you?"

"Not really," Doris eventually admitted.

Betty looked exasperated as she took a long drink from her tea and fixed Doris with an annoyed look. "Then why all the fuss about getting hold of it?"

Doris's expression had changed to a sheepish one. "Um, because it's tradition," she repeated. "Besides, it may be like Betty's cranberry sauce. I might like it this time."

"Are all Americans as annoying as you?" Penny laughed.

Doris shook her head. "I'm a special case."

"Bloody head case, more like it," Mary decided, causing everyone, including Doris, to laugh.

A knock at the back door interrupted the conversation, and before anyone could even glance up, it opened to admit Lawrence. The silence could be measured in milliseconds before Mary shot to her feet and flew into his arms, nearly knocking him off balance.

"Don't mind me," Ruth told the pair as she stepped past them into the kitchen. "Hi, everyone, sorry about this pair. You wouldn't think they only saw each other last night! Hope you don't mind a couple of visitors."

"By the looks of it"—Penny pointed at the two who were still connected at the lips—"someone doesn't mind."

"So what brings you around?" Betty asked as Ruth took a seat and automatically filled up a cup from the teapot.

"Believe it or not, Lawrence there wanted to see

you!"

Unsurprisingly, Lawrence failed to react upon hearing his name.

"Shall we leave them to it?" Ruth asked, pushing back her seat and taking up her cup. Everyone else, after glancing over at the loved-up pair, shrugged their shoulders and followed Ruth into the lounge.

Once all had settled into seats, Betty asked Ruth, "Any idea what Lawrence wanted to speak to me about?"

Fortunately, the man himself, together with Mary firmly gripping his hand, chose then to join them. "I've got it, Ruth." Settling down on the floor, his back against the sofa Betty and Penny were sitting upon, he waited until Mary was seated too, leaning against his side. Fishing into a pocket in his jacket, he brought out and displayed a small brass key. "Ring any bells?"

Betty immediately leant forward, and Lawrence placed it in her hand. Seeming lost in her own world, Betty let a few minutes pass before she spoke. No one dared to interrupt her thoughts whilst she was so engaged.

"I must be getting old. I'd forgotten I'd given you this." She looked up from the key, expectation upon her face. "What did you find out?"

"First, let me apologize again for not being able to give you more information until now. I know my being called back as soon as the hangar dance finished was incredibly rubbish timing."

"I'll say," huffed Mary, tightening her hold on his hand. "We barely had a chance to have a goodbye kiss!"

"So you were making up for time just now?" teased

Doris.

"I decline to answer, on the grounds I may incriminate myself."

"You sounded a little too practiced there, Mary," Betty joined in.

Lawrence patted Mary's arm. "If I were you, I'd stop whilst I was ahead."

"Back to my key?" Betty suggested.

"Right, sorry, Betty. The key. It's as we thought, definitely a key to a safe deposit box. From what my contact told me, though, it's no ordinary safety deposit box from your standard bank. It's a high-end—posh, if you will—bank." He looked up to find everyone else staring at Betty as well. "Does this make any sense to you?"

Betty turned the key over and over in her fingers, as if doing so would help unravel the key's secrets, before, with a bemused expression upon her face, she told him, "I haven't a clue."

Chapter Three

Doris let out a groan of pleasure, laying her hands over her stomach.

Slowly, Penny turned her head toward her friend, laying it against the rear of the sofa. "Mind if I add something?"

"Go right ahead," the American agreed, closing her eyes and wriggling around in an effort to get comfortable.

Penny let out an even bigger groan. "I don't care what anyone thinks, unless I loosen my belt, I'm going to explode!"

"Anyone want a turkey sandwich?" Mary asked, kicking the lounge door open to allow a large platter of said sandwiches precede her into the room.

Both occupants of the sofa turned their heads and pried open their eyes to glare at their friend. "Only if you want to be known as the first person in history to be convicted of murdering someone with turkey as the weapon," Penny informed her.

"Thank heaven." Mary surprised them both with her reply as she placed her load down on the table. "Betty and Ruth insisted I ask, but if I'm telling the truth, I could barely stand to be near them. It's the smell of turkey!"

Doris and Penny squidged together to make some room, and both patted the space they'd made. "Come on. We may as well all die together."

As all three lay back and tried to wish their stomachs to stop churning, another low groan made them open their eyes. Standing in the doorway was Shirley. The redhead, usually so scrawny she seemed in proportion to her height, now appeared to be a few months pregnant.

"Is this where we come to die?"

As though summoning the last of her strength, Penny waved a hand vaguely. "Claim a seat and join the living dead, Shirley."

With a heartfelt moan, the younger woman followed her friend's advice.

It was this pitiful sight the rest of the Thanksgiving crowd came into the room to find.

Ruth planted her hands upon her hips, whilst Betty stood behind her and rested her head on her friend's shoulder. After glancing around at the girls, each now doing her best to outdo the others with various expressions of pain, she burst out laughing, shortly joined by Betty. Trying to look over the two's shoulders at the cause of the hilarity, Jane and Thelma, together with the menfolk, Walter and Lawrence, eventually had to resort to nudging the two into the room.

"Oh, my God!" Ruth managed to get out. "What happened here?"

The sofa's inhabitants all eyed her but were unable or unwilling to raise their heads. Shirley, taking the hint though closing her own eyes, made certain her voice portrayed how much discomfort she was in as she told them, '"Death by turkey."

"Short and sweet," Betty commented, when it became obvious they weren't going to get anything else out of the four.

Walter, looking splendid in his best suit and tie, went and sat down on the floor, taking Doris's stockinged feet in his hands and proceeding to massage them.

"If only you could work your magic on my stomach, love," she groaned, wriggling her toes with pleasure.

After a minute, Doris seemed to have forgotten anyone else but her boyfriend was in the room, and her moans and groans were such that Penny cracked open an eyelid and raised her voice so she could be heard, saying, "Other people around, you two!"

Walter dropped his fiancée's foot like a hot potato. Mary leaned forward and pinched his cheek. "Aww, you're so cute when you're embarrassed."

"Isn't he?" Doris agreed, leaning forward to kiss her man on his head. "Oh, big mistake!" she uttered, flopping back and clutching her stomach again. She put a hand in the air. "Everyone! I have an announcement. If I ever say I miss Thanksgiving again, you have my permission to…to…to drown me in cranberry sauce!"

"Ignore those four," Thelma said, dragging in a couple of chairs from the kitchen, closely followed by Lawrence with one more. "You've only got yourselves to blame!" she said loudly enough the sufferers could hear. Her lack of concern was treated with the disdain it deserved, and ignored. "Anyway, Walter, don't you think you should give Doris your present? Before she drops asleep completely?"

As Walter himself seemed in danger of falling asleep, Lawrence stretched out a foot and gave his friend a none-too-gentle kick. "Wakey, wakey!"

Walter jerked fully awake. "Hmm. What's up?"

"Go and get Doris's present, mate," Lawrence reminded him.

Removing his hands from Doris's foot, which elicited a grumble, Walter heaved himself to his feet and disappeared into the hall. Sounds of rummaging issued into the lounge, followed by the sound of something tinny hitting the floor, followed by Walter swearing. A few moments after, he reappeared bearing a large newspaper-wrapped package.

"Sorry about the wrapping paper," he told her, pressing the package into hands stretching blindly into the space before her face. Bending down, he kissed her on the forehead. "Open your eyes for a few minutes more, love." He waited for her to do so, thankful he didn't have to pry them open with his fingers. "You should know too that despite what Lawrence just said, this is actually from Betty. She's the one who arranged and obtained it."

Blushing, Betty squirmed in her seat and told him, "You didn't have to tell her."

Doris slowly focused on the package she found in her arms, while Walter shook his head. "Yes, I did, Betty. You did all the work. I don't know what you did to get it, but all of us will benefit from it, indirectly," he finished somewhat enigmatically.

As near awake as she was likely to be, Doris tore the newspaper off and became fully awake in a split second. "Where on earth…? How did you…? I've been looking for so long…!"

Hearing Doris all a-fluster was rare enough to have the power to cut through the turkey-addled brains of her friends. Mary and Penny each found the energy to open a single eye, and Shirley, being younger than everyone else present, managed both.

"What's she got?" Shirley asked, proving even if you had both eyes open, you still might not see.

"Coffee! A huge tin of coffee!" Doris shrieked. Suddenly, her stomach ache was consigned to memory, and she leaped to her feet, bounding over to where Betty sat, startled. Launching herself at her landlady and friend, she fell into her lap and did her best to cuddle the life out of her.

Eventually, Betty managed to extract herself from the over-exuberant American and tried to remind her, "Don't you think you should be thanking Walter? It's his present!"

Unwilling to let go as yet, Doris blew a kiss toward Walter. "I think what he said is true. I also think it's so sweet, so very sweet of you to try to give him the credit. And Walter"—she fixed her beau with a toothsome grin—"I love you all the more for making sure I know whose present it really is."

"Question," Jane stated, getting the attention of everyone who was awake, Penny and Shirley having dropped back asleep. "How many cups do we allow Doris each day?"

"What!" Doris nearly shouted, stopping herself barely in time, as she still sat on Betty's lap and her mouth was right next to Betty's ear.

Aware how close she'd come to being deafened, Betty asked, "Doris, lovey, would you mind going back to Walter?" With another hug and a slobbery kiss on the cheek, Doris heaved herself off her friend's lap and moved back, with considerably more effort than she'd used going in the opposite direction. Once she'd massaged some life back into her thighs, Betty gave everyone her opinion. "Now, don't shoot me, but I think she should be rationed." She hastened to add, "For your own good," as Doris opened her mouth, undoubtedly to protest. "Two cups a day, one first thing in the morning and the second soon after she gets home from work."

"Sounds good to me," Penny agreed.

"I think we could handle a Doris fueled by that amount of caffeine." Jane nodded.

Thelma added, "No argument here."

"It doesn't affect me," put in Lawrence, as he was present, "But a Doris fueled by anything more than two cups would be more than even the Luftwaffe could handle."

"Sounds fair," Walter decided, earning himself a sharp clip around the ear.

"Hey! Whose side are you on?" Doris demanded, settling back into the sofa, crossing her arms, and pouting.

"I think he's on the side of sanity, for the sake of both the village and the base," Jane stated.

"And I don't get a say in this?" Doris wanted to know.

"Everyone looked at each other and, as one, faced Doris and said, "No!"

****

By ten in the evening, the girls had been packed off to bed. Not because any were particularly tired, since they'd done nothing but lounge around and moan about being overfull. For a while, they resisted, until Jane pointed out they were all on duty in the morning and she wouldn't accept turkey-poisoning as an excuse for

25

not being able to fly or, in Shirley's case, wield a spanner.

Lawrence kissed his girlfriend Mary good night and then left with Ruth and Shirley to walk the short distance along the river to home.

"So, Betty, I don't mean to tease," Jane began.

"Yes, you do," Thelma said. "Or, if you don't, I jolly well will."

"About what?" Betty didn't know what her two friends were talking about. Jane and Thelma glanced at each other and held a silent conversation, causing Betty to demand, "Come on! Out with whatever it is."

Thelma blew out a breath. "Major Jim Fredericks."

Betty tried to put a look of confusion upon her face, asking, "What about him?" She failed completely, as her blush betrayed her.

"We've been talking about it—"

"You have, have you?" Betty interrupted.

"Yes, we have," Thelma carried on, refusing to be put off. "We've been talking about all the wonderful food you talked him into giving you."

"What about it?"

"Well, we don't think even guilt would persuade someone to hand over a turkey."

Betty didn't answer, but she folded her arms across her chest and, if it were possible, went an even brighter shade of red.

"No, we don't," Jane agreed. "I seem to recall seeing the two of you setting the floor alight at the hangar dance. I never knew you could foxtrot."

"Forget the foxtrot," Thelma said. "I could have sworn I saw you two doing the—what's it called?—jive!"

Betty was obviously caught, and her two friends could see her mind seesawing back and forth. Finally, she released the breath she'd been holding in and slumped back into her chair. "If someone will put on the kettle, I guess I may as well tell all."

Thelma hurried to fill up the kettle and put it on to boil. She leant back against a worktop and fixed Betty with an inquiring smile. "And?"

"So I didn't tell the whole truth. When Doris mentioned about missing Thanksgiving…" Jane snorted at the outcome from this, and both Betty and Thelma nodded in agreement. "I sat down and quickly decided there was only one place I could possibly get a turkey. All our farmers have cows, and I think she'd have noticed the difference. So I gave him a call, and as soon as he realized it was me and I was a friend of Doris's, he immediately became so apologetic again, I just blurted out what I was trying to put together. He even offered a turkey before I could ask."

"Which doesn't explain the wonderful dancing," Thelma felt the need to point out as she turned to pour the hot water into the teapot. "You'd already met before all this."

"I'm getting there," Betty advised, tutting. "I felt bad. I felt I'd pushed him into sending me the food, even though I barely had to ask. You spoke to him, Jane, so you know he's lovely." A few months earlier, Doris had been accused of stealing a handkerchief belonging to a Hollywood film star serving in the USAAF at RAF Polebrook. Jane had liaised with Jim Fredericks, who was the adjutant of the Bomb Group the movie star served with. "After everything arrived, I called to thank him, and we had a good chin-wag. He only realized I'd been his dance partner after we'd been talking for five minutes."

"Hang on," Thelma said, pushing a fresh cup of tea in front of her. "You mean to say you didn't tell him your name when you danced? Didn't you speak?"

"When you danced so wonderfully," Jane added.

"Months before," Thelma also added.

Betty was blushing furiously again. "It never came up. We didn't seem to need any words."

Jane took a sip of her tea and regarded Betty rather calculatingly. "Well, well. I've never seen this side of you before, Betty. Where on earth did you learn to dance?"

Betty's blush disappeared, to be replaced by a clouded, hooded look, and it took a while for her to reply. When she did, her friends almost wished they didn't know. "At the orphanage. Eleanor insisted. She said it would make us...nimble." She wiped away a tear.

Abandoning their cups of tea, Jane and Thelma immediately got up from the table and gathered their friend, from both sides, into a warm and loving hug.

"I'm sorry, Betty. I didn't mean to upset you."

Drying her eyes with her cardigan sleeve, Betty gave both her friends a soggy smile and ushered them back to their seats. "It's okay, and you didn't. It's actually one of the few happy memories I have of the place. It seemed I hadn't forgotten what I learned, or rather, my body seemed to remember it can pick up dances very quickly."

"It remembered very well." Jane gave her a huge smile and patted her hand.

"And when he realized you were his Cinderella?"

Thelma wanted to know.

Chuckling at being likened to the fairytale character, Betty took a sip of her tea. "We may have spoken most days since, on the phone," she admitted.

"You dark horse!" Thelma laughed.

Betty turned to face Jane, preparing to be teased by her boss, too. She was a little surprised, though very happy, when Jane simply smiled and told her, "I couldn't be happier for you. If any of us deserves to find happiness, it's you."

Thelma snapped her fingers. "Oh, much, much better. I so agree!"

Jane then did slightly tease their friend with, "You do know we will want to hear all the juicy details, don't you?"

Betty flopped back into her seat, wondering what she'd got herself into. Then she remembered how hearing Jim's voice on the phone made her feel, and how it had felt to feel his strong hands around her waist and the happiness pouring through her as they whirled around the dance floor. Shaking herself, very reluctantly, out of the joyful memory, Betty observed the expectant faces of her friends. She may have to warn Jim the vultures, friendly but still vultures, were circling.

In the happy afterglow of an evening spent with good friends and unusually excellent food, she listened absently as someone padded down the stairs. There was a click as the lounge door opened, and then the radio came on low, but audible enough for Betty's good hearing. It didn't matter it wasn't the big band sound she so loved, since it was happy-sounding music. Contented, for once, Betty closed her eyes, and in her mind's eye, she was soon back smooching to "Moonlight Cocktail" by Glenn Miller, held by the powerful yet gentle arms of a certain American major.

Chapter Four

Having to put off the party for the Home Guard didn't go down very well with Ruth. She'd originally hoped to have the get-together in her back garden, in the parts not given over to her vegetable patch, as soon as she'd pulled herself together after coming to terms with what had happened to her son. The problem with this, of course, is how do you come to terms with finding out your offspring's been badly hurt and there's nothing you can do about it?

Her son, Joe, the original editor of the *Hamble Gazette*, had been captured as part of the British rearguard at Dunkirk back in 1940. She still didn't know the full details of how he'd been injured, as he refused to elaborate in his letters, which made it all the harder. Heaven forbid, if he'd been injured, or worse, back in Dunkirk, she might have known more, and perhaps that would have made it easier to understand. Only he hadn't, so she didn't. Just how do you lose a leg in a POW camp? She'd lost count of the number of people she'd called up, trying to find someone who could find out more—anything—for her, but with no luck. Even requests for information from the Swiss Protecting Power hadn't given her any leads. They said they'd requested information from the German authorities but had only received the bare bones back— shot whilst attempting to escape.

Only one of her circle of friends, Shirley Tuttle, could partially understand what she was going through. Her husband, Ted, had been captured in North Africa, and the younger woman had only just found out he was alive and not dead, as she'd been led to believe, in November last year.

However, even talking together and sharing the letters they received didn't help. It was one thing agreeing she could do nothing about the situation, but quite another to live with that reality. She was even waking up in the middle of the night in a cold sweat lately, something she hadn't shared with anyone. With Lawrence back now, she wasn't certain how much longer she could keep this secret. As Shirley made so much noise, a little like a buzz saw, when she slept, she'd only woken her up once, and explained it off as some random nightmare. Lawrence made just as much of a racket, but he being a policeman she didn't think she'd be able to convince him so easily.

So, rather than find herself in the situation where she had to explain the insomnia, she suffered silently instead. Recently promoted to Detective Inspector, her nephew was too astute to be fibbed to. Plus, so far as she was concerned, you don't lie to family. Perhaps if she talked things over with him, she'd be able to find some balance. Setting out the breakfast things, a pot of tea, toast, and eggs—which reminded her, the chicken coop still needed rebuilding—she put her head about the kitchen door and yelled, "Breakfast! Get it whilst it's hot!" and was rewarded by the thunder of feet upon the landing.

"Thanks for the shout, Ruth," Shirley said, pulling out a chair and sitting to finish tying the ribbon on her ponytail. "Blinking alarm didn't go off."

By comparison, Lawrence ambled in, still in his ancient dressing gown, hands thrust into pockets more holes than anything else. "As I'm up." He beamed a smile at his aunt through an unshaven face. "Thanks very much, Aunty."

Wondering how she was going to get him alone for a chat, since for some reason she'd forgot about Shirley, Ruth was saved from the quandary by Shirley swallowing her tea in a few gulps, then piling her eggs between two slices of hastily buttered toast. Jumping out of her seat, she kissed Ruth on the cheek. "Sorry to run. Lizzie's loaning me some flying manuals before she goes off, and I want to have a flick through before I start work."

Torn between her desire to be alone with her nephew and her instinct to tell Shirley to sit down and eat a proper breakfast, the choice was taken from her by the mechanic rushing out of the kitchen, grabbing her coat and bag from the hall stand, and charging out the front door, a shouted, "Bye!" echoing behind her.

"What have I missed?" Lawrence asked, a piece of toast in his hand.

Not wishing to make light of Shirley's considerable achievement in soloing in a station Tiger Moth, Ruth also wanted to turn the conversation around to her son as soon as possible. "You remember Shirley soloed before you had to go back to London?" Lawrence nodded as he shoveled some eggs into his mouth. "She's off in a few days' time for official flying training in the ATA. Assuming all goes well, she'll go on to Haddenham for lectures and advanced flying training."

Lawrence let out a whistle and cast his eyes to where Shirley had briefly sat beside him. "Well, well. Our Shirley really has come far, hasn't she?"

Despite her desire to get off the subject being discussed, Ruth couldn't deny his words. "She's certainly done herself proud."

Lifting up his teacup, Lawrence had a quick sip before putting it back down. "What's on your mind, Aunty?"

Ruth changed her mind about taking a bite of toast.

"I'm not known as the sleuth of the yard for nothing, I'll have you know."

Ruth was glad she hadn't been drinking her tea, else she'd have snorted hot tea down her nose. "I doubt if anyone's called anything of the like," she commented. "However, you're right. I do want to talk to you."

"About?"

"Two things. First, and it's rather silly, but as you're here, you should know I'm...I'm not sleeping well—still." Lawrence raised an eyebrow, yet kept quiet. His police training told him to let her continue talking. "I'd hoped to have got used to my poor Joe having lost a foot by now."

As she had to stop for a deep, calming breath before continuing, Lawrence could guess where she was going here. However, when someone needed to get something off their chest—or conscience, in the case of suspects, so far as police work was concerned—let them talk. Even if a certain amount of waffle and repetition was involved. In his aunt's case, he sensed she was feeling guilty at being powerless to help. Not surprising, so far as he was concerned. Whilst he'd been back in London, probably slightly abusing his new status of police inspector, he'd tried to see if there was anything anyone could do to help either his aunt or her son. The frustrating answer had been as he'd expected. If he was feeling guilty, Lord alone knew what the poor chap's mother was going through!

Ignoring his cooling tea—there'd be time to make more later—he pushed his cup aside. "I've been thinking about Joe whilst I've been away," he began. "Even wrote to him myself. Wishing him all the best, you know. Anyway, I don't believe you should try and get used to it. Hear me out," he hastened to say, when Ruth showed all signs of interrupting. "The only thing you can do, I think, is carry on. Trying to get used to it is impossible, whilst he's not here. Your imagination is probably running wild as to what—what his leg looks like. I can't tell you how to go about changing your way of thinking, and you'll be thinking about what he looks like until the day he walks through the front door there. I do have a suggestion. Something a colleague of mine in the force did after he was injured in Norway."

Intrigued in spite of herself, Ruth took up a knife and buttered herself a slice of toast. "Go on."

"Bear with me here," Lawrence asked, "as this is going to sound rather silly, but he swears it helped him. If it did, I don't see a reason it couldn't help you."

If not intrigued by now, Ruth was certainly very curious and motioned with her free hand for him to continue.

"He held a funeral…for his foot."

Whatever Ruth may have been expecting to hear, it wasn't this. Crumbs flew everywhere! Hurrying to push himself away from the table, Lawrence gently pounded his aunt on the back until she waved him away.

Grabbing a cloth from the sink, he swept the remains of her slice of toast into his hand and gave the kitchen table a quick wipe-over. "Sorry. I guess I should have warned you."

Woken from his slumber by the sound of his owner coughing, Bobby sleepily staggered in from the lounge, where he'd been having a post-nighttime snooze, and raised half-open brown eyes toward her. Upon seeing no sign of a sausage or piece of toast coming his way, he turned his tail toward Ruth and Lawrence, flicked it in disdain, and wandered back to the sofa.

The two humans, having watched the canine interlude with some interest, turned back to what they'd been discussing.

"You know," Ruth said, "I think you've hit the nail on the head. It's such a strange idea, such a strange thing to do, but it sounds like just what I need."

Lawrence contemplated the lady before him. For the first time he could remember since her son had been maimed, she had a genuine smile upon her face. He had to be sure, though. "I've got to check," he told her. "You did understand what happened, what my mate did?"

She obviously did, and was crying with laughter. She nodded, as she wasn't quite capable of speaking, though she eventually managed to catch her breath enough to tell him, whilst flapping her hands in front of her face, "I did! When can we arrange it?"

It took Lawrence a few minutes to sort his thoughts out, as in all honesty he never thought his suggestion would be taken up, although what he'd told Ruth had been the truth. His friend had joined up at the outbreak of war, been sent to Norway, and lost his foot in an air attack during what had been a disastrous undertaking. When he'd been discharged, he'd been in a bad place. Not knowing what he would do, he'd stumbled into the pub he used to frequent when he'd been in the police in Westminster at the exact moment his old colleagues had entered. Even their delight at seeing him alive, as rumors had been rife about what had happened to him and they'd heard he was dead, hadn't been enough to bring him out of his depression. Things didn't change until a colleague Lawrence vaguely knew from Records came in and took his friend aside. Five minutes after, the Records chap had then brought him back to the group and stayed for a pint of beer before walking back out without revealing a word he'd said, merely whacking his walking stick against his leg, which made a weird ringing-bell sound. A few months later, after Lawrence had secured his place back in the Metropolitan Police, he'd taken him aside. The Records chap had lost his lower leg in the trenches of the Great War, and as he'd been carried away, his last sight had been of his colleagues burying his leg in Flanders mud and erecting a small cross above it.

"What a story!" Ruth exclaimed. "Is he still working in Records? I'd love to do a story on him!"

Pleased to see his aunt happy again, Lawrence snaffled some toast before it got too cold, and replied, "You know, I think old Charley is still there. I'll call work up later today and see what he says."

"Wonderful!" Ruth declared, clapping her hands together.

Bobby, as sleepy as before, stumbled back into the kitchen, barked once in their direction, and turned back to the lounge.

Lawrence asked Ruth, "Since when's he been in such a mood?"

Ruth didn't seem to have noticed Bobby particularly and ignored the question to reply to Lawrence's previous statement. "Brilliant. Let me know once you have, please?"

"I will. And we'll sort out a foot funeral for Joe. You'll write and tell him?"

"You bet I will," Ruth replied. "Now, I wanted to ask you something else, remember?"

"You want to know what I'm doing here."

"Show off," Ruth informed him. "You could have guessed."

Lawrence looked at the clock on the wall. "It's coming up to nine, Aunty. How about we finish up here, and I'll walk you to the office. I'll tell you on the way."

"Bugger!" Ruth exclaimed, also throwing a glance the clock's way. "You're right. I'd better shake a leg, or I'll be late."

****

Ten minutes later, Ruth and Lawrence were strolling along the riverbank, toward her newspaper office in the center of Hamble.

"You're here because…" Ruth prompted.

"I'll tell you shortly. First, you remember my little accident?"

Ruth frowned, and Lawrence was a little surprised he wasn't actually swatted around the head. He'd been injured and nearly killed whilst conducting an investigation in London a few months back and had come to his aunt's to recuperate. Once they found out the circumstances and the extent of his injuries, neither Ruth nor Mary were one bit happy with him. Everyone had taken to calling it his "accident" as otherwise arguments would have been all too common.

Lawrence's brow creased at seeing her expression. "I can, er, see you do. Anyway, I wanted to let you know. Not only have we caught the gang who were stealing the lead from those church roofs, we've also arrested the one who caused my injuries."

Ruth stumbled to a halt, nearly causing Lawrence to trip over Bobby's leash. Gripping him by both elbows, she fixed him with a determined stare. "Tell me again!"

Lawrence, knowing his aunt needed to be certain he was telling her the truth, returned her stare. "We've got the bugger."

For a second, he thought her legs might go from beneath her. Wiping away a single tear, she squeezed his arms once and then, taking one of his hands, turned back toward work. Whilst walking, he filled her in on what had happened.

"I never told you about my assistant, my sergeant. Durrell's his name. A bit old for a sergeant. I was never quite sure if he had the wherewithal to become an inspector—you know, as he seemed to like muddling along. Anyway, I thought they'd killed him too, as the last I saw, he was lying in a heap, blood everywhere. He was in the next bed to me in the hospital. Seems I was wrong about him. Whilst I was down here, he discharged himself and went in search of the one responsible for our injuries. This in spite of a broken arm and a knife wound to his neck which just missed his jugular."

By now, they'd been led by Bobby to the door of the *Hamble Gazette*. Walter stood outside, his key just in the lock, when they turned up. He opened his mouth to wish them both a good morning, but something about the intensity of the way Ruth was listening to Lawrence held his tongue.

"I'll be going back to London next week. I've to testify against the man who murdered his colleague and tried to do the same to both myself and Durrell. He's turned on his masters in an attempt to save himself, so we've got everyone. The trial will take a while, and then I'll be back."

"Back?" Ruth asked, puzzled.

Lawrence treated her to a semi-feral grin. "You don't get rid of me so easily! Durrell's taking over my post, and I'm moving into this area. A detective inspector position has come up at Portsmouth. So you'd better be on your best behavior, Aunty. Hamble will be within my sphere of responsibility!"

Chapter Five

Penny had managed to see a little more of her husband, Tom, since his squadron had come out of the special lockdown they'd been on for the last month. All Tom would say on the subject was they'd been undergoing training for a mission which had now been scrubbed. Tom, though, hadn't been allowed to take part. Wounded around the same time Doris had become engaged to Walter, he'd recovered nicely, except for where a bullet had creased his skull. Unable to hide the headaches he got after leaving hospital, he'd been grounded by the station medical officer until they went away.

Now, as December arrived, he was still grounded. Being unable to fly whilst his colleagues went back on operations put him in a foul mood, something even the frequent phone calls with Penny didn't much help. She could tell he was careful not to lose his temper with her. She also knew him well enough to know how angry and frustrated he was. It didn't help things when his navigator and friend, Flight Sergeant Stan Atkins, was assigned to a new pilot. She shared his fears. Typically, pilots new to operations were at a much greater risk of being killed, even on normal operations, than experienced ones, and no one with experience liked flying with a rookie. The last time they'd spoken, two nights ago, Tom had told her Stan and the pilot (whose name he couldn't even remember) had flown five missions. She'd found out exactly how worried for his friend he really was, when she commented, without giving it a thought, on how well things were going. Tom's voice had raised, but in the same breath lowered to normal, though she could almost hear him gritting his teeth as he tried to explain how Stan had beaten the odds thus far, but the odds were getting longer.

Penny could understand and shared her husband's worry. She was very, very fond of Stan. She'd met him only a few times, one of those when she and Jane had turned up at RAF Hospital Ely to find him sitting outside Tom's room. He'd still had wounds which hadn't been tended to, such was his determination to make sure his friend was going to be all right. The last thing she wanted was for anything to happen to him.

All this didn't prevent her from being a little angry at Tom, though. He'd made the mistake of not telling her, his wife, about the headaches. She'd only found out about them when she'd called his office and his phone was answered by some pilot officer who let slip Tom was seeing the medical officer. As any good spouse would, she'd pumped him for more information—he'd probably argue she bullied him—and he eventually told her why Tom was there. After the ear-bashing she'd given her husband when she managed to get hold of him later, she wouldn't like to be the pilot officer. Penny felt a little guilty, but she would do so again in a heartbeat! Her husband and his health were the most important things in the world to her.

"Enough," Penny told herself, picking up her alarm clock and checking the time again.

She'd been awake for an hour now, umming and

arring about getting up. It being nearly seven in the morning and with the alarm about to go off, she threw back the covers, threw on her dressing gown, slipped her feet into her slippers, and hurried to the bathroom. Ten minutes later, she was on her back on her bed, struggling to do up the zip on her skirt. "Come. On," she muttered between gritted teeth. The damn thing had been getting tighter in the last few weeks. She'd have to cut back on the bread and butter.

"About time too!" Doris commented as Penny joined them for breakfast. "Any longer, and I'd have had your egg."

"Only if you'd beaten me to it," Mary chipped in, bashing the top of her hardboiled egg in and sprinkling a little salt over it.

"Enough," Betty, the voice of reason, told them. "Are you feeling all right, love?" she asked Penny as she sat down heavily in her seat.

Mustering a smile plainly intended to placate them, Penny pushed her egg away and helped herself to a slice of toast. "Sorry, Betty. I don't feel I can face an egg today."

Obviously having listened to what Betty had said a few moments ago, both Mary and Doris batted their eyelashes at their landlady. Knowing she wouldn't be the winner if she chose one over the other, Betty fished a thruppenny bit out of her pocket. "Doris, you call. Heads or tails?"

"Tails," the American said as the coin spun through the air.

Betty caught it and slapped it down on the table. Slowly, she took her palm away to reveal—heads. Mary immediately drew Penny's egg toward her, not giving her friend any time to try an argument.

Considering she'd lost the toss, Doris took a moment for a proper look at Penny and didn't give the lost egg another moment's thought. "Are you sure you're all right, Penny? Betty's right. You look a bit off color."

Munching on her toast, Penny waved away her friend's concerns. "I'm fine. Perhaps a little sad to say goodbye to Shirley," she mused.

This caused everyone to eat the rest of their meal in silence. It wasn't until a loud rapping at the front door, accompanied by much barking from Bobby, caused everyone to put down their cups.

"Only us!" Ruth yelled, closely following her voice into the cottage.

Behind her filed Lawrence, Walter, and a rather quiet-looking Shirley. Whilst Lawrence went to kiss Mary a good morning, Betty, Penny, and Doris all came and gave their friend Shirley a huge hug each.

"I'm going to miss you," Betty told the redhead when her turn came along.

By now, Shirley had tears in her eyes but was making a conscious effort not to let them fall. Still held in Betty's embrace, she sniffed loudly and, with a very wobbly lip, enunciated as loudly as she could so everyone in the room could hear her, "I'm going to miss you most of all, Betty. When you'd have been quite within your rights to send me away, you chose to give me a chance to make amends. Few other people would have done so. I still don't think you know how much you mean to me, but because of your kindness, I've found a home and hope." By now, Shirley wasn't the only one with tears building up. Lawrence excused himself from the room, though everyone could hear him blowing his nose from the hall. "I hope you don't mind my saying this, but you've become much more than a friend to me, Betty. You're the next best thing to a mother I've known since my own one died."

The only sound in the room, apart from Bobby snuffling around the floor for crumbs, was various people sniffling, followed by the taking out of handkerchiefs and the wiping of eyes.

Blowing his nose with a sound to rival a trumpet, Walter told his boss, Ruth, "Who needs theatre, when we've our very own Shakespeare right here."

Doris put her arm around her fiancé. "I've always said you had a kind heart, my love."

Finally releasing her hold upon Betty, Shirley stood back and looked at the new watch upon her wrist, a good-luck gift from the two households. "I hate to say it, everyone, but if we don't leave now, Jane may decide to go off without me."

****

"I was beginning to think you'd changed your mind!" Jane told Shirley when the younger girl and her farewell committee joined her outside the flight line hut.

Throwing decorum to the winds, Shirley rushed into Jane's arms. "This was one morning I was never going to be late." She then stepped back and put her bags on the ground between them. "Thank you for believing in me, Jane. I still can't believe I'm actually off to flying school!"

Penny and Doris stowed Shirley's bags in the Magister and joined the rest of the group.

"Where's Lizzie?" Shirley asked, looking around.

"I'd hoped to say goodbye to her too."

"Sorry," Jane told her. "She's on an early morning delivery. She wanted to be here, but as she couldn't, she asked me to tell you this. She expects to see you back here flying with the Pool before too long."

"Oh, God!" Shirley exclaimed. "I'm going to well up—again!"

"Then perhaps we'd better get going."

Shirley went around once more, hugging and kissing all her friends before turning to face them, her back to the trainer in which Jane was going to fly her up to Haddenham. There she would live whilst being bused to Barton-le-Clay, slightly north of Luton, to officially train up to solo standard. Once accomplished, she would stay at Haddenham for advanced training and aviation lectures.

"Ruth!" she called, and when she had her attention, asked, "Would you give any letters or postcards from my Ted to any of the girls, please? Jane said she'd forward them on to me. It's too difficult and wouldn't be worth it to send him a change of address."

"Of course I will," Ruth assured her.

Jane looked at her watch. Clapping Shirley on the back, she told her, "Come on, trouble. We really need to get going."

Amidst much shouting and tears—mostly from Walter and Lawrence, everyone was most amused to note—Shirley disappeared into the hut to quickly change into the flying suit she was borrowing. A few minutes later, she was strapped into her seat in the front cockpit, with Jane behind her.

Not long afterward, Shirley was enjoying the early morning calm. There were a few seagulls still in sight, though not much else was in the clear blue sky.

"Asleep yet?" Jane came on the intercom to ask.

"Not yet, boss," she replied.

"Just as well. I've cramp in my left arm. You're going to have to take over."

A cloud of butterflies broke out in Shirley's stomach, and she nearly forgot to answer.

"I can't! I'm not qualified!"

Jane's calm voice told her, "Listen very carefully, Shirley. I think my cramp will go, but not until we're about to land. Do you understand?"

This was one of those moments when a light bulb could have gone on above Shirley's head. Thus far, Shirley had only flown Tiger Moth biplanes, very benign and forgiving as planes go. Jane was giving her a chance to get a head start on some of what she would be taught, and she'd be a fool not to take advantage. She wracked her mind for the correct expression, even though she'd used it often enough when Third Officer Lizzie Banks had taught her. It came to her before Jane decided to change her mind.

"I have control."

Chapter Six

Since Shirley's declaration from her heart on Monday, Betty's mind had been spinning around and around. Never married and with no children, she hadn't known quite how to respond, if she were truthful with herself. Fortunately, Jane had decided they needed to take off. She hoped Shirley hadn't noticed her lack of response. The closest relationship she'd ever had with anyone had been with her sister, the late Eleanor. Her vocation when Eleanor was alive hadn't been conducive to relationships of any kind. She'd been attracted to numerous men, but the constant possibility of being sent to jail for fencing stolen goods had always put her off pursuing them.

Now it appeared she had the next best thing to a daughter, and she wasn't sure how she felt about it. At least with Shirley being away for a while—though they expected her back for a few days over Christmas—gave her time to sort out those feelings.

Thinking of feelings, she took advantage of her lodgers being at Ruth's, giving her a hand with whitewashing the rear of her cottage. The blast damage from the near miss of the German bomb a few months ago had been repaired, thanks to the kindness of the local Home Guard and other tradesmen around Hamble, yet the soot and smoke damage needed to be cleaned and painted over before winter set in. Apparently, Ruth was expecting a delivery of whitewash on Saturday morning—"Don't ask where from," she'd advised Betty when she asked—so everyone else was mucking in (pardon the expression, she thought) with finishing off the scrub-down of the plasterwork.

Reaching up to the top of her wardrobe, she took careful hold of the box containing her sister's things and carried it downstairs to the kitchen table. A mild Friday evening, she left the back door open, something she'd never do with the front one, as otherwise the whole house would be filled with midges in no time. The only wildlife which entered through the back door was small, four-legged, black-and-white, and furry, plus cute as anything.

"Hello there, Bobby," Betty said, reaching down to give the spaniel a scratch behind his ear, his favorite place. "Come in. Let's see if we can find you a biscuit."

Five minutes later, Betty was sitting at the table, nursing a cup of tea, whilst Bobby was contentedly sleeping off a dog biscuit or three from the stash Betty always kept tucked away for him. "Right. Let's have a look."

Ever since Lawrence had confirmed the key was for a bank safety deposit box, trying to figure out where it could be from had become a bit of an obsession. Turning it around and around in her fingers hadn't revealed anything to her, as it hadn't to Lawrence. It seemed to be a brass key of no particular importance.

What was contained in the box it would open, however, was another matter. The first thing they needed to do was to find out where that box was. This information was proving to be elusive.

Looking at the box before her, Betty knew a last

chance when she saw it. Eleanor had never lived anywhere permanent and, for safety's sake, had always been the one to contact her if she needed to utilize her particular skills. The safest method for both of them it may have been, but Betty had still found it frustrating. It meant she had no way to contact her sister if she had an emergency, which she'd never been happy about. However, as the price to pay for their continued freedom, she'd accepted it. If there were any clues about the key to be had, then this was the one place it had to be. She'd already run her fingers through Eleanor's scarf and bobble hat. Not even running a magnet over them had revealed anything.

Taking off the lid, Betty laid her sister's death certificate aside straight away. She needed to put it with the rest of her private papers. Pausing, she scolded herself and pulled it back. About to turn it over, she was interrupted by someone coughing behind her. Turning, she was confronted by the Air Transport Auxiliary Mystery Club itself!

"Had some thoughts, Betty?" Mary asked.

Whilst Penny and Mary joined Betty at the table, Doris swirled the teapot around and poured out a cup each for her friends before she knelt down at Betty's side and put on her sweetest smile. "I know I've already had my two-cup ration, but can't I please have one more? It'll help the little gray cells."

"Don't think quoting Hercule Poirot will get around me."

"Please?" Doris allowed a little whine to enter her voice and added some batting of her eyelashes for emphasis.

Betty looked at her friends. "What do you think?

Should we risk a hyper-Doris?"

Quite aware how much they could annoy and wind up their friend, Penny stroked her chin whilst Mary pretended to say something, only to close her mouth before repeating the act.

This went on for the best part of a minute before Doris lost patience. "Do you really want me to sit here complaining how much I hate tea every few minutes?"

"She does make a good argument," Penny stated.

Betty nodded. "True. However, if we give in once, won't we set a precedent?"

"A very good point," Mary agreed.

Doris threw her hands up in the air. "Oh, I give in! Have it your way." So saying, she poured herself a small—very small—cup of tea, sat down, and uttered her perennial words, "Doesn't taste like coffee," before taking a small sip.

Everyone except Doris smiled.

"Now Doris's ritual is out of the way, ready for a little sleuthing?" Betty inquired. Her friends all nodded, though Doris's agreement was more of a grimace as she gagged down her tea.

"What are we looking for?" Penny asked, though as Betty's key lay before them on the table, she was pretty sure it would have something to do with it.

"Take everything out of this box. If it's got writing on it, read it. Don't worry, as there shouldn't be anything personal. Besides, I haven't any secrets from you lot. Even if I did, I wouldn't for very long, knowing how nosey you are!"

This time, all three did treat her to a big grin each, knowing they were all as close as any loving family, so the words were only said in jest.

"Basically, see if you can find anything mentioning the key," Betty finished.

****

Ruth found a dispirited bunch when she popped her head around the door an hour later, as everyone had been through each item, just in case anyone had missed anything. "Any of you seen Bobby?" she asked. In answer to her question, there came a doggy snore from under the kitchen table. Ruth ducked her head but came back up quickly as he broke wind and everyone pushed their seats back rapidly and rushed to the door for some much needed fresh air. "You haven't been feeding him those dog biscuits again, have you, Betty?"

In between gulps of evening air, Betty nodded. "I keep forgetting they give him wind."

"So what's everyone doing?" Ruth asked once the air had cleared and they were all able to retake their seats. "Oh, and thanks again for your help tonight, girls," Ruth added, beaming. "You sure you're still all right to come over and paint tomorrow?"

"Try and stop us!" Penny told her.

"We were looking through Eleanor's things," Betty explained to Ruth. "All Lawrence could say about the key is that it's for a bank safety deposit box, but I'm sure you already know that. We've been looking to see if there's any mention of a key in any of her documents, or anywhere else."

Ruth leant forward with interest. "Any luck?"

"Nothing," Doris supplied.

"Want another pair of eyes?" Ruth offered.

Betty shook her head and reached out to squeeze her friend's hand. "Very kind of you to offer, but we've all been through everything, effectively, four times, and have still come up blank."

Ruth sat back in her chair and reached down to fondle the ears of her still sleeping spaniel before asking, "You're certain you don't have anything else of your sister's? Anything at all you may have put away? Don't answer straight away," she cautioned. "Think about it for a few minutes."

All was quiet, except for the snoring dog, whilst Betty gave Ruth's question serious thought, knowing how important the matter was. Eventually, her head shot up and her eyes turned to the ceiling.

"What've you thought of?" Doris asked.

Instead of speaking, Betty got to her feet and rushed out of the kitchen and up the stairs.

"Don't move," Ruth warned them, stopping both Penny and Doris, who had gotten to their feet to follow her.

From the sounds of things, Ruth was rummaging in the airing cupboard. There came the sound of various things being thrown to the floor and an odd muttered curse before they heard a loud, "Ah-ha!" Shortly, Betty reappeared and almost reverently laid a Sidcot flying suit upon the table, moving the resealed box of Eleanor's effects out of the way.

Even Bobby didn't dare interrupt the silence. This was what Eleanor had been wearing when she was killed. Ruth didn't think she'd seen it since her friend had come into the house with it draped over her arm after the police had released her things. Certainly none of the girls had seen it before.

For their benefit, as they hadn't ever known Eleanor, Betty briefly explained, "This is actually my suit. Only I haven't worn it since my sister…borrowed it. I haven't even washed it."

"And you think there could be something, some clue, somewhere in it?" Doris asked, reaching forward, only to stop herself from touching it without Betty's permission.

"Go ahead," Betty told her. "Take a look."

Whilst Mary, being obviously very careful, pulled the suit toward her, Ruth took hold of one of Betty's hands. "You okay?"

Betty shrugged. "Memories, just memories."

"I never knew you were a pilot," Doris said.

Betty shared a look with her old friend Ruth before replying, "I took my wings off my ATA jacket after my sister's death." Even as she was saying the words, she reached out with her free hand to gently take the suit from Mary's unprotesting hand. "After she...died, I didn't want to fly again. Jane was very understanding when I came here, and even though I'm officially on the roster of active pilots, she's never pressured me into starting up again." This was news to the younger pilots, and as one they all raised their eyebrows, though none spoke. After another moment, Betty looked around at her friends and let a smile grace her lips. "You know, perhaps I should speak with Jane. Maybe it's time I got back in the cockpit."

"We're all here if you need us, Betty." Mary beat everyone else to replying. "Whatever you decide."

Ruth got to her feet and, taking up the flying suit, stood next to her friend. "Why not try it on? See how it feels."

Everyone could see Betty steeling herself, but almost as if she'd made her decision before she could second guess herself, she disappeared back upstairs.

When she'd gone, Mary pointed out, "I hadn't finished searching yet."

Ruth patted her hand. "There'll be plenty of time, don't worry."

"Did any of you know Betty flew?" Penny asked.

"Not a clue, Doris replied, whilst Mary shook her head. "Did you, Ruth?"

"Only what Jane told me about her request. I didn't think I should ask her why she didn't fly."

Further conversation was foreshortened by Betty rushing into the room, an excited gleam in her eyes that wasn't missed by anyone at the table.

"Has anyone got any tweezers? I can't find mine," Betty stated.

"You've found something?" Penny asked, jumping to her feet and rushing past Betty to grab her bag from the hall stand. Coming back, she dumped the bag upside down on the table. Sorting through the strewn contents, she found what she was looking for and handed Betty a pair of blunt-nosed tweezers.

"I don't know," she answered. "I pulled it on, and it felt good, apart from something cutting into my left thigh. I've checked, and there's nothing in the pocket, but it still feels like there's something small and square there. I can feel a cut in the lining, though. I think, whatever it is, it's in there."

Penny knelt next to Betty. "Hold still, then." She found the cut Betty was talking about, took the tweezers, and gently inserted them. Everyone held their breath. After a few seconds, Penny slowly withdrew the tweezers. Clasped between the ends was a piece of white card. Fighting the urge to look at it, she handed it up to Betty and hurriedly got to her feet.

Not looking at anyone or anything else, Betty held the card between her fingers and lifted it to her face.

"What is it?" Ruth asked, unable to keep silent any longer.

Looking at her friends, Betty, her eyes shining, turned it so they could all see. "It's a business card—for a bank in London."

Chapter Seven

"It's a real shame Shirley couldn't be here," Doris stated, hugging Walter closer to her side.

"Perhaps," Walter half agreed as they finished Doris's tour of the rear of Ruth's newly decorated cottage. "Remind me. Where did Ruth get the whitewash from again?"

Lawrence slapped a hand onto his friend's shoulder. "Just who's the policeman around here?"

Doris treated her favorite detective inspector to a kiss on the cheek, whilst Walter contented himself with a firm handshake.

"I don't really want to know," Lawrence backtracked. "Merely curious."

"As Ruth reminded us, repeatedly, whilst we were slapping the stuff on, don't ask," Mary chipped in, chinking her bottle of Guinness against Doris's.

"Careful now," Lawrence said to everyone. "Here comes the hostess."

"Careful about what?" Ruth asked as she stopped in front of them. "Where the whitewash came from? Don't ask."

"Told you," Doris told him, deeply satisfied.

"How's everyone enjoying themselves?" Mary asked, hoping to break the line of conversation.

Ruth joined everyone in looking around. It wasn't the party she wanted to have, but as a thank-you to

Hamble's Home Guard, it more than served its purpose.

A few months ago, a German bomber had jettisoned a bomb whilst flying over her cottage after raiding nearby Portsmouth. Fortunately, the explosion was far enough away that no real damage occurred, but most of the tiles of her rear roof had been blown off, together with all the windows blown in. Peppered with shrapnel and debris, the rear of the dwelling had taken the brunt of the blast and had looked a mess.

Walter, a recently joined member of the Home Guard, had led the charge of the platoon toward the fire the bomb had caused in the field behind Ruth's cottage, and with their aid the fire had been extinguished before it could do any real harm. Going above and beyond the call of duty, so far as Ruth was concerned, they'd turned up during the next couple of days and put in place temporary repairs to the roof and all the holes left by her sudden lack of windows and doors. Because of this, she and her lodgers—Lawrence, at the time, and the now departed Shirley—had been able to move back in after only a few days.

Today was proving to be a rare November Sunday afternoon—it wasn't raining. A decorating table, covered with a white sheet, stood near the open back door, laden down with all the food and nibbles Ruth had been able to drum up. Betty and her team had chipped in as well—the sausage rolls were the first thing anyone had seen Penny bake and seemed to be going down well. Ruth's specialty rock buns were nearly all gone, though the less said about the pumpkin soup the better. It had seemed like a good idea to use up some of the pumpkin left over from the Thanksgiving lunch and still taking up space in Betty's icebox.

However, it seemed no one was brave enough to try the orange concoction.

If she'd been worried about there being enough food to go around, she needn't have. Most of the Home Guard appeared to be married, and even under wartime restrictions nobody liked to turn up without bringing something. Some couples brought bottles of stout or beer. Others were just as welcome with homemade wine of various and lurid varieties, some of which Ruth was trying to gather up the courage to try. Spam hash and fritters had been presented by at least three families, currant buns (mostly sans currants) were piled high, and there were even a couple of apple crumbles, which in particular were proving very popular.

Ruth turned back from appraising the gathering and smiled. "Considering there's a fair few more people than I'd reckoned upon, I think it's going well."

"I think it's going very well," Home Guard Sergeant Matthew Green announced, stepping up to join the group, a bottle of beer in one hand and a plate of food in the other.

"Hello, Matthew. Enjoying yourself?" she asked.

"Everyone's having a great time, thanks. This was a great idea!"

Ruth leant her head over and, for just a second, looked about to kiss him on the cheek. Indeed, Lawrence had opened his mouth to speak but stopped himself as his aunt thought otherwise of her action and took a small step back. "Well, there are more people than I thought. It seems half the village has turned up, but it feels like it's what everyone needed."

A burst of laughter from where Ruth's makeshift chicken coop stood made all their heads turn.

"I see what you mean," Mary said.

Matthew looked around before asking, "Where's young Penny? I'd have thought she'd be here."

"She went to see her husband," Doris supplied. "It seems she's got something to tell him."

****

"You know, darling," Tom Alsop said, his arm tight around the shoulders of his wife, "one of these days, you're going to get yourself shot down."

"What a strange thing to say."

"Claiming you've got engine trouble, only so you can pop into an operational base to see your husband? Someday, you're going to meet a military policeman you can't talk your way around."

"Never going to happen. Our Doris taught me a few tricks," she replied, full of confidence, though she did notice the way her husband's eyebrows shot up. "Don't worry. You know Doris is a real sweety. Plus, she is engaged, so she's nearly a respectable woman."

"As if," Tom teased her.

Penny rapidly elbowed her husband in the stomach. "Don't toy with Doris. Not only is she wilier than anybody else I know, I love her like she were my own sister."

To show there were no hard feelings, Tom took his wife by the hand and pulled her to the side entrance of his squadron's hangar. Wrapping his arms around her, he lowered his head and touched his lips to the cherry red ones of his wife. If anyone else was around, neither would have cared as they proceeded to make up for lost time.

When they finally parted, Penny's lips were swollen and even slightly sore. She cared not a jot, as sometimes she forgot how it felt to be in her husband's arms. In those times, she felt the pain of living apart from him all the more. It was only by reminding herself she wasn't the only woman separated from her husband by the war that she kept from screaming out at the injustice of it all. The thought reminded her of the conversation she'd been meaning to have with him on their belated holiday a few months ago.

"Come on." She grabbed hold of his hand and pulled him toward the door. "We need some privacy. Careful!" She swatted him on the arm when he waggled his eyebrows suggestively at her.

A minute later, Penny had only just closed the door of Tom's office, not even getting so far as to open her mouth, before there was a knock on the door. "Bloody hell!"

"Let me," Tom told her, thinking so long as it wouldn't affect the outcome of the war he'd shoot whoever it was, he opened the door.

"Hello, Wing Commander Alsop." Sharon Coates, the girl who worked in the squadron canteen, thrust her head through the small opening Tom left. "Penny! I thought so. Anyone care for a cup of tea?'"

Penny had met Sharon earlier in the year when she'd delivered the horrible news about Tom's brother Sam, who was killed when the ship he was serving on had been sunk. Last she knew, the young woman, nearly eighteen, had begun stepping out with Tom's navigator and friend, Flight Sergeant Stan Atkins.

"Yes, please," Penny answered and then asked, as she was curious and couldn't help liking the girl even though they'd met only a few times. "How're things with Stan?"

Fighting the blush which immediately sprang to her cheeks, the girl muttered what sounded like, "Fine," and rushed off, presumably to organize the tea.

Whilst she thought about it, Penny asked her husband, "How are they doing? He's treating her well? How's his recovery?"

Taking her by the hand, Tom led her to one of his two semi-comfy armchairs and sat her down, taking the one beside her. "She's been treated very well," Tom assured her. "No one makes a cup of tea quite like Sharon, so everyone on the squadron is suddenly behaving as if they're her father. Stan wouldn't dare to do anything to upset her—half the lads would string him up if they lost her cuppa."

"Good for them," Penny declared, squirming in her seat, trying to get comfortable. "Mind you,'" she told him, moving to lean toward him and finding it much easier to do so in her flying suit than in her skirt, "if she ever fancies a change, we'd take her in a flash. Our new mess manager, Mavis, can't make a cup of tea for toffee."

"We'd better be careful, then," Tom decided, taking his wife's hand in his.

"And his wounds?" Penny asked again. When her husband had been wounded, so had Stan. When she got to the hospital, she'd found out how close a friendship the two had as, despite his burns, Stan had waited outside Tom's room until he could be assured his boss and friend was going to be all right. How could you not feel affection for someone when they did something like that?

"Pretty much healed. Don't say anything. I know what you're going to say—why's he flying, then, if he's not completely healed." Tom hushed her when she would have interrupted. "We've a shortage of navigators, and Stan's the best on my squadron. Believe me, if I could get away with grounding him too, I would. I am keeping an eye on him, though. Sharon makes sure I do."

Penny grinned. "Good for her. Now, how are you, Tom?"

Before he answered, Tom made certain the door was closed. Whilst he was standing up, he hurriedly untucked his shirt to show his wife his chest. "You can barely see them now."

From where she sat only a few feet away, Penny decided he was being deluded if he thought he was healed. Cut up when his Mosquito had been hit, she could still easily make out the red lines where the shrapnel had smashed into her husband's body, and she had to work hard to get rid of the queasy feeling in her stomach. Forcing a smile, she looked up at her Tom. "Looks much better."

She'd said the right thing, and he made himself presentable, kissed her on the forehead, and took back his seat. Just in time, too, as there came a knock on the door, and again without waiting for a reply, Sharon nudged the door open with a tray containing a teapot, two mugs which had seen better days, and a chipped plate with a few sorry-looking biscuits.

"Sorry about the biscuit selection, boss," she said, setting the tray on the small table between the two of them. "The Naafi's running a bit short."

"Don't worry. Thank you, Sharon," Tom replied. Sharon took the unsaid hint and, smiling, closed the door behind her. "Shall I be mother?" Tom offered.

Raising her cup to her lips, Penny sniffed and then took a sip. Unable to prevent a satisfied, "Ah," from escaping her lips, she took a longer sip before putting her mug down.

"The perfect temperature, the perfect taste," Penny declared. "Even without sugar."

"Don't you go telling her," her husband retorted. "If she leaves, we'll lose the war tomorrow."

"Well…" Penny began and then remembered what they'd been discussing, not to mention what she still had to talk to him about, and reluctantly put the glorious cup of tea from her mind. "Let's agree those wounds don't look too bad. Now, about these headaches…"

Upon her mentioning this, her husband's mood turned. He didn't immediately say anything, yet he sat back in his seat and crossed his arms and legs.

Penny leant forward, reaching for one of her husband's hands—which he, reluctantly, gave to her, though she was the one who found herself rubbing her thumb in his hand to comfort him. "It's no use pretending it doesn't exist, Tom. I know now, and I am very, very annoyed at you for not telling me. I ask you, having to bully it out of one of your pilot officers!"

"Yes, well," he stammered, at least having the honesty to look sheepish.

"Shall we agree, to begin with, you should have told me? I shouldn't have had to find out as I did?" Tom nodded his agreement. "Good. So, how is it? I assume from the mood when I bring it up, you're still grounded?"

"Until further notice," Tom muttered, picking up his tea and frowning.

Sensing the conversation could easily turn sour and not wanting to spoil any of the precious time she could get with her husband, Penny moved from her chair and sat on his lap. Automatically, one of his arms snaked around her waist. The movement reminded her, as if she needed reminding, of the urgent matter she needed to discuss with him.

"Tom, can you lock the door?"

Though he raised a questioning eyebrow, Tom reached out a hand and turned the key in the door.

"Thanks."

"What's wrong?" he asked, searching her face as she turned on his lap, the better to face him.

Taking a deep, steadying breath, Penny looked him square in the eyes. "How do you feel about children?"

Chapter Eight

"There's something wrong," Walter uttered as soon as Ruth walked through the door of the *Hamble Gazette* the first Monday morning in December, "but I can't put my finger on it."

The paper usually put out only one issue a week. However, after reading the Beveridge Report—properly titled "Social Insurance and Allied Services," only this was such a mouthful it had quickly become named after its author—Ruth had decided its contents needed to be summarized and reported to her readers, most of whom wouldn't have heard of it but would be affected by it.

Ruth did a twirl, making certain her coat was open and her neck exposed. "Ta-da!"

Walter shook his head and slumped back into his seat. Bobby, released from his leash, took up his spot of the week, shuffling his body under Walter's feet. "No, I give in."

Ruth hung up her coat and took her own seat. "My scarf? I always wear my powder blue scarf with this pullover." At least he was a better reporter than he'd make a policeman, she thought. "It's chosen this morning to go missing."

Scratching Bobby's neck with his toes, having slipped off his shoes, Walter mused, "Haven't quite a lot of clothes gone missing from both your place and Betty's? I seem to remember Shirley mentioning she'd lost a scarf at the hangar dance. I don't suppose it ever turned up?"

Ruth shook her head. "No. We turned the place upside down, but never found it. Chances are, she simply lost it on a walk sometime and forgot. Though perhaps it's still somewhere in her belongings back at the cottage."

"Ah, well." He shrugged his shoulders before looking back up. "Have you heard from her?"

"Betty told me she received a letter from her the other day. I'm glad you brought it up. Everyone's going over to Betty's tonight for a reading. Are you on patrol?"

Taking out a small notebook from his top pocket, Walter flipped a few pages over before shaking his head. "I'll be there," he told her.

"Good. Seven o'clock all right?"

"No problem. I can start packing tomorrow night instead."

"Sorry. Packing?" Ruth asked puzzled.

"My fault," he said. "I had notice from my landlady last week. Her son's been invalided out of the Army."

"Oh, no!" Ruth uttered, her hands flying to her mouth. "Has she told you what happened?"

"Well, I didn't like to pry, but she did mention he'd been shot."

Ruth couldn't answer back straight away. Hearing about this tragedy reminded her of Joe, her son, captured by the Germans and now lying injured in a prison camp.

Realizing the effect the conversation was having upon his friend, Walter got to his feet, put the kettle on, and perched on the edge of her desk. Slowly, he leaned forward and pulled Ruth's head onto his shoulder. There were no tears, no shudders shaking her body. There was nothing, no reaction. This wasn't good. He really wasn't sure what to do. "Ruth?"

"Hmm?" Finally, she looked up, having to draw back so she could see Walter's face. "Oh, I'm sorry. I expect you know what was on my mind," she stated.

Walter kissed the top of her head before letting her go and going to make the tea. "Here you go," he told her, handing her a cup. "You've the last of the sugar, but I thought you needed it more than me."

"Thanks, very thoughtful." Ruth smiled back. After sipping her tea steadily, she eventually composed herself enough to ask, "Where does this leave you? Do you have somewhere to stay?"

Walter shrugged his shoulders. "I'd heard the Victory had a room going spare."

Ruth frowned, and Bobby barked in his sleep. Slowly, a smile actually crept onto her face. "Nonsense, at least whilst Shirley's away, I've a room free. You should come and stay with me."

Walter gave the offer some thought before turning a grin toward her. Sometimes, Ruth made it so easy to tease her. "Didn't I hear Betty saying she was going to partition her loft for Celia? I could ask if I could stay there."

However, Ruth wasn't the editor of a newspaper for nothing. "Firstly, until you're married, you will not live under the same roof as your Doris, engaged or not. Secondly, Celia's due back in a few weeks, so you'd have to move back out. No, come and take Shirley's room. I would say you can have the room Lawrence normally takes, but I've found the window doesn't fit since the bombing. We missed it when we were taking stock, and it'd be a bit like living in an icebox."

"Won't Shirley be back for Christmas, though?" Walter asked.

"Hmm. I don't know. I'll get Betty, or one of the girls, to ask. You have given me an idea, though. Come back with me tonight before we go around to Betty's. I haven't been up to my loft for yonks, so I've no idea what's up there, but how about we see if we can make it into a place where you could be happy sleeping?"

"Ruth, I've never said so, and don't take this the wrong way, but after having to bunk down at Mrs. Dunn's place, I'd be happy anywhere."

Contenting herself with a raised eyebrow, Ruth pushed her empty cup aside and picked up her notepad. "Come on, this article won't write itself, and the sooner it's done, the sooner we can get back to the cottage and see what we can sort out. What have you got so far?"

Back at his desk, Walter picked up his own pad. "I've been playing around with headlines. How does this one sound? It's only a work in progress, mind you—The Welfare State."

****

"You wanted to see me?"

Betty looked up from the paperwork occupying her, a little surprised to see Jane standing before her desk in the flight line hut. Not normally nervous, Betty temporarily forgot what she wanted to talk to her about. Then she noted a Tiger Moth trundling by, and she chided herself for being silly and smiled up at her friend.

"If you've the time?" Betty asked.

Jane pulled up a chair. "For my friends? Always. What can I do for you?"

Betty cleared her throat. "Where to start? You know how much I've appreciated what you've done for me, looking after me, so to speak, whilst I haven't felt able to fly." Jane didn't answer but raised an inquiring eyebrow, urging her to keep talking. Betty took a deep breath and, before she changed her mind, asked Jane, "Can you put me back on the active flying roster?"

Jane nearly slid off her seat. "Well, not what I was expecting to hear today. I have to ask, what brought this on?"

Betty got to her feet, opened the door to the hut, and went and stood out on the wooden decking. An Anson was beginning its landing approach, and as Jane joined her, they both watched it come in for a perfect landing and begin to taxi past. From the pilot's seat, Penny waved to the two of them.

"I'd forgotten how beautiful it is, you know, flying." She turned to face her friend, an expression of determination upon her face. "I want that feeling again." Then she proceeded to explain, "We were looking through my sister's things, trying to find any clue about the key."

"The Miss Marples ride again, eh?" Jane stated, resting her hand upon Betty's shoulder.

"The girls do seem to have a twinkle in their eyes again, yes," Betty agreed. "Anyway, we found a business card from a London bank. Of all places, it was hidden inside the lining of my old flying suit."

"She was quite something, your sister," Jane told Betty with a wide smile, shaking her head.

Betty just returned her smile.

"So I now need to ask, when are you off to London?"

Betty had the good grace to shrug her shoulders. "Very perceptive. It's not something you want to discuss over the phone. I've been waiting until one of the girls has a day off which coincides with one of mine, and then I'll call up in time to make a personal appointment."

Jane and Betty had been friends for a long time, so Jane didn't hesitate. "Come on, you." She took her friend by the arm. "Let's go back to my office."

Once back in the ops hut, Jane opened the door of her office, and the two sat down. "First things first—getting you back flying. We'll have to make this official, so as soon as you get back from London, Thelma can take you up in a Moth, and as soon as I'm satisfied you're not going to crash us into a hill or something, I'll want you to solo. Next step, back up in the Magister, followed by our old Spit. If all goes well, we'll have you out on deliveries within the following week. Now..." She fixed her friend with a look to brook no argument. "This doesn't get you out of your current job, so you won't be going on deliveries every day. Understood?"

Betty nodded.

"I'll tend to use you as cover for when we have girls on leave, or there's a flap on. It's what someone with your job would normally be expected to do anyway. Sound good?"

Betty grinned like the cat that got the cream. "Sounds very good to me, boss."

"Good." Jane nodded and pulled her desk diary toward her. Opening it, she licked her fingers. "Now,

71

let's see when we can get you and one of the girls on the same day off."

****

"Get those scissors to work, Penny," Doris advised as soon as her friend came through the front door, even before she'd had the chance to hang up her coat and bag.

"Again?"

"Again," agreed Mary from where she sat on the floor, surrounded by the remains of newspapers.

Penny sighed and flexed her fingers. "All right, all right. I'll go up and change and be right down."

As Penny hurried up the stairs, Betty shouted, "Fish pie in twenty minutes!" after her.

Five minutes later, Penny joined her friends sitting on the lounge floor to cut out strips of newspaper and help to glue together what she believed was going to be the world's longest paper chain.

"You do know we've still got about three weeks until Christmas, don't you?" she asked pointedly of Doris.

Doris, who appeared totally oblivious to the piece of paper she'd glued to her left ear, looked at Penny as if she'd completely lost the plot. "I know. We are so behind where we were last year! If we don't get a move on, we'll never get all the decorations up."

"We're behind," Mary felt the need to point out whilst shaking the front page of last week's *Hamble Gazette* free from her hand, "because we don't have Shirley to pressgang into the production line."

Everyone's moaning was for show, as Doris's enthusiasm for Christmas was legendary, even though they'd only had one together so far. Considering how

72

difficult food and presents were to obtain, she seemed to be going all out on the homemade decorations. Already Betty's lounge and hall were strung about with so many streamers and paperchains that the ceilings were barely visible. The holly tree in Ruth's garden had been virtually stripped bare—with Ruth's permission, of course—and both cottages were festooned with its branches. This did mean an occasional yelp was heard as someone accidentally brushed up against a sprig of holly, but Doris refused to let any be taken down. Ruth's house was taking shape in much the same fashion, though she had insisted the holly in her place was limited to the lounge. Everyone in Betty's, barring Doris, was in full agreement with her. The one thing they all did agree with was the greenery, as Doris had also raided the trees lining the riverbank, making the places look Christmassy and livening up the dreariness of the dull evenings. Wartime shortages or not, it was evident Christmas was coming to both of the riverside cottages.

By the time seven o'clock rolled around, the fish pie had been consumed, the washing up done and dried, and the lounge was full to bursting. Ruth had turned up with Walter and informed everyone he was going to be her temporary lodger. He was promptly inundated with offers of helping him move his things in. After he'd reassured them everything he owned could fit into a couple of suitcases, the room settled down, and Betty pulled out Shirley's letter.

"Everyone ready?" she asked, taking up position before the window.

To the accompaniment of much nodding, Betty began to read:

"*Dearest Betty,*

"*Before I forget to say, thank you very much for sending on to me my Ted's letter. It was waiting for me when I got to my billet. Such a treat—he even said he was behaving himself!*

"*I've been here five days, and I don't think my feet have touched the ground. They've got us flying all the hours God sends, and probably a few more besides—and I'm loving it! I soloed, officially, as my instructor said, yesterday and now have my license. I can't believe it. Honestly, if you'd have asked me if this all would have been possible last year, I'd have said world peace breaking out with Hitler dancing a tango down Pall Mall with Churchill would have been a better bet. I can't thank you all enough. Please ask Jane to thank Lizzie for me.*

"*I can't say where we're billeted, but it's a lovely old manor house, I think you'd call it. I share this big old room with ceilings so high I can't touch them even when I bounce on my bed. Please don't tell anyone I do this. There're three other girls in my room, and they're all a little bit older than me, so I've been taken under their wings. I don't think they want to see me get into trouble. Mind you, I did tell them some of what we got up to last year—don't worry, Betty, I'd never tell anything I shouldn't—and since then, I think they've been hoping I'll lead them into an adventure of their own. I think it should be me who's looking after them!*

"*Speaking of adventures, good luck with finding out about you-know-what!*

"*Now I've soloed, I've started on the Magister, and then it's the classroom. That's the bit I'm not looking forward to. I know you all went through the books with me and tried to drum it into my thick head, but I can't help but be worried. I don't want to let you lot down. I know I have a lot of work in front of me before I can wear my wings.*

"Oh, I have learned one thing already. The mechanics here don't like the trainee pilots tinkering with the engines. The one on mine a few days ago didn't sound great when I started it up, so I shut down and had the engine cowling open and was up to my elbows when I was yelled at to leave well enough alone.

"I'm going to stop now, Betty. I'm not much of a letter writer. Pass on my thoughts and love to everyone, please, and I'll write again soon. I hope to hear from you too and assuming we get Christmas leave, see you soon.

"Lots of love,
"Shirley"

Doris nudged her fiancé in the ribs. "Are you going to tell her you're sleeping in her room, or shall I?"

Chapter Nine

Betty had been up and down, then up and down again in a Tiger Moth since she'd gotten in to work the next morning. Jane, true to her word, had taken over Thelma's and Betty's duties so Thelma could take her up and get her used to the feel of an aircraft again. And Betty felt flying again was the best decision she'd made in ages. At least since her sister had died. As soon as she got back behind the stick, something slid back into place inside her. When the slipstream struck her face once again, she needed all her composure to avoid yelling out a whoop of sheer joy and exhilaration and couldn't help but wonder what she would feel like once she got her hands on a Spitfire.

By midmorning, the exhilaration hadn't worn out, but her body was feeling the pace. She had forgotten how tiring flying could be. She didn't care, though, and couldn't wait for her tea break to be over so she could go back up. Thelma said she'd been pleased everything had come back so quickly, as she'd never seen Betty fly before. If she came back tomorrow and did as well or, in Thelma's own words, "Didn't prang the bloody thing," then she'd let her go solo on Thursday.

Betty knocked back her tea, earning a look of reproach from Mavis, and then rushed back to the flight line hut, her throat still burning from the hot liquid that had done its best to scald her throat.

"Hello. Martins Bank of Lowndes Street?"

After finally being put through to someone who seemed to be in some sort of charge, Betty asked if they had safety deposit boxes, and then if they had one under the name of Eleanor Palmer. She had to endure a tedious wait whilst the woman on the other end of the phone went away to obtain (Betty presumed) a list of those who held a box at the bank. Five minutes—timed by Betty's watch—later she was back, and Betty could hear her leafing through pages before she heard, "Ah-ha!"

Betty didn't wait further. "You've found something?" At which she was told, yes, there was indeed a box registered under her sister's name. Swallowing hard, Betty said her sister was—dead. There were a few seconds of quiet from the other end of the phone, but not as many as would have been likely pre-war. Probably Betty wasn't the first person who'd told the same story. A few perfunctory condolences followed before the woman went back to what were obviously prepared lines for this situation. Once it was settled who was asking, Betty was informed to bring evidence of who she was to the bank.

There was another, "Ah," but no follow-up "Ha," this time.

"What's the matter?" Betty asked. The woman at the other end then asked if Betty was aware the Lowndes Street branch of the bank had actually been destroyed back in the Blitz of 1940? Unsurprisingly, Betty wasn't, and she began to say she'd been a little busy that year...and then stopped. If this woman had served in the bank back then, there was every chance she'd been in London during the bombings and therefore had been through her own fair share of hell. She didn't deserve any sarcasm. So Betty simply said no, she didn't know. The woman—Betty remembered her manners and found out she was called Mrs. Potter—then went on to tell her it was still titled the Lowndes Street branch, but it had actually moved to 48 Sloane Street. Fearing they were going around in circles a little, Betty asked why she was bringing up the bombing. Mrs. Potter said that when the old building had been destroyed, a good number of the bank's assets had also of course suffered, including a fair proportion of the safety deposit boxes. Betty felt an ice cube settle in her stomach.

As Mrs. Potter told her this news, she apologized for having to ask her to wait again, as she needed to go and find another book, one which contained the list of surviving boxes.

"There you are!" Thelma poked her head around the hut's door. She pointed at her watch. "You're late!"

Betty held the phone handset to her chest. "Sorry. I'm on the phone to the bank." Thelma frowned, so Betty told her, "I'll explain in a minute." Thelma nodded her head and left her to her call.

Mrs. Potter came back on the phone and thanked her for waiting. Not realizing she did so, Betty held her breath. Luck was on her side, however, and she was told her sister's box had indeed survived, apparently one of only twenty to have done so. Obtaining the new address and making a note of what identification she'd need to bring, Betty made an appointment for Thursday at midday and thanked the woman profusely for her help. Tucking into her top pocket the piece of paper with the appointment information, Betty allowed herself to slump back into the chair and let out the breath she hadn't known she was holding in.

Once she'd got her heartbeat back down to normal, Betty heaved herself to her feet, plucked her flying helmet up from where she'd dumped it on her desk, and headed out of the hut to find Thelma.

"Care to explain why you're late, First Officer Palmer?" Thelma asked from the wooden steps where she sat, trying to appear annoyed with her friend.

Betty bowed before her. "My apologies, First Officer Aston. Permission to plant my, as Doris would say, fanny?"

Laughing at Betty's choice of words, Thelma gently pulled her friend down beside her.

"Even though we don't actually have time, as such," Betty began, "I couldn't put it off any longer. You know the brass key of my sister's we found? Well, we found a bank card for a London branch of a bank, hidden in my flying suit, and I was phoning up to find out if the bank has a safety deposit box under her name."

Thelma leant forward, elbows on her knees, "And?"

"And I'm going to have to miss flying on Thursday, sorry."

Betty had been preparing for an argument, as Thelma was being very keen and helpful, but instead, she got a huge smile, and an offer. "Do you need a backup woman?"

Returning her grin, Betty clasped her friend's arm and pulled her close. "It's very kind of you to offer, but Jane's already arranged with Doris for her to come along." Thelma looked a little deflated, so Betty explained why she was taking Doris along.

Thelma gave it some thought and then said, "I can see why a brash American could be handy."

"I am sorry," Betty told her again.

After a few seconds of silence, Thelma gave her a squeeze. "Right. I was, if I'm being honest, hoping to get involved in this mystery. I saw what happened last year and was a little jealous. I felt a bit on the outside looking in."

"I didn't realize. Oh, my love, it wasn't any fun," Betty stated, placing a hand over her side where she'd been stabbed.

Thelma's free hand flew to her mouth. "Oh, Christ! No, I know, believe me. However, this doesn't sound like anywhere as dangerous a mystery as last year, if you'll pardon me," she added, knowing Betty had come very close to joining her sister in the ranks of the dead.

"Don't let it worry you. Look, if you can get Thursday off, by all means, join us.

"You mean it?" Thelma asked, all wide eyes.

"Of course!"

Thelma jumped to her feet and pulled her friend up also. "Come on, then. What are we waiting for? Let's go and speak to Jane. Then we've got about three hours and a bit of decent light left, so let's get into the sky. If you're going to solo tomorrow, we need to be back up as soon as possible."

****

As the train pulled into Hamble station, Detective Inspector Herbert Lawrence stepped off, put two heavy cases down on the platform, and stretched his back to work the cricks out of it. Catching the early, early morning train from London so he could surprise Mary had seemed like a great idea when he'd thought of it at nine o'clock the previous evening, but not so much now at just past seven in the morning. The worst bit? Honestly, he wasn't sure what the worst bit was. If truth be told, he wasn't a morning person. Unless he managed to get eight hours' sleep a night, the first few hours of each day always seemed to pass in a haze. It could be a bit of a problem, being a detective. He'd been permanently tired these last five years.

With one last groan, he rubbed his eyes and set off on the short walk back to his aunt Ruth's. By the time he stood outside The Old Lockkeepers Cottage, debating whether or not to knock on the door instead of going straight to Ruth's as he'd planned, he felt a little more alive, the early morning air reinvigorating him. Refreshed, he decided to knock after all, there being no reason he could think of why she shouldn't be awake.

"Lawrence!" Penny cried, as she opened the door.

"Did you say 'Lawrence'?" Mary put her head around the corner from the kitchen.

Putting his other case down, Lawrence opened his arms just in time to accept the onrushing Mary. "What are you doing back so early? I wasn't expecting you back until later tonight, maybe tomorrow!"

"Should I go back to London?" he asked, kissing her neck and eliciting an excited squeal from his girlfriend.

"Not at all," she breathed into his neck, "though you'd better stop before Betty hits you over the head with her gas mask case!"

Playing safe, Lawrence released his hold and stepped back. Exactly as Mary had warned, Betty stood in the kitchen doorway, twirling her gas mask case.

"Good morning, Lawrence."

"And a good morning to you too, Betty," Lawrence replied as Betty turned back into the kitchen. "She's a little scary, sometimes," he whispered into Mary's ear.

"A big, strong policeman like you? Scared of a little lady like Betty? Really! What would all your colleagues say?"

"I'd say, 'Come and meet this little firebrand who used to be a fence and survived being stabbed.' "

Mary, none too gently, hit him in the arm and treated him to a serious look. "You can never tell anyone about Betty's past! Do you understand me?"

Understanding she needed to know how seriously he took her words, Lawrence took both her hands in his and looked deep into her eyes. "I understand. Don't worry. She's very special to me too."

"Pleased to hear it," Betty told him, clapping him on the shoulder and making him jump. "Mary, we need to get to work. If I'm late today, Thelma may not let me solo, and I've places to be tomorrow. Lawrence?" She looked up at him. "If you want to talk to Mary anymore, you'll have to walk in with us."

Lawrence didn't have to think about it. "Mind if I leave my cases here, Betty? I'll pick them up later."

"Of course."

Shortly after, Lawrence was walking along the riverbank, arm in arm with Mary, following Betty, Doris, and Penny.

"I don't suppose anyone will tell me why Doris has a duck waddling along at her feet?"

"Quack! Quack, rrrr!" went the fowl in question.

Doris turned and bent down to stroke the noisy fowl. "Well, during what I'm calling 'The Case of

Gable and the Handkerchief,' this fiendish fowl happened to cross my path when I was walking home. Without knowing what I was doing, or so this lot would have you believe, I picked it up and walked along stroking it. Ever since, whenever he sees me, he follows and won't leave until he's had a bit of a fuss from me."

"Very strange, Doris," Lawrence finally told her as they reached the turning toward RAF Hamble. "You're lovely, but strange." After Doris had bent down and stroked her duck goodbye, he added, once safely out of hearing range, "What does Bobby think of him?"

"Bobby?" Penny said. "Whenever he sees that duck, he chases it into the river. Mind you, I don't think he'd know what to do with it, if he did catch it."

"How long are you back for this time?" Mary asked as they neared the entrance gate.

Allowing the others to go ahead, Lawrence folded his arms around her neck whilst Mary did the same around his waist. "Good, Ruth didn't tell you."

"Tell me what?" Mary asked.

"I expect to be around for quite a while."

Mary's eyes widened.

"Unfortunately," he continued, and she shrank a little, "not in Hamble. I've been made the head Detective Inspector in Portsmouth. So you see, I may not be living here, but I won't be far away and will be doing my best to spend as much time as I can with you, my likely odd working hours allowing."

"How wonderful!" Mary enthused.

"You'd better be careful, you and the rest of the ATA Mystery Club, not to step out of line. You're under my jurisdiction now."

Unsure if he was serious or not, Mary gulped.

Chapter Ten

"Why're trains never on time in this country?" Doris moaned, as they stepped off onto Waterloo's platform, immediately getting jostled by a multitude of civilians and service people from all walks of life and from all over the world.

"Be fair," Thelma said, rubbing her upper arm where a Lee-Enfield rifle had banged against her as it slipped off the shoulder of some private who didn't even notice. "We're only late because of some army convoy crossing in front of the train."

Doris skipped rapidly back to avoid getting an army boot on her foot, yelled at the back of the officer who'd nearly crippled her, "Watch where the hell you're going!" and promptly returned his stare with venom. If he wanted to get into a shouting match, neither Betty nor Thelma fancied his chances. Once he'd decided discretion was the better part of valor, she answered Thelma in typical Doris fashion, "And that's an excuse for not checking the train timetable?"

Betty kept quiet and slipped into step behind her two escorts. She knew the main reason for Doris's bad temper. They'd deliberately got on an early train from Hamble, knowing there were likely to be delays and wanting plenty of time to spare before Betty's appointment.

However, there were delays, and there were delays.

Leaving Southampton late had cost them twenty minutes, and some cows which had managed to get onto the line took another fifteen. The unexpected army convoy was what had cost them the best part of an hour, which had led to all their frayed nerves. Doris, though, wasn't one for keeping what she was feeling inside, and it seemed anyone who got in her way, at least if the train station crowd was anything to go by, was going to get informed what she thought of them. A quick discussion the previous evening about whether or not to go in uniform had ended up with Betty casting the deciding vote. She was very glad they were in civvies now, as otherwise she'd have half expected complaints to eventually wind up on Jane's desk.

"If you step on my foot one more time!" Doris was squaring up to a Royal Navy sailor who must have been a foot taller than she was, if he was an inch. He'd made the mistake of actually stepping on Doris's foot. Thelma had dropped back to stand next to Betty, though she had an expression of great amusement upon her face. When Betty looked behind the outhouse-sized sailor, his friends seemed to have similar looks. Everyone, especially Doris's opponent, could see he was in a no-win situation. Nobody in their right mind would challenge this chap to a fight—half his left ear was missing, and he had a vivid red burn covering most of his neck.

"You'll what?" he replied, obviously deciding he needed to take part in the confrontation, though equally obviously not wanting to do anything physical to the diminutive woman before him.

Doris took another step forward. She was now nose-to-collarbone. "Or I'll chew your ankles off!"

To be fair to the sailor, he was smarter than he looked—this wasn't difficult—and at hearing her words, he immediately creased up with laughter, swiftly joined by his mates. Sweeping off his cap, he took two steps back, then bowed and swept the cap downward in one swift motion. "Please, accept the apology of this humble servant of His Majesty's Royal Navy."

Every one of his mates made the same gesture with their caps, and in delight Doris clapped her hands together and grabbed the large sailor around the neck as he made to straighten up. "Apology accepted, my good man," she added in a terrible attempt to impersonate an upper-class English lady.

"Some film star's going to try the same awful accent one of these days and is going to be slaughtered!" Thelma declared, shaking her head.

Doris didn't appear to hear her as, by now, she was gallantly accepting a handshake and a swift kiss on the cheek from each of the sailors. As they turned to go, all waving heartily, she called after them, "Keep yourselves safe, boys!" a sentiment both Betty and Thelma greatly agreed with, so joined in the waving.

By the time this strange incident had happily passed, there was a temporary lull in the crowds, and they were able to make their way toward the Underground without further incident. "It's a very good thing Walter wasn't here," Betty commented.

They found where they needed to go, a short walk once they got off the Piccadilly Line from Knightsbridge. The Martins Bank of Lowndes Street located on Sloane Street didn't look too hard to find.

Accepting her ticket, Doris cheerily told them as she made toward the escalators, "He'd have made mincemeat of him!" Betty and Thelma both stumbled upon hearing this and had to hurry to catch their American friend up. "Come on," she shouted. "We're going to be late unless we get a move on."

****

They would have been late, too, if they hadn't been able to drag Doris away from the twinkling delights of Harvey Nichols. November in wartime or not, the store was doing its very best to pull in the customers from the bleak London streets. Only by promising the American they would pop into the store later did she allow herself to be led away, though not without the odd wistful glance over her shoulder.

According to Thelma's watch, after they'd backtracked up Sloane Street having missed their turn from Lowndes Street and sighted the sign for Martins Bank, they had five minutes to spare until Betty's appointment. Opening the door, they were met by a woman in her early fifties, dressed in the off-bottle-green uniform of the Women's Voluntary Service.

Holding out her hand somewhere in the middle of the threesome, she ventured, "Ms. Palmer?"

"Betty," she replied, taking the proffered hand and shaking it briefly before following her to a little area set aside for interviews and minor meetings.

"Forgive the rather cramped conditions," Mrs. Potter said after introducing herself. "We've not as much room here as we used to, but we'll make do. Would your friends care to join us?"

Betty turned her head and raised an enquiring eyebrow at them both.

Thelma shook her head, knowing this was something Betty should at least try to get through on

87

her own. "We'll be here if you need us," she informed her, taking Doris by the arm and steering her to some free seats against the far wall.

Betty nodded her understanding and jutted her chin out a little more as she took the seat before Mrs. Potter's desk.

"You've brought the items to prove your identity?" she asked Betty without preamble.

Not feeling much in the mood for small talk either, Betty took out an envelope from her bag and pushed it across the desk. Taking the papers out, Mrs. Potter spent a few minutes studying them and comparing the information on them against what her records showed. Apparently satisfied, she looked up and smiled. "Well, all seems to be in order. I assume you'd like to see the contents?"

Betty's gift of speech seemed to have deserted her, so she nodded, got to her feet, and followed the WVS lady through a door and down a short corridor to another door. Once that was unlocked, they found inside a simple wooden table. Taking a set of keys from her pocket, Mrs. Potter held them up before her until she came to the one she wanted.

"Do you have your key, please?" she asked.

Betty took her small brass key out and passed it across.

Comparing the two, Mrs. Potter frowned before looking across at Betty. "Were you aware the ID number on this key's been very carefully filed off?"

Not willing to reveal anything about her sister if she could avoid it, Betty shrugged and was happy to find she wasn't asked for any more information. Without further ado, she was handed her key back.

"Well," Mrs. Potter told her, "let's open up."

So saying, she turned her back and bent to insert her copy of the key. A moment later, she straightened and laid a long, narrow steel box on the table. Stepping back, Mrs. Potter said to Betty, "I'll just step outside the door. Please knock when you've finished, and I'll come back in and lock the box away."

"Thank you," Betty managed, finding her voice.

Once she'd gone, Betty laid her hands on the lid, stroking the metal as if to do so she could communicate with Eleanor, so she could tell her what she was going to find without actually opening the lid. When this failed to work, she took a deep breath and lifted the lid. Whatever she'd been expecting—jewels, cash, the odd rolled-up stolen master painting—didn't materialize. Instead, all she could see was a single piece of white paper with her name scrawled in her sister's copperplate script.

Taking it out, she couldn't resist the urge to thrust her hand inside the box and then, when this revealed nothing else, she tipped it upside down. This didn't reveal anything else either. Unfolding the paper, Betty began to read.

****

Ten minutes later, Betty had dragged everyone into a tea shop, shushing Doris into silence when she complained about it not being Harvey Nichols.

"I need a little time, Doris," Betty told her, leading her and Thelma to a table in a corner and ordering a pot of tea and three cups from a passing waitress as she went.

Once they'd settled and Doris had been persuaded of their impending visit to the department store, Betty took out the piece of paper she'd taken from the deposit box and laid it before them.

Thelma reached out and, when Betty didn't object, pulled it toward her and turned it over, though she didn't open it. "Is this all?"

Betty pursed her lips. "That's all." The tea then arrived, so they waited for the waitress to leave before Betty took the paper back and opened it out.

Thelma and Doris both read what was there, looked at each other, and then each took up the paper and re-read it.

You are not alone!

Contact a solicitor called Alistair Burrows, London.

As the three made their way out of the bank, heads close together in deep conversation, none of them noticed that the smartly tailored man who'd held the door open for them was following them as they strode back toward the underground station.

Chapter Eleven

"Cheer up, Penny, you'll find something," Doris advised, riling Penny even more.

"But we've only a week to go, and I've not got Celia anything for Christmas! No matter where I look, I can't find anything suitable." Penny slumped face down on her bed and thumped her pillow in frustration. After a minute or so of beating it up, she flipped over, taking the pillow with her and hugging it to her chest.

Doris sat on the end of her friend's bed. "Why's it so important? I know you left her on good terms, but you weren't close before."

Penny threw the sorely abused pillow into the air and punched it on the way down. It went sailing over Doris's head and was neatly caught by Mary as she came into the room. "What did this poor pillow ever do to you?" she asked.

"It was there," Penny unwittingly paraphrased George Mallory. "And I wasn't actually aiming at you."

Mary gathered her friend up and hugged her. "And we both know who always loses in a pillow fight, don't we?"

Unbeknownst to either, Doris had picked up the pillow from where Mary had hastily discarded it and promptly whacked her two friends around the backs of their heads. "The two of you!"

Penny raised an eyebrow at Mary, and the two of

them darted out, and a few minutes later, both were back with pillows of their own. Lines were drawn.

Backing up until she was against Penny's wardrobe, Doris raised her pillow. "If that's how you want it to be, have at it, you varlets!" cried Doris.

Penny went in low, aiming for the American's knees, and at the same time, Mary aimed for her friend's head. "I think we'll have to, if for no other reason than for your mangling of the English language!" Mary declared, failing to spot Doris's pillow aiming for her left ear.

"Ouch!" Mary muttered, retreating a little.

Doris got halfway through a cry of triumph but was cut off as Penny chose her distraction to swing her pillow around and land a resounding strike upon Doris's head, making her knees wobble. Before she could recover, Mary came back and connected with her other ear. Briefly making a recovery, Doris managed to catch Penny a glancing blow off her left shoulder before both Mary and Penny swung and connected at the same time, on the top of her head and her stomach respectively.

Staggering backward toward Penny's bed, at the same time holding up her free hand to fend off the relentless assault from her friends, Doris fell onto the covers. "Get her!" Mary yelled and launched herself on top of the squirming American. After a moment's hesitation, Penny joined her, and with one girl sitting on her chest and one pinning her knees, Doris was soon pleading for mercy.

"You were saying?" Mary demanded, jumping deftly off to stand beside the bed and holding out a hand to help Penny off Doris's legs.

Doris struggled up onto her elbows and fixed her two friends with a death stare. "That was hardly the same thing. It took two of you to beat me!"

The distinct possibility of the whole thing degenerating into a full-blown argument was nipped in the bud by a burst of laughter. All three heads turned to find Betty leaning against the door frame, red in the face from holding in her laughter for nearly too long.

"Oh, why did you stop? That's the funniest thing I've seen in years! Can we set up a weekly match?"

Doris looked at Penny, who looked at Mary, who shared a nod with the other two. A little too late, Betty realized the danger she was in and took to her heels, her three friends close on her heels.

****

"So what brought that on?" Betty asked, flicking a strand of loose hair back behind her ear.

Wiping a hand across her mouth, Mary put down her glass of water and stared across at Doris and Penny, who were also drinking heavily from their own glasses. She shook her head and replied, "You know, I haven't got a clue. It just kind of happened."

"I remember Penny throwing a cushion at my head. It hit Mary, and things progressed from there," Doris added.

Giving up trying to put her hair right, Betty aimed an eyebrow at her younger friends. "So I was…what? Collateral damage?"

All three exchanged looks, and when none of them could think of any other excuses, Penny took it upon herself to say, "Kind of. Sorry, Betty."

Getting up, Betty put on the kettle. She was a great believer in the healing power of a cup of English tea. "I suppose it's one way of blowing away the cobwebs," she told them, chuckling to herself, before noticing what the time was. "Come on, you lot," she told them, taking the kettle off the plate and turning off the gas. "We're going to be late unless we leave now, and I for one don't want to try using a pillow fight as an excuse."

Betty's warning galvanized everyone, and in a few short minutes, everyone had put on their remaining uniform parts, pinned their hair into what could be considered a reasonable shape, and were out the door at the same moment Ruth and Walter were passing the gate.

Walter exchanged a glance with Ruth before deciding to ask, "Is it worth asking why Doris has a feather in her hair?"

Before anyone could embarrass her further, there was a loud, "Quack!"

Doris, still with the feather she'd missed sticking out of her hair, bent down to pick up her perennial aquatic companion. Straightening up, she tucked him under her free arm, and with Penny on one side and Betty and Ruth on her other, they all set off down the riverbank. Walter, even though he'd seen and been part of the same strange procession, still shook his head every time he saw it. Each morning, the self-same duck, come rain or shine, waited for the American, ever since she'd picked him up whilst in a temporary fury a few months ago. It was now a tradition, yet still one of the strangest any of the group had ever been a part of.

"A very good morning, Duck," Doris told the fowl, beginning to stroke its back.

"You've named it now?" Ruth said. "Since when?"

Doris turned her face to the newspaper editor.

"Why not? He's a friendly little soul."

Penny reached out a hand to stroke him and was immediately rewarded by it snapping its bill at her, forcing her to hastily pull her hand out of the way. "Maybe to you," she muttered, checking she still had the same number of fingers.

"But, Duck?" Ruth prompted.

"He comes only when it suits him, so why give him a proper name?" Doris stated as they came to the bend in the path where one path led toward RAF Hamble and the other led into town.

"Makes sense," Mary replied, whilst making a grab for Ruth's arm. "Cats only come when they feel like it too."

"Right." Doris beamed back.

"You lot go on," Mary asked, hanging on to Ruth's arm. "I need a word."

Once everyone had nodded and made off toward the airfield at a slower pace, to give her a chance to catch them up, Ruth sent Walter ahead and waited until everyone was out of earshot before asking, "I assume you're wondering when Lawrence will be back?"

Mary grinned. "Am I so transparent?"

Ruth squeezed her arm and returned the smile. "Only to those who love him."

"And?" Mary prompted. She was pressed for time, and she'd also noticed her friends had stopped a little way up to wait for her.

"He'll be back tomorrow," Ruth revealed, and then when Mary gave all signs of squealing, pressed a hand to her mouth. "Too early in the morning, my dear."

Looking a little embarrassed, Mary bit down on her lip. "Sorry."

"Apart from the obvious, is there any particular reason you need to see him?"

Mary nodded. "I haven't told Betty about this," she began. Before Ruth's eyebrow could morph into a verbal protest, she raced on, "She told us last night about the message she found from her sister. I think we're going to need the help of a policeman to track this solicitor down."

"Solicitor?"

"Mary!"

They both looked up toward where Betty had shouted out and was waving at them.

"I think that means I'd better go," Mary said to Ruth, waving a hand toward her friends.

"Quick explanation!" Ruth demanded, gripping her friend's hand.

"We think it's a clue."

"A clue to what?" Ruth queried.

Mary shrugged her shoulder. "We don't know. The only other line on the note hinted she wasn't alone."

Ruth looked over Mary's shoulder and locked eyes with Betty, who twitched her eyes back to Mary, then back to Ruth. With a brief nod, Betty yelled out Mary's name again.

"I think I'd better go."

****

Penny was standing half in and half out of the flight line hut. She was fully dressed in her Sidcot suit and flying helmet, parachute in one hand and overnight bag in the other. "Do you think she'd mind?" she yelled again, striving to be heard over the whine of the Cheetah engines.

"I can't hear you!" Thelma shouted back, even

though she could.

"Come on!" Mary put in, marching up and attempting to pull her friend toward the Anson awaiting them. "Lizzie says the engines will overheat unless you put a shake on," she shouted into her friend's ear.

Penny snapped her head around. "I'm trying to get Thelma to let me borrow an aircraft!"

Mary took a step back and rubbed her ear. "Have a word when we get back," she told her and pulled her friend by the hand until they were at the door of their taxi.

Penny turned and shouted, "I'll speak with you when I get back."

"Okay!" Thelma waved.

"That she bloody well heard," Penny muttered to herself as she allowed Mary to shove her into the aircraft, where she hunkered down next to Doris, not to speak a single word until they got to the maintenance unit. Then she made up for lost time.

"What the hell is that?"

It was a very apt question.

Penny wasn't alone, amongst the pilots Lizzie had dropped off, to be on her hands and knees and staring at the strange objects strapped to the underneath of the Spitfires they were due to fly north. Beneath each normally smooth fuselage was a tank-like object. She felt a tap on her shoulder as she reached out a knuckle to rap it.

"It's called a Slipper tank," Doris supplied as Penny looked up.

"A what?" Mary asked.

"Slipper tank," Doris repeated and then elaborated. "It's an extra fuel tank, gives the plane a heck of an increase in range."

Mary frowned. "I thought we were only going to Scotland. I didn't pack for anywhere else." She threw a skeptical look at her overnight bag.

Doris helped Penny to her feet. "Don't worry," the American said. "We're only taking them as far as RAF Woodvale. I've a feeling we wouldn't want to be going with them any farther."

Doris's statement sobered them. Hamble was mounting a major effort today, and after watching the rest of the girls walk off toward their mounts, Penny leaned in close and almost whispered, "Convoy?"

Mary nodded. "They're either covering a convoy, or something secret's up, and if so, I'd rather not know what," she ventured, then clapped both her friends on the shoulders before giving Penny a quick hug, knowing her husband's brother had been killed on convoy duty. "Come on, the sooner we get these crates up there, the sooner we'll be back. At least it's the only delivery we have to make today," she added, reaching down to pick up her kit from where it lay at her feet.

****

Mary slammed the phone down, which earned her a full-bodied stare from the RAF flight sergeant on duty in the operations room. They'd already handed their delivery chits to him, so she grabbed her things and stormed out of the room, found where Doris and Penny had ensconced themselves on the steps of the hut, and flopped down beside them.

"When's the taxi due in?" Penny asked, leant back on her elbows with her eyes closed.

It had been an uneventful flight, albeit a long and tedious one. There had been a rain squall to navigate around just after they'd passed the Midlands, and nothing else of excitement occurred at all. Flying as a threesome, they'd taken their turn and shared the role of lead aircraft for part of the trip, which kept them all alert enough to avoid any danger of getting lost. Liverpool was quite a big city to miss, and Jane would never have let them hear the end of it if they had got lost. As they approached their destination, though, they had dropped back behind the others and followed them in to safe landings. Now they were all anxious to get home, and because of this, Mary's news wasn't best received.

"It's not."

Both girls' heads snapped up to look at the bearer of bad news.

"You're kidding!" Doris said, shaking her head.

"So what do we do now?" Penny wanted to know.

Mary flopped down between the two and filled them in. "Jane says she's very sorry. Our Anson's gone unserviceable, and the other's busy at the other end of the country. I'm sorry, girls, but it's going to have to be the train."

At that moment, an American Jeep pulled up next to them and a corporal shouted over at them, "You girls for the station?"

Penny and Doris looked at their companion.

"Jane's work. As soon as she knew what was going on, she arranged for transport to the station and for these…" She fished out of her inside pocket three train warrants and handed one each to Doris and Penny.

"Shouldn't we change?" Mary asked, glancing down at herself. All three were still in their flying suits.

"Did the others?" Doris asked, looking around and

ignoring the driver, who'd begun to lean on the Jeep's horn. "I don't see them anywhere. Hey, corporal," she turned and shouted over at the driver, throwing in her best eyelash-bat to get him to lay off the horn, which worked. "Did you drop off any of our colleagues?"

"A mate of mine did, hon."

Doris frowned and considered her options. Why did every British man, the first time they met an American girl—she could tell—go all Hollywood? Their American accent was worse even than her best English one. However, as she needed information off him, she couldn't kill him—yet.

"Did they go in their ATA uniform, or as we are?"

The corporal, very annoyingly, leant back in his seat, and all three quite clearly saw his gaze rove over them.

Penny picked up and flicked a small stone which hit him on the forehead. "Eyes up, or risk losing the ability to ever have children," she shouted.

He cleared his throat, rubbed his forehead, and at least pretended to be serious, though his answer didn't leave them much time to think things over.

"Well, seeing as they all arrived a good twenty minutes before you lot, I only saw the back of them as my mate sped off to the station." He shrugged.

Mary walked over and leant on the rear of his seat, forcing him to bend his head back to see her, "So what you're actually saying is, you have no idea what they were wearing?"

"Um…" The corporal cleared his throat and was rewarded by Mary swatting him around the back of his head.

"If those eyes even leave the road whilst you're

driving us to the station," she began, "it may be the last sight you ever see. Do we understand each other?"

Not certain if he had permission to speak or not, the corporal swallowed hard and nodded.

"Good boy." Mary patted his cheek. "Now, how long until the train leaves?"

Risking a glance at his watch, he replied, "If we leave now, you might just catch the three-thirty train."

Whether to change or not was now answered for them. All three exchanged glances before grabbing their gear. Doris, thinking it would be a good idea for their chances of making it alive to the train station for Mary to ride in the rear, hopped in the front.

"Well, what are you waiting for, boy?" she added for his benefit. "Let's get these doggies rolling!"

Chapter Twelve

With everyone out on deliveries, Betty, Jane, and Thelma were taking advantage of the quiet, trying to enjoy one of Mavis's cups of tea in the mess.

"It's coming along nicely, don't you think?" Jane pointed at the collage.

Thelma leant as close as she could without actually getting out of her seat, peering toward the top right-hand corner. "Who drew the Kilroy?"

The tips of Jane's ears turned a fetching shade of red. "I think my Frank may have had a hand in that."

"You think?" Betty smirked.

Jane took a sip and mumbled, "All right. He's to blame."

"Well, I like it," Betty assured her friend, patting her on the hand.

"More than the tea?" Thelma asked, pushing hers to one side.

Jane looked behind her. Fortunately Mavis, purveyor of the world's worst cup of tea, was busy wiping down her work surfaces and was out of earshot. "Between you and me, I can't remember how she got the job."

Betty, also checking that Mavis couldn't overhear, asked, "Did we check she could make a cup of tea at the interview?"

"No, you didn't," Mavis announced, having

appeared out of nowhere. Giving their table a quick wipe, she disappeared back into the kitchens.

"How did she... I didn't hear her... Is she a ghost?"

No matter what they thought of, none of them could come up with a plausible explanation as to how their mess manager could suddenly appear by their side. They eventually decided there could only be something ethereal about her, so perhaps treating her as such would be for the best.

"We really do need to find someone who can make a decent cup of tea. After a hard day's flying, our girls need something decent to come back to."

Jane nodded her agreement with Thelma's statement, adding, "If you've any ideas, I'm open to them."

They sat there in silence for a few minutes before Betty delved into a pocket and, after a small hesitation, placed the note she'd retrieved from her sister's safety deposit box on the table.

"Is this it?" Jane asked.

Betty nodded. "Go ahead, read it."

"Is that all? The name of a solicitor," Jane stated, a moment later. "It's not much to go on."

"I suspect that's what Mary was speaking with Ruth about when we came in this morning. I think she wants to bring in Lawrence."

Jane slumped back in her seat and looked up at the ceiling. "Don't tell me," she uttered, shaking her head. "Another mystery?"

Thelma leant in and nudged her friend. "I know. Isn't it exciting?"

****

"Did I ever tell you two how much I hate trains?" Penny asked her friends as she squeezed out of the toilet to join them.

"Have you lot finished yet?"

Doris turned her best evil stare at the owner of the voice. As was the norm these days, the train was crowded. Even with Doris doing her best to spur their driver on, the three had missed the three-thirty train and had to wait for an hour for the next one heading south. Typically, the station toilets were out of order, so they'd had to wait until they got on the next train to find one so they could change out of their flying suits and into their ATA uniforms. Though they didn't often wear them, all admitted they were more comfortable and smarter for wearing on the train, plus Jane didn't like her girls traveling in their flight suits.

"Yes, we have. Sooo sorry to have broken up your little card game, guys," Doris informed them. "You may have your office back."

The four army privates didn't know how to react to her sarcasm. When the three girls got onto the train, they'd stood out like a sore thumb in their flying suits, and when Doris had banged on the door of the first toilet to ask how long the occupant would be, the one she'd just spoken to had opened the door. The card game in play had been the last thing she'd expected, but Doris, being Doris, had recovered quickly and had literally dragged them out so she and her friends could change.

"Even now," Mary told her American friend, "you can still surprise me."

The three of them were now occupying space originally meant for two in the compartment. It was cozy, but at least they were together. The rest of the compartment was taken up by a vicar—there's always one, an unwritten rule—a young naval officer who was deep in whispered conversation with someone Penny hoped was his mother, given her age, and an elderly couple who were both fast asleep against each other's shoulders, snoring gently.

Despite the long day, no one was tired, so naturally the conversation came around to what they knew about the new mystery.

"But it's not new, really, is it?" Penny protested, as she took out her remaining sandwich and flask of cocoa.

Doris polished off her corned beef and washed it down with her remaining cocoa too. Licking off her remaining cocoa moustache, she put her flask away before replying, "I suppose you could look at it like that. Mind you, this could be much more Miss Marple than what happened last year with Betty's sister."

"How so?" Mary asked, wriggling a little trying to get more comfortable.

"What's that in your pocket, Mary?" Doris asked, also wriggling. "There's something sticking into my side."

Arching her back, Mary shoved a hand in the pocket and took out a penknife. "Sorry," she told her, shifting the offending item into her overnight bag.

"What I meant," Doris continued, "was what went on last year, with a great deal of hindsight, was a lot more dangerous than I've ever read in one of Mrs. Christie's books."

"I don't know how you can say that," Mary broke in. "There always seems to be plenty enough murder and mayhem in the books for me."

Immediately Mary closed her mouth. She knew the cat was out of the bag.

"Since when did you read Miss Marple?" Doris asked, whilst Penny looked at her friend with a newfound interest.

"Yes," she said. "Enlighten us."

Knowing she'd been caught, Mary settled back between her friends, enjoying the warmth they provided in the chilly compartment. "I'll only say I ran out of things to read back in April, and as there were a few of them lying around, I thought I'd see what all the fuss you lot made about them was about. They are rather exciting, aren't they?"

Trying and failing to playfully pinch her friend, Penny settled for laughing. "Welcome to the club!"

"So," Doris started, "as the newest member of the ATA Mystery Club, what are your thoughts?"

Before Mary could enlighten them, the elderly couple snorted in their sleep and the gentleman of the two began to drool. The young man and his very friendly mother covered their mouths with hands and tittered. The vicar folded up the newspaper he'd been reading and laid it aside. "I've always been a little partial to Miss Marple myself," he announced in a surprisingly high-pitched voice.

A natural respect of the clergy prevented anyone from telling him to mind his own business, so no matter how much they all wanted to discuss Eleanor's message instead, they found themselves caught up in a surprisingly entertaining discussion on the cases the fictional detective solved. In spite of this, all three were very glad when they pulled into London's Euston

Station. With a quite warm goodbye shared between the four, the young naval officer and his mother having departed with undue haste as soon as the train pulled to a stop, the girls left the vicar to wake up the sleeping older couple, waving away their offers of assistance.

A hurried journey across central London to Waterloo Station later—thankfully, uninterrupted by any air raids—they were safely tucked away on the Southampton train, though it wasn't until they were on the connection to Hamble that they managed to get a carriage to themselves.

"I'd try and hold it in, if I were you, girls," Penny advised, pulling the door shut behind her. "It's not out of order, but it'd be cleaner and safer to hang your bum outside than to try using that toilet."

"Wish we hadn't stopped off for that beer now," Doris mumbled. "It wasn't a patch on a Guinness anyway."

"You can hold on until we get to Hamble?" Penny asked.

"I'll bloody well have to." Doris chuckled.

"Seriously," Penny broke in, "whilst we've the compartment to ourselves, what are we going to do about this note of Betty's?"

"Short of speaking with Lawrence," Mary supplied, "I can't think of anything else we can do."

"That's what you were talking to Ruth about this morning?"

Mary nodded, immediately going red.

Penny nudged Doris in the ribs. "Methinks someone also wanted to find out when Lawrence will be back for her own purposes."

Mary nudged Penny a little harder than Doris had

been nudged. "So sue me. I miss him when he's away."

Both Doris and Penny enveloped their miserable friend in their arms.

"We know you do, hon," Doris agreed.

Mary wiped away a single tear and laid her head on Penny's shoulder. "I'm not being fair, Penny. I'm sorry. Here I am, moaning about my boyfriend not being around enough, when your husband's in danger nearly every day."

Not knowing quite how to respond, and not wanting to say the first thing to come out of her mouth in case it was the wrong thing, Penny held on to her friend for a while. Eventually, she told her the only thing she could—the truth.

"They're more alike than you give them credit for, Mary," she began. "There's no difference between getting shot at by the Germans or being thrown out of the first floor of a bombed-out building by some East-End gangster."

The door of their compartment chose that moment to slide open. Standing in the open doorway was a slim, black-suited man with very little hair and a grin which strongly reminded Doris of a shark she'd once seen being hauled out of the ocean—predatory and too full of teeth for its own good.

"Good evening, ladies. I regret disturbing you, but may I have a word?"

In case any of them were inclined to say no, he drew back his jacket to reveal a revolver, tucked into the waistband of his trousers.

Chapter Thirteen

From behind his office desk at Portsmouth Police Headquarters, now located at the Municipal College since the Guildhall had been destroyed in an air raid in 1941, Lawrence imagined he'd only have to close his eyes to see RAF Hamble, see his Mary taking off on her deliveries. Of course, he'd have to sweep away a bunch of trees and develop the ability to see over twenty miles, but it was a nice thought. A knock at his door ushered in his secretary, a nice woman of indeterminate age, likely in her early thirties to mid-fifties, with a nice demeanor and a nice line in tea. Nice seemed to fit her perfectly. However, it also meant he knew he'd never stand a chance of remembering anything about her.

After she left him a cup of her "nice" tea and a couple of biscuits he picked up and immediately put back down as likely to give him a stomach ache, Lawrence's phone rang. "Detective Inspector Lawrence," he answered.

Ten minutes later, he was running down the steps of the building, yelling over his shoulder at his secretary, who had run after him on her "nice" legs after he'd slammed the phone down, that he was off to RAF Hamble and could be contacted at the Station Commander's office. Jumping in his car, he hit the dashboard in frustration when it didn't start first time. "Come on!" The threat worked, and it started. Then came the problem of finding his way around a city which had quite a few streets simply no longer in existence. Cursing as he had to backtrack a number of times when one was too many, he eventually found his way onto the road leading to Hamble.

In his rearview mirror, he caught a fleeting glimpse of his sergeant's car closing up behind him. Perhaps he should see about commandeering—this was another person whose name he'd have to learn—that car? It certainly seemed faster than his! As he drove, doing his best to ignore a distinct clonking noise somewhere in the engine, he could feel his heartbeat begin to settle down.

When he'd received the call from Jane, he'd been certain his heart would shoot through the roof and he'd drop dead. The ten-minute call had mostly consisted of him asking her to repeat herself, as he found it very hard to believe the information his ears were receiving. It hadn't helped that her conversation included such words as "gun" and "kidnap attempt," and when Jane had told him his Mary had been involved, he'd acted instinctively. Though aware he should have, perhaps, assigned the first contact to his detective sergeant, he'd spluttered out that he'd be there as soon as he could and was halfway down the stairs before that thought had struck him. By then, nothing was going to stop him.

****

"Are you sure we can't begin the interrogation?" Doris asked, flicking aside the flap covering the peephole to the same cell Ralph had occupied last year.

"Come away from there," Jane advised her from where she stood next to the open door of the guardroom.

110

Penny, perched upon the edge of the desk, twiddled with a pencil as she pushed a revolver a few more inches away from her. "I agree with Doris. Why do we have to wait for Lawrence?"

"He is tied up and handcuffed," Mary pointed out, pushing the revolver back in Penny's direction. She sat on the opposite end of the desk from Penny.

Closing the door, as it had begun to rain, Jane pulled up a chair and sat between the pair. "Listen to me—and this includes you, Doris," she said pointedly, causing the American to come and stand next to her friends. "There will be no—repeat, *no*—interrogations before Lawrence gets here. We need to do this by the book, so we can find out exactly what he wanted with you." She shook her head and fixed Walter with a glare, not for the first time. "Honestly, Walter, I'd have expected this from this bunch, but to rope you in? Why didn't you call the police last night? If you'd have done the correct thing, we wouldn't be in this mess now!" Walter, still in full Home Guard uniform, did his best to blend into the background...and failed. Jane shot him one more evil glare before turning her wrath on the girls. If she was honest with herself, she was taking out her relief they were alive in the form of a telling-off to end all telling-offs.

"Tell me again, girls, as it doesn't look like Walter here is going to enlighten me." Walter did his best, again, to become invisible. "What happened? I want to make certain I can prevent Lawrence from arresting the lot of you."

Doris did her best to look affronted. "That's not fair, Jane! We didn't pull a gun on him. We're the wronged parties here."

"And, again, how come he's the one tied up and with a bump the size of an egg on the back of his head?"

"It's not our fault he didn't think Mary was a threat and turned his back on her whilst he was tying me and Doris up," Penny protested.

Jane eyed Mary's overnight bag suspiciously. "Exactly what do you keep in there? House bricks?"

Mary hopped off the desk, took up her bag, and held it open before Jane.

"I'll be darned!" Before Mary could stop her, Jane thrust a hand into the bag and came out holding up one slightly cracked brick.

Mary shrugged, took the brick from Jane, and after giving it a quick lookover, put it back in her bag. "You never know," she said by way of explanation.

Penny flashed a smile. "Well, me and Doris are certainly glad you do. Heaven knows what would have happened if you didn't."

"Well said!" Doris put in.

Exasperated, Jane ran a hand through her hair, causing it to stick up in all directions. "And he never told you why he was pulling a gun on you?"

"We were assuming he was going to get to that," Doris replied, "after he'd tied us up. Only Mary didn't let him get that far."

"And why our local bobby wasn't notified?" Jane persisted.

"We talked about this whilst we were waiting to get into Hamble," Penny put in.

"Yes," added Mary, "and the only thing we could come up with—"

"As he was unconscious," interrupted Doris,

unable to resist grinning.

"As he was unconscious," Mary agreed, "was that whatever he wanted, it must be something to do with Betty's sister."

"Go on," encouraged Jane, thinking she could see where this was going.

"Well, she's the only one of us—apart from Thelma, and we think her past wouldn't be relevant—who's got any connection to anything remotely serious, crime-wise that is."

"Yes," Penny agreed with a shrug. "We can't think of anything else."

Unseen by them all, whilst the girls had been doing their best to explain their actions to Jane, the door to the guardroom had opened.

"They're probably right, you know."

"Betty!" shouted Penny, Mary, and Doris at the same time, jumping up and rushing to hug her, nearly knocking her over in their enthusiasm.

Jane raised an eyebrow. "How much did you hear?"

"Enough."

"And?"

Betty allowed herself to be led over to the seat Jane had vacated. "And, I think they're probably right. I can't be certain, but I had this feeling, after we left the bank in London, that we were being followed. I had the odd look behind us, but I never saw anyone."

"You're certain of that?"

"Lawrence!" Mary shouted, causing Penny to choke on the cup of tea she'd just picked up.

For a few moments, Lawrence allowed himself to slip into the role of concerned boyfriend, holding his girlfriend as tightly as possible. Reaching up a hand, he stroked his fingers gently down the side of her cheek. "Are you sure you're all right?"

Mary nodded. "Never been better," she assured him.

Over the top of her head, Lawrence glanced across at Penny and Doris. "And the pair of you?"

"You're kidding," Doris told him, doffing her head toward the girl in his arms. "We've a wonder woman on our side. We've never been better."

At a cacophony of noise outside the door, Lawrence barely had time to release Mary before Detective Sergeant Terry Banks barged into the room. If anyone could be described as a lanky bag of bones, it would be Lawrence's number two. His other distinctive feature was a pair of the thickest bottle-bottom glasses anyone in the room had ever seen.

"Boss. What the hell?"

Taking a moment, Lawrence thought of how best to get out of the hole he'd dug himself. He knew how he'd feel if he had a boss he barely knew suddenly run out on him whilst only yelling a vague reason and directions over his shoulder. However, he'd worry about building bridges when he had time.

"I'll apologize to you later, Terry," he told him. "For now, get your notebook out." He reluctantly moved away from Mary and spoke to Jane. "Am I right in thinking the culprit's in the cell?"

"Same one as Ralph," she informed him. "I think you know the one." She held up a key to him.

"Need a hand?" Doris offered, with what could only be described as a grin fit to send a shudder down any villain's back.

****

"But I keep telling you! I never drew my revolver!"

Lawrence threw a glance and a raised eyebrow toward where his assistant Terry Banks lounged against the wall. To all but the untrained eye, he appeared to be so laid back as to be almost asleep. However, Lawrence was much wiser, and though he barely even knew his first name, the inspector could see how his sergeant's limbs were taut, ready to spring into action at a moment's notice if required. His ill-fitting suit did much to hide his state of readiness, though their prisoner wasn't in a condition to notice.

Much to his amusement and no little satisfaction, Lawrence had found him tied up and in handcuffs in the cell, his clothes disheveled, and nursing a major headache and a lump that clearly shone through his hair, where Mary had whacked him with the brick. He'd been so proud it had taken all of his self-control to prevent himself from turning back, taking her in his arms, and, damn the audience, kissing her to rival Rhett Butler.

"You still haven't explained why you were carrying a revolver in the first place," Banks asked again, breaking Lawrence out of his daydream.

Their prisoner tried to bring up a hand to wipe the sweat from his brow, but as they hadn't uncuffed him, this was impossible.

"Nor why you tried to accost three women on a train."

Lawrence decided to see what would happen by making it clear he considered this to be a personal matter. Marching purposely forward, he placed both hands on the man's shoulders and lowered his face until he could look him in the eye. "Listen closely." He glanced at the man's identity card to ascertain his prisoner's name. "Mr. Adams, I'm only going to say this once. You need to think very carefully. One of the women you attacked…"

"I attacked?" Adams tried and failed to pull back from the glare he was facing.

Lawrence gripped his prisoner's shoulders tightly and physically dragged both him and the wooden chair upon which he sat a few more inches toward him. "Yes, you attacked! As I was saying," he continued, "one of them is my girlfriend." He paused to let this news sink in, and Lawrence went on as soon as he felt his prisoner recoil as much as his circumstances allowed. "So I'm sure you can see I have reasons to know why you would threaten her."

The sudden quiet was broken by two things; Banks made a big display of cracking his knuckles, closely followed by Doris's shouting, "Ready for me to play bad cop yet?"

****

A mere fifteen minutes after Doris's attempted intervention, the cell door opened. Out marched both Lawrence and Banks. Behind them, visible just before the door closed, Adams sat slumped back in the chair. Barring the one caused by Lawrence's Mary, he didn't bear a mark, yet his body displayed nothing but total defeat.

"Can someone take him a cup of tea?" Banks asked of the room in general, and when no one took notice of him, he glanced at his boss, who moved his lips to frame one word. Sheepishly, he tried again. "Can someone take him a cup of tea, please?"

Jane nodded her head in approval. "Penny, put the kettle on."

Still reeling slightly under her boss's earlier telling off, Penny made off to fill the kettle.

"Banks?" Lawrence turned to his aide. "If you'd be so good as to write up your notes, I'll be with you shortly."

Nodding, the sergeant made his way to the desk and, with a polite, "May I?" took Mary's place. For her part, Mary happily moved to wrap an arm around his superior.

Doris, never much of a one for authority, blurted out, "What did you find out?"

Jane waved her excitable American friend into silence, and with obvious reluctance, Doris ran her hand through her hair and slumped down onto the desk, nearly knocking Banks's elbow in the act. She uttered a hurried and not really meant, "Sorry."

Lawrence asked Jane, "Do you have the key to his cuffs?" He jerked a thumb over his shoulder.

"Girls?" Jane asked, raising her voice and casting her eyes over her pilots.

Betty put a hand in her breast pocket and handed the key to Jane. "I thought I'd better keep hold of it." Jane passed it to Lawrence.

Noting the way Doris's eyes were flicking back and forth between the cell door and the key, Lawrence made certain he put the key safely into his pocket. He settled himself against the wall and satisfied himself that Banks was indeed writing up the notes, though he knew he'd be listening in to hear how his new boss handled this strange situation, as he wasn't yet aware of how close he was to this bunch of civilians. Lawrence told those present of what they'd got out of the prisoner. He didn't miss how all his friends gave him their full attention. Even Doris didn't make a move toward the door, let alone try to pick his pocket for the key. He wasn't sure she had the skill, but he wouldn't have put it past her.

"That solicitor's name," he asked, turning his head toward Betty. "What was it again?"

"Hold on," Betty replied, dipping her fingers into her pocket, fishing out a card, and reading out, "Alistair Burrows."

Sergeant Banks looked up from his notes and opened his mouth as if to protest, but was silenced by a raised eyebrow from his boss. Penny noticed this and patted Banks on his shoulder, which only served to confuse him more. He put his head back down and started up with his notes again.

Lawrence nodded with some satisfaction. "Apparently, this chap used to work for him—though, and we shall be checking his story, he was sacked a week ago for stealing confidential information."

Betty did her best to ignore the sudden feeling someone had plunged her into an ice bath. "What kind of…confidential…information?"

"The address of a client." He focused entirely upon Betty. "By the name of Palmer."

Chapter Fourteen

"How's Walter settling in?" Penny asked Ruth on the Monday as they walked to work.

"I am right here," the young man in question felt compelled to point out, tapping Penny on the shoulder.

"Of course you are, honey," Doris told her fiancé, giving his free hand a squeeze, whilst shifting Duck under the other arm, where it proceeded to spit and quack, in a very intimidating manner, at Mary and Betty.

Mary shook her head and hid a little behind Betty, "I really don't know how you put up with that thing."

"He's a sweety," Doris replied, absently stroking Duck's head.

As normal, whenever the subject of Doris's feathered friend came up, especially when the psychopathic aquatic fiend was present, the subject came back around to the connection between the two. Doris was the only one he'd allow near him, as he seemed to believe he was some kind of guard goose. Nobody really thought he understood human speech, but Mary, Penny, and Betty all thought he took umbrage at their voices.

After an incident a week ago when Mary had nearly stepped on his foot and he'd chased her into the Old Lockkeepers Cottage, she'd suggested he'd make a wonderful Christmas dinner. Doris had been lost for words, before finding her voice and letting Mary know exactly what she could do with that particular idea. Betty had noted she hadn't been aware the American had known so many Anglo-Saxon words and expressions.

Though they'd quickly made up, Mary still wasn't Duck's biggest fan. From her position behind Betty, she nodded down toward Ruth's feet. "Sweety? Look at Bobby. He's cowering behind Ruth's legs!"

Distracted by the argument, everyone looked down, and the spaniel was, indeed, shivering. Ruth bent down and stroked his back, receiving a soulful brown-eyed look up in return. She straightened up and told Mary, "Sorry to disappoint, but he's a little cold. That's all."

Bobby, the local furry hero, pulled at his leash as if to emphasize his desire to get into the office of the *Hamble Gazette* and settle beneath Ruth's editor's desk next to her electric fire.

Ruth herself let out her own small shiver. "He's got the right idea. Come on, Walter, say goodbye to Doris, and let's all get in from the cold."

"Here's hoping there are no biplanes today," Doris muttered before kissing Walter on the cheek and joining her friends on the short walk to RAF Hamble.

As they came within sight of the guardroom, there seemed to be an altercation going on. Standing next to the chap on guard was the sergeant in charge of the guardroom. His hands were on his hips, with one twitching toward the holster for the revolver he wore on his right hip. Before the two, their backs to the approaching girls, were two men wearing rather grubby raincoats of indeterminate color, one of whom had a camera swinging from his neck. They saw it as he turned to talk to his companion, though they were too far away to hear what was said.

"Morning, Sergeant!" Betty called when they were about five paces away.

Still somewhat distracted, the sergeant barely glanced up initially upon hearing her cry, though when he looked up a second time, a small smile made an appearance. "Miss Palmer. Perhaps"—he stepped slightly to one side so Betty could come and stand next to him, whilst the other girls stood to one side—"you could tell these *gentlemen* of the press that they can't come on base?"

The man next to the one with the camera turned to face Betty, but when he spotted the other girls, his gaze alighted upon Penny, where it stopped dead. Ignoring Betty's outstretched hand, though in fairness it's doubtful he even saw it, he quickly strode over to stand directly before Penny, who to the surprise of both Doris and Mary was doing anything but look at him.

"It is, isn't it? It's Penny Blake!" When she didn't reply, his expression grew quizzical, and he threw a quick look over toward his companion, who merely shrugged. He tried again. "Don't you remember me? Gerald Wilks. I'm from *The Post* magazine. I did a few stories on you before this lot all kicked off."

A beat before Doris spoke, Penny found her voice, and though her smile appeared forced, she held out a hand, which the reporter took between his own. "Yes. Sorry, of course I remember you. How are you keeping, Gerald?"

She got a shrug in return, though his smile appeared warm and sincere. "No point in grumbling, eh?" He looked around him, and upon seeing both Betty and the sergeant were now sporting identical hostile expressions, he hastily cleared his throat. "Yes, well. I mustn't take up too much of your time."

Doris, never one to be shy in stepping forward, did so, fixing the unfortunate man of the press with a glare more akin to one of a protective mother as she asked, "So what can we do for you, Mr. Wilks?" Mary stepped to Penny's other side so the reporter was in a semi-circle of slightly hostile natives. Betty came to stand a few feet behind him, completing the circle, gripping his shoulder and forcing him to turn to face her.

Correctly recognizing he was now addressing the ranking individual, Wilks cleared his throat. "I too would like an answer to that question," Betty informed him. "The sergeant here has told me you've been talking nonstop about Penny since you arrived ten minutes ago and wouldn't take no for an answer when he, quite rightly, refused you entry to the base."

Wilks threw a glance of help toward his photographer, who instinctively, as if he knew potential trouble when he saw it, stepped back. With that movement it became clear he had only one arm, so perhaps he did recognize when to be wary.

The cornered reporter ran a finger around his shirt collar, his eyes darting from side to side, but escape eluded him. "It came to my attention that Penny, here, had joined up, and me and my editor still remember her from before the war. You were quite a flier!" he said to Penny in a voice obviously aimed at endearing him to her. When nobody's expression lightened, he added, "Though I can see you didn't actually join up."

All four girls took a step toward him, leaving him

with no escape now. If they'd been human Bobbys, all four would have had their hackles up!

Betty shook her head, and Doris spoke more softly than she'd intended, probably a good idea. "I take it you do know what the Air Transport Auxiliary is?"

At least the reporter appeared to have a sense of self-preservation, as he hastily tried to make amends for insulting nearly everyone present. "Of course, of course! I didn't mean anything by it."

"Certainly bloody seemed like it," Doris said, not bothering to keep her voice down this time.

"Just tell us why you're here!" Penny snapped, linking her arm with Doris's.

"Yes, good point, I will," he stammered. "When we heard about Penny, here, we decided it would make a good story. You know," he went on, warming to his task. He started to wave his hands around but realized he hadn't room. "*Pre-War It-Girl Flies Spitfires*, that kind of thing."

Penny, almost instantly followed by Mary and Doris, turned their backs on him and moved toward the gate, the girl in question telling him as she moved off, "Sorry. That's all behind me. I'm not interested."

"But..." Wilks began, making to follow them before Betty stepped in front of him, placing a hand firmly on his chest.

"You heard the lady. Thanks, but no thanks. Now, I suggest you be on your way so I won't have to pretend not to see what the sergeant here would like to do to you and your photographer."

Whether Wilks was going to say something to the contrary, the pop of the sergeant unbuttoning the flap on his holster was enough to make him change his mind. Retreating to his companion's side, he called, "No hard feelings, Penny! You know where to get hold of me if you change your mind," before, with one last backward glance, sloping off toward Hamble.

Betty hurried to join her friends, who hadn't got very far and were now in conversation with the guard sergeant. She clapped him on the shoulder when she reached them. "Good job, Charley."

Now the intruder had been seen off, he reverted to first names. "My pleasure, Betty. Livened up the morning, eh?"

Penny actually leaned in and kissed him on the cheek. "Yes. Thank you, Charley."

Doris stood muttering and running a hand through her hair as the two men disappeared from sight. "I wonder how he found out you were here?"

Charley revealed, "I can help you there, miss. When he realized we wouldn't let him in when he first got here, the two of them had a chin-wag they thought was out of my hearing—mistake. I'm afraid it was your sister, Penny."

"What?"

Charley stopped himself from taking a step back. After all, he wasn't in trouble—he was merely the one passing on the news. "Not directly," he hastened to add. "That Wilks bloke's daughter goes to the same school as your sister and happened to mention what happened when you flew her back."

"I guess that explains why he was here," Penny said, and then a cloud settled over her and in a voice that would have frightened Hitler, she declared, "You wait until I get my hands on her!"

****

"You believe he's the same one who was following you when you came out of the bank, then?" Jane asked, grimacing as she regretted taking a sip of one of Mavis's cups of tea.

Just about to bring her own cup to her lips, Betty saw her friend's expression and hastily, hoping Mavis wouldn't spot her, pushed her cup away from her. She'd have a cup from the flask of Bovril she'd brought in with her that morning. After seeing her friends off on their first delivery of the day, she'd gone to find Jane, to fill her in on what had just occurred at the guardroom, but also to find out when she could begin deliveries. Jane had other ideas, and as soon as she'd joined her friend, had brought the conversation around to the previous day's incident.

Betty sat back and gave the matter some thought before finally telling her, "I think so. I mean," she tried to clarify, "I had a feeling we were being followed, but I didn't mention it to Thelma or Doris at the time, and though I kept glancing behind me, I never got a clear view of anyone shady."

"And you haven't felt like you're being followed since?"

Betty shook her head, absently and by force of habit taking a sip of her tea, instantly regretting it. "No, nothing like that. But if it is the same fellow, how come he was on that train?"

Jane smiled. "There, I can help you. It was simply one of life's coincidences. As well as the name and address of that couple, he also obtained your address." Jane let her friend mull that bit of information over, letting her take her time to reply.

"I've been wondering about that, though you'd

already know this," she eventually said. "I know it's my last name, but I've no idea what the connection would be between it and me. I don't have anyone, now Eleanor's gone. I'm not counting my parents, as they never wanted anything to do with me." Fortunately, Jane knew about Betty and her sister being placed in an orphanage, as their parents wanted only boys. "Did he say anything else?"

Jane shook her head. "Nothing Lawrence told me, anyway."

Betty let out a sigh of exasperation and slumped back into her seat. "I guess there's nothing else for it. I'll have to make a visit to this solicitor."

"It seems so," Jane agreed, picking up her cup and then, at Betty's hasty shake of her head, pushing it away. "When do you want to go?"

Whilst Betty thought this over, Mavis appeared as if by magic at their table. "Not thirsty?" She glared at the two virtually untouched cups.

Jane turned on her best smile and hoped the mess manager would fall for it. "We're not thirsty after all, it turns out," she told her and was rewarded with a disbelieving, "Hurumph," as the older woman took up the cups and, amidst much rattling, transported them back to her kitchen.

"Before you answer," she said, turning back to her friend and ignoring the continued rattles and crashes coming from the depths of Mavis's domain, "what was it you wanted to ask me about?"

Betty had to think hard for a few seconds. "Oh, well, two things. Firstly, I wanted to let you know there was a small incident down at the guardroom this morning."

After she'd told Jane what had happened, Jane shook her head and informed her, "*The Post*? I'll give their editor a call and warn him off. It doesn't sound like we'll have any more trouble from them, though."

"Penny'll be pleased to hear that," Betty agreed.

"And the second?"

"After everything that's happened, it almost seems not worthwhile mentioning," Betty said with a shrug.

"Mention away," Jane prodded.

"Well, I was hoping to find out when I could go back on deliveries."

Jane gave her friend a wry smile. "If it weren't for all this malarkey, I'd have said tomorrow. All your reports have come in top class."

"And now?"

"And now...I think you need to go and see this solicitor first, don't you? The last thing you need is something going around in your mind, taking some of your attention, when you're flying. Agreed?"

Reluctantly, Betty nodded, wondering what on earth a solicitor could want with her.

Chapter Fifteen

"Mr. Burrows is ready to see you now." The secretary, who in a strange brown floor-length dress resembled nothing more than a Christmas pudding, held open the door to the inner sanctum of the elusive Alistair Burrows, solicitor and possible holder and revealer of secrets.

Mumbling reluctant thanks—they hadn't even been offered a cup of tea, and it was now nearly one hour past the time of the appointment Betty had made—the two friends strode purposefully into a smartly appointed though sparsely furnished and surprisingly small room. Lining one wall were row upon row of leather-bound books. After the briefest of glances, Betty knew she wouldn't understand the contents of any of them. Mind you, she would bet anything that the mere attempt at reading any of them would be enough to cure anyone's insomnia. As they made their way toward the single desk, which was placed before the floor-to-ceiling window crisscrossed with tape at the end of the room, its occupant stood up and held out a hand.

Betty hoped she'd been able to keep from her face the same distaste Thelma must have felt as she shook his hand. The girls shared the quickest of glances out of the sides of their eyes and wiped their hands on the sides of their skirts. Both would agree later that neither had experienced such a sweaty handshake before. Their host, however, appeared to be either unaware of this personal problem or didn't care.

Exceptionally tall and likely the wrong side of seventy, with a pince-nez balanced on the end of his crooked nose, he'd attempted to hide his thinning pate by combing overlong strands of hair from one side to the other. Contrary to the man's off-putting physical aspect, the wide smile that accompanied the welcoming hand appeared genuine.

"Miss Aston," he said with a slight bow of his head toward Thelma before she was able to say anything and then turned his full attention to Betty. "Miss Betty Palmer, I cannot tell you how pleased I am to finally meet you. You have no idea how much like your brother you appear."

Betty almost missed her chair.

Thelma helped her to recover her balance and take her seat, whilst resisting the urge to say any of the half dozen questions that were fighting to escape her lips. Betty patted her friend's hands in thanks, keeping hold of one between both of hers for comfort. She opened and then closed her mouth twice and, when no words would come, squeezed Thelma's hand.

Assuming Betty would want to know the same answer to the same question as she did, Thelma took the helm and simply asked, "Who?"

Mr. Burrows frowned as he retook his seat, the smile slipping from his face. "I'm sorry. Aren't you here in response to Marcus's request?"

Betty tried to find her voice again and failed. Proving that you shouldn't judge someone by something like sweaty hands, the solicitor flicked a switch on his intercom and leant forward. "Miss

Fanshaw, three cups of tea. As quickly as possible, please." He then asked Betty, "Are you all right, Miss Palmer?" He filled a glass with water and pushed it toward her, and Betty gratefully emptied it.

"I'm...I'm not sure," Betty stammered. "Would you mind repeating what you just said?"

Before he could speak, the door opened, and in came his secretary with a tray bearing a very welcome pot of tea. "Thank you, Miss Fanshaw. That will be all," he dismissed her, and only when she'd closed the door behind her did he speak. "Where were we? Oh, yes, you do bear a remarkable resemblance to your brother, Marcus Palmer. He's been wanting to meet you for a while now."

Betty nodded, but still turned to Thelma for assurance before speaking again. "I've got no idea whom you're talking about," she told him, gratefully accepting the cup of tea the solicitor held out for her. "Thank you."

Before replying, Mr. Burrows took a long draft from his cup. "Perhaps, before you explain why you wanted to see me, I let you know of my connection to Marcus. To put it simply, I am the Palmer family's solicitor. Or, I should say, I was, as unless circumstances change, I shall not be doing business with the family after the Pilot Officer's commission finishes." As he finished, he sat back expectantly.

Taking another sip of her tea, Betty then took the card out of her pocket and placed it across the desk for the man to see.

Raising an eyebrow for permission, to which Betty nodded, he picked up the card, his eyebrow going even higher toward his receding hairline at realizing his name was on the card. He then turned it over and saw what was written on the reverse. "Very…enigmatic," he commented, pushing it back to Betty, who scooped it up and put it swiftly back into her jacket pocket. "I don't recognize the handwriting," he continued. "Could you enlighten me?"

"It's my sister's, Eleanor's. I only came across it myself very recently, though I have no idea how long ago she wrote those words."

"Hmm." Mr. Burrows twiddled a pen between his fingers before looking back across the desk where Betty and Thelma were waiting a little impatiently. "I'm afraid the name Eleanor Palmer isn't one I'm familiar with. Perhaps if I could talk to your sister?"

Betty shook her head, fighting away the icy feeling that always came to her stomach whenever the subject of her sister came up. Though she was beginning to get used to it, she didn't expect it to go away anytime soon, if at all. Nevertheless, she squared her jaw and informed him, looking him straight in the eye, "I'm afraid that's impossible. She was murdered last year."

Her choice of words, though enough to cause the solicitor's eyes to widen, didn't appear to shock him as much as she thought it would. Maybe he was tougher than his years implied.

"I'm sorry," he said simply, before getting up from his chair, turning his back upon his visitors, and staring out the window for a few moments. Turning back, he was stroking the remnants of his wispy, gray beard. "There is one possibility, though," he added, sweeping past them at a surprising rate of knots to yank open the door. "Miss Fanshaw, would you please bring in the list of clients of my late brother? Thank you." He shut the door and retook his seat. "My brother, before he passed last year…" He waved away the ladies as they began to utter the usual platitudes. "Natural causes, I assure you. Anyway, my brother was my partner and had his own list of clients. I admit, I haven't had inclination nor the need to look through most of his papers. Now may be as good a time as any, eh?" he told them with a small smile.

Betty took a deep breath. "I feel I should warn you, Mr. Burrows. My sister had a, shall we say, rather shady occupation."

Proving there was more to him than first appearances would say, the solicitor merely gave her a small nod. "When one has lived and worked in London as long as I have, you cannot honestly say that all of your clients are totally honest. My brother, certainly, wasn't above taking on certain clients of dubious persuasion."

Further conversation and possible revelations were brought to a temporary halt by the appearance of his secretary, who deposited a buff-colored folder on his desk. After waiting for her to leave the room and close the door behind her, the solicitor picked up the folder and opened it. Taking out a single piece of paper, he replaced his pince-nez and perused, presumably, the list of clients.

"Well, well," he muttered, before laying it down and looking at his clients with renewed interest. "There is, indeed, one Miss Eleanor Palmer here."

Thelma felt Betty's fingers tighten once more upon her hand. "Does it say what he did for her?"

"I'm afraid this is just a list. It doesn't give me anything of use, apart from her name," he informed them, shaking his head. He got to his feet and opened the top drawer of a filing cabinet, where he rummaged around for a minute before taking out a thin envelope. Placing it on the desk, he turned it over to reveal a bright red seal. With a crack, he opened and tipped out its contents. This turned out to be one crisp white envelope, addressed to Betty. The solicitor didn't hesitate, but immediately passed it into Betty's trembling hands. "The handwriting appears to be your sister's."

"Go on," Thelma told Betty when she turned her face to her friend, "open it."

Betty did so, though it took her two goes before her fingers managed to worm their way under the flap.

****

"...and even though it wasn't my fault the engine blew up, she still grounded me for two days! I ask you, how can that be my fault? It's not like I meant to fly into that gaggle of geese. They popped up out of the clouds and flew into me before I could do anything! She didn't even ask me if I was all right!

"I don't mean to complain, but it doesn't seem fair.

"That's all for now. I still hope to see you all at Christmas.

"Love to all and a big hug for Bobby!

"Shirley

"xx"

"Would I be right in saying you haven't yet got around to telling her you've given away her room?"

Walter was on the floor, leaning against the seat where Doris sat, her trousered legs either side of him. The only people missing from the usual crowd were

Betty and Thelma, who had taken the Tuesday afternoon train into London to keep their appointment with the solicitor. Despite it being December, the front windows were thrown wide open, at Doris's impassioned pleas, due to the almost over-powering stench of vinegar permeating the air. Naturally, everyone was digging in to newspaper-wrapped portions of fish 'n' chips—large, naturally.

Putting their absent trainee-pilot's letter aside, Ruth dipped an extra-large chip into a pool of brown sauce and waved it in the air. "Not as such, no."

Doris leant forward and rested her head on top of her arms, on top of Walter's head, "So, that's a no, then."

Ruth finished her chip before replying, "I suppose you could put it that way."

"I don't think she'll be very happy if she comes back and has to go into the icebox," Mary said, "and, just putting this out there, I for one am not sharing with her. I don't think my ears could take her snores again!"

Penny snorted Guinness out her nose as she tried to laugh and drink at the same time.

"Here." Mary passed her a handkerchief.

"I really don't mind moving in there whilst she's here," Walter declared.

Ruth shook her head. "It's my fault. I'd said we'd have a look at the attic when I offered you a room, Walter, and I haven't done so."

"Everyone's been busy," Walter tried to say.

"That's no excuse," Ruth told him, shaking her head again. "I should have found the time."

Behind Walter, Doris scrunched up her empty wrapping, heaved herself to her feet by stepping over her fiancé, and stood in the middle of the room. Looking around at her friends, who were gazing up at her with curiosity, she lobbed the ball of paper toward a waste bin in the corner of the room, missing by a mile. Hurrying to retrieve it, she put it in the bin by hand this time and then resumed her pantomime pose.

"Do you want to play charades?"

Doris stuck out her tongue to show what she thought of Penny's comment.

"No, we are not going to play charades, Penny."

"So, the reason for the stance is…"

"I believe you Brits have an expression," she began and then, when all she got in return were mystified glances, said, " 'No time like the present.' Come on! Everyone finish up, and let's go and take a look at Ruth's attic."

Nobody moved.

Doris stamped her foot in impatience. "Well?"

Finally, Ruth got to her feet, threw her finished wrapper into the bin, with considerably more precision than the American, and clapped her hands together. "It's not the worst of ideas," she said before turning to address everyone else. "Come on, we've still an hour of good light before blackout. Walter, if you would go out the back, there's a ladder in the shed we'll need."

Whilst Walter hurried out through the kitchen to obey his new landlady, everyone else followed Ruth up the stairs to the landing.

"It's not a large hatch, is it," Jane decided, looking up at the wooden hatch in the ceiling, a mere few feet across.

"My Walter's not fat. He'll be fine," Doris decided.

"Who said I'm fat?" Walter demanded from

halfway up the stairs, the ladder over his shoulder.

"I suggest you get your ears looked at, honey," Doris half shouted down toward him. "I said you're *not* fat."

"That's all right then." He carefully made his way toward them and leant the ladder against the wall. "Any idea what we'll find up there?" he asked Ruth.

Ruth pushed her glasses onto the top of her head and frowned. "Probably a lot of cobwebs." She shrugged, earning herself a playful swat on the arm from Jane. "Hey! I can't remember the last time I was up there."

"I brought up a torch," Walter announced. "I assume there's no electricity up there?"

Ruth shook her head.

"Right, stand back then," he continued. "I don't suppose anyone else wants to go first?"

His fiancée shook her head and leaned it against his arm, fluttering her eyelashes at him. "No fear. I'll face anything Hitler wants to throw at me, but show me a spider, and I'm the world's biggest coward."

With a foot on the lowest step, Walter leant down and kissed her on the forehead. "And I love you in spite of that major failing."

"You'd better!" she replied, smacking him hard on the backside as he lifted the hatch. Doris passed him the torch even whilst she kept a firm hold on the ladder.

"Girls," Penny said, keeping her voice low, "I need to speak to you—now."

****

Ruth handed the letter back to Penny and let out a breath she hadn't been aware she was holding.

Doris had stayed upstairs holding the ladder, with

Jane for company, so Penny felt more able to speak freely than when the words had tumbled out of her mouth. Though she trusted her, Jane was still her boss, and there were certain things she didn't want her to find out, at least not until she had no choice. Hence her decision to pass around the letter she'd received that morning from her husband Tom.

"Well?" Penny asked. She was perched on the edge of her chair, wringing her hands together nervously at what everyone would say.

"How far gone are you?" Ruth wanted to know.

Chapter Sixteen

Detective Sergeant Banks knocked on the open door of his new boss's office and marched up to his desk. He laid a report in front of Lawrence and then took a seat. "Report on my interrogation of that bugger we picked up at Hamble, boss."

Before speaking, Lawrence got to his feet and went to the hotplate he kept by the window. Holding up a rather battered kettle, he asked, "Care to join me, Banks?"

It had taken the rather mild-mannered sergeant only a short while to become very fond of this habit of his new boss. Virtually every time he delivered a report, or made any other visit to see him, he was offered a cup of tea. With his previous superior, he had seemed to be on endless trips down to the canteen, something he liked to blame for the lack of meat on his bones. His biggest problem now seemed to be worrying about making sloshing noises as he walked, but at least his boss made an excellent cuppa.

Banks crossed one leg over the other. "Don't mind if I do. Many thanks, boss."

Whilst they waited for the kettle to boil, Lawrence picked up the report and scanned through it, his eyebrows gradually rising until, just before he put it back down, his eyebrows nearly hit his hairline. His neck had also taken on a bright red sheen of anger which Banks could quite understand. He was a policeman, after all, and he had witnessed the close relationship his boss obviously had with one of the ladies—Mary, he thought her name was. To give his boss some time to think, he got up and went to make the tea. By the time he'd finished, Lawrence was back behind his desk.

"Thanks very much." Lawrence acknowledged the mug placed before him and prodded the report. "This is right? That piece of…scum actually admitted this?"

Banks cradled his own mug in his hands. The weather was too cold for Banks, and he'd found since turning the wrong side of forty that he felt it worse in his fingers, so the warmth was welcome. "He didn't want to," he informed Lawrence, "though why he waited a full day, I don't know."

"Me neither," Lawrence put in and then added, probably forgetting he wasn't alone, "but at least I can tell Betty something now, and perhaps Mary will stop annoying me for news." As soon as he'd finished speaking, he seemed to remember where he was, but when he looked up, Banks was looking innocently out the window. Lawrence cleared his throat. "This is good work, Banks, very good."

"Sorry it took so long," Banks told him, then took a long draft from his mug. "Do you mind if I ask you something?"

Lawrence swallowed before settling back in his seat and nodding. "Feel free."

"How well do you know this Betty Palmer?"

Lawrence smiled and took up his cup to warm his own hands before replying. "Quite well, I like to think," he began, before elaborating. "She's a very good friend of my Aunt Ruth, who runs the local newspaper, the *Hamble Gazette*, so I've known her for quite a few years."

"Sorry to say, boss, but my senses spiked when I was around her."

When he didn't add anything, Lawrence filled in the blanks, though being careful not to reveal too much of what he knew about Betty's past. "I'll only say this—don't ignore your senses. However, know this. So far as Betty is concerned, that's all in the past and I trust her completely. Is that good enough for you?" Lawrence asked, fixing his sergeant with a firm stare.

When he didn't answer straight away, Lawrence knew he'd made a good choice for his number two. Anyone who'd answered immediately wouldn't have really thought things through, merely telling the person who'd asked what they believed they wanted to hear. Indeed, when Banks did eventually answer, what he said truly satisfied Lawrence.

"I'll reserve judgment, but if you say you trust her, I'll trust you."

Lawrence got up from his desk and held out his hand. "Good enough for me."

Without hesitation, Banks got to his feet and shook his boss's hand, sealing a new level of trust between the pair.

****

Somewhat to her surprise, Penny was still flying. Admittedly, she hadn't spoken to Jane. Indeed, only Ruth knew of her condition, as she hadn't even confided in her best friends, something which didn't sit well with her. Not even as a child had she had such friends to tell everything to, but she'd lost count of the number of times she'd come close to telling them her secret, either on the walks to and from base or in the evenings.

Betty's problems, which only seemed to be multiplying, had taken front stage and allowed Penny to put her own issue on the back burner. The main problem was Tom. Her husband, still grounded because of the after-effects of the wounds he'd suffered earlier in the year, had taken to phoning her each night once he was sure she'd be home. She was regretting, a little, telling him her suspicions before she was certain. This was one of the problems with wartime marriages, she was finding out—you spent so little time with your partner, some subjects you would have talked about before even contemplating marriage went by the wayside. Penny hadn't given second thoughts to children. Obviously, Tom had, as he'd been delighted when she'd told him she suspected she was pregnant.

The biggest immediate problem was that he expected her to give up flying. Somehow, she wasn't shocked to discover, she found the very thought terrified her. Flying had been her life before the war came along, and now—now she truly believed she was performing a vital service to her country and felt sick at the thought of leaving it.

Undoing her harness, Penny wished she hadn't thought about being sick, as her stomach made a loud grumbling noise and started to churn. Hurriedly, she heaved herself out of the Anson's pilot seat and stumbled toward the exit, making it to the open door just in time.

"I didn't think the snacks were so bad anymore," a voice declared.

Wiping her mouth on the back of her glove, Penny raised her head, and as her vision refocused, she found she'd nearly been sick all over her boss's shoes. "Sorry about that, Jane," she told her and then gripped the door frame as another wave of nausea hit her, making her head swim.

Fortunately for her, Jane was watching closely and darted forward to steady her friend, making certain she didn't fall out of the plane. The ground wasn't as soft as in summer, and an early evening frost was beginning to settle in. "Steady, there," she told her. "I've got you." Waiting a few seconds for Penny to pull herself together, Jane kept hold of Penny's elbow as she made her way onto terra firma.

Close up, Jane could see the young woman was decidedly gray in pallor, and a frown creased her forehead. Looking her up and down, she then glanced around to check no one could overhear. They were quite alone, as Penny's passengers had already hurried into the flight line hut. She hooked Penny's hand through her arm and led her off in the direction of the ops hut instead.

Once they were safely ensconced in her office, Jane gently pushed a slightly protesting Penny into a chair, poured her a glass of water, and waited until her friend had drunk it down. "Better?"

Penny placed the glass on Jane's desk and gave her a weak smile. "A bit," she admitted.

Jane sat down behind her desk and allowed her face to slip into boss mode. "Is there something I should know?"

Penny couldn't keep the guilty expression off her face. She didn't help herself by automatically placing her hands over her stomach, at which Jane's other eyebrow went up.

"How long?"

Penny shrugged and finally placed her flight bag on the floor before replying, "I'm not sure," she admitted. "Probably a couple of months."

"Does Tom know?"

The memory of his last letter, which she still hadn't replied to, or telephoned him about, caused the corner of her mouth to turn up. "I've told him my suspicions."

Jane jerked back into her seat. "Suspicions? You mean you haven't seen a doctor yet?"

The buzz of a Tiger Moth's engine as it flew low past the hut caused Penny's eyes to flick to the window.

"Ah!" Jane said, steepling her hands together and allowing herself a wry smile. "I see."

"Hmm? Sorry," Penny said, refocusing on Jane.

"I think I see the problem," Jane told her. "You don't want to give up flying."

At hearing the words, Penny let her head droop before looking up and asking, "Do I have to?"

Jane came and perched on the edge of her desk, as close to her friend as she could. Taking one of Penny's hands in hers, she looked her in the eye, her heart heavy, as she didn't want to be the one to break her friend's heart. Nevertheless, she knew regulations better than anyone else. "Let's get you seen by a doctor first and take things from there. At least you'll know for certain then."

****

"So how was your first day back on the job?" Thelma asked.

The question was quite unnecessary. As she well

143

knew, her friend was literally bouncing up and down in post-flight excitement, but she wanted to hear what her friend had to say.

Betty let her flying suit drop to the floor of the flight line hut and hurriedly hung it up before sliding her pullover off. In a thrice, she'd donned her uniform trousers and jacket. The hut had no heating, and it wasn't a pleasant place to be in few clothes on a cold December evening. Sitting down, Betty bent over to tie up her shoes. Once done, she leant back against her locker and allowed a grin to fix itself upon her slightly oil-smudged face.

"I'd forgotten how much fun this is! The sense of freedom it gives you," she gushed before closing her eyes. "Plus, I flew my first Spitfire today." She opened her eyes and made certain to catch the eye of each of her friends. "I can now see what you mean. You don't fly them, do you? You strap them on and become a part of them!"

Thelma clapped her hands together in delight. "Girls, we have another convert."

The door opened and wafted in a cold evening breeze.

"Shut that door," yelled Thelma and Doris as one.

"Sorry," muttered Penny as she slumped down on the wooden bench between Mary and Thelma.

"What was that all about, with Jane?" Mary asked her friend as Penny slowly began to undo her flying suit.

When she didn't answer straight away, Mary playfully prodded her friend in the ribs with her elbow. "Cat got your tongue?"

Penny looked up, and for an instant, the normal

twinkle in her eye was there, but if you blinked, you'd have missed it. "Perhaps it'd be more appropriate to say, 'Frog got your tongue.' "

Thelma and Mary looked at Penny as if she'd lost her marbles, but Doris and Betty both gave audible gasps, as if they were twins, and flew to her side, bumping both Mary and Thelma aside in their haste.

"Hey!" Mary yelled. Her friends ignored her.

"How long?" Betty asked the usual question.

Meanwhile, Doris enquired, "You're sure, honey?"

Mary and Thelma put two and two together at the same time.

Penny did her best to climb into her closed locker, her eyes wide in moderate alarm.

Betty was the first to notice and swatted all three girls' hands away from where they were simultaneously reaching for Penny's. "Girls! Give her some room!" She matched actions to words and shuffled a good six inches to one side. After a moment, Doris did the same, and the others stopped in their tracks. Once she was satisfied Penny wasn't about to climb the hut's walls, Betty, putting every ounce of authority she possessed into her voice, instructed, "Penny, you finish getting changed, and the rest of us will be waiting outside for you. We can talk when we're back home."

Giving none of the others a chance to argue, she picked up and put on her uniform jacket and hat, took up her flight bag, and with a *very* pointed stare at her friends, strode to the door and held it open. Doris, Mary, and Thelma all looked at each other and, wisely, didn't utter another word but merely did the same. Betty closed the door behind her.

Left alone with her thoughts, Penny mechanically

went through the motions of getting changed. It took her two goes before she realized she'd been trying to get her legs into her jacket. Eventually dressed, she rested her hand on the doorknob, took a couple of deep, calming breaths, attempted and failed to put a welcoming smile upon her face, and opened the door. Her friends were waiting outside. Not a word was spoken the whole time it took to walk back to the Old Lockkeepers Cottage, and for this small mercy, Penny was grateful, as it gave her some time to get her thoughts into some kind of order for the questions about to come her way.

Sitting on her bed, Penny took up Tom's picture from her bedside table. Taken at the hangar dance at RAF Polebrook not long back, it had been the same day she'd discovered her husband was a Wing Commander. She'd been delighted, if not a little annoyed he hadn't told her before about the promotion. In it, she was beaming from ear to ear, and she'd had a wonderful time. Her husband didn't exactly look like he was chewing a bee, but it wasn't far from it. He was miffed about being grounded because of the headaches. Despite this, she still loved the picture for the memories it brought back to her every time she set eyes on it. Rubbing her sleeve on the glass to buff it up a little, Penny gathered her thoughts and muttered aloud, "Don't force me to make a choice, Tom."

Chapter Seventeen

Her girlfriends were waiting for her in the lounge. Penny caught sight of the bottles of Guinness set before them and the open one at an empty seat between Thelma and Betty on the sofa. From the slight nod of her head, she surmised this was Doris's idea. Trust her American friend to try to put a smile on her lips, she thought. Her lips twitched. Taking her seat, she raised her bottle, ignoring the glass next to it, and took a long pull. Since Doris had come into her life, she'd spent many an evening eating fish 'n' chips accompanied by a cool bottle of Guinness, and the liquid was a welcome relief. By the time she allowed herself to flop back into the pillows, a third of the bottle had gone. Unsurprisingly, a loud belch quickly followed. This actually broke the nervous atmosphere that was pervading.

"Someone needed that!" Doris announced, raising her bottle in salute.

"Certainly hit the spot," Penny announced.

"Forgive me for asking," Thelma asked, actually putting up her hand as she nervously continued, "but should you be drinking?"

By way of a reply, Penny reached for her bottle and clutched it to her chest. She fixed her friend with a semi-serious glare. "That's an old wives' tale. Plus, I don't see the doctor until tomorrow."

"So you're really not sure yet?" Mary asked.

Penny shook her head and looked around the room. Farthest from her, Betty was regarding her with a quiet assurance, obviously waiting to see what else was said. Doris too appeared calm, but the way she kept raising her bottle to her lips without actually drinking betrayed her. Penny would bet she'd someone in her past who had found themselves unexpectedly pregnant too. As for Mary, her eyes kept bobbing all over the place, the situation being out of her comfort zone. Ah, well, she knew they were here for her, and that's what counted.

"Do you need someone to come with you tomorrow?" Betty asked.

Penny shook her head and shot her a reassuring smile, or what she hoped was one. "Thanks for the offer, Betty, but I'd rather go on my own, if that's all right."

"You're sure?" Doris asked.

Penny nodded. "As sure as I can be. Jane took the trouble to make me an appointment with the station doctor on the quiet. He's sworn to keep this secret, on pain of death from Jane."

This news broke the tension, and everyone burst out laughing, even Penny, though she was, admittedly, last. Eventually, once everyone had dried their eyes, Penny put her now empty bottle down and stood up. "I'm only going to say this once. I'm still me, so if you could all stop treating me like an invalid, I'd very much appreciate it."

"Of course, sister," Doris immediately replied, soon echoed by her other friends.

"I've got to ask, though," Mary piped up, "what Tom thinks. I assume you've told him?"

Penny sat back down and let out a breath of frustration, mixed with annoyance.

"Need a top up?" Thelma passed her bottle to Penny, who took a hefty swig before passing the remains back.

"Thanks," she said and, head bowed a little, took out Tom's letter, which she'd been carrying around with her ever since it arrived. "I haven't been able to pick up the phone and discuss it with him yet—"

Doris interrupted, "You mean you haven't had a chance to phone him yet?"

Penny kept her eyes down, and her voice became barely a whisper, so the others had to lean in to hear. "More like, I haven't plucked up the nerve to."

Betty shook her head. "This isn't you, Penny."

Penny flopped back into the cushions once more and kneaded her eyes with her balled-up fists. "I know. I know! I'm not being fair, you don't need to tell me, but he's not being fair either." Now she'd begun, Penny found that she couldn't keep her fears and worries in. "He knows how much I love flying, and it's not like this was planned. I don't want to give up my job! I'm where I belong. What do I know about babies?"

Everyone looked at everyone else before Doris spoke up and asked a remarkably sensible question. "Have you told Tom all this?"

Penny hurled a cushion at her friend, who deftly fielded it before tucking it down in the side of her chair. "You know I haven't." She got to her feet and plonked herself down on Doris's lap, where she buried her face in her friend's shoulder and mumbled something.

"Could you try again?"

"I said," Penny tried again, moving her head

slightly away, "will you help me?"

Doris, with a big effort, heaved her friend off her lap and, grabbing her by the hand, pulled her out into the hall. Picking up the phone handset, she handed it to Penny. "No time like the present."

****

Ruth placed her hands on the small of her back, bent over backward as far as she could, rotated her hips, and let out a groan.

"And I believe that's nature's way of telling us it's time to pack it in for the night." Leaning on a spade he'd used to fill in a posthole, Matthew Green followed up his observation by copying Ruth. The groan he let out matched hers. "In fact, I think my body would agree." Going over to where Ruth stood next to the newly completed henhouse, Matt brushed the dirt off his hands as best he could before holding out a hand, which Ruth unhesitatingly took. "Do you think Mary will like it?"

Ruth dug her nails slightly into the back of his hand until he winced, and she released her pressure. "Don't tease her. It's not her fault she's scared of chickens."

Matt shook his head. "I still find that hard to believe. I mean…it's a chicken! What's the worst it can do? Peck your feet?"

Shouldering her shovel, Ruth set off for the back door. The light was fading, and the wind was strong enough off the Solent that she was more than happy to call it a night. It had taken a long time to get hold of all the materials to repair and rebuild after the bomb blast which had so nearly caused the loss of her beloved cottage, and then a while longer before Ruth and her friends could find the time to clear up the damage and put things back to how they used to be. Now, the henhouse was back, and she could transfer her remaining chickens from the temporary pens she'd knocked up. At least the vegetable garden and the rabbit pen had been up and running for a few weeks.

"Do you want to go and wash up?" Matt asked, filling the kettle.

Looking down at her hands, Ruth kissed him on the cheek before making her way upstairs, shouting as she went, "Good idea. I've half of the garden under my nails."

Ten minutes later, they sat around the kitchen table. Ruth was digging under her nails with the end of a pair of scissors, and Matt was dunking a biscuit in his tea. Another ten minutes passed, and though Matt had by now finished both his biscuit and tea, Ruth was still busy with her scissors, her tea seemingly forgotten and her eyes staring off into space.

Matt coughed and then, when this failed to elicit any response, he reached out and gently removed the scissors from Ruth's unprotesting fingers. "Penny for them?" he asked. "What's brought this on? I'm not saying you were chattering away outside, but it's like you're a different person."

After a few moments, Ruth let out a sigh, gave her fingernails one more glance, and cupped her hands around her now lukewarm cup. She looked up into Matt's warm and concerned face, her eyes flicking over the Home Guard battledress jacket hung on the back of his chair. "I think that's exactly it," she told him and in answer to his questioning gaze, elaborated, "Perhaps I need to be someone else."

Without hesitation, Matt reached across and took hold of her hands, gently rubbing his calloused thumbs across the backs of her hands. "It's taken me long enough to find you, Ruth, and one 'you' is about all I think I deserve, but I'm here, so tell me what you mean, and let's see what we can do about it—together."

"Together," Ruth mumbled, allowing a small smile to break out. She returned the pleasurable pressure to his hands. "I feel there's more I can do. You know," she went on, "for the war effort."

Matt turned her hands over, brought them to his lips, and gently pressed a featherlight kiss to each fingertip. "Personally, I think running a newspaper is more than enough. However..." He released one of his hands to hold it up as Ruth had been about to interrupt him. "I'm not stupid enough to try and persuade you otherwise. What did you have in mind?"

Ruth laid her free hand on his stubbled cheek. "What did I do to deserve you?"

The grin that split his face, made him look ten years younger than his mid-fifties. "I could tell you, but then you'd send me out on my ear!" This did earn him a slightly pinched cheek. Rubbing it, he asked, "So, ideas?"

"Well, I was thinking about joining the ARP."

****

After finally managing to get through to her husband, Penny held the phone slightly away from her head and motioned for Doris to come and sit next to her. Immediately realizing what she intended, her friend shook her head and made to move to take up a seat on the stairs. However, Penny grabbed and held her firmly by the arm and pulled her down to sit on the floor with

152

her. "Stay, please?"

Doris was about to protest when she saw the tears in Penny's eyes and felt any further objections drain away. Making herself as comfortable as possible, Doris lifted her arm and Penny scrunched down, leaning against her side and holding the receiver so it rested between them.

"Penny?" came Tom's voice, making them both jump.

Penny's lips twitched as she noticed Doris firmly clamping her mouth shut to stop from saying a greeting.

"Hi, Tom!"

"What happened to you?" he asked without preamble, adding, "Where've you been?"

Forcing oneself to make a phone call you weren't prepared for was one thing, but it had the additional unwelcome issue of making you think on your feet. Usually, Penny was good at making snap decisions or dealing with unexpected situations, but nothing in her past had prepared her for anything so delicate and personal. However, now the call had been made… "I've…I've been thinking."

"About what? What's there to think about?" he asked straight away.

Penny's arm around Doris's waist tightened in annoyance. "About this whole…baby…thing."

Brief silence occurred before Tom eventually said, "Don't you…want a baby?"

Almost at once, Penny replied, "Of course I do!" Before he could say anything with the breath she heard him take in, she got in, "Only I thought it would be something we talked about—planned, you know. It's come as a complete surprise. Plus," she added, realizing how it would sound, "I'm not actually seeing the doctor until tomorrow morning, so we're not even certain I am—pregnant." It was the first time she'd said that particular word out loud, and it didn't sound right.

Both girls could hear him take in a couple of deep breaths before he managed to say, "Do you really think you're pregnant?"

Before answering, Penny cocked her head to the side and raised an eyebrow at Doris, who promptly raised hers back. Taking a deep breath of her own, Penny told him she believed she was, which elicited an excited little yip from her husband. That caused Penny to smile until, remembering her husband's letter, she squashed it. "That's by the by, at least until tomorrow. I have to say, I'm not happy about you making the assumption I'll stop flying—resign from the ATA and come to live with you."

"But surely it only makes sense," Tom said, his voice rising slightly.

Penny required a small prod in the ribs to find her voice. "Perhaps," she allowed, "but I can't help but feel I'm being pressured into something I'm not prepared for."

"Don't you want us to live together?" Tom pressed and then, obviously unaware he was speaking to more than one ear, coyly suggested, "I look forward very much to the day when we can wake up together on a regular basis."

Doris clamped her free hand to her mouth, desperate to prevent a snort's escape.

Despite the extreme closeness of her best friend, Penny couldn't help but agree that the suggestion held tremendous merit. "Of course, that would be wonderful, but I would have preferred for the opportunity to present itself somewhat less…unexpectedly."

When Tom next spoke, there was hesitancy in his voice which sent a shiver down Penny's spine. "You must do as you feel right, of course. Know that I love you, but on this matter, I can think of no other outcome."

"But I…" Penny began to say, but she trailed off, as the line had gone dead.

Chapter Eighteen

Betty, ever so carefully, used the old towel beside the oven to take out the brick heating these last few hours before she went up to bed. She laid it on the kitchen table, and there she wrapped it in another towel she kept for the purpose of placing it in her bed. Her parcel safely tucked under her arm, she popped her head around the door to the lounge.

"I'm going up to bed, girls. See you all in the morning."

All three were huddled up together on the sofa, and upon hearing Betty's words, only Mary and Doris looked up. Penny was between them, and it didn't go unnoticed by their landlady and friend that she didn't look up. Moving the towel and its contents to beneath her other arm, Betty crossed the floor to stand before them. Juggling her bedwarmer, Betty pulled up a stool and sat before them.

"Penny, love, what's wrong?"

Penny gulped a couple of times before giving up trying to speak. Doris filled Betty in on the cause. This time, Betty did drop the brick, narrowly missing the toe of her slippered left foot.

"Have you tried to call him back?" Betty asked, pushing the brick to one side with her foot and kneeling beside Penny.

"He's not taking her calls," Doris told Betty,

wincing a little as Penny grabbed her hand and squeezed.

Betty frowned. "Something must be going on. This doesn't sound like the Tom Alsop I've come to know. He's normally so understanding and supportive. Is there anything you can think of, Penny? Anything at all?"

With a couple of deep, hard swallows, Penny managed to find her voice. "There's only one thing I can think of. He's still grounded. The doctors won't allow him to fly until his headaches go away. It seems that was the main thing on his mind whenever we talked, before...well, before this came along." She laid her free hand on her stomach. "He can't wait to get back on ops."

"But you're happy he's safe on the ground. Aren't you?" Mary asked.

"I am." Penny sniffed. "I think that may be part of the problem, though, now you say the words. Here I am, flying around in all kinds of weather, and he can't."

"You think he's what, jealous?" Doris asked, gently prising a couple of Penny's nails from the palm of her hand.

"Sorry," Penny muttered and ran a hand through her hair. "It's possible."

"It'd certainly explain why he's acting the fool," Betty added. "Look, the best thing to do is to go and talk things out with him. It never does any good to let these things fester."

"He could..." Penny swallowed, coughed, and then sneezed before carrying on. "He could refuse to see me..." Having voiced her fear, Penny threw herself into Doris's arms.

Betty tucked her brick back under her arm, stood

up, and kissed Penny on the top of the head. "I don't think so. You leave things with me," she assured her friend. "If memory serves, you were hoping to persuade Jane to let you take a Magister to pick up Celia tomorrow afternoon. Yes?" When Penny managed a nod, Betty continued, "Well, you leave this with me. I'll speak to her and explain things. I'll get you permission to drop into Marham first, and then you can go and pick up your sister."

Penny looked up with grateful eyes at Betty who, knowing she wasn't capable of speaking at that moment without bursting into tears, gave her a half-smile and nodded to the others as she left the room for bed.

****

With the still-hot brick safely wrapped in its towel, Betty pulled her blankets up to her neck and reached to her bedside table to pick up the book she was reading. Her fingers brushed the letter from her sister she'd received at the solicitors. She'd opened it but been unable to read much of it at the office. She had sensed both the solicitor's and Thelma's frustration, though neither had questioned her decision.

Picking it up now, she turned it over once, twice, but there were no clues to indicate what it could contain. There was nothing else for it. If she prevaricated any longer, they'd enter her name as the new definition for the word "prevaricate" in the dictionary.

Taking a deep breath, she glanced up, making sure her bedroom door was shut. Good, as she didn't want to share this moment with anyone else. She took out the single piece of paper, and began to read silently, taking it slowly, one word at a time.

Jan. 10th 1942

My darling Betty,

It is my dearest wish that you are never in receipt of this letter, because if you are, then that means you found my other letter/note/whatever—I never was any good at explaining myself in words, was I? You've met the Burrows brothers now, I expect. I do hope you like them, as they were responsible for my personal affairs, things I didn't want to bother you with. These were mostly what I did with my share of our...takings. There are instructions at the end of this letter as to where you may find and take control of what is now yours.

However, and I fear you will now become rather angry with me, and I am so very sorry, my dear, dear Betty, so very sorry for keeping this from you. If he hadn't specifically made me promise on a Bible, I hope you can believe I never would have done so otherwise. I would have told you in an instant.

We have a brother! His name is Marcus, and he's a pilot in the RAF. What a coincidence, isn't it? He became aware of us when our parents—sorry to call them that, I know you hate even thinking of them, like I do—let slip our existence. He wouldn't go into the full details of when or how that happened, but by pure luck we had the same solicitors (what's the odds?) so when he mentioned our names...well, let's just say it saved him a lot of work tracking us down, not to mention money.

We met a few times, and he seems a pleasant enough young man, though perhaps a little naive. He actually brought up us reconciling with—his parents. I soon put him right on that!

I shall say one more thing on that subject—it seems

*that dear father has a gambling habit in which his
success is not matched by his luck. In fact, it appears he
lost his seat in the House of Commons because of his
debts to certain disreputable bookmakers.*

*I don't know if that is the reason why Marcus
wishes to become acquainted with us. To find some way
of extorting money out of us? I don't know, but I don't
believe it, either. As of the date of this letter, I have not
discovered.*

*As you have no doubt figured out, it has become a
habit of mine to write uncalled-for letters which I hope
will find their way to you upon the event of my death.
This is another, but also the last. I wrote one of these
every month to give to my solicitor for safekeeping. The
others were destroyed, each in turn when I handed him
the new one.*

*If you wish to contact our brother, then you should
get back in touch with Mr. Burrows and ask him to look
up a file with this reference—291166. I'd rather not
give his details here.*

*And so, my dearest Betty, my sister, I will sign off
with the hope that we do not meet for a long, long time.
Make good use of the money that I have left you, and do
with it as you will.*

I will always love you,
Your Eleanor
xxxx

Turning the letter over, Betty saw a number of
bank details. All the names were of establishments in
London including, she was amused to note, the name of
one place from which Eleanor had stolen a rather
splendid diamond necklace amongst other items from

its safety deposit boxes. The irony wasn't lost on her. Whatever she found, she would move to a place they hadn't frequented. Sense dictated it.

Folding the letter, trying to ignore it was dated the month Eleanor had died, she placed it back in its envelope and tucked it inside the cover of her book. She was ready to lose herself in *The Body in the Library* once again. Miss Marple was about to begin interviewing the Guides, and Betty was anxious, however much she enjoyed this novel, to begin the next. *The Moving Finger* had lain unopened on her dressing table since she'd bought it last month. She'd lost count of the number of times she'd had to smack the fingers of one of the other women to prevent them from taking it and reading it before her.

****

"Come in!" Jane said, pulling open the door to her office and ushering Betty into the room.

"I'm sorry," Betty immediately apologized.

Jane was not alone. Lawrence sat before the desk, a cup of tea to his lips seemingly forgot. At hearing her voice, he immediately put the cup down and jumped to his feet.

"Betty! What a coincidence this is! We were just discussing you."

Jane grabbed her gently by the elbow and shut the door behind her. "Yes, don't go. Take a seat, please."

Unable to keep a suspicious expression from her face, Betty allowed her friend to steer her to the seat next to Lawrence. "And I was the subject of discussion because…?"

Jane and Lawrence exchanged looks before Lawrence pushed a brown envelope toward her. "Read that."

A couple of minutes later, Betty was slumped back in her seat and being urged to finish off Lawrence's cup of tea. Eventually, she looked up into their concerned faces and wiped a hand across her brow. "Well, I'm not sure what to say."

"I find the expression 'Bugger me' about covers it," Jane suggested, getting a slight chuckle from Betty in response.

"Yes, I think that sums it up nicely."

"Of course, I don't know anything about your parents," Jane supplied, "but anyone who hires a cheap private investigator to warn someone off from knowing they have a brother, well…"

Betty gratefully took hold of one each of Lawrence's and Jane's hands. "I don't think there are words," she agreed. "I must admit, though, even taking into account what little I know of them, it hardly makes me champ at the bit to meet them, ever."

"And this brother?" Lawrence asked. "I did notice you didn't seem surprised."

"That's why you're such a good policeman." Betty laughed slightly and took out the letter she'd read the previous night, placing it on top of the police report she'd just read. At their querying eyebrows, she told them, "It's a letter from my sister. Apparently, she was in the habit of writing one a month to leave with the solicitors. That's the last one she ever wrote. She says our brother, Marcus, as you already know"—she indicated the police report—"had found out about us, and by sheer chance, his solicitor was the same one Eleanor used. She'd even met him a few times."

"Did she say why your parents were so desperate to

stop him from contacting you?" Lawrence asked, police hat on.

Betty fixed him with a serious expression. "Lawrence, I appreciate you're doing your job, and I won't do anything to hinder your investigation—I assume you'll be contacting...them?" she asked. When he nodded, she continued, "Can we agree not to call them *my parents*? I don't want anything to do with them. How about *the Palmers*?" Betty suggested.

Lawrence swiftly agreed. "I'm sorry, Betty. I should have thought. "So what's your next step?"

"Funny," Betty said, "that's exactly what I was going to ask you."

To fill the silence which this caused, Jane asked Betty, "What can I do for you? Something tells me it's not anything to do with Lawrence's investigation."

"I came to ask a favor for Penny, actually."

Jane frowned and took her seat behind her desk. "I don't suppose this has anything to do with Penny and her sister, has it?"

Instead of replying straight away, Betty turned her attention to Lawrence. "I don't suppose you'd give us a few minutes, Lawrence? I could really do with talking to Jane in private."

Lawrence got to his feet with a smile, pulling on his overcoat. "Say no more. I came over to fill both of you in on what we'd found out. You turning up allowed me to kill two birds with one stone. I'll be off now." Picking up the report, he opened the door to Jane's office. "Ladies, keep safe, and I'll see you both soon."

"Drive safely!" Jane called after him, and with the shutting of the door, the two were alone. Once he'd left, Jane turned her full attention on her friend. "Go on.

163

What does she want?"

"Well, she'd like your permission to borrow a Magister and go to pick Celia up for Christmas."

Jane didn't answer straight away, but instead steepled her fingers and regarded her friend over their top, before asking, "I expect you know of her—situation."

"To be fair, nothing's been confirmed yet. She's only seeing the doctor this morning. Well"—she brought her wrist up to look at her watch—"right now, actually."

"She should be grounded, at least," Jane pointed out.

Betty nodded, though she didn't smile. "If it's positive."

"If it's positive," Jane agreed.

"So, in the meantime, would you have any objection to her request? If it helps, she could also do with going via Marham to see her husband."

"Tom?" Jane lurched forward, concern etching her brow. "What's wrong? Is he okay?"

"Physically?" Betty said, shaking her head sadly. "I'm not sure. The problem is, she spoke to him on the phone last night, and he hung up on her when she wouldn't agree to immediately resign from the ATA. Now, he won't take any calls from her, and she's worried sick, even more than she has been."

"Has she tried this morning?" Jane asked.

"Yes," Betty answered. "Twice, before we came in, but same result."

Jane immediately picked up her phone. "Let me try."

Matching actions to words, Jane wasted no time in

calling up RAF Marham and getting herself put through to Tom's squadron. However, upon her request to be put through to him, the person at the other end told her he wasn't taking calls from anyone at Hamble. No amount of pleading would change his mind, so knowing a fruitless task when one presented itself, she put the phone down.

"He's being an awkward sod, all right," Jane told Betty. Getting out of her chair, she turned her back to stare out the window. It was nine in the morning, and the last taxi aircraft was just taking off. Coming to a decision, she turned back to Betty. "Go and tell Penny that once she's finished at the doctor's she's to take up a Magister—I'll tell you which, when you come back—and go and kick some sense into that husband of hers! She can then go and collect Celia."

Betty was out of her chair, a half-formed, "Thank…" nearly out of her lips when Jane's next words cut her enthusiasm down to size.

"But tell her that depending upon what the doctor's report says, when she gets back, she'll be grounded until further notice."

Chapter Nineteen

"How many times do you intend using the old, 'I'm ATA, so I don't have a radio, sorry to just drop in' routine?"

Penny hadn't seen her husband look so angry, ever. "I thought, it being Christmas Eve, I'd be able to get away with it once more," she told him, but he didn't appear to hear.

At this moment, her husband was striding ahead of her toward the hangar his squadron was housed in. She supposed he had reason to be angry, having had to explain to the station commander that their unexpected visitor wasn't lost after all but was his wife, on a visit. His temper wasn't improved by the knowledge she was intent upon them talking through the situation they were in. She hadn't said so in so many words, but the first words she'd said when she'd jumped out of the rear cockpit of the Magister had been, "We need to talk."

Opening the door to his office, he impatiently waved Sharon Coates away when she had the nerve to pop her head out from the canteen and wave a teapot at them. Slamming his door behind him, he threw his hat toward his desk with such force it bounced off and ended up in his wastebasket. Normally quite fastidious about appearances whilst on duty, it showed the level of his annoyance when he flopped down into the chair behind his desk without bothering to fish it out.

Penny was more than annoyed at his choice of seat, as she'd been expecting him to take one of the easy chairs they'd occupied the last time she'd been in his office. With little choice, she pulled out the wooden seat on the other side of his desk, not troubling herself with the squeak it made, and sat down. Seeing Tom didn't seem in any hurry to begin the conversation, she took a few moments to take in her, at this moment, very annoying husband.

With the bandage still wrapped around his head, he looked a little like a half-dressed mummy. She suppressed a shiver and vowed to give that film a miss if it came around again. From what she could see of his forehead, there appeared to be a permanent frown etched upon it. Well, Penny thought, steeling her resolve, with the way she was feeling toward him right now, it wasn't her place to smooth it away. Love could be cruel at times, and this was going to be one of those times.

"Tom," Penny began and then, when he didn't lift his head from the hand he was resting it upon, slapped the desk and snapped at him, "Tom!" Now she had his attention, Penny came right out with what she wanted—needed—to say. She'd had plenty of time on the flight over to decide on what words to use, and she only hoped she'd be able to get through to the man she fell in love with, not the one who was behaving like an oafish bore. "Here is what I've decided." Her opening choice of words had the effect she hoped, as his head snapped up, leaving his supporting arm hanging there. "If—and neither of us will know until the results of the test I had this morning come in…"

Annoyingly, Tom broke in to ask, "And when will

the results be back? When will you know?"

Penny huffed, as the answer didn't give her much room for maneuver. "I'll know in the morning."

"Will you phone and let me know?" he asked, now leaning forward.

"It depends," Penny half-snapped, still annoyed her carefully prepared speech was being interrupted. "Will you take my call?" Her swift reply caused Tom's jaw to flop open. She was secretly pleased at this reaction. Assuming his answer would be in the affirmative, Penny went on. "As I was saying. *If* I am pregnant, then I will have to stop flying."

If she'd have felt in any way like weakening in her resolve, her determination was reinforced by the sight of the grin upon her husband's face. It could only be described as belonging to one who believed they'd won everything they wished for. She loved her husband, despite his actions of late, but she wasn't about to give up on her beloved flying that easily.

"However, I believe Jane would let me continue working for her, even if I am pregnant, though not in a flying capacity." Even as she said the words, she could feel her heart clench, as she had no intention of giving up flying without a fight. "Look, you can't expect me to give up my job completely. I love you..." She was happy to see that his expression did indeed soften upon hearing this confession. "But I'm also doing a job I love, one that's vital to the country. Surely"—she began to play her trump card—"you of all people can appreciate that?"

Once, twice, three times Tom opened his mouth to speak, but on each nothing came out. His eyes were glazed, and Penny had no doubt he was indeed, as she'd hoped, thinking back to when they'd first met. She'd delivered a Mosquito bomber to Marham, and Tom had been sent up to lead her in. Only he'd been flying a type of aircraft, a Mustang, she wasn't familiar with. The mix-up used to make them both laugh, and though she felt a little guilty for using it against him, considering his behavior she didn't feel all *that* guilty.

Hesitatingly, Tom allowed the fingers of a hand to crawl across the desk. Hoping for a gesture of reconciliation, Penny leant forward and reached out one of hers. Tentatively, Tom first rested his fingers on hers and then, when she didn't pull away, gradually clutched her fingers in his. Lowering his head, he raised their entwined hands to his lips and kissed her fingers.

Looking into her eyes, he asked, "Have I really been such an ass?"

"Yes," Penny told him, though she did allow the corners of her mouth to turn up slightly. No point in totally alienating him, not if she wanted to keep her marriage alive, and that was one thing she was certain of. No way would she let anything come between them. "Now, can you tell me why?"

Getting to his feet, though keeping tight hold of Penny's hand, Tom moved over to the comfy armchairs, making certain his wife was seated before taking the other. With his free hand, Tom scratched the top of his head where a small tuft of hair poked through the bandaging. He let out a deep sigh. "It's Sam."

Puzzled, Penny asked, "What's Sam got to do with this?"

Tom's brother Sam had served in the Merchant Marine and been killed earlier that year. She'd never met him, but from how Tom had talked about him, the

169

two of them had been as close as brothers could be. Still, she couldn't make a connection between Tom's strong feelings on her possible pregnancy and his late brother.

If she were a betting lady, Penny would have wagered her husband had quickly wiped a tear away. "It was always Sam who was keen on marrying, perpetuating the family line," Tom began, steeling himself and glancing at the curious gaze of his wife. "Before I met you, I was a happy bachelor. You corrupted me—in a good way," he hastened to add. "Then Sam…died…and all of a sudden, the weight of continuing the family line fell to me. Well, what with the war and us seeing each other so irregularly, there never seemed a good time to bring up the, ah, subject. Then, you told me of your suspicions, and I believe I went off the deep end, as your friend Doris would say."

"I won't disagree with you," Penny told him, after giving his speech some thought. Stroking the back of his hand, she told him, "You should have told me. Even in a letter or over the phone, you should have said something, Tom. Do you really feel that strongly about us having children?"

With a final squeeze, he let go of her hand, settled back into his seat, and stroked his chin in thought, eventually looking up into Penny's patient, expectant face. "I do, yes. However…"

"However?" Penny took a turn to interrupt.

"However, I bitterly regret behaving as I did, and I certainly should not have demanded for you to give up your job and move up here to be with me."

"Oh, Tom." Penny reached up and stroked the face she so dearly loved. "You do know how much I wish we could be together, don't you?" She waited for him to nod before going on. "Well, let's see what happens, shall we?"

Realizing this was the best offer he was likely to get, Tom nodded, leant over, and after a slight hesitation, kissed Penny firmly on the lips. After a moment, she allowed herself to relax into the sensation of enjoying the taste of her husband's lips upon hers. She fought to conquer the idea of where they could end up if she allowed her body to behave as it dearly wished to do. It had been too long since they'd slept together, and her body was reminding her of its needs.

Breathlessly, she pulled away, hoping she could speak coherently. She looked deep into his eyes and found what she was hoping for behind those long lashes she was so envious of. "Are we…okay?"

In a voice which made her wish more than ever they were anywhere more congenial to how she felt, he told her, "If you'll forgive me, then, yes."

"I forgive you," she told him and leant in, deciding her body could take control for a few more minutes.

Unexpectedly, Tom pulled away, a look on his face of, if not horror, then one of dawning realization.

"What's wrong?" Penny asked, alarm tinging her voice.

"Today's Christmas Eve."

"Right," Penny agreed, waiting to see where he was going.

"And you said you'd get the test results tomorrow…"

"Right," she said again and then stopped, her hand flying to her mouth as his meaning became clear. "We won't get the results tomorrow."

"Right. Day after Boxing Day?"

"I'll speak to the doctor when I get back," Penny promised.

Tom nodded, satisfied, and then drew her back into his arms. "Now, Mrs. Alsop, where were we?"

****

Penny could still taste Tom's kisses upon her lips as Celia's school came into view. She was about a half hour late in arriving due to "circumstances beyond her control" and, leaning over the side of the cockpit and seeing what looked like the entire school being out to greet her again, felt a pang of guilt. Deciding to blame the weather, if she was asked why she was late, she circled the school once and then, when the main driveway had cleared, brought the Magister in to land.

To her surprise, the headmistress, dumpy yet eternally enthusiastic Samantha Garret, clad in what seemed to be her usual tweed, was standing ready with a set of wooden chocks. No sooner had the plane rolled to a halt than the lady darted under first the port wing and then the starboard, securing a chock under each wheel. Post-flight checks over, Penny shut down the engine and took off her flying helmet, leaving it on her seat as she hopped out of the cockpit, onto the wing, and thence onto the ground.

Barely had her feet touched the ground when she felt a pair of arms wrap themselves around her from behind, closely followed by a loud voice squealing, "Sis!"

"Miss Blake!" shouted the headmistress.

"Yes?" both Penny and her younger sister said at the same time.

"The younger Miss Blake," Samantha amended. "I

know you're happy to see Penny, but please let her go for a short while."

Released from her sister's embrace, Penny gave Celia a brief kiss on the forehead before turning to face the beaming headmistress. "Miss Garret," Penny said, holding out a hand—which was ignored, and she found herself in another, slightly less enthusiastic, embrace.

"Don't be silly. Call me Samantha," she was told. "You can't go through a near-death experience as we did and not be on first-name terms."

"Samantha it is," Penny agreed. Personally, she thought her friend was slightly over-exaggerating things. Yes, on the brief flight she'd treated Samantha to on her last visit they'd spotted German airplanes high above them, but their own plane hadn't been noticed by the enemy. Penny looked around, and though there weren't as many students and teachers around as before, there was still quite a crowd. "I'm a bit surprised to see so many here today. I thought school had finished lessons yesterday."

Samantha linked her arm through one of Penny's, and with Celia on her other side, they started walking toward the school's main building, an old manor house. "There wouldn't normally be this many girls around, my dear, no, not at all, only once word got around you were flying in to pick up Celia, well, it seemed everyone's transport arrangements had to be put back for a day."

Once they were settled in her office, Penny felt compelled to say, "I'm very sorry for any trouble I've caused, Samantha. I didn't realize my coming would have this effect. I haven't prevented you from going away, have I?"

A steaming pot of tea was waiting for them on the headmistress's desk, and so as Celia dutifully poured out the tea for her elders and then took her own to a seat a little farther back than her sister's, Samantha replied, "Not at all. My sister doesn't finish work until tomorrow, so I won't be leaving until tomorrow anyway."

Taking hold of her cup and saucer, Penny brought it to her lips, blew on it, and took a deep and refreshing gulp, luxuriating in the hot liquid as it rapidly warmed her still very cold throat. Her silk scarf could only do so much against the cold as she flew. With half the welcome drink gone, she placed the cup down and, tipping her head to one side, regarded her sister. "So has this one been behaving herself?"

Celia was kneading away at her throat and had already finished her own tea. "I've been a paragon of good behavior, I'll have you know!" she protested.

Samantha wagged a finger at Penny's sister. "Only because we've had you so busy you haven't had the time to get into trouble."

"It worked, then?" Penny asked.

"Certainly did…and my floors have never been so clean," Samantha agreed.

Celia looked from one to the other, though as she turned her whole body instead of just her head, the process appeared forced, perhaps even painful.

"Are you okay?" Penny asked.

Turning her head toward her elder sister once more, Celia again looked not quite right, but she nodded, only once, and said, "I'm fine, just a little anxious to get back to Hamble, that's all."

Taking into account both her own possible

condition and the time of year, Penny turned to the headmistress. "If you don't mind my asking, are there any illnesses going around the school?"

Samantha didn't need much thinking time. "A few colds, some girls complaining of feeling stiff, nothing out of the normal, but you have to keep in mind this is an old building, and keeping it warm is a very difficult task. I think I'd be right in saying that the years we don't have any snuffles or sniffles is when we would notice."

No matter how nice she found sitting in the warm and comfortable room, talking to someone who, if she lived closer, could easily become a good friend, Penny was very conscious she was on the clock, so to speak, and really should be getting off back to Hamble. She tried not to dwell on the fact it could be her last flight for a while. Finishing her tea, Penny got to her feet and held out a hand to Samantha.

"I'd really, really love nothing better than to stay and chat, Samantha, but I must be getting along. I hope you don't mind?"

"Not at all," the headmistress assured her, also getting to her feet and pumping Penny's hand firmly between the two of hers. Still shaking her hand, she addressed Celia. "Pop up and get your baggage, Celia," she told her, "and we'll meet you at Penny's aeroplane."

Ten minutes later, Celia had—with some difficulty, Penny noted as her sister pulled it over her head—donned a thick white pullover she'd borrowed off Doris, followed by a flight suit, and was strapped into the front seat of the Magister. Gradually Samantha was able, with the willing aid of her remaining staff, to clear

175

the excited students from the drive, and Penny, with a little visual difficulty because of her sister's constant waving at her school friends, turned the plane around and lined it up for takeoff.

"Come back and visit soon!" Samantha was able to shout above the din of the engine, and Penny gave what she hoped was an encouraging smile back. She had a sinking feeling it could be a while before she would be able to do so.

Chapter Twenty

"I'm bloody glad I've finished cleaning," Walter announced as he walked into Ruth's kitchen, pulling a large cobweb out of his hair.

"What on earth were you doing?"

"Shirley!" Walter exclaimed upon seeing the person at the table nursing a cup of tea. "I never heard you come in. When did you get back?"

"Go and wash your hands first," Ruth told him as he made to come and give his friend a welcoming embrace. "Then you can give her a hug."

"Was it Walter responsible for all that banging and crashing we could hear?" Shirley asked as Walter turned on the tap. "What were you doing?"

Walter turned around, rubbing his hands dry on a towel. "You've not told her?" he asked Ruth.

Ruth shook her head. "She's only been in a half hour," she explained. "I thought I'd let the poor girl warm up a bit before telling her about the new arrangements."

"What arrangements?" Shirley wanted to know, looking at each of them in turn, then up at the ceiling toward where all the noise had been coming from.

"Do you want to, or shall I?"

Taking a clean cup from the draining board, Walter placed it before an empty chair and poured himself a cup of tea before taking his seat. After a long, refreshing draft, he set his cup down again. "I'll let her know," he said.

Shirley looked deeply suspicious and sat back, crossing her arms. "Would someone tell me what's going on? Please?"

Walter spread his arms wide and grinned. "Hello, housemate!"

It took her a minute or so before she was able to find her voice. "Wait! Let me get this straight. You're moving in? Here? Where?"

Walter stuck a finger directly up toward the ceiling. "The loft."

"The loft?" Shirley shook her head and asked Ruth, "He did say the loft?"

Ruth nodded, struggling to keep a smile from her face. "He did indeed."

Shirley cranked her head back as if she could look through the ceiling. "But there's no window."

"I admit, that is a bit of an issue," he said. "However, I only expect to be sleeping there, so it shouldn't be much of a problem. Besides, I've spent the last few days cleaning it up, laying down floorboards, and putting up some storage. I've a camp bed that's surprisingly comfortable, so it'll do."

"Until you marry Doris, and she buys the two of you a castle," Ruth put in.

"Until I marry Doris, and..." He stopped himself just in time. "Very funny. For your information, she's seen a windmill, whilst out flying, that she quite fancies."

"Well, I guess all I can say is...at least I've still got my room." Shirley grinned.

****

"I'm so very glad to have caught you, Mr. Burrows," Betty said down the phone, wiping a hand across her forehead. "Yes, I've read my sister's letter. No, nothing in there to bother your good self with, though I may engage your services in relation to my late sister's estate once I've thought it through over Christmas. However, there is one thing I should like your aid with." Betty paused and reached a hand down to move Bobby from off her left foot, which had gone to sleep. "That's right, Marcus. Is he still seeking to make contact with me?" Betty gulped down some of the cold early evening air coming in through the open window of the flight line hut and was considering whether to get up and close it when the solicitor answered. Her hands all of a sudden broke out in a tremble as she took in what he told her. "I see. Well, I don't know why Mr. and Mrs. Palmer"—she still refused to acknowledge their relationship—"would wish to stop him from contacting me, so the next time he contacts you, please provide him with my telephone number."

She quickly rattled off her home telephone number, and, with hands that by now she was barely capable of controlling, bid him a goodbye and a Happy Christmas and placed the receiver back in its cradle. Lost in thought, Betty felt a weight on her lap and looked down to find Bobby was awake, his head resting on her knee, his big brown sorrowful eyes regarding Betty's distraught face with what she believed to be concern, or as close to it as he could manage.

Reaching a still-trembling hand down, she ruffled a floppy, furry ear, and the friendly Cocker Spaniel leaned into her fuss, eyes now rolling back in pure pleasure.

"I suppose the deed's done now, eh?" she told him. "No going back now. I wonder what he's like?" she mused.

"What who's like?" came a voice from the doorway of the hut, causing her to nearly fall off her chair.

"Hell's bells, Jane!" Betty half-shouted, placing her other hand over her heart, though she did notice she had at least stopped shaking.

Jane threw Betty's hat toward her, where it landed on the blotter before her. "Come on, time you got off home."

Placing her hat on her head, Betty joined Jane as they left the hut, Bobby trotting along between them as they made their way toward the station exit.

The guard on duty was leaning on the counterweight to bring the gate up when Bobby startled them all by beginning to bark his head off. The girls and the young man on guard all immediately turned their heads skyward, expecting to see Nazi aircraft screaming down at them at any minute. All three stood there for a good couple of minutes, and nothing happened.

"Maybe he's not foolproof?" Jane mused, rubbing her aching neck and then looking down at where Bobby was still making a racket.

Betty knelt down next to the dog and, stroking his back, tried to get him to calm down. "It's all right, Bobby. We'll let you off."

As she finished, the dog huffed, and launched himself at some bushes. Instead of a swarm of Messerschmitts or Heinkels, he proceeded to back out of the bush dragging an angry-looking man Betty immediately recognized.

"Gerald Wilks! What the hell are you doing back here?"

The man in question was quite unable to answer, though, as Bobby had fixed his teeth around one of the man's ankles and seemed determined to bring his find for the ladies' inspection.

"Ouch! For fuck's sake! Get this dog off me!" Wilks was yelling, reaching down to try to prise the dog off him, but hastily withdrawing his hands at the menacing growl that greeted his attempt.

Jane reached out to stop Betty from moving toward the man now hopping toward her. "Not yet," she told her with a shake of her head. Glancing behind her, she ordered, "Brown. Cock your rifle and take aim at this...person."

Without hesitation, the guard did as Jane ordered, leaning his elbow on the gate for support. The sound of the rifle being cocked was enough to shut the man's protestations, though not his occasional yelp of pain. Jane nodded her head to Betty who, understanding her meaning, told the dog, "Bobby, drop!"

Like the reasonably well-trained dog he was, Bobby immediately let go and, with a fine growl of warning, trotted back to Betty's side, where he turned and sat between the two women.

"What right did you—" Wilks began to yell, but the words died in his throat as the combined growl and bark from Bobby and the way the guard cleared his throat and rattled his rifle, persuaded him it wasn't in his best interests to complain further.

Jane marched up to where he was trying—and, for

181

the most part, failing—to balance on one foot. Keeping out of arm's reach, she asked Betty over her shoulder, "If memory serves, isn't this one of those newsmen who tried to accost Penny the other day?"

"This is the reporter," Betty informed Jane, coming to stand beside her friend, whilst making certain she wasn't in the guard's line of fire. Bobby added an extremely menacing growl and raised his hackles for good measure. Betty and Jane both patted him on the top of the head. "Good boy," Betty told him.

Jane crossed her arms. "Right, Mr. Wilks. Tell me exactly what you're doing skulking in those bushes. And make it quick, as you're holding up my tea."

Wilks was looking at the ruined leg of his trousers, bloody and ripped and almost certainly beyond repair. "Look at the state of my trousers! And my leg!"

"I don't give my aunt's fanny for either," Jane told him. "Answer the question."

Wilks stood up straight, making the mistake of stamping his injured foot. "I don't have to answer anything. There's no rule against sitting in a bush," he finished, his voice trailing off a little as he realized how lame his words sounded.

Betty flashed him a very feral grin. "Oh, but you do, and you know it. Now, last chance, answer Jane's question."

Stubbornly, Wilks stood still, closed his mouth, and didn't utter another word.

Jane looked at Betty, who simply nodded, knowing what her friend would do. She turned to regard the man before her, arrogance simply radiating from every pore. "Nothing to say?" He, indeed, had nothing to say. "Very well." She turned to Betty. "Betty, please would you go and get the guard commander. Tell him we have a prisoner for him, and he's to put him in the cells until the morning. Of course, if he decides to talk, and I'm satisfied with his explanation, then we can let him go. If he says nothing by eight in the morning, then we'll call the police and have him charged with being a suspected spy."

That got his attention. "Spy? Me?" he blustered. "What...what nonsense!"

Jane half-turned back to face him. "You can give me the real reason you're here? Though I think I can guess."

"If you can guess," Wilks said in a very haughty voice, "then why do I need to say anything?"

Fed up with being messed around, Jane gave Betty a nod, and she needed no second invitation. Within a minute, there came a bustling noise from inside the guardroom, and very swiftly and efficiently Wilks found himself bundled into the building. "The coldest cell you've got," Betty yelled after his departing, protesting back.

"You can't do this! It's Christmas Day tomorrow!" he kept yelling, but everyone ignored his protests.

When the guard who'd covered them came back out, Jane held out her hand to thank him. "Thanks for your help, Brown. I'm staying around Betty's tonight, so whatever the outcome, please have someone give me a call there tomorrow morning."

Picking up her overnight bag, Jane linked arms with Betty and, with Bobby trotting along ahead of them, strolled off toward Betty's cottage.

"What shall we tell anyone we meet if they ask why Bobby has half a trouser leg hanging from his mouth?"

****

"What's all that shouting?" Mary muttered, switching off the light in Betty's lounge and then twitching the blackout curtains aside a little and opening the window.

A very loud quacking echoed around the room, closely followed by what sounded like someone shouting, "Help!"

"What is it?" Celia asked, laying a hand upon Mary's shoulder.

"You wouldn't believe me if I told you," Mary began and moved aside. "You'd better see for yourself."

Taking her place, Celia poked her head out of the window and immediately burst into peals of laughter. "Oh, my good God!" she cried, turning her head back toward Mary, now joined by Penny and Doris, who were wondering what was going on. "You've got to see this, Sis!"

Penny squeezed in and also promptly laughed out loud.

"Hey!" Doris said. "Don't keep all the fun to yourself."

"I think," Penny decided, leaving Celia to enjoy the show, "you need to get outside, Doris. Duck is holding Betty and Jane to ransom."

"Again?" Doris uttered, shaking her head.

Celia kept her head out the window so she could continue to enjoy the show as she asked, "Is this a normal thing these days?"

"Not usual," Penny replied. "Maybe a couple of times a week."

"Tell them I'll be out in a minute," Doris asked, heading toward the kitchen.

"What's she going to do?" Celia wanted to know.

Mary leant over and switched on the wireless set, then sat down to let it warm up. "You see, Duck is rather fond of our Doris, but he's also very anti anyone else walking along what he considers to be his riverbank. Doris is the only one he'll allow near him. Sometimes, like now, it takes a few pieces of bread before he'll allow anyone to pass."

Celia promptly dissolved into yet more hysterical laughter.

A few minutes later, Doris came back into the room, closely followed by both Jane and Betty. Celia had by now nearly recovered herself and promptly launched herself into Betty's arms, hugging her tightly.

"I've missed you," Celia told Betty's shoulder.

"Me too," Betty told her, kissing her on the forehead as she came up for air. "I swear you've grown!"

Penny looked up from where she sat next to Mary. "I do hope not. I'm not certain I can let out her skirt any more."

Chapter Twenty-One

"What the hell's that racket?"

Penny, with a none-too gentle elbow, pushed a groaning Celia out of the single bed they were sharing. "Why don't you go and find out? And, while I'm at it, what are you doing in my bed?"

Picking herself up off the floor, Celia pulled on her dressing gown from the end of Penny's bed, hurriedly tied it around her waist, and opened the bedroom door. Turning back to where her sister was slowly waking up, she stuck her tongue out. "I was freezing in that front room," she told her and pulled the door shut behind her as a pillow flew in her direction. Cracking open the other eye, Penny glanced at her alarm clock. "Six-thirty! On Christmas morning! Somebody had better have a damn good excuse," she muttered and then let her head flop back down.

Her attempt to get back to sleep was flummoxed by the pounding of feet upon the stairs, and her bedroom door flew open again. Without opening her eyes, presuming her sister had come back, Penny told the intruder, "Go back to the sofa and leave me be!"

The edge of her bed dipped—and dipped a lot more than if it had been Celia who'd sat down. Curious, without sitting up, she opened both eyes and was greeted by the extremely surprising sight of Tom leaning over her, his face split in a huge grin. She went from half asleep to wide awake in a second, and before he had a chance to react, Penny had flung her arms around his neck and was kissing his lips for all she was worth. Neither noticed Celia poking her head around the open door, her mouth hanging open before, with a slight shake, she silently left, closing the door to give them some privacy.

Making her way back downstairs, Celia opened the larder door, bent down, and carefully pulled out the Christmas tree she'd made the previous day. Her sister had offered to help, but she'd insisted she wanted to make it alone, and now, in the early morning sunlight, she was quite pleased with the result. She actually thought the biggest surprise was when she brought the chicken wire from out of her backpack. She didn't have enough to make the old six-foot tree they used to have at their parents' house. However, she'd rapidly pushed that thought to the back of her mind when Penny had accidentally let the comment slip out.

Taking her two-foot tree into the lounge, she stood there for a minute, deciding where best to put it. All in all, she decided, her sister and her friends had done as good a job as could be done in wartime with the homemade decorations. Plenty of newspaper streamers, probably too many, were hung around the coving and crisscrossing the windows together with various small branches with their green foliage, interspersed with holly and their bright red berries. The room shouted the word "Festive!"

Deciding the table under the window next to the wireless would be the best place, she took the empty fruit bowl into the kitchen and placed it upon the table there. Then, carefully so as not to snag the lace doily, she placed the wire tree on the window table, turning it this way and that until she was happy the best side was facing into the room. Once she was happy with that, Celia glanced around the room, deciding where she could take some paperchains and foliage without it being missed. She stepped back to critique her efforts and nearly jumped out of her skin when she bumped into someone.

"What the…"

"Language, young lady," Betty's voice admonished her.

The girl waited a moment for her heart rate to settle back down before turning around. Betty's face was aglow. "You like it?"

Betty kissed Celia on the forehead and wrapped her in a huge hug. "I love it! Happy Christmas, by the way."

"Happy Christmas to you too," Celia said, pecking Betty on the cheek.

"Were you warm enough in here last night?" Betty asked as she went in for a closer look at the tree.

Celia hesitated for a second, trying to decide whether she should tell the truth, and then, as it would only be for another two nights—seeing as sharing a bed with her sister would no longer be an option—saw no point in hurting her sister's friend's feelings. "Snug as a bug in a rug," she announced.

With one more glance at the new Christmas tree, Betty touched Celia on the elbow. "Care to help me prepare some breakfast?" With a nod, Celia followed her into the kitchen, where she was put to work cutting up the bread for toast, whilst Betty started the kettle boiling and laid out cups and cutlery. Whilst waiting for the tea to brew, Betty took a seat. "I'd have crawled into my sister's bed, if it were me. It gets perishing in that front room in the small hours at this time of the year."

Celia touched her cheeks and was surprised her hands weren't burnt when she took them away. "It's true what Penny says, then—not a lot gets past you, does it?"

Betty shrugged. "My cottage. Who was that trying to break the door down?" she asked.

Celia turned four slices over to brown the reverse before answering, "Tom."

Betty frowned before replying, "Tom. Tom, as in Penny's husband?"

"That's the one."

"I didn't even know he was coming," Betty stated, giving the teapot a quick stir with her spoon.

"Judging by the expression on my sister's face, neither did she."

"Well," Betty said, "we'll undoubtedly hear more on that when they come down. In the meantime, be a love, will you, and go and wake up the others. Tell them the toast will be cold if they don't hurry. By the way, don't forget Jane's on my bedroom floor, so be careful when you open the door. I'm sure if you bang her on the head, I'll be the one who never hears the end of it."

****

Once everyone had partaken of breakfast and Tom had explained, "I managed to get a late twenty-four-hour pass," everyone settled in the lounge. Even with Celia's blankets put away, everyone had to squeeze together to get in.

"It's a real pity Ruth's cottage isn't joined to yours, Betty," Tom said from where he sat on the floor at Penny's feet. "Then we could knock the two together."

"Speaking of…" Doris said, scrambling to her feet, and waving to visitors in the shape of Ruth, Shirley, and her fiancé, Walter, as they came down the path to the front door.

"What about your family, Mary?" Celia asked, oblivious to the immediate interest both Penny and Betty showed at her words. She wasn't to know that despite having known her for more than a year, neither really knew much about Mary's family and, after some questions when they'd initially met had been politely rebuffed, all three of her best friends had stopped asking.

"Oh, look!" Mary declared. "It's coming up to nine-thirty. Someone switch the wireless on. I've been looking forward to *Flodden's Band* all week!"

Suspicious, Penny picked up the current copy of the radio schedule and opened it to Christmas Day. "Thought so. Don't you mean *Foden's Motor Works Band*?"

"That's the one," Mary agreed, clapping her hands together. As she couldn't look at anyone, no one was fooled.

Celia looked at all and sundry, seeing that even Ruth's group had picked up on the atmosphere in the room and noting that, despite both Walter and Ruth having their arms half raised in greeting, not a word was said. "Did I, uh, say something wrong?"

Every head turned toward Mary, who, after making a few perfunctory twiddles of a knob on the wireless set, let her head hang down and followed up with a deep sigh.

"I did, didn't I," Celia stated and then, bursting into tears, she fled the room.

"Oh, heck," Mary said, hurrying after her.

"Leave it!" Penny stated, making to get to her feet.

Mary stopped at the door, turned back, and then laying a firm hand on Penny's shoulder, pushed her back down into her seat. "No. I'm the one who upset her. I'll go. Please?" she asked when Penny looked like arguing.

Aware of how upset her sister had been when she ran out of the room, Penny thought quickly before deciding, "All right, but I'm right here if you need me."

Not wasting any more time, Mary turned back, and the next thing everyone heard was her voice calling Celia's name from out in the back garden.

"We didn't cause that, did we?" Ruth asked, still hovering with her lodgers in the doorway.

"'Course not," Betty assured them. "Go and hang your coats up. Whilst you do, the men can go and get some chairs in from the kitchen." When neither of the men seemed inclined to move, she took matters into her own hands. "Come on! Put those muscles to use!"

A few minutes later, the lounge was more crowded than ever, giving the impression that everyone was sitting on top of each other. To be fair, Doris had taken up her usual position at Walter's feet, and Tom had followed suit at his wife's.

"What was all that about, then?" Walter asked.

"Celia asked about Mary's family," Penny supplied.

Ruth, the newspaper editor in her coming to the fore, leant forward. "Did you learn anything?"

Jane shook her head a little before saying, "No. We'll have to wait and see what, if anything, she says when they get back inside." In an obvious attempt to change the subject, she turned her attention to Shirley. "Well, and how's Trouble doing?"

"You heard?" the trainee pilot asked.

"Of course! Don't worry, though," Jane told her, leaning in and pretending to confide in her by cupping her hand over her mouth, though she didn't bother to keep her voice down. "I was grounded a couple of times myself."

"Really! What for?" Shirley couldn't stop herself from asking.

Jane held up two fingers and lowered the first. "Flying with a broken wrist…"

"And you had a go at me for wanting to fly with a broken foot!" Doris half-protested, waggling a slipper-clad foot.

Jane carried on, choosing not to get into an argument with the American. "The second time, I put itching powder in my instructor's blankets when she made me take my solo test a second time."

"You did what?" Penny shouted, accidentally kicking Tom in the process.

"My point is, don't be put off. Believe me, if I—if we," she amended, to take in Betty and her other friends, "didn't believe in you, we wouldn't have put you forward. True, you could have volunteered without us, but there's no harm in accepting help. Just keep on with your lessons, try not to break too many aircraft, and you'll be qualified in no time. I mean, look how far you've come in such a short time!" Jane spread her arms, and Shirley went beetroot red.

"Who's come far?" Walter asked as he leant back and rummaged in a trouser pocket.

"Ouch!" Doris let out as her fiancé sat on her foot.

"Sorry, love," he muttered as he fished a piece of paper out of his pocket. He held it out for Jane to take. "Here. I took a message for you. The chap from the camp came to our place instead of here."

"Is that about the bloody reporter?" Penny asked, leaning forward and resting her arms on top of her husband's head.

"Don't mind me," he mumbled, unable to keep a wide grin from his face.

"I won't," his wife said, kissing him on top of the head, then moving his bandage back.

"Any idea when they'll let you take that off?" Betty asked.

Reaching up, Tom scratched at the tuft of hair poking out of his bandage, clear irritation showing upon his face. "Not a bloody clue," he muttered and slumped back against Penny's legs. She wrapped her arms around him and, with a swift glance around the room that told everyone not to ask him any more questions for a while, carefully placed her chin on his head, whispered into his ear and, whilst paying attention to the conversation, began rubbing his tension-ridden shoulders.

"Seems to be a day where we upset people," Doris announced.

"Who's upset now?" Mary asked, coming back into the room.

"Where's Celia?" Doris asked, trying to look around her friend.

Mary glanced behind her before telling them,

193

"Gone upstairs to clean up."

"Is she all right?" Doris asked.

Mary came and sat down beside her. "She's fine. We're fine."

"Ah-ha!" Jane suddenly announced, making most people in the room jump. "I knew it!"

"Knew what?" Betty asked.

Jane looked up and passed the note across to Penny. "It's from the guard commander. It took most of the night, but he finally cracked. Seems he'd persuaded his editor he could get an exclusive with Penny, here. Appears he managed to get double his usual rate."

"Ha!" Penny laughed, screwing up the note and throwing it into the roaring fire. "That'll teach him!"

"Why'd he wait so long just to tell us that?" Walter asked. "It's not exactly a life-changing admittance, is it?"

Penny told the room, "The problem is, he knows he's going to be in big trouble with his editor when he gets back."

"Because he didn't get the story?" Mary wanted to know.

Penny shook her head, then nodded. "No, well, yes, I'm sure he will, but he'll really get it because he's spent the advance he got and can't afford to pay it back."

Doris patted Penny on the knee. "Well, I don't think we'll be seeing him again."

"Seeing who?" Celia had just walked into the room and surprised everyone by coming and sitting at Mary's feet, resting one hand lightly upon her knee. Though seen by all, a couple of raised eyebrows were all the reaction this choice brought forth.

"Just a reporter I used to know. Turned up uninvited, looking for a story," Penny filled her sister in on what they'd been talking about. "Which reminds me, I have to tell you off about this," she told her.

Everyone noticed the way Celia's hand tightened its grip on Mary's knee. "Would I be right in thinking this is something to do with my friend Lucille Wilks?"

"Most certainly," Penny agreed.

Celia nodded very slowly. "Would it help if I promised to be more careful in future?"

"It would make our life a little easier," Penny told her, as her girlfriends all nodded in agreement.

Celia hung her head as she told everyone, "I'm sorry. She only told me her father was in the news business *after* I'd told her what you did before the war. I really will be more careful, honestly, Pen," she added, as her lower lip started to quiver.

Hastily, Penny clambered over her husband and flopped down on the floor next to her sister and took her in an embrace. "Come on, no need to get upset again. It's all sorted. Put it from your head, and let's enjoy the day."

"Quite right!" Mary said, leaning forward and catching both Celia and Penny in an awkward hug.

"Come on," Betty announced, casting a glance out the window. "Everyone into the kitchen. The dinner's not going to make itself."

****

"Why didn't we think of a wire tree?" Doris asked, as she sat at the kitchen table enjoying a cup of coffee.

Everyone else, including Walter—though not Tom who, along with Penny, had been tasked with getting some carrots from Ruth's larder, as Betty had decided she wouldn't have enough—were crowded around the table, busy with various cooking and baking tasks. Doris had initially offered to help, but after seeing the complete mess she'd made of her first two attempts, it had been unanimously agreed that she should not be trusted with a knife. There had followed a vote, from which she was excluded, and she'd been nominated as washer-upper. As nothing was ready to be washed up yet, she'd decided to treat herself to a cup of her diminishing stock of her favorite drink.

"I don't think it would have made much difference," Betty told them. "If you all remember, we were working at maximum pelt over the whole of last Christmas. We were so busy I sometimes wonder why we didn't bed down on base."

Celia opened her mouth, but instead of words, she quickly turned her head away from the pile of potatoes she was busy peeling and started to cough. Everyone waited for her to finish, but when she didn't and instead rushed out through the back door with her hand over her mouth, everyone looked at each other before Betty quickly wiped her hands and rushed after her.

To the accompaniment of much gut-twisting noise, those left did their best to get on with their tasks until Betty came back inside. Beneath her arm, and being held up by Betty, was Celia.

Penny and Tom, his arms full of carrots, chose that moment to open the front door, with Penny immediately catching sight of her sister. Celia's gray pallor and sweat-soaked forehead were visible even when viewed through the hall and across the kitchen. Her hand was also holding and rubbing at her throat.

"Celia!" Penny shouted, rushing to her wretched

sister's side. For her trouble, she received a weak smile. "Betty?"

"Come into the lounge," Betty urged the sisters. "The light's better."

A clatter of kitchen implements followed as everyone else around the table stood up.

Betty turned her head and told them, "And where do you lot think you're going? Are any of you doctors? No? I didn't think so. Back to work, or there'll be no lunch. And can someone put the joint in the oven? Horse meat takes a bit longer to cook." With her orders delivered, Betty gently led Celia into the lounge, waited for Penny to come in behind her, and when she had, asked her to close the door. "There's a candle on the sideboard," she said and, once Penny had lit it, led an unprotesting Celia toward the window.

"What's going on?" Penny asked as Betty took the candle from her.

Ignoring the question for now, Betty asked Celia, "Open wide, lovey," and turned her slightly so she had the best natural light, then added that from the candle. She bent down and peered into Celia's mouth. "Uh-huh," she mumbled, adding for good measure, "that explains it."

Celia pulled away from Betty's gentle yet firm grip. "Explains what?" she asked and then gripped her throat, as if she wished she hadn't spoken.

Betty addressed the sisters, Celia having gone to Penny's side and laid her head on her sister's shoulder. "How long have you had a sore throat?"

"Only for the last couple of days," Celia replied.

"Well, with that plus the redness on your tonsils," Betty began, "the fever you have and the vomiting, I'd

197

say you have strep throat."

Penny hugged her sister a little tighter to her side. "What makes you so certain?"

Betty turned her back on them and looked out the window, her shoulders heaving as she took some steadying breaths. Finally, she turned back to her friends. "Eleanor had it when we were in the orphanage. At least the nurse they kept on knew her job," she explained with a shrug. "Well, nothing else for it." Betty made firm eye contact with Celia. "Upstairs with you. A couple of days' bed rest and you'll be fine."

"But Christmas lunch?" Celia moaned, turning her best pleading eyes up at Betty.

"You can still eat," Betty assured her, "but it's bed rest you need, and no talking."

"No…" Celia began.

"…talking," Penny finished for her. "Up to bed. I'll bring you up a book, and lunch when it's ready."

"A Miss Marple?" Celia asked, brightening slightly.

Betty planted a kiss upon Celia's fevered brow. "As it's Christmas Day, and because—only because—you're sick, I'll let you have first read of her new one."

"You've a copy of *The Moving Picture*?" Celia asked, glancing around the room.

"Up to bed," Betty repeated. "I'll bring it up shortly."

Celia allowed Penny to lead her upstairs. As she reached the top landing, Penny shouted down, "Can I read it after Celia?"

Betty shouted back, "Not bloody likely!"

Chapter Twenty-Two

"Can someone get the door?"

Doris looked over her shoulder, no easy task, as the kitchen table was crowded, now Christmas lunch was about to be eaten.

"I never heard anything," she answered, prodding Walter in the ribs. He promptly shuffled his chair backward until he could get out.

"You've got him well trained," Ruth remarked.

"Who wants to bet Celia won't touch a bite?" Penny asked, accepting the bowl of sprouts from Mary. "When I took her plate up, she'd made a good start on the book already."

"So long as she doesn't tell me who did it," Betty mumbled.

"Regretting lending her it?" Tom asked, slightly taking everyone by surprise, as he hadn't said a word since Betty had tasked him with peeling and cutting the mountain of carrots.

Betty shook her head and then, after a moment's thought, nodded. "Yes, well, no. A bit, I suppose."

"So long as you're certain!" Shirley laughed.

Walter came back into the kitchen. Wedging himself back into his place, he passed an envelope across to Betty.

Turning it over in her hands, she found no clues as to the sender, only her own name on the front.

"Before you ask," Walter volunteered, "I looked outside, and there's no one around. Whoever left that, their shoes must have rubber soles."

Betty passed the carving knife and a fork to Tom. "Can you do the honors, Tom?" Then she got to her feet, and next thing everyone knew, they could hear her footsteps as she went upstairs.

****

After turning the strange letter over and over and holding it up to the light, Betty was no farther along in finding out who had sent it. Sighing, she worked a fingernail under the flap and slit it open. Inside, it contained a single sheet of pale blue paper, which she extracted and unfolded.

My dear sister,

This is your brother, Marcus—and now, I don't know what to say!

Well, at least you now know of me, and from this letter, you'll surmise that I did go back to my solicitors and they supplied me with your contact details. I hope you'll forgive my taking the coward's path, as I don't think I could bear telephoning you, finally hearing your voice, only for you to put the phone down. At least this way, you have the option of reading this letter and then throwing it in the fire and not contacting me by return. If you do decide upon this course of action, I would at least request that you leave a message for me with Mr. Burrows informing him you have no wish to be in contact with me. If that is the case, I shall, reluctantly, respect your wishes.

In the scale of things, this is probably the strangest letter I've ever written, and with my—our—family...

Betty couldn't stop the disparaging noise that came from her lips. So far as she was concerned, Mr. and Mrs. Palmer were no relations of hers!

...that's saying something! No matter, hopefully it'll lead to something better.

You should know my parents are aware I've tried to contact you, though I never told them about meeting up with Eleanor. I am very, very sorry to hear of her death. I'd only just begun to get to know her, so, of course, I'm nowhere near as affected as you are and cannot begin to imagine how you must feel. I've lost pilot friends, but it's not the same. I was shocked to hear from Mr. Burrows that she was murdered!

I shall stop here. The solicitor told me you have my phone number, and so, I hope you will consider telephoning me, Betty. I would love to not only get to know you, but also hear more about Eleanor. I really liked her. She had spunk!

Yours,

Marcus

How long Betty sat there, she couldn't say. Only when there came a persistent knocking on her door did she come to her senses. Getting up, she opened it, the letter still in her hand.

"I thought I'd come and see how you are."

If she'd been more her normal self, Betty would have realized it would be Jane on the other side of the door. "Come in," she said, stepping aside and shutting the door behind her.

Jane waited for her friend to sit down, then shuffled along until she was up against her. "Everything

201

okay?"

Without hesitation, Betty handed Jane the letter. "Read this."

A minute later, Jane wiped a hand across her brow and handed Betty back the letter. "So that's your brother."

Betty nodded. "What do you think I should do?"

Jane shook her head and held out a hand for her friend to take. "I'm kind of glad that's not up to me to say."

"Then let me rephrase. What would you do?"

Jane sat waiting, soothingly stroking the back of Betty's hand whilst she stared out the window, not moving until a bird flashed past, startling her. Slowly, she turned back to face her friend, a smile upon her face, even as she dried a tear leaking from her eye.

"Have you worked out what you're going to do?"

Betty nodded. "I have."

"And?" Jane prompted when Betty didn't elaborate straight away.

"I think I need to wish someone a Happy Christmas," she said. With a final squeeze of Jane's hand, she leaned over and retrieved the letter she'd received at the solicitors, then got up and opened the bedroom door.

A raucous, off-key round of "Jingle Bells" echoed up the stairs and assaulted their ears.

"Before or after you eat?" Jane asked. As Betty opened her mouth to speak, her stomach interrupted and let out a very loud grumble. "After, I think would be best."

Just then, Celia opened the door of Penny's room and told them, with one hand covering an ear, "If you can get that lot to stop singing, I promise to be a good patient."

Laughing heartily, Betty and Jane made their way back downstairs, determined to see how loudly they could sing and how long it would take for Celia to come and complain.

****

"...shall not rest from our task until it is nobly ended."

"You're sure he's got a stammer?" Doris asked from where she lay before the fire, stretched out on her back with Bobby, Ruth's Cocker Spaniel, lying on his own back, both with stomachs too full of food to do much else than lie as still as possible.

"Oh, yes," Jane replied. "He's quite famous for it."

"But he's still the King?"

"Naturally," Jane agreed.

"With a stammer?" Doris persisted.

"Walter, throw a cushion at your fiancée, please?" Mary put in.

"He wouldn't dare," Doris replied, closing her eyes and allowing Bobby to snuggle into her shoulder. Before she could say anything else, a cushion hit her in the face, though she only had the energy to half wave an arm in protest. "If that was you…"

"Don't look at me," Walter defended himself. "I know which side my bread's buttered on."

"What about presents?" Doris asked, cracking open one eye, careful not to disturb the sleeping dog.

"What about them?" Betty asked.

"Aren't we going to open them?"

"I don't know about you, but I'm too tired to move at the moment, and mine are only homemade, I'm afraid."

"And mine," said Jane.

"Same here!" added Mary, and Penny nodded too.

"So how about we all wait until later this evening?" Penny suggested. "Maybe Celia will feel up to coming down for a short while."

"Jane," Tom asked after a pause, "we seem to be missing a member of your gang."

Raising a cup to her lips, Jane decided she couldn't even take a mouthful and put it down on the floor. "If you mean Thelma, she drew the short straw and is manning the phones on base today."

"Awful bad luck," he commented. "What's she having for Christmas lunch?"

Betty sat up straight. "Good point."

"I mean no disrespect, Betty, the meal was wonderful, but horsemeat's not beef."

"I'll bet it's still better than anything they'll rustle up in the canteen today," Penny put in.

Tom heaved himself to his feet, stretched out his back, and suggested, "We've some leftovers. How about we make up a plate and take it in for Thelma?"

Betty clapped her hands together. "Excellent idea. I'm a bit ashamed of myself for not thinking of it first. Who's going to take it up?"

"I'm on my feet," Tom declared, "and to make things easy, I volunteer my Penny to get us onto base." He prodded his wife with his foot, which caused her to let out a loud snore.

Doris threw her cushion at Penny this time. "Hey! I know your snore, and that isn't it."

Ten minutes later, Penny was following Tom toward the front door, a covered plate in her gloved hands. As he opened the door, a man in uniform nearly fell in.

"Steady as you go, old chap."

Leaning a hand on the doorframe to steady himself, the man looked up. Something about him rang a bell. He was wearing the uniform of an American major, and Tom was pretty certain he'd seen him before, though not enough to think of him as a friend. He didn't think he'd been around him that much.

A cough brought him back to his senses. "Major Jim Fredericks, sir. At your service," the major said, holding out a hand. The other, Tom noted, held a brown parcel.

"Of course!" Tom shook the hand and stepped aside to let him in.

"This is where First Officer Betty Palmer lives?" the American asked.

At that moment, the lady in question came out of the lounge and stopped dead in her tracks at seeing who had just crossed her threshold. "Jim? What the hell are you doing here? I thought you were working over Christmas!"

Ignoring Tom and a slightly surprised Penny, Jim strode toward Betty, took her in his arms and planted a kiss as delicate as gossamer upon her lips. Brief it may have been, yet Betty couldn't have felt happier unless it had been from Clark Gable himself—which, she reminisced, Jim could perhaps have arranged a while back.

As Tom closed the door behind him and Penny, he heard the newcomer say, "Look, I brought some Spam!"

****

"Knock, knock! Anyone awake in here?" Penny called, sticking her head around Jane's office door.

Looking a little like a startled deer, Thelma looked up from the newspaper she was reading. "What on earth are you doing here? Is that Tom?"

"Delivering a pretty decent Christmas lunch," Penny told her, setting down the plate before her. "I don't imagine what you had from the mess was very edible today."

"You could put it that way," Thelma agreed, licking her lips in anticipation and accepting the knife and fork Tom offered her.

"A very happy Christmas, Thelma," Tom offered, leaning across the desk and kissing her on the cheek.

"Why, thank you very much," Thelma replied, her cheeks coloring a little. "The two of you have certainly made my day, I must say."

After allowing her friend to take a few bites, Penny asked, "Anything happen today?"

Thelma swallowed before answering, "Nothing to speak of, really. We've had a few planes turn up in need of refueling, but nothing to talk of. Oh, we did have some RAF type come over the R/T a short while back, asking if we were Chicksands! Obviously I didn't reply, but there's someone who's going to get his feet wet, unless he's careful."

"Sounds like we've had a more exciting time, even taking into account it's Christmas Day," Tom mused.

Thelma stacked a fork with a sprout, the last of her horsemeat, and some mashed potato, all dripping with gravy, and piled it into her mouth. Tom believed she meant to say, "What happened?" Only she was difficult to understand, and he hoped she'd have the sense to clean up the gravy splatters she was making all over Jane's desk.

"Betty had a letter hand delivered that was from her brother."

Thelma's eyes went wide, and Penny and Tom were treated to the fascinating spectacle of their friend struggling to swallow her huge mouthful of food.

Sensing she had something urgent to say, Penny hurried around to rub her friend's back, hoping she wouldn't have to slap her friend on the back if she started to choke. First aid had never been her forte, so perhaps her husband would do the honors, if need be. Fortunately, after swallowing, Thelma took a long swig from her glass of water and, apart from a resemblance to a beetroot, appeared fine. After a few gulps, she proved Penny right.

"I'm the biggest idiot!"

"Not what I was expecting to hear," Tom grumbled.

"No, wait, I mean to say"—Thelma stumbled over her words—"one of those pilots who landed to refuel...he's still here."

"And..." Penny prodded, not knowing what her friend's point was.

"And, oh, patient one," Thelma told her, "instead of waiting by his aircraft, or going to the canteen like any normal pilot would, he told me he had an errand to run. He then jogged off toward the guardroom."

"I still don't follow you," Tom told her.

Thelma rolled her eyes and, not for the last time, wondered if her newfound love of Miss Marple wouldn't be the end of her. "Think about it," she advised Tom, unable to keep some exasperation out of her voice. "What errand would he have to run at a strange base? Especially a non-RAF one? Who could he know here? I've certainly never seen him before!"

"What makes you think this has anything to do with Betty's letter?" Penny wanted to know.

"Because, until you mentioned it, I didn't stop to wonder why he had a letter in his hand as he ran off."

Penny and Thelma exchanged a wide-eyed look.

****

Five minutes later, having persuaded Tom to man the phones, Penny and Thelma burst into the canteen.

"Do you see him?" Penny asked, looking around the seemingly deserted room.

"Oi! You two born in a bloody barn?"

Looking around, the two found the owner of the accusation bearing down on them. Mavis was waving what they both hoped was an empty teapot at them as she stormed toward them from the kitchen. She kicked the door closed, giving both pilots a view of the door, which seemed to have a small dent in it where the mess manager's foot had connected.

"Sorry, Mavis," Penny apologized.

"There he is!" Thelma tapped her on the shoulder and, leaving a not-quite-silently stewing Mavis behind them, strode over to where a man in RAF uniform had appeared. They hadn't seen him, as he'd been crouched down admiring the collage Jane had set up, and had been hidden behind a table.

Hearing approaching footsteps, he straightened his uniform jacket and turned around. "Hello," he said but didn't give his name.

"Pilot Officer," Thelma began, "I thought I'd let you know. Your kite's all refueled. You can take off when you like."

"Awfully good of you to let me know," he answered, holding out a hand to shake in thanks.

"Our pleasure," Thelma told him.

Unable to hold herself in anymore whilst Thelma went through the polite chit-chat, Penny tapped her friend lightly on the shoulder.

Thelma took the hint. "Did you manage to get your, er, errand done?"

Penny gasped as she witnessed the tips of the young pilot's ears go bright red, exactly the same as Betty's did.

He ran a finger around his collar. "I, um, did, yes, thank you."

"You didn't have any trouble finding the Old Lockkeepers Cottage, then?" Penny couldn't stop herself from asking.

The pilot's dropped jaw was all the answer the two girls needed.

Penny held out her hand. "Pleased to meet you, Pilot Officer Marcus Palmer."

Chapter Twenty-Three

"We've picked up a stray, Betty!" Penny yelled as she opened the door.

"Do they know they enter at their own risk? You've told them about your sister's strep throat?" Betty yelled back, leaning around the kitchen door with what looked suspiciously like an American major's uniformed arm around her waist.

"I'm perfectly aware you're the boss," stated another voice. "Yes, I'm strangely also aware you should show yourself willing, being the new boy on the job. Doesn't mean I have to be happy about it, though."

"What's going on here?" Penny asked, still standing in the doorway.

Mary held her hand over the telephone and glanced up. "I'm having a mild discussion with my boyfriend."

Penny raised an eyebrow. "Mild?" and deftly avoided Mary's flailing legs as she stepped over her friend, who sat on the floor, leaning against the wall. "Give my love to Lawrence," she told her, risking patting her friend on the head.

"Who's the stray, then?" Betty asked as she came around the corner hand in hand with Jim.

"Before I answer," Penny answered with an enigmatic waggle of her eyebrows, "have you called your brother back yet?"

Betty ignored Jim's quizzical expression. "Not yet.

I'm not certain if today's the right day to make it. He may be at, well, you-know-who's place, and I've no inclination to speak to them."

Quickly making stop-type signs with her hands behind her back and hoping Betty couldn't see, Penny made certain. "But you do intend calling him?"

Betty nodded firmly. "Of course."

"In that case," Penny replied, turning back to the door, "I think you can come in," she called. "Just mind the idiot sprawling all over the hall," she added. Mary stuck her tongue out at her friend.

Penny waved an encouraging gesture, and through the open door, with Tom closing it behind him, came a rake of a man, with a wispy moustache, in the uniform of an RAF Pilot Officer. Taking off his chip-bag hat, revealing—unusual for an RAF officer—closely shorn ginger hair, he appeared to be barely out of his twenties.

"Marcus Palmer," Penny began, doing her best to ignore the sharp intake of breath from Betty who, by the look of pain which had suddenly appeared on Jim's face, had just dug her nails into his hand. "I'd like to introduce you to your sister Betty."

Penny hadn't shouted at all, but her announcement coincided with a lull in the wireless program, and so more than one head appeared around the lounge's door. From out of the handset, Lawrence's voice could be heard saying, "Mary! Mary? Are you there?" whilst the Mary in question sat doing her best goldfish impression.

Recovering her composure, Betty stepped over Mary, grabbed her coat and a scarf and, with a mumbled, "Follow me," to the newcomer, strode past Tom and made toward the gate.

Marcus stood there, looking back and forth between Betty's receding back and Penny, not certain of what he should do.

Penny made the decision for him. Hopping over the still immobile form of Mary, she shoved Marcus out the door with the command to, "Get after her!" before she pulled her husband inside and shut the door.

Celia had somehow missed the unfolding drama and her voice could be heard to ask, "Can we open presents yet?"

****

Having managed to avoid Duck, Betty strode on until she came to the turning which led to the Hamble airbase and, in the other direction, to Hamble itself. With her mind whirling, she didn't know which direction she should go. Caught in two minds, she was still looking this way and that when she sensed Marcus had caught up with her.

After standing with her back to him for a minute, she turned around and took a first look at someone who was a blood relative yet also someone she knew less about than yesterday's toenail clippings. The man appeared on the point of bolting, and it struck Betty that he must be as apprehensive, if not a little frightened, as she was. Reminding herself that he hadn't done anything wrong—you could choose your friends but not your relations, let alone your parents—she tried to put to the back of her mind this fact and pasted what she hoped was a welcoming smile upon her face. At his half-step back, she gave up the smile.

She asked the first thing which came to mind. "What happened to leaving it up to me whether I contact you or not?" closely followed by, "Do you know what Elle did for a living?"

Taking off his hat, he tucked it in his pocket and wiped his brow. "Hi, I'm Marcus." This was accompanied by a winning smile Betty wagered made him very popular with the ladies.

Whether it was the way he said it or what appeared to be the genuine smile accompanying it, Betty let out a breath she hadn't realized she'd been holding. With a smile of her own, Betty held out her hand, which was immediately shaken warmly, firmly.

"And I believe I'm your sister, Betty." With the tension hanging in the air somewhat broken, Betty gave a still slightly nervous chuckle. "That's probably the silliest thing I've ever said."

"Would it help if I told you I'm very glad you were the one to say it?" Marcus asked.

"Probably not."

"Didn't think so. Want to try again?" Marcus replied.

Betty shook her head. "I think I'm okay, actually. You?"

"Not sure I should be here," Marcus admitted.

"Because you may think I think you're a liar? After what you wrote in your letter," Betty ventured.

Marcus let out a whistle. "You believe in telling it as it is, don't you."

Betty shrugged. "Always."

"Good," he surprised her by saying. Marcus crooked his arm. "Shall we take a slow walk back along the river whilst we talk?"

Deciding he was unlikely to murder her—which, considering the events of the previous year, wasn't much out of the realm of possibility—Betty laid a hand on his arm. "As good an idea as any."

"However," Marcus said as they began their walk, "you may have to protect me at some point. There's this mad duck which tried to attack my foot somewhere along here."

His words relaxed her, and as Betty gripped her companion's arm, her step lightened. They'd gone but a dozen paces before Betty reminded him, "My questions?"

"Your questions," he mumbled, patting her hand. "Well, I wrote the letter after I'd heard about Eleanor from the solicitor. It never left my pocket, to tell the truth." He shrugged. "This was a spur-of-the-minute thing," he told her. Then, upon noticing her raised eyebrow of disbelief, he added, "Honestly! I was on patrol, and we happened to be passing over Southampton, and I decided to do something rather stupid, something I'm certain my boss will have my hide for if it gets out. I claimed I was low on fuel and told my boss I'd have to put down at Hamble to top up."

"And he believed you?" Betty asked, voice and raised eyebrow disbelieving.

"Perhaps. I mentioned something about a possible fuel leak, so I'll have to put the kite down as unserviceable when I get back, but my mind told me to throw caution to the wind—and here I am."

"But how did you know where I live?" Betty wanted to know.

"Don't tell him off, but I persuaded Mr. Burrows to give me your address, and when I got to the guardroom, I persuaded the chap on duty to give me directions. Please don't tell him off either."

"Hmm," Betty mused, thinking it over and finally saying, "Well, I don't suppose any harm's been done. I was, after all, going to phone you."

Marcus let out a sigh of relief. "I'm very glad to hear that. I would have left here and now, if you'd said otherwise."

Betty looked at him out of the corner of her eye, eventually nodding. "I believe you. So, what do you know about Elle?" That was twice she'd used her old nickname for her sister in a very short space of time, after not having used it since she'd died. It felt both strange and comforting at the same time.

Marcus noticed her smiling and wanted to know, "What is it?"

Betty slowed her pace a little, and Marcus matched her steps. "Hmm? Oh, nothing much. It's only that I haven't called my sister by her nickname since she died."

"And how does it feel?" Marcus asked. "Good?"

"Yes. Surprisingly so."

"So that's a good thing?"

"Yes, yes, it is."

They continued their stroll, until Marcus remembered he hadn't answered her question. "I know she was a—how do I put this without getting thrown in the river?—jewel thief, I think is how she described herself."

"And?"

"And she was very careful to make sure I knew she was a high-class thief. What happened?" he blurted out. "Who killed her, and why?"

Betty dug her heels in and took her arm back.

"I'm sorry," he hastened to say. "I didn't mean to

upset you. I've a habit of saying what's on my mind."

Stepping before him, Betty regarded him and could see no deception there. Taking a fortifying deep breath, she laid a steadying hand, more for her than for her brother, upon the arm she'd been holding.

"No, it's all right. It's good you know who she became. We had to support ourselves after…" She hesitated and then plunged on. "It was after we left the orphanage those people left us in."

Marcus shifted awkwardly from foot to foot.

Nevertheless, Betty carried on, assuming Eleanor had told him about how they'd ended up in that establishment. "Elle was the strong one, physically, and also much more beautiful than me, so she elaborated upon what we'd learned."

"You didn't…" Marcus asked.

"Become a thief?" Betty ended for him. She shook her head. "Let's say my skills lay in different areas."

Marcus was silent for a few seconds before a light bulb appeared to go on behind his eyes. "You were her fence!"

Betty's brows knitted, and she opened and closed her mouth twice before finding the correct words. "You don't sound shocked."

Marcus shrugged his shoulders before holding out his hand toward Betty, who took it without hesitation. Together, they turned and restarted their walk. "I've seen films," he said by way of explanation. "Plus, it makes sense, at least to me. You did what you had to do, and, assuming what Eleanor told me is the truth, you only stole from those who were—how did she put it—on the wrong side of the law."

"There were, and still are, plenty of those," Betty

said.

Marcus then asked again, "What did happen to her? If you can bear to tell me, that is. I'd only begun to get to know her, and, well, I'd love to have known her much better."

Betty squeezed his hand and found that place she liked to go to when having to talk about her sister's murder. "She was killed by a doctor who was being blackmailed by someone we stole a set of pearls from. He was trying to get them back, and, well, she was in the wrong place at the wrong time. I don't want to go into details. It's still too raw."

"Was her killer caught?" Marcus asked gently.

Betty's grin could only be described as feral as, recalling the satisfaction she'd felt at striking the doctor around the head with her frying pan, she told him, "Oh, yes. We got him—him and his blackmailers too!" She felt him squeeze her fingers this time.

"Good for you!"

They strolled on for a few more minutes until they came within sight of her cottage. Betty opened her mouth, but strangely, a loud quack was heard instead of her voice. Looking around, they both caught sight at the same time of Duck advancing upon them, wings outspread, and his face, if it were possible, looking very menacing.

Gripping Marcus's hand, she broke into a swift trot and practically dragged him through her gate, slamming it just in time.

The front door opened as they stepped up to it, Jane standing aside to let them both in. "I was watching out for you," she admitted.

"Good thing you were," Betty thanked her.

"Are you two picking on Duck?" Doris shouted from the lounge.

Ignoring the question, Betty took off her scarf and hung it and her coat up, gesturing for Marcus to do the same with his hat.

"Everything all right?" Jane asked, stopping her friend with a gentle, yet firm hand as Betty made to walk past her.

Looking back to where Marcus was standing regarding the pair quizzically, Betty let a slow smile grace her lips. "Yes. Yes, I think it is."

****

"There you are!" Celia remarked in an exasperated voice, getting to her feet from where she'd been lying with her head upon Bobby's side. "We've been waiting for you."

"Don't tell me," Betty commented. "Bobby hasn't moved since we went out."

"He lets us know he's alive every now and then." Ruth laughed, getting to her feet as the amiable spaniel chose that moment to demonstrate how he let them know he was still in the land of the living.

"Oh, my God!" Betty exclaimed, waving a hand in front of her nose and turned to fix Doris with a withering glare. "I told you we shouldn't feed him sprouts!"

Doris shrugged and snuggled down a little farther into Walter's shoulder, quite content with the way his hand was stopping her from falling off his lap. "You get used to it."

"See what you're saddling yourself with?" Penny laughed.

"No complaints here," Walter answered.

Ruth, probably wisely, decided to change the subject and went to stand next to Betty, though her attention was focused upon Marcus, who had appeared behind his sister and had, judging by his grin, heard the previous conversation.

"Care to make the introductions, Betty?"

By way of reply, Betty grabbed Marcus's hand and ushered him before her until they were in the middle of the room.

"Marcus Palmer, my brother." Looking up at him, a certain level of pride in her expression, she added, "Brother, I should like you to meet my extended and slightly deranged family."

"Are we ever going to open these presents?" Celia's voice whined, breaking the moment.

Chapter Twenty-Four

Celia had finally gotten her way, and everyone still around sat with a present or two, most wrapped in newspaper, on their laps. Marcus had given his apologies, turned down Betty's offer to walk back with him, telling her they'd speak soon, and was on his way back to Hamble. He explained he was only supposed to be refueling his aircraft and was certain his boss would be tearing him off a strip when he got back. How late he was would determine the amount of trouble he would be in. Upon hearing that, Tom surmised Marcus would be pulling orderly officer duty for at least two weeks. Penny had slapped her husband around the back of the head, telling him he wasn't on duty and to mind his own business.

"No!" Celia shouted as she tore the paper from her present from Betty, who'd told her to open that one last of all so, naturally, she'd picked it to open first. "*Five Go Adventuring Again*! I'd heard a new one was out." Carefully laying the book down, she launched herself at Betty and gave her a huge hug and then kissed her on the forehead and both cheeks. "Thank you so very much! I promise to take very, very good care of it."

"Good," Betty told her, pleased as punch with the girl's reaction. "I'd heard they were good stories."

Celia was examining the book's cover. "You're welcome to borrow it after I've finished," she offered.

220

"It's not Miss Marple, but they're fine stories," she told the room. "By the way," she added, looking up whilst gripping her new book tightly to her chest, "thank you so much for letting me borrow your new Miss Marple. It's wonderful! I won't"—she made the sign of the cross over her heart—"tell you who did it, promise!"

Betty mentally rolled her eyes and assured Celia she'd love to borrow the new book.

Midway through the frenzy of unwrapping which followed, Jim Fredericks, who'd sat shaking his head in undisguised amazement at the apparent joy everyone was showing, couldn't stop himself from voicing this out loud. Everything came to an instant stop. Betty, who'd been leaning contentedly upon his shoulder until he spoke, jerked upright and turned to look him full in the face, her own visage a picture of disappointment.

"I've no idea how things are over in the States, Jim, but over here not only do we have to 'make-do-and-mend' for a lot of our civilian clothes, but since Christmas 1940 most of the gifts we give out are either homemade or secondhand, and people are grateful for what they receive."

Looking around, Jim's gaze danced over what was in everyone's hands. Doris had given each of her friends a new thick white jumper, perfect for keeping them warm in the unheated cockpits they flew in, whilst for her fiancé she had gotten some socks and a rather badly hand-knitted balaclava helmet, telling him she didn't want him to catch a chill when he was out on guard duty. By coincidence, Walter gave each of the girls a pair of thick socks so their toes wouldn't get cold. Jane took the presents for Thelma and placed them on the hall table so she wouldn't forget them when she left tomorrow.

Without hesitation, Jim got to his feet and looked around the room, making certain to catch everyone's eye. "I'm sorry," he began, "very sorry. I don't get off base much, and I guess I expected everything to be the same as before the war. I keep forgetting you Limeys—sorry—have been fighting a while longer than we have."

Tom raised the bottle of brown ale he was drinking in salute. "Glad to have you with us!"

Jim raised his own bottle—which, quite noticeably, contained more ale than anyone else's. "Here's to being over here!"

Everyone raised theirs, joining in the toast, before Jim finished his apology.

"So, if you'll forgive this Yank—"

"Hey!" Doris protested. "I'm supposed to be the Yank around here!"

"You're my Yank," Walter told her, pulling her back to him as she squirmed around.

"Well, you have to say that," Doris told him, playfully ruffling his hair. "Mind you, I do love your present."

"What did you get her?" Mary asked. "You were moaning your head off since the beginning of December, trying to figure out what to get her. After all, what do you get a millionairess?"

"Yes," Jane agreed. "What did you get her? I was watching you pair, and I only saw you pass her an envelope."

"Can I?" Doris asked Walter, who nodded. Taking the envelope from where she'd tucked it down the side of her chair, she took out a piece of paper. With a loud, wet kiss to Walter's cheek, she announced, "Walter's got us a marriage license!"

Penny clapped her hands together. "So you've set a date at last!"

The engaged couple looked rather sheepish, and both shook their heads before Doris answered for them both, "Not as such."

Slouching back into her seat, Penny shot them both a look. "I give in. When you do decide to get married, at least give me a few hours' notice."

Because nobody had expected Tom to turn up, the only person who had a present for him was Penny, who, grabbing a protesting Celia's hand, commanded, "You've had more than enough excitement today, young lady. Back to bed. You know what Doctor Betty told you." With that, she took her sister upstairs to her room. After a few minutes, she came back down and handed Tom a small box.

"Go on," she urged as he looked at her. "It's all right if you didn't get me anything."

Instead of replying, Tom nipped into the hall, fished in the pocket of his uniform jacket, and was back in a jiffy. Curiously, he handed her a very similar-sized box.

"On three?" he suggested.

Penny nodded and, as he said, "One," didn't bother to wait for the following numbers.

Onto both their palms they tipped out of their respective boxes identical Saint Christopher medallions.

"Great minds think alike!" Penny announced.

Tom gave his wife a hug and told her, making certain everyone could hear, "Well, this one's getting his head right again."

Penny pulled back a little, then leant her forehead against her husband's. "I'll go and see the doctor as soon as his office is open. No rest for the wicked, eh?"

"There is for you," Jane felt compelled to say. "Remember what I told you?"

Penny was unable to keep a pout from her face as she replied, "I haven't. Only I haven't had anything confirmed yet, so I can fly tomorrow."

"Let's wait and see what tomorrow brings, shall we?" Jane suggested, not wanting the discussion to turn into a disagreement.

Hoping to distract Penny, Tom set his wife down in his seat and went to hover over Betty before bending over and kissing her on the cheek. "I haven't had the chance to say so yet, Betty, but thank you so very much for not chucking me out on my ear, what with turning up out of the blue like this. I'll be out of your way in the morning, don't worry."

Betty reached up and gave his cheek a friendly stroke. "Don't be daft. We're all very happy you were able to make it. Sorry you'll have to bed down in here tonight, though. Blame Celia for being so inconsiderate as to get ill!" she added with a smile.

"You can have my bed, if you like," Ruth offered.

Penny immediately rushed over and, dragging her friend to her feet, enveloped her in a bear hug. "That's so kind of you, Ruth, but no matter how tempting, we wouldn't dream of throwing you out of your bed on Christmas night."

Tom came over and joined in the hug, though clearly he was a little more tempted than his wife to take Ruth up on her offer.

Jim got to his feet, pulled down his uniform jacket

to straighten it, and held out a hand to Betty, helping her to her feet.

"I hate to spoil the party, but I really should be going. The colonel lent me his car, and I should make it back before it's too late. I don't think Marcus will be the only one on the receiving end of a telling-off today."

"I'm sorry you have to go, Jim." Betty walked into his arms, not one bit self-conscious, even with the eyes of her friends upon her—until Doris waggled eyebrows at her. Then Betty took his hand and led him into the hallway.

Taking down his cap from the coat rack, he placed it at the regulation jaunty angle so favored in the movies, bringing a smile to Betty's face, a smile which she was struggling to keep in place. Her burgeoning relationship with Jim had taken her by surprise, and if anyone had asked and, if she'd felt brave enough to admit it, she'd have told them she was having a hard time accepting that she deserved his—attention? Whatever this was? She wasn't sure yet.

She stood at the open gate while Jim opened the door of the olive-drab sedan and came back with a small package, which he handed to Betty. She pushed it back, saying, "I can't. You've already been so generous. Not only today with all the Spam, but for Thanksgiving."

To her surprise, Jim laughed. Though he took the package, he also showed her what was in it.

"Ah," Betty said, going a little red. "Hold on." She turned her head and shouted out, "Ruth! Can you come outside a minute?" And to Jim she advised, "I think you need to give this to her yourself."

A moment later, Ruth trotted out to join them. "You hollered?"

"Here," Jim said, "is a little something for Bobby. We need the air raid warning system on top form, after all!"

Her brow furrowing, Ruth took the brown bag from him, laughing delightedly when she saw its contents.

"Shippems meat-and-fish paste! I'll put some on his toast for him," she told Jim and gave him a quick hug in thanks before popping back inside, leaving the two alone.

"Guess I'll really have to go," Jim said, though he didn't take his arms back from where he'd wrapped them around an unprotesting Betty, her head buried in his shoulder. He kissed the top of her head, and she made a little happy sound before dragging her eyes up to look into his.

Surprising herself, as they'd only shared the odd quickly caught kiss before, she grabbed the back of his head, nearly knocking his hat over his eyes, pulled his face down to her level, and fixed her lips upon his. Tentative at first and then, when she felt him responding with an equal measure of enthusiasm and tenderness, she deepened the kiss, feeling something awaken in her heart, something she'd long assumed would never happen to her. Time stood still for them both, and though her lips were rapidly growing numb, she cared not one jot and could have stayed as she was until the world stopped turning.

What eventually ended the moment was whistling and clapping coming from somewhere in the air. Looking urgently around in case the Germans were being unsporting and they were in the middle of a raid, both located the source of the interruption at the same time.

Hanging out of an upstairs window, Celia had obviously been watching the pair and hadn't been able to stop herself from adding her opinion.

Jim laughed and gave Betty one last lingering kiss before he climbed into his car, rolled down the window, and shouted up at their unwelcome audience, "Remind me to thank you the next time I'm around!" Then, with a toot of the horn, he drove off.

After watching until the car disappeared from view, Betty allowed her face to assume the expression that had scared the wits out of all the other children when she was in the orphanage. With this in place, she turned her head, gazed up at where Celia was still watching, and told her, in a voice edged in ice, "I think I'll come up and *thank you* right now, young lady."

****

"Whose idea was it to go out carol singing?" Betty enquired, throwing an unsmiling glance behind her.

Bringing up the rear, her collecting tin nearly dragging on the ground, Doris raised her head. "I tried to tell you I couldn't carry a tune."

"Yes, you did," Mary agreed, turning and walking backward as they neared Betty's cottage. "Only, we didn't think you meant it."

"Last time I heard a racket like it, Bobby had cornered a cat," Ruth said.

"Maybe we could use her as an air-raid warning siren if Bobby's not around," Penny added, reaching down to ruffle the spaniel in question, who leant into her hand and nearly tripped over his long ears.

"Surely that sound's against the Geneva

227

Convention," Walter suggested after another minute, not realizing the time limit for Doris to take the banter in a good way had expired and thus earning himself a kick in the backside.

"I wouldn't," Penny warned him as he began to turn around to argue.

Celia, having announced she was bored of being alone whilst the others were getting ready to go to work that morning, had decided she'd hole up in the lounge for the day with her book. As the dejected group came up the path, she pulled open the door for them. "How did it go? Make much?"

It wasn't until Doris, bringing up the rear, slammed the door shut behind her that anyone replied. "It depends."

Gathering her cardigan around her a little tighter, Celia hurried back into the lounge to reclaim her place on the sofa whilst everyone divested themselves of the many layers they'd worn to go out carol singing.

"Tea, everyone?" Betty's voice sang out from the kitchen, having her priorities right. As everyone, even Doris, replied in the affirmative, she put the kettle on and prepared the cups before taking off her coat and bobble hat. "To answer your question, Celia, I'm afraid what we collected won't help the evacuees much."

Ten minutes later everyone's noses, barring Celia's, were starting to look a little less like Rudolph's and their hands were cupping their hot drinks, blowing into them so they could get them down without burning their throats.

"So?" Celia asked, leaning forward a little impatiently. When she didn't receive an immediate answer, she persisted with, "Something's up. Come on, what happened?"

After another silence, Doris couldn't help herself. "Come on! It's not all my fault."

"What's not all your fault?" Celia wanted to know.

"I tried to tell them," Doris said with a pout.

"Still not any clearer."

"I suppose if we'd have paid any attention to what Doris told us, Celia," Mary began, "we may have made a bit more."

"Could someone, please, explain to me what happened?" Celia pleaded, nearly tumbling off the sofa.

Doris stood up, threw a sloppy salute to all and sundry, and explained, "I can't sing. This lot didn't believe me, and so, well, let's say we didn't start getting much in our tin until I was relegated to conductor and head tin-rattler."

Ill or not, Celia nearly fell off the sofa laughing, though this may have been because Doris looked so affronted by her own admission.

"Don't you think it'd be a good idea if Celia disappeared back up to bed, Penny?" she suggested. "You know, before something happens to her?"

Celia did her best to stop laughing, partially succeeding as her sister pushed herself out of her seat and held out a hand toward her. "I can take a hint," she said. "Besides, Betty already told me off yesterday, and I think one telling off is enough for me. Doris, I'm sorry for laughing and"—she shot the rest of her sentence over her shoulder as she nipped past Doris, who managed to give her bottom a half swat—"that you can't sing."

Chapter Twenty-Five

"Anyone seen my slip?" Mary called as she turned her room upside down, again.

Doris and Betty both poked their heads around the corner of their doors, in the dual act of doing up their uniform jackets. "When did you last see it?" Doris asked.

"It's not my only one," Mary mumbled from the depths of her chest of drawers. "But it's my favorite one."

"What's your favorite one?" Tom asked, as his head popped up on the stairs, causing Mary to squeak and half-close her bedroom door. "Oops, sorry, Mary," he said, turning a little red.

"She's lost her slip," Betty explained.

"Her favorite," Doris added.

Tom nodded, not really understanding, as he wasn't party to the various items of clothing which had gone missing over the last year or so, including his wife's best bra. "Is the bathroom free?" he asked, holding up his shaving kit.

"Help yourself," Betty told him. Going up on her tiptoes, she kissed him on the cheek. "We'll be gone by the time you've finished. Drop Penny's key off at Jane's office when you're ready, will you?"

Tom placed his towel and kit on the floor and surprised Betty by giving her a big hug. "Thank you again for a wonderful Christmas, Betty. I hope I wasn't too much of a misery-guts?"

As he gave Mary and Doris each a quick hug, Betty told him, "So long as you've sorted things out with that lovely wife of yours."

Turning back to Betty, he took her hand. "I promise. She's put me right—we'll be okay."

"You'd better!" Doris told him, though the grin upon her face was enough to show him she was joking.

Picking up his things, he looked over the small band of fellow pilots and felt his chest swell with pride. "You lot be careful up there, okay?"

"We promise," Mary volunteered for the group.

****

Penny flopped down onto the seat, her thoughts in turmoil, and suddenly everything being said to her seemed to be as if it were coming down a long tunnel. She felt the need to put her head between her legs as her vision began to darken at the sides. With an extreme effort, she fought off the impulse to pass out, beads of sweat breaking out upon her forehead. A hand—she didn't know nor care whose—pressed a glass of water into her hand as she felt her heart rate returning to normal. The water went down—nectar couldn't have been more welcome.

"Penny?" A man's voice, possibly her husband's, spoke. "Penny!"

Over and over it repeated until her hands flew to her temples and she screamed out, "Who the hell else would it be?"

As her vision cleared, she focused upon the form of Doctor Raymond Barnes, who stood leaning against the medical center's wall. He appeared to be twisting his stethoscope between his hands and regarding her with a worried expression.

"Miss Blake," he started to say and stopped at an annoyed cough from Tom. "Sorry. Mrs. Alsop, can you hear me now? How are you feeling?"

She found Tom holding one of her hands and, if it were possible, looking even more worried than the doctor. Had her reaction been *that* bad? Tom opened his mouth, but she squeezed his hand to forestall him, answering, "Pregnant. I'm feeling…pregnant."

Tom seemed to be searching her face, trying to gauge how she felt about that feeling. To give herself some thinking time, she squeezed his hand and mustered up a small smile. How did she feel? Well, confused, for one, but was she happy? Her husband certainly appeared to be happy, no matter how hard he was trying to hold it in, obviously waiting for her reaction before sharing his. Taking her hand back, she laid it with her other one across her belly, stroking her stomach, wondering if she could feel some connection to the life growing inside her. Closing her eyes, she tried and tried, yet felt no different. Perhaps it would come later? Yes, of course. The love had to come later.

Deciding she couldn't put off speaking any longer, Penny opened her eyes and searched out those of her husband. He nodded at her in encouragement. "Penny?"

"I'm fine," she told him and then, when he didn't react, she went for, "We're having a baby!" with more enthusiasm in her voice. At hearing this, he threw his arms around her.

"Let's go find Jane," he told her, his head next to her ear.

Only the good doctor, who she'd trust not to say

anything, could see how her face had fallen upon hearing those words. When would she fly again?

****

"How's Celia?" Jane asked tentatively, peering from the open flight line hut's door over to where Penny sat at Betty's desk.

Jane had moved it herself so her friend would have the best view of the airfield she could. This wasn't turning out to be the best idea she'd ever had. Since she'd come in and been informed what she would be doing, as Betty was now back flying full time and her job was vacant, she'd developed a frown, even deeper than the one she'd been wearing since she'd waved her husband off the previous morning. When the first Anson of the morning took off with Betty at the controls, her face had, if it were possible, become even more morose. If it would help, Jane thought, she'd suggest moving the desk to somewhere Penny wouldn't be able to see the aircraft take off and land. She didn't think it would.

When she failed to get a reply, Jane coughed, loudly, and tried again. "Penny! How's Celia?"

Finally, Penny looked up, and Jane could see the effort it took for her to muster a small smile. She put down the pen she'd been using to write in a log book. "I'm sorry, Jane, I'm being rude. Celia, yes." Penny scratched her head before looking up once more. "She's much better now. I think she's even looking forward to going back to school. Says she wants to give her friend Wilks what for." She laughed, a small laugh but a real one. "Well, she didn't quite use those words, but I've told her off for using bad language, and I don't want to get told off by you for repeating what she really said."

233

This was the first time Jane had heard Penny laugh since the possibility she might be pregnant arose. The thought wasn't nice, and Jane did her best to put it to the back of her mind. Her friend needed her support now more than ever.

Since taking command at Hamble, Jane had hardly been able to do any flying. Only by seeing how Penny was reacting now did she realize how much she missed it—she felt like someone had punched her in the teeth. Swallowing hard to try and get rid of the bad taste in her mouth, Jane managed to say, "Sounds like she's getting better."

Penny nodded, and Jane noticed she couldn't help but look out through the window before replying, "I phoned her school earlier to explain why she wasn't back. The headmistress—awfully nice lady, though perhaps a little on the batty side—understood and is going to get the school nurse to do her best to check if any of the other girls are ill."

"Big job!" Jane commented.

"I certainly don't envy her," Penny agreed. "I think Celia should be well enough by tomorrow for me to fly her back."

Jane's head jerked up, and as she did so she saw the expression on Penny's face. Her friend had just realized what she proposed. Jane was about to open her mouth, though without knowing what she was going to say, when there came the roar of aero engines much bigger than those of the largest aircraft usually at the airfield, their own Avro Anson taxies.

"What the hell's that?" Penny half-shouted, looking out the window, then turning back, a wide-eyed look upon her face, to announce, "It's a Yank C47! I'm not certain, Jane, but if I recall their markings right, it's from Frank's group."

Curious to beat all else, both women left the relative warmth of the hut and headed toward the hard standing where the twin-engined transport aircraft would stop its taxiing. Hands over their ears, they waited for the engines to shut down and then a minute more for the rear door to open. Out jumped a captain in the USAAF. As he landed, he waved a hand in their direction, obviously having noticed them.

"Do you recognize him?" Jane asked Penny.

Penny waited until their visitor was a little nearer. Only when he was merely ten yards away did a bell go off in her head, and she nodded. "I think it's First Lieutenant Pete Gabrowski—well, now, a captain—and I've probably completely messed up his surname, Jane. He flies with your Frank, I think."

"Ma'am," the captain said with a touch to his cap, having obviously heard what Penny said. "And you pronounced it just fine." He held out his hand to Jane first, and his demeanor immediately gathered a dark aura. This didn't go unnoticed by either woman. "I'm really sorry I'm not here to deliver ice cream this time, Ms. Howell," he told her, shaking his head.

"Tell me," Jane ordered without preamble, a sinking feeling in her stomach, correctly surmising the young man had come to see her.

Pete glanced around before refocusing on Jane. Even with no one else within hearing range, the ground crew having chocked up the C47 and then been waved off by another American standing in the transport's open door, he asked, "Is there somewhere more…private, where we can speak?"

Jane shook her head. "Whatever you have to say, you can say in front of Penny. I trust her with my life." Penny opened and closed her mouth, not quite knowing what she could say to such a moving statement.

"If you're sure," he agreed after a moment. He reached into his uniform jacket and pulled out a crumpled envelope, turning it over and over in his hands before finally, and quite reluctantly, handing it over into Jane's slightly shaking hands. This task done, he looked her in the eye, bowed his head slightly, and told her, it seemed all in one breath, "I'm very sorry I wasn't able to deliver this news before now. We only got back from—overseas—yesterday, and they kept us busy late into last night, or I would have called. But I wanted to do this in person. I'm really, really sorry. Jane, Frank's plane was shot down on the twenty-third." He held up a hand as Penny opened her mouth to ask the obvious question. "No, I'm afraid there's no question of survivors. His plane took a hit from anti-aircraft fire smack-bang in the cockpit."

Jane didn't appear to be on the verge of breaking down, though neither did it look like she could say anything in response.

"Thank you for coming to tell us in person, Pete," Penny managed to say. "We understand it must be very difficult for you, losing someone who's your friend. How are you doing?"

Pete shrugged his shoulders and ran a hand through hair much longer than she'd seen on any serviceman for a long time. "Day to day, just taking it day to day." He looked over his shoulder before turning back. "I've lost count of the friends I've lost, and I'm sure we'll lose a few more before this hell is over."

Jane must have been listening, as she nodded her head in what Penny assumed was agreement, before saying, "I'm sorry too, Pete, and as Penny says, you have my eternal thanks for taking the time to come and tell me in person. I will remember your kindness."

"Will you and your companion stay for some tea?" Penny asked, not knowing if she wanted them to stay or not but slipping into typical British politeness mode.

"No, thanks." Pete shook his head. "We have to get back. We're not here for long, and there's a lot to do before our—next job," he finished.

Putting his cap onto his head, he snapped to attention, saluted Jane, and with an about-face, marched back to his plane.

Penny's gaze followed the American as he boarded the transport. She watched as its engines turned on, and as it taxied out and finally took off. It wasn't until it had disappeared from sight that she turned to speak to Jane, only Jane had disappeared.

Chapter Twenty-Six

"Did you hear what happened yesterday in the Arctic?" Ruth asked Walter as soon as he came through the door.

"Good morning to you too, Ruth," he said, shrugging off his overcoat and hanging up his hat on the coat stand before switching the kettle on. Ruth, always in editor mode when in her office at the *Hamble Gazette*, wasn't terribly good at making tea, or so Walter insisted, so he always made the front office's brew. "No, we had a quiet night reading, remember? There wasn't anything either of us wanted to hear on the wireless."

Ruth snapped her fingers. "Of course, what with finding this out, it completely slipped my mind. It's a pity Shirley couldn't stay any longer, but this flying course seems to have turned her into a right little chatterbox."

Walter nodded and poured the water into the teapot, gave it a stir, and presented Ruth with a steaming cup of nice, fresh tea. "It is quite a change. So what's this news that's got you so excited?"

Ruth put her cup down, her eyes ablaze with a hunger he hadn't seen since she'd found out her POW son had lost a foot during a bungled escape attempt. Whatever news she'd found out must be big to get this reaction.

"A big naval battle took place yesterday evening, somewhere off the North Cape—that's off the coast of northern Norway—and the Royal Navy sank the *Scharnhorst*!"

Walter nearly dropped his cup, barely managing to avoid spilling its contents all over his desk. "You're joking?" he eventually managed to say.

"Not one bit," she assured him.

"So that's why you wanted us in the office so early!" he surmised.

Ruth nodded. "I want to bring out a special edition. Give our readers something to celebrate. What do you say?"

In answer, Walter took out his notepad and a pencil. "Ready when you are, boss. Let's give our readers a real treat!"

"Did you hear?"

The words were heard before the person who uttered them came through the door.

"Lawrence!" Ruth exclaimed, jumping to her feet. "What a lovely surprise." She got to her feet and gave him a hug, whilst Walter took his opportunity to shake his friend by the hand.

"Sorry you couldn't make it for Christmas," he told him. "Mind you, I've got to ask—have your ears recovered from that roasting your Mary gave you?"

Lawrence raised his fist and then smiled and immediately lowered it before letting out a quick chuckle. "If I wasn't in such a good mood—"

"Because?" Ruth asked, as she poured the last of the tea out for their unexpected visitor.

"Have you heard about the *Scharnhorst*?"

"That's why the boss has me in early," Walter told

him. "We're going to put out a special edition. A kind of celebration, you could call it."

At hearing Walter's words, Lawrence became a little somber. He took the seat across from Ruth and stirred his tea—for something to do, more than anything, there being no sugar on offer. He finally looked up with a sigh.

"What is it?" Ruth asked. "You were all excited when you came in. I mean, it is good news, so why the change of mood?"

"No, I'm with you that it's a good thing." He nodded. "I've information you probably don't have yet. It puts a different perspective on it."

Walter looked puzzled. "What could be different? We sank a Nazi battleship, one that's been a thorn in our side since the war began. What could be wrong about that?"

Lawrence shook his head. "You slightly misunderstand me, mate. I quite agree the sinking is good. How could I not? No, it's the casualties." He stopped when he noticed Ruth had gone pale at his words. "Ruth," he asked, turning to face her, "are you all right? I'm sorry. I didn't mean to upset you."

Ruth took a long, slow drink of her tea before mustering a smile. "I know you didn't," she assured him. "Until you mentioned casualties, I'm ashamed to say I hadn't stopped to think about them."

It looked like she wasn't the only one, as Walter was nodding his head in agreement. "Winter in the Arctic Sea—it doesn't bear thinking about. A person wouldn't last long in those seas. Is that what you meant?"

Lawrence very slowly nodded in agreement. "All I

can say, and I'd rather you didn't put this in your article, is that there were only a few dozen survivors."

Walter swallowed. Ruth went, if it were possible, even paler. She reached out and ran a finger across the picture of her son, Joe, a POW, as with the other hand she wiped away a stray tear. Lawrence went into nephew mode and perched himself on the edge of her desk.

"How's he doing?"

Ruth looked up, recognizing his presence, and accepted his reassuring hand on her shoulder. "He's fine," she began automatically and then shook her head. "Well, maybe not. His new leg's not a great fit, and it's causing him some trouble. I suspect," she added, "that he's making light of it for my sake. His main complaint, though, is that since he lost his leg, the Germans have given him a different job in the camp, so he's pretty much alone whilst his mates are out working all day."

"We'll have him out of there before he knows it," Lawrence told her, overdoing his duty of trying to cheer her up.

"You can be a dear boy at times," she told him, patting him on the cheek.

"Only at times?" he asked, reverting back to his best cheeky persona.

"I think it's all down to Mary," Walter put in, earning him a nod of agreement from Ruth and, after a moment's thinking time, from Lawrence.

"If you're sure you're all right?" he asked his aunt, who assured him she was. "Then I'd better get off. I've some making up to Mary to get along with."

As the door jangled shut, causing Bobby to raise his head and crack open a single eye before going back to sleep in his place beneath Ruth's desk, Walter took up his pencil and declared, "Right. Back to work."

As Walter bent over his notepad, Ruth couldn't resist saying, "There are two t's in battleship."

****

"You can go in now," the redoubtable Miss Fanshaw told Betty with a wave of her hand toward the office door of solicitor Alistair Burrows.

Having waited ten minutes past her appointment time, again, and without being offered any kind of refreshment, again, Betty didn't bother to thank the secretary this time as she passed her desk and slammed the door shut behind her.

Looking up from a piece of paper in his hand, Mr. Burrows heaved his elderly bones to his feet and held out a—thankfully—dry hand for Betty to shake. "Sorry to keep you, Miss Palmer," he told her warmly. Then he noted the expression upon his visitor's face. "Should I surmise my secretary hasn't offered you a cup of tea yet?"

Betty settled herself down in the plush yet slightly fading green leather chair across the desk. "You must be some kind of clairvoyant, Mr. Burrows."

"If I were, I would have won the football pools years ago, Miss Palmer." He shook his head with a smile. "No, I'm just someone with a secretary who hates everything. I would change her, only I've decided to retire once both your and young Marcus's business is concluded."

"Really? I get the feeling you would be the type of gentleman who would become bored if you weren't working," Betty found herself saying, a little surprised to find she cared.

His finger hovering over the intercom, the solicitor seemed to be considering her words. "Miss Fanshaw. Two cups of tea and a selection of the best biscuits we still have, please. Soon as you can," he ordered, releasing the button before his secretary could say anything. Only then did he respond to Betty's statement.

"Perhaps, perhaps. I expect time will tell. Perhaps I could take up teaching again, to pass the time? I expect there is a call for that profession now. Anyway"—he gave his full attention to Betty—"you didn't come here to discuss my plans. What may I do for you, Miss Palmer?"

Betty was about to tell him the purpose for her visit when the door of his office opened and in walked Miss Fanshaw carrying a tray bearing two cups, a pot of tea, and a small—very small, Betty noticed when it was placed between herself and the solicitor—plate of rather dry biscuits. Both of them waited until the bearer had left the office.

Mr. Burrows picked up one of the brown effigies purporting to be a biscuit, sniffed it, and swiftly put it down. "Perhaps...just the tea?" He poured them both a cup of what at least looked to be tea, pushed one before Betty, and took one for himself.

Betty picked it up, sniffed it—it smelled like tea—and took a tentative sip, hot, wet, and not tasting very much of anything. Typical wartime tea. She put the cup down.

"I've read the letter my sister left me." She gave him a summary of what Eleanor had said about Marcus, though not troubling him with details. When she got to the part about Eleanor's estate, she asked him to arrange to move all the contents of her sister's various accounts into one central account. She knew she could do this herself, but it would take a great deal of time, she was positive. Her sister had been like her in not being in the habit of splashing her cash around. Being brought up in an orphanage taught you the value of money, as you never had any. No, whatever he charged her for performing this service would be well worth it.

By this time Mr. Burrows had drunk half his tea— and absently nibbled on one of the biscuits before hastily spitting it out into a bin. "Sorry," he mumbled, wiping his mouth. He gave her a firm nod of his head. "Certainly, I can make those arrangements. Where would you like the contents moved to?"

Betty had first thought, when the idea had come to her, about simply having everything moved to the account where her wages from the ATA were deposited. However, some little voice inside her told her to open a new account with one of the big banks. That way, she'd have better access to the funds for the scheme she was mulling over. Keeping this part to herself, she asked him if he could open a new account for her.

"If that is your wish, then I suggest we take a walk to the local branch of Lloyds. I shall need access to your account, albeit temporarily. Obviously, you should revoke this as soon as the task is complete." Betty nodded, finishing her own tea. What he'd said seemed logical to her. She was about to open her mouth to ask him something awkward, but he could obviously read minds. "With my limited understanding of your background, Miss Palmer, I feel I should provide you certain…security assurances that I can be trusted to deal with your funds." He took up a pen and proceeded to write. "Here is my home address, which, I am certain, you could easily check up on, should you so desire. As your sister could attest if she were here, I can promise my family are worthy of your trust."

Betty held up a hand. She didn't need to hear more, though she decided she might very well trail him when he went home at the end of the day. It would do no harm.

"Thank you, Mr. Burrows. That is more than good enough for me." She held out her hand to seal the deal.

****

After taking a rather slow walk with him into the City to open an account and make all other necessary arrangements with the bank, Betty went off alone to visit each bank on her sister's list, deciding now was as good a time as any to make a summary of Elle's assets.

By the time she'd finished, she really needed the glass of stout she was polishing off in a pub off Leicester Square. She'd done well enough from being her sister's fence, in addition to acquiring her beautiful little cottage—now with its houseful of wonderfully eccentric girls. Her sister, though…well, her sister was quite a bit better off. Obviously, she hadn't passed on everything she'd stolen. Never mind, Betty shrugged. Water under the bridge and all that. If anything, it added considerably to what she was planning. Look out, Errol Flynn!

The rest of her morning was spent back at Mr. Burrows' office, where she laid out her plan for most of her sister's estate. The idea had only come to her over Christmas, and so far she had only the bare bones. Bare bones or not, when she'd finished telling him, the elderly man had a tear in his eye and had to excuse himself from the office for a few moments to compose himself. When he came back, he shook her hand warmly and promised, as she asked, not to breathe a word to anyone.

An hour later, feeling quite drained, she bid Mr. Burrows a hearty and heartfelt goodbye, ignored the purveyor of stale biscuits, and making certain her coat was done up tight, opened the door leading out onto London's cold, damp streets. Outside, huddled under a large black umbrella, was Marcus! Delighted to see her newly found brother, she opened her arms wide and cried, "Marcus! What are you doing here?"

Though he returned her embrace with warmth, something was missing from how his arms felt around her. Her intuition told her to be on the alert, and she trusted her intuition. It had kept her alive back in the orphanage, and it continued to do so. Stepping back, she looked around, trying to make sense of her feelings. She realized then that Marcus hadn't answered.

"What are you doing here?" she replied, noting he was in uniform.

"I'm sorry," her brother said, his voice hard to hear over the hustle and bustle of London's traffic.

He didn't look up as he spoke, seeming intently interested in shuffling his shoes. "For what?" Her ears picked up the approach of footsteps, and what sounded like the clunk of a cane, approaching from behind her.

Turning, she saw a couple in their mid-fifties. Their clothes looked as if they'd once been the height of fashion, but to her sharp eyes, they hadn't seen the inside of a cleaner's in a while, and their wearers too looked as if they were slightly past their best. Betty, prepared to turn and run if they showed the least hostile intent, watched as they continued toward her. Even with the limited view she had of their faces, half-hidden under the umbrella they were sheltering under, something was naggingly familiar about them, and she didn't like it one bit.

To her surprise, Marcus stepped away from her and, as the couple came to a halt, stepped around next to the newcomers. He inclined his head to the woman and shook the man's hand. His words, when they came, took her breath away.

"Mother. Father."

Chapter Twenty-Seven

"If I open my mouth any wider, you could fly a Tiger Moth into it," Celia moaned, as the station doctor asked her to open up again. "How'd you find out I had strep anyway?" she asked, not getting an answer, as he was too busy poking and prodding around the back of her throat.

"Your sister had the good sense to ask me to check you out before allowing you to leave, young lady," Doctor Barnes informed her, throwing his tongue depressor into the bin. He turned to the waiting Penny. "You can tell Betty, when you next see her, she did a good job. I'd say that Celia here did indeed have strep throat—which, I'm very happy to say, is very nearly cleared up." He turned and bent down to look Celia in the eye. "I expect you to keep warm, and there is to be no strenuous exercise for the next week. Understood? I'll give you a note you can hand in to your headmistress."

After Penny made certain her sister thanked the doctor, the two made their way over to the flight line hut. As they neared, there came a piercing whistle, and they caught sight of Jane waving at them beside an Anson which had just come out from having an engine change. Puzzled, Penny grabbed her sister's hand and the two walked over. As they came within earshot, Jane spread her arms wide and declared, "Your taxi awaits, young lady."

Penny hadn't gotten around to telling her sister she was pregnant, for reasons she couldn't fathom, so to be greeted by the sight of Jane in full flying gear confused the younger of the sisters.

Celia's head turned from Jane to her sister and back again. "You're not flying me back, sis?"

Jane cocked an eyebrow. "You haven't told her." It wasn't a question.

"Told me what?" Celia asked. "Where's your flying suit?" she asked her sister.

Instead of replying, Penny told her, "Get your things and give me five minutes alone with Jane." When Celia didn't do as Penny asked straight away, Penny added, "Please?"

Once she was satisfied she wasn't going to be interrupted, Penny turned to her friend and asked, full of curiosity, "Care to tell me what's going on?" She flicked Jane's flying helmet.

"Well, though you can't pilot a plane, I see no reason you can't tag along whilst I test fly this crate and, if we happen to take a detour via Celia's school…"

She didn't get any farther. Jane found all the air being knocked out of her as Penny threw herself around her, nearly sending her tumbling over.

"Thank you, thank you," Penny told her once she'd released her vise-like grip. "I was wondering how I was going to get her back today. It's way too late for her to catch a train back."

"It is?" Celia asked, having come up behind the pair unnoticed.

"It is," Penny agreed. "So if you can climb aboard this plane"—she waved a hand behind her in the general direction of the Anson—"Jane's going to ferry us up to your school."

Celia crossed her arms. "Not until you tell me what's going on. Why can't you fly me? You don't look injured," she declared, having looked her sister up and down. "In fact, if anything, I'd say you were positively blooming with health!" Celia wasn't her sister's sister for nothing, and as soon as the words were out of her mouth, she took in how Jane was hovering over Penny, in a most protective way. Her hand flew to her mouth.

Penny nodded and began to say, "Yes, I…" but never had the chance to finish, as Celia let out a squeal and launched herself into her sister's waiting arms.

"I'm going to be an aunt!" she yelled out.

****

"You're certain your headmistress said the driveway's wide enough?" Penny shouted so Celia could hear her over the racket of the Cheetah engines.

Celia nodded, shouting back, "She's positive."

Penny tapped Jane on the shoulder and told her what they'd just discussed. After managing to prise her sister from her neck, she'd had the thought to call up and ask the question, the Anson being a bit bigger than the Miles Magister single-engine aircraft she'd previously used. It also had a wider undercarriage track, and Penny had wanted to make certain. From memory, she personally thought they'd have a bare few inches either side. Jane shrugged her shoulders by way of a reply and turned her attention back to flying. Penny settled back in her seat, silently agreeing with her friend. They were kind of committed, so they'd wait and see. If Penny were flying, she'd circle a couple of times, perhaps even do a dummy landing to check, and she had no doubt Jane would do the same.

Penny hadn't experienced Jane's flying before and if the take-off hadn't been the smoothest, she hadn't found fault with the flight since. Looking at her watch, she estimated they were about ten minutes away from being in sight of the old manor which was serving as the school. She was about to pass on this information to Jane, not that she reckoned she didn't already know, when something else struck her. Nothing to do with the flight, yet it could conceivably impact on her living arrangements.

"You did give Betty back her book, didn't you?"

Celia gave her sister a knowing smile, replying, "Yes, I left *The Moving Finger* on Betty's bed. You'll still be able to read it."

Her sister did indeed know her very well.

As she'd figured, spot on ten minutes later they were over Celia's school. Settling into the co-pilot's seat to Jane's right, Penny looked across to her friend's side as they banked the plane low and to the left, skimming a bare ten or so feet above the driveway. Taking the plane back up, Jane did the same again, and once she'd climbed back up to five hundred feet, put the plane into a gentle banking turn so she could talk over their options.

"What do you think?" she shouted, so Celia could hear from where she was leaning over the back of their seats.

"I think we should put a parachute on her and chuck her out," Penny shouted.

Both Jane and Penny were looking at Celia when this was suggested, and both grinned as they saw the blood drain out of the girl's face.

It took Celia a full minute before she registered their malicious grins. "Why, you evil…"

Jane held up a hand to stop her. "Don't finish that sentence, unless you want Penny to carry out her threat."

Whether because she thought her sister might carry out her threat or because she was distracted by the view she was treated to when Jane pushed the nose down and lined up for landing, Celia didn't answer and hurried to strap herself in.

As the wheels touched down, Penny glanced out her side window and thought her estimation of a few inches of clearance on each side was going to be about right.

The Anson had barely rolled to a stop when a stout little tweed-clad apparition jumped up in front of them a couple of times, holding up her thumbs. Penny recognized the figure of the headmistress, Samantha Garret, of whom she'd become quite fond on the two times she'd met her. Once she was certain she'd been seen, the headmistress ducked down, waved a couple of blocks of wood in the air, and Jane, understanding what she intended, gave her a thumbs-up of her own.

Post-flight checks over and the engines switched off, Jane and Penny took off their flying helmets, left them on their seats, and clambered into the rear, where a slightly ashen-faced Celia was fumbling to pick up her things.

"Need a hand?" Jane asked, unable to stop another smile from appearing.

Once they'd opened the door, they were engulfed in a wall of sound which turned out to be the entire school clapping. Celia, perhaps in an attempt to divert the attention from how ill she felt, raised a hand in acknowledgement, whilst both Jane and Penny went over to an undercarriage wheel each.

"An inch," Penny called.

"Maybe two," Jane replied.

As they joined Celia, Samantha appeared in their midst, reaching out and grabbing Jane's hand and pumping it up and down vigorously before doing the same to Penny, whilst Jane massaged some life back into hers.

"Wonderful landing, Penny, my dear!" she enthused. "Absolutely wonderful! To tell the truth, I wasn't one hundred percent certain there would be room."

Penny grabbed her arm before she could say any more. "Most kind, Sam." She remembered the bundle of energy which was Celia's headmistress had insisted she call her so. "But it's my boss who actually landed her." Penny did the introduction. "Samantha Garret, I'd like you to meet my boss and very good friend, Flight Captain Jane Howell."

Slightly afraid of permanent damage to her hand, Jane bent down and kissed Samantha on the cheek, which delighted their host. "Oh, any friend of Penny's is mine for life too. Come," she announced. "I'm sure you've time for a warming cup of tea." At Jane's dubious expression, she leant in and, with her hand hiding her lips, confided, "Last of my pre-war stock? Tempted?"

A cup of pre-war tea was such a treat both Jane and Penny nodded their heads immediately.

"Excellent, excellent," she told them, clapping her

hands before turning back and facing the crowd, most of whom were still milling around, poking, prodding, and generally investigating the Anson as closely as they could. "Attention!" she shouted, startling Jane so much she jumped—Penny and Celia knew what was coming and had covered their ears. "Attention! Everyone except those I detailed to stand guard duty—back to the school!"

Jane watched through widened eyes and slightly open mouth as the order was instantly obeyed. Within a very short space of time, the headmistress and the pilots—Celia having been swept up by her friends—were alone, apart from a group of ten of what looked like the biggest girls in school, accompanied by what had to be one of the teachers.

"Miss Thorpse," Samantha called to the teacher, with an accompanying gesture of a finger, "we'll be back in thirty minutes. Please make sure the plane is safely down to the other end of the driveway, so my friends can take off."

As she led Jane and Penny toward the school, Jane had to check. "This Miss Thorpse. She, um, knows what she's doing?"

"Oh, yes, don't worry about anything, my dear," Samantha told her, not breaking her step. "Her parents run a farm, you know."

When no further explanation was forthcoming, both Penny and Jane looked back over their shoulders and were slightly relieved to see the teacher stood near the tail, in supervisor mode, whilst the girls slowly pushed the Anson back down the road.

****

With the taste of the best cup of tea, even including

that served at the Ritz, still fresh in their mouths, Penny and Jane each gave Celia a hug goodbye.

"Be good, and remember what the doctor said—no strenuous activity for a week."

Samantha patted Penny on her elbow. "I'll make certain of that. Don't you worry."

"Thank you, Sam," Penny told her before bending down to accept a strong hug. "It's always a pleasure meeting up with you."

A little less enthusiastically, Jane also accepted her hug, with Penny and Celia stifling their amusement. "A pleasure too, Sam."

"I do hope to see you both before too long," she said. "In the meantime, keep safe, and may God watch over you."

Samantha's version of a ground crew had done a very good job in positioning the Anson, and once they were in the air, Penny and Jane settled into companionable silence. Then, just as they were flying over Winchester, Jane's voice came through Penny's earphones.

"I wanted to apologize for disappearing on you yesterday," she began, hurrying along to prevent Penny from interrupting. "No, it has to be said. Despite the—situation—it was unprofessional."

Penny didn't give her a chance. "Nonsense. I don't know what I'd do if it were me, but it's quite understandable."

Next to her, Jane shook her head. "Nevertheless, I am sorry."

"We haven't had a chance to talk since yesterday," Penny said. "I didn't want to say anything whilst Celia was around, but if you need to talk…"

In the silence which followed, Penny could sense her friend was mulling things over before saying anything. Finally, she heard Jane clearing her throat. "The letter, from Frank," she began. "It actually contained his diary. It had an inscription inside which said, *Deliver to Flight Captain Jane Howell in the event of my death.*"

She stopped her tale as she pointed out the window at a bank of fog, undoubtedly coming up off the Solent and not unusual at nearly seven in the evening. Penny told her she'd also seen it, and together, given the fog and the growing darkness, they began to keep a closer eye out the windows.

"Anyway," Jane picked up, "apparently, he bought it the day after our first real date. On that date he wrote, *I've met the woman I'm going to marry.*"

"This bloody fog," Penny said out loud, as she could tell Jane was swallowing like crazy, trying to keep her emotions in check. Eventually, she risked saying, "I'll take her, if you want. We'll talk, just the two of us, when we get down. Okay?"

Jane didn't have time to reply before all hell broke loose.

As they flew through a particularly dense patch of fog, both jerked in their straps as something dark and moving at considerable speed flashed past their nose. Both their heads moved as they tracked the path of whatever it was. Coming out the other side of the fog patch, both gasped.

From being on their own, on a quiet and uneventful stooge back to base, they found themselves flying too sedately and at right angles between a Nazi He111 bomber and—too late for any evasive action—the incoming fire from an attacking British Spitfire. The control yoke in Jane's hands jerked and twitched at the same moment they both felt cannon shells striking the tail of the Anson.

"Bloody hell!" they both cried at the same time, with Penny making a wild grab at the yoke in an attempt to help Jane control the damaged plane.

"Look out!" Jane cried, jerking the column to the right, having spotted the bomber's upper gunner firing back.

Whether he was aiming at the Spitfire or deliberately at them didn't matter. What mattered was that they were hit, this time by enemy fire. Some of the gunner's fire went through the side of the cockpit, and other bullets smashed into the instrument panel. At first, it didn't appear to be as serious as what they'd already suffered, but then Jane's attention was drawn to the smoke beginning to pour from the left engine, and the control yoke gave another, deeper, longer shudder.

"Buggeration! Penny!" Jane yelled. "Give me a hand." When she got no immediate response, she looked to her right, and her heart nearly stopped.

Penny was slumped over the control yoke, and Jane was shocked to the core to see blood pouring from a wound in her friend's upper arm.

Chapter Twenty-Eight

The shock of seeing her friend shot, unconscious, and bleeding was almost enough to cause Jane to lose what little control she still had over her stricken aircraft. Torn between wanting to help Penny, if it were still possible, and needing to nurse the Anson along, she mustered her wits, pulled her friend back until she was resting against the back of her seat, checked the harness was secure, and placed a couple of fingers on the side of Penny's neck. To her relief, she found a pulse, faint but present. Tugging her scarf from around her neck, she stuffed it none too gently into the area of Penny's wound, getting unwonted satisfaction when she got a groan of pain as she did so. At least it confirmed her friend was alive.

A sixth sense caused Jane to pull back on the control yoke barely in time to avoid taking the top off a tree. Shifting her helmet, which had skewed around until it nearly covered one eye, Jane hit Send on her radio, using Hamble's frequency. "Mayday! Mayday! This is Howell. Have the medics ready. Wounded on board!"

A part of her knew her RT procedure wasn't right, but most of her didn't care. She was just thankful they were in the Anson as, unlike the aircraft they delivered, it at least had a radio. Jane knew her work was dangerous, though nothing had prepared her for actually being shot at. Beside her, Penny groaned again, and her head lolled over to face Jane. Knowing the aircraft needed as much of her attention as possible, Jane nevertheless risked a glance. Penny's face was beyond pale. Before turning back, she looked across at her makeshift bandage and stifled a gasp—blood had already soaked through it.

Desperately, she tried to fly and apply pressure at the same time, but the combination of the damage done by the Spitfire's cannon to the Anson's rudder and rear control surfaces, together with the engines appearing to be on the point of dying, made that impossible. Knowing Penny's life, not to mention her own, was firmly in her hands, Jane forced herself to pay full attention to getting them down in one piece.

Flicking the radio switch, she was met by silence. One more part of the aircraft had died on her. The intermittent fog was still causing visibility problems, as if she didn't have enough to be getting along with, and upon coming out of a particularly dense patch, she was relieved to find she was alone in the sky. This was quickly replaced when she looked down through the window and found she was much nearer the ground than was comfortable. After nearly hitting that tree, she'd pulled back on the yoke and thought she'd managed to coax enough out of the engines to gain her a little height and time. It appeared she was wrong. She was also off course to make for Hamble—and to put the icing on the cake, the fuel warning light had just come on.

Jane had no choice. She'd have to get down, and quick. With the limited control she had of the Anson, it'd be best if this didn't entail any violent maneuvers.

Hell, with the state the plane was in, even a gentle turn could be enough to tear it apart.

Desperately glancing around, all the while aware of the fact that Penny's life could be slipping away, she spied a field a few degrees to her left and about four to five miles away. With no actual airfields in sight, she took the best bet of a bad deal. As gently as she could, she twitched the control yoke until the nose was pointed more or less at the field. From what she could see, a farmhouse with some outbuildings was on one side and, as she got nearer, a stream was on the other.

Penny twitched and moaned again. Jane really needed both hands on the yoke to maintain any semblance of control, but she did rest a hand very briefly on her friend's knee, trying not to worry it felt cold to her touch even through the layers she was wearing. "Hold on, Penny, hold on," she muttered.

Down the Anson went, cutting through the air with the grace of a brick. With a last cough and puff of black smoke, the left-hand engine died, forcing Jane to jam her foot on the opposite rudder bar to try to correct the sudden loss of power. Gritting her teeth against the strain, Jane wiped the sweat from her brow. As the ground got nearer, now only a mile or so off, she squinted at the field. Something about it didn't look right. Something was there which she wouldn't normally expect to see in a field. If she didn't think she was going out of her mind trying to cope, she'd think the field had sprung a tiny forest.

"Bloody hell!" she shouted.

With only a few hundred yards to go and way too low on both height and power to pull up and look for somewhere else, she now knew what she was seeing. If she'd been in her right state of mind, not only wouldn't she have been trying to land there, but she'd have remembered about the defenses that sprang up around southern England back in 1940. What she and her crippled aircraft were about to hit head on was a field full of stout wooden stakes.

Before she had time to contemplate doing anything else, the Anson slammed into the hard ground and immediately bounced ten feet back into the air before coming down again with a smack that rattled Jane's teeth. Her left hand flew off the yoke and her arm smacked into the side of the cockpit. Something snapped, and she couldn't stop her yelp of agony. Whatever part of her brain still working sent her right arm into Penny's upper chest, trying its best to stop her from being thrown about too much.

An almighty jolt started the plane spinning to the left, closely followed by something similar to the right, and the plane straightened back up. Blinking something wet from her eyes, her pain-raddled brain just about registered that both wings had been torn off by the stakes. The screech of metal was mind-numbing, and just as Jane thought her head might split open, the nose of what remained of the Anson struck a pole head on and juddered to a halt.

Desperately wanting to do nothing more than to put her head back and go to sleep, Jane fought the urge. Cradling what she knew was her broken left arm to her chest, she slapped her harness off and wiped her head again, the back of her hand coming away bloody. Filing this away—she'd worry about what was causing the blood later—she heaved herself out of her seat with some difficulty and, wobbling a little, leant over Penny.

Greeted with a moan, she let out a sob of relief. She was still alive!

A quick glance out both sides of the cockpit revealed both wings had indeed been torn off. Pulling down the zip of her Sidcot flying suit, she gritted her teeth and tucked her broken arm inside, the suit acting as a makeshift sling. Never had making her way out of an Anson been so difficult. More than once she knocked her arm against the various protrusions, causing her to cry out in agony. Whilst she made her painful way out, she watched her footing, so as she approached the exit door and raised her eyes, she got another shock. Neither the door nor the fuselage was present. Instead, the tail was completely missing. A jagged-edged hole was before her, with the remains of the tail and what looked like an engine a hundred yards behind.

Struggling the last few feet until she stepped out onto the hard, torn-up grass they'd plowed, Jane fought for breath, her arm causing her intense pain and the blood dripping from her forehead getting into her eyes and causing vision troubles. With her good arm leaning against the remains of the fuselage, she opened her mouth and yelled, "Help!" twice, a third time.

Surely someone from the farmhouse had heard the crash? Opening her mouth, she was about to shout again when her dimming vision caught what could be a light in what she thought was the direction of the farmhouse. There it was again! It flicked once, twice, and then steadied. Feeling hope rising in her, she yelled again, "Help! Over here!"

In the gathering dark, Jane saw the light was now joined by another, and she thought she heard voices.

"Are you all right?" The shout came from whoever was making their way toward her.

Jane almost sagged in relief, almost. If she weren't in such pain, she'd have laughed at the typical, daft question. A surge of pain in her arm jolted her back to reality, and mustering the last of her fading strength, she called out, "Get a doctor! My friend's been shot!"

****

A light was shining in her eyes so, naturally, she tried to raise an arm to bat it away but found the action hurt too much. Somebody said something, and she felt the next stab of light go through her skull, or so it seemed. She turned her head, or thought she did, as she couldn't see anything except the light—and now that had gone, and all was darkness again.

With the light gone, she let out a groan and was rewarded by someone saying, "Hold her! Don't let her move!"

Why should she move? If she moved, or tried, it hurt like nothing she'd ever felt before, and she had no desire to feel that pain again anytime soon. When she'd tried to raise her arm, it had felt like someone was trying to rip her guts out. The memory brought forth another groan, and her eyes snapped open.

"Penny," a familiar voice cried.

"Hold her!" a voice she didn't recognize demanded, and Penny found the command wasn't aimed at her. A moment later, she really wished it had been, as something was pressed to her stomach, and with an accompanying scream, her body automatically tried to twist itself off whatever she was lying upon.

"I said to hold her!"

Through waves of pain, Penny felt a cool hand

upon her brow, and then a familiar face swam into view. Her lips tried to say her name, but nothing except another scream came from her mouth.

Jane's hand laid a damp towel across her forehead, and Penny thought she heard someone say, "I wish you'd let me splint your arm."

"Not until I know about my friend."

The voice giving the orders, unfortunately out of her sight, now said, "Look. There's an ambulance on its way, but if you don't stop getting in the way, two things are likely to happen. Firstly, that bandage my wife put around your forehead won't stop that gash from bleeding, and more importantly, if you don't stop talking, you'll distract me while I'm trying to tend your friend's wounds. So stand still, close your mouth, and be ready to hold your friend down if I tell you."

"What about the blood between her legs?" Jane's voice actually sounded abnormally calm.

Without apparently needing to think about it, the other voice said, "There's nothing I can do about that. It's too late. But if I don't stop this arm bleeding, it won't matter anyway. I always find it a surprise how much a human limb can bleed."

How long his ministrations lasted, Penny didn't know. This was the one thing she was glad about, as she could swear she could feel each and every cut and prod the doctor made.

"Tighter! Hold her tighter!" was the order.

After a subjective eternity, the pain began to relax and the voices became fainter and fainter. In fact, she could feel her body begin to relax. Whatever had been done to her must have worked. With a sigh, she let the pressure she'd been putting against the various hands holding her down slacken off until a warm feeling came over her, and she closed her eyes and decided that going to sleep would be a good idea.

****

"Penny!" cried Jane, feeling her friend's fight begin to leave her.

"Blast!" exclaimed the doctor who'd been working on her arm. "Get out of the way!" he ordered, shoving Jane out of the way and swiftly slapping Penny around the face.

This brought an immediate rush of blood to her face and an inrush of breath. Penny began coughing.

"Thank God," the doctor muttered. Once he was satisfied his patient was stable, he moved back to her arm. "When I'd nearly finished, too," he complained. Without looking up, he snapped, "Hold her again. Not long now."

Five minutes later, during which Jane was heartily glad her friend kept breathing but also didn't struggle again, the doctor stepped back and flopped onto a chair next to the kitchen table.

"Saul," he said without looking up. "Thank you. Now, please go outside and wait for the ambulance. They shouldn't be long."

The man he addressed, who'd been helping Jane and the doctor—and, she now saw, the farmer and his wife, presumably—hurried outside without a word.

Jane looked down at her friend to find her awake and staring up into space. "Penny! Can you hear me?"

After asking again, Penny's eyes briefly focused upon Jane's concerned ones before closing. Sweat was running in rivulets down her face, and upon her forehead a bruise of epic proportions was developing where her face had been accidentally whacked against the aircraft's fuselage as she'd been extracted. Quite rightly, Jane could now acknowledge, trying to follow the doctor in relaxing, it had been ignored as it wasn't life-threatening. Taking her friend's hand with her good one, Jane did her best to ignore the bloody mess her arm was, and the less she looked at the stain between Penny's legs the better.

Jane had luckily crash-landed on the outskirts of a village, unseen from the sky, in which lived a doctor who'd been a medic in the Great War and now served the local area. At hearing Jane's shouts to get a doctor, the farmer's wife had run off immediately, whilst the farmer, himself a veteran who'd served in the hell of the trenches, had done his best to stanch Penny's wound until more help arrived and they could carry her into the farmhouse and place her on the kitchen table, where the doctor performed his emergency surgery.

"Penny," Jane said again, leaning down. When her friend didn't reply, she looked over at where the doctor still sat, drinking a glass of water. "Is she going to be all right? Aren't you even going to check what caused that?" Jane pointed a shaky hand at the stain.

The doctor finished draining his glass before looking over into Jane's concerned face. He appeared to be giving his answer some thought, though he eventually shrugged his shoulders. "The bleeding has stopped. There's nothing I can do about it." When Jane's eyebrows shot up, he hastily added, "She's going to need more surgery and then a long period of recuperation."

"What about my baby?"

Everyone in the room's heads swiveled to the

patient, who had surprised all by speaking.

It may have been the tiredness he'd naturally show after performing the makeshift emergency surgery, but the doctor's face fell, and he slowly yet emphatically shook his head, and Jane knew in that moment what had caused the blood loss and why he hadn't tried to treat it.

Chapter Twenty-Nine

"Ready?" Matt Green yelled.

"Ready," Ruth replied, holding out a hand to catch the roll of tape he threw up to her. "I tell you this," she said tearing off a strip. "I was beginning to wonder if I was ever going to get these windows taped up! You know how difficult it can be to get hold of this blinking tape these days."

"I do wish you'd let me do these upstairs windows," her boyfriend muttered, though not low enough that Ruth didn't hear him.

"I would be happy for you to play the gallant boyfriend," she informed him as she finished the last cross on her own bedroom window, "if you didn't suffer from vertigo. Honestly, you did make me laugh, clinging to the ladder when you were only on the second rung."

Looking down at his feet, Matt, in all seriousness, informed her, "I'll have you know I fell off the second rung of a ladder when I were a nipper, and it broke my leg."

Ruth performed a fireman's slip down the ladder, forcing Matt to hurriedly step back before she landed on his feet. Turning around, she reached out and grabbed him by the lapels and planted a kiss upon his lips, before wrapping her arms around his neck.

"Why didn't you tell me? If I'd known, I wouldn't

have pulled your leg."

Matt squeezed her and playfully slapped her on the backside. "Yes, you would."

Ruth laughed. "You're right. I would've—only not so much."

Half an hour later, they'd finished taping crosses on all the rear windows and stood back to admire their work.

"Much better," Ruth remarked. "You'd never know the place had suffered any bomb damage at all now. Come on," she told him, taking him by the hand. "I think you deserve a cup of tea. I take it you've time before you go on parade?"

"Always make time for a cup of tea, my love," Matt let her know. "It's part of what makes us British."

"What makes us British?" Walter asked as he looked up from the kitchen table where he was reading a manual called *Lewis Machine Gun for the Home Guard*.

"Glad to see you're taking that job seriously, Walter," said Matt as Walter's sergeant in the local unit of the Home Guard.

"Kettle's on," Walter remarked before replying, "You gave me the thing. Seems only sensible to read the manual. Any problems with the windows?" he asked.

"All done," Ruth announced. "We make quite a team," she added, batting her eyelashes at Matt.

"Speaking of teams," Walter said, getting to his feet to pour the hot water into the teapot, "there's a card from your son on the mantelpiece."

Without uttering another word, Ruth took to her heels and was back within moments, clutching the precious piece of card in her hands, eyes locked upon its contents. Walter and Matt both exchanged small smiles of understanding whilst Walter stirred the pot and then played mum, pushing a cup in front of Matt and another where Ruth took a seat next to her boyfriend. Finally, she looked up, her expression the usual mixture of pride and sadness she had whenever she heard from Joe.

"How is he?" Walter asked, cupping his tea.

"That's what I hate about these postcards. You can't fit much news on them," Ruth remarked. "He says he's okay, and that his leg isn't causing him as much trouble. I think he asked who won the FA Cup."

"He must mean the Football League War Cup," Matt decided. "Tell him Blackpool, when you reply. I don't think that'll fall under giving away state secrets," he added, getting a small chuckle out of Ruth.

"Oh, there's also a couple of letters for Shirley from her Ted," Walter informed her. "Shall I drop them in to Betty's on our way out?"

A sharp knock at the back door was followed, without preamble, by a slightly out of breath and a little distressed Betty.

Putting the postcard on the Welsh dresser, Ruth pushed herself out of her seat and hurried to where her friend stood in the open doorway. "Betty! What's wrong?" she asked, taking her by the hand and closing the door before drawing the blackout curtain across again.

Walter and Matt exchanged pointed looks with Ruth, quickly surmising her need. Getting to his feet, Matt retrieved his uniform jacket from his chair back, pulled it on, and placed his side hat on his head. "Come on, Walter. Let's make an early start for the hall. Odds are the Women's Institute will have left the chairs strewn all over the place. You and me can clear up before the rest of the platoon get there."

Without a word, Walter also donned his jacket and hat. Both kissed Ruth on the cheek before quickly making their exit.

Believing nothing like a nice, fresh cup of tea would help wash any troubles away, Ruth ushered Betty into the seat Matt had vacated before taking a clean cup off the dresser and pouring her best friend a brew.

"Take your time, drink that up, and then, when you're ready, tell me all about it."

As soon as she put her cup down, Betty fixed her friend with a wide-eyed stare and blurted out, "I saw my parents!"

****

Jane wasn't the best of patients. More than one nurse at Southampton General Hospital had told her so. It had taken the threat of being sedated by a rather irate doctor to get her to sit still long enough to take an x-ray. This showed she'd suffered a clean break and wouldn't need an operation, which momentarily put a smile upon her face before he then informed her she would need to have a plaster cast. She took some morbid satisfaction when he took a step backward when her face turned to fury at being told this.

"I'll do you a deal," she tried, as a nurse helped her slot her arm into a sling whilst the necessary arrangements were made. "As soon as I know my friend's going to be all right, I'll let you plaster any part of me you want, but not until then."

The doctor, a tall chap with glasses as thick as bottle-bottoms, summoned up his courage and stepped next to her. He made to put a friendly hand onto her good shoulder, yet changed his mind when she turned her glare up a notch. "Jane, believe me, your friend couldn't be under better care. The surgeon operating on her is a personal friend of mine, and he's damn good. You really don't want to know what kinds of surgery he's had to do since this war started, and if I had to have an operation, he's who I'd want to perform it."

Jane had the good grace to relax a little.

"However, you must allow us to do our job. I'll do you a deal, and this is my only offer," he added, turning the tables on Jane. "You allow us to clean up your head wound—which, by the way, will need a few stitches—and then we'll bring in the chap to plaster your arm. You're lucky. Not only is it a clean break, but another inch higher and it would probably have snapped your elbow. As it is, you'll only need a cast below the elbow."

"And my friend?" Jane asked.

"I'll send one of my nurses up to the operating room. You should be aware, by the way, that she has much better things she could be doing with her time. She'll get you an update on how the operation's going. Deal?"

Jane knew when she'd been boxed into a corner and held out her good hand. "Deal, and"—she turned her head to address the two nurses for whom she'd made life awkward ever since she'd been admitted—"I'm sorry for being horrible to you."

Neither nurse looked like they were much out of their teens, but Jane wouldn't wish to imagine what they'd gone through during the aftermath of the bombing Southampton and the area had suffered. The one who appeared hardly old enough to be out of school answered, "Don't worry about it. I'll go up and see what I can find out about your friend. I know what it's like, so I'll be as quick as I can. Sally'll get you the good painkillers to take home with you when you're ready."

Before Jane could ask if that meant she'd not had the good stuff yet, the girl was gone.

"Right," the doctor said, grabbing her attention. "You sit still whilst Erin here cleans up your head wound. I'll be back shortly, and we'll get you sewn and plastered up."

"He's not as funny as he thinks he is, is he," Jane commented, once the doctor had left, and as Erin began to clean her forehead, whatever she did caused Jane to jerk back in pain.

"Sorry about that, love," Erin told her, getting back to the job, "but you're right, he isn't a very funny man."

Jane decided it would be best, and less painful, if she kept her mouth shut until the doctor came back.

It took about twenty minutes to apply the plaster cast to Jane's lower arm. Even with the painkillers she'd been given, she still couldn't stop the odd flinch of pain. Each time she did, the doctor—"Call me Simon," he'd told her, smiling, when he'd accepted the plaster and bandages—seemed to flinch in sympathy.

Jane was soon sporting a white, wet cast and a nice white bandage to protect the five stitches put in just before Simon started with her cast. She'd semi-jokingly asked if he could put the bandage on at a jaunty angle, but he merely confirmed his nurse's statement by not complying with her wishes. As the nurse was splitting the end of the bandage and beginning to tie a knot, the door flew open and in strode the nurse, Sally.

Jane's head began to turn but Erin held it in place, forcing Jane to swivel her eyes instead. "How is she?"

Sally glanced over at the doctor, who gave her a nod. "I popped my head in, and after they'd told me off, they gave me an update. The surgeon reckons it'll take about another hour, but he can't see any serious problems. Does she know about her baby?" Sally asked and upon Jane managing a nod now the bandage was tucked in, carried on. "Her arm's fine—that village doctor did a very good job, the surgeon said. However, he believes a combination of the shock of being wounded and an impact to her stomach caused her to miscarry. He's tidying up, but he can't say for sure if she'll ever be able to have another."

Jane hung her head and immediately regretted it, as it started to ache. Should she tell them about Penny striking the control yoke? Would it make any difference?

The doctor laid a hand on her shoulder, breaking her train of thought. "Is there someone, her husband, we should call?"

Slightly awkwardly, Jane reached up and back to squeeze the fingers on her shoulder. "I think I should do that. It's my fault, after all."

Perhaps he had no sense of humor, but he proved he had a good heart with his next words. "That's silly. From what you told me earlier, there's no way you could have known a battle was going on before you came out of that fog."

Whether it was her feelings of guilt or the delayed

shock, all of a sudden tears began to pour out of Jane as she told him, "Probably, but she shouldn't have been up there in the first place. I'd grounded her as soon as I knew about her pregnancy, but I still let her come with me to fly her sister back to school. If I'd have put my foot down, she wouldn't have been hurt!"

"Can you get us some tea, please, Sally?" Simon asked, before taking Jane by her good arm and gently leading her through the door, down the corridor a short way, and into his office. "Sit down," he ordered. "Here," he took out a handkerchief from his pocket. "I promise you, it's clean," he added with a smile.

In the time it took Jane to get herself back under control and cleaned up, Sally had brought them some tea and backed out of the office. "Sorry," Jane said.

"Nonsense." The doctor waved away her apology. "There's nothing to be sorry for, a quite natural reaction. In fact, if you hadn't reacted like that, I would be worried. Tell me…" He picked up his tea and took a quick sip, grimacing. "Never will get used to the lack of sugar. Sorry, where was I? Oh, yes, tell me, would you have been able to stop her boarding the plane?"

"Well, no," Jane admitted. "But maybe I should have made her drive, or take the train, or…"

"If wishes were horses," he finished for her. "Stop trying to second-guess something you can't change. There is nothing and no one to blame. It's the war, and these things happen. I'm sure she'll be fine and won't even think about blaming you," he ended with a smile.

"But what if she can't have children? That'll be my fault!"

"Stuff and nonsense." The doctor waved away her latest statement. "I know it's going to be difficult, but you must stop these thoughts. She's going to need her friends, especially over the next few days. Now, you rest for a few minutes whilst I see if I can rustle you up something to eat. You need to keep your strength up."

Whatever the cause, as soon as the doctor left her alone, it felt like a cloak of heavy darkness laid itself upon her shoulders, and Jane felt compelled to place her head down on her arms upon the doctor's desk. Closing her eyelids wouldn't do any harm whilst she waited for him to return, she told herself.

"Flight Captain Howell. Flight Captain Howell. Jane! Can you hear me? Time to wake up!"

"A few more minutes, mum," Jane murmured, shrugging her shoulders to try and rid herself of whoever was shaking her.

Whoever was a little more forceful on the next try and didn't stop until Jane's eyes fluttered blearily open. Raising her head, slightly awkwardly as her cheek had half stuck to her new cast, she looked up into the smiling yet still anxious face of Simon, the doctor. Ignoring the headache and the dull throb from her broken arm, she demanded, "What time is it?"

"Half six in the morning."

If he was going to say anything else, he didn't get the chance, as Jane shot to her feet shouting, "Half bloody six?" She fixed the doctor with a look which if her hair were made of snakes would have turned him to stone. "Why on earth did you let me sleep through the night?"

Placing a cup of tea on his desk, he stood up to Jane and explained, "We tried to wake you up a few times, but you refused to react, so we decided to leave you to wake up in your own time."

"Penny!" Jane exclaimed, going to slap her head and finding her arm of choice encased in plaster. She shook the arm in frustration before asking again, "How's Penny?"

Simon smiled this time, and Jane felt a little of her anger and annoyance slip away. "Ah, there, at least, I have good news. She came through the surgery fine, had as good a night as we could hope for, and has just this moment woken up."

Jane made to move past him, but he stopped her by stepping into her path. This was just as well, because after a single step, she began to sway. Taking her gently but firmly by her good arm, the doctor led her back to his office seat. "Sit down and drink that." He indicated the cup of tea. "Don't ask questions, but I've rustled up some sugar. You need it."

The doctor found that a night's rest hadn't done much for Jane's humor. Stubbornly, she said, "I'd like to see her."

He shook his head. "Later. Drink up first, doctor's orders." He pushed the teacup into her hands. Once she had drunk a good half of her tea, he moved the telephone across the desk toward her. "Now, do you want to call her husband?"

Giving her privacy, Simon left her alone in his office. Putting the tea down and picking up the handset, she found her hand was shaking. Who should she call first, Tom or Celia?

Chapter Thirty

Thelma collided with the unexpectedly locked door of the ops hut. Rubbing her elbow, she tried again, in case she'd somehow twisted the handle the wrong way, despite her knowing it only turned the one way. Frowning at the locked door, she strode back to the guardroom and signed out the spare key. Whilst there, she asked if anyone had seen Jane, as her friend and boss was usually in well before her. She raised an eyebrow when no one had.

On her way back to the hut, Thelma glanced over at the aircraft being rolled out in readiness for the day. As usual, she passed a few Tiger Moths and a couple of Miles Magisters. Only when she subconsciously counted off the Avro Ansons did she come up short. She counted again—one was definitely missing. With some effort, after looking closer at their registration identifications, she came to the conclusion that the missing plane was the one Jane and Penny had taken up on the test flight cum taxi ride for Celia.

Taking to her heels, she quickly found the maintenance manager and asked him if he was aware of this.

"I was wondering about it myself," he admitted.

"Didn't you stay around until they came back?" Thelma demanded, knowing there should have been ground crew on duty to turn the aircraft around after the flight. From the way the man ran a hand through what little hair he had and did his best to avoid her eyes, she knew she wasn't going to like his response. "Well?"

"Well," he eventually replied, "it's like this..." He trailed off as Thelma fixed him with her best steely-eyed glare. Coughing, the poor man attempted to find his voice again and managed, "It was Brian's birthday yesterday, and Jane knew a bunch of us were going to meet up at the Victory after work. Well, she told me that if she wasn't back by seven, last night, to stand everyone down, and she'd lock up the plane herself when she got in."

"And yet no sign of her plane."

"No, ma'am," he agreed, hanging his head.

Thelma sighed, sensing a mess coming up. "Right. You'd better get along with the pre-flight checks. I'll get to the bottom of this," she told him and, turning her back before he had a chance to reply, strode off toward the ops hut. However, she didn't get more than a few yards before she spotted Betty and the rest of the Mystery Club members waving and running toward her. Pointing, she indicated for them to meet her at the ops hut.

Getting there first, Thelma unlocked the door and left it open for those following her. The thunder of feet on wooden flooring announced her friends' arrival.

"Do you know where Jane is?" she asked at the same time as Betty blurted out, "Have you heard about Jane and Penny?"

Not quite understanding what Betty meant, Thelma asked the second question she wanted the answer for before her mind had the chance to process what it had just been told. "That Anson Jane took, to take Penny's sister back yesterday, is missing. Do you know anything about that?"

Instead of answering, Doris took Thelma by the hand and led her to the nearest seat, pushing her down before telling her, "That's what we're here about."

Thelma looked closely at Doris and noticed the twinkle normally ever-present upon her face had slipped away. Ceasing her protests, she leant forward to where Betty had perched upon the edge of a desk, very aware Doris had left a hand upon her shoulder. Whatever was coming, it wasn't good. Feeling the blood drain from her face, she gathered all her courage and said, "You'd better tell me."

Doris and Mary both came and stood either side of Betty, their faces the same hue as hers, Thelma was sure, and leant in toward the older lady in support. No, whatever she was about to learn wasn't going to be anything she wanted to hear.

"Thirty minutes ago, we had a telephone call from Jane..." Betty had to put up her hand to stop Thelma from interrupting. "She's at Southampton Hospital. The short version is, they crash-landed on the way back from dropping off Celia. Penny was shot..." Thelma let out a gasp of disbelief, and Betty took the opportunity to take a few welcome lungfuls of air. "And Jane broke her arm in the crash."

Thelma couldn't keep silent any longer. "How..." She gulped and began again. "How was Penny shot?"

"That's the long version," Mary filled in, when it became clear Betty couldn't speak any longer. "They came out of a patch of fog just outside Winchester, right into a fight between a Spitfire and a Nazi bomber. They got caught in the crossfire."

"Christ!" Thelma breathed out, wiping her forehead. "You said Jane told you this? Where are they? Is Penny—is Penny going to be all right? What about the baby?"

There seemed like an interminable wait before someone spoke. Each of her friends seemed to be looking at another and then back again. Finally, Betty spoke again. "We...don't know," she admitted with a shake of her head. "Jane was able to tell us she'd phoned Tom and Celia, but then she had to go. The doctor needed the telephone. She did ask you to take over, and she was going to sit with Penny until her family could get there."

"We're her family too!" Doris couldn't help snorting out, to which everyone in the hut immediately nodded their heads. "However," she added, slightly out of character for Doris, "we can tell them both that once they're safe back here."

Thelma stood up, straightened her jacket, and looked over her friends. "Right. Don't take this the wrong way—you all know how much I love the lot of you, but we need to get to work. For one, all of us rushing down to the hospital won't accomplish anything other than having Jane bring us up on a disciplinary once she's back."

Everyone let out a slightly strained chuckle that did little to relieve the nervous energy pervading the room.

"So gather around and pick up your delivery chits." She glanced down at the papers on her desk, cleared her throat, and quickly wiped her eyes, which everyone pretended not to see. "Now, I wouldn't normally have to say this." She drew herself up to her full height. "I want you all to be totally professional up there today.

'By the book' is the rule today. I want to see everyone back here safe and sound when the day's work is done. Finally, do not speak of what's happened to anyone else. I need to speak to our superiors, apprise them of what's happened. Now, go out there and make Jane and Penny proud of you."

****

Lawrence never thought he'd find himself missing London. When he'd been offered this post, he'd jumped at the chance. The promotion meant he'd been doing something right, and secondly, of equal importance, it meant he was much nearer his Mary. Or at least, that was supposed to be the idea, so far as the latter was concerned. However, everything seemed to have conspired against them spending much time together— or barely any time at all, as things were turning out. In fact, the most they'd been together was the previous day, when he'd taken the day off and turned up unexpectedly. Of course, in his need to see her, he'd forgotten to tell Mary, and she had, naturally, spent the day flying around the country. So he'd actually spent more time in the dubious company of Mavis and her undrinkable tea before being rescued in the early evening. Yes, the long walk they'd taken had been enjoyable, but Mary had been tired, and so the day had ended earlier than he'd wanted.

Twirling his pencil between his fingers, Lawrence looked out the window but saw only Mary's face. "Wake up, dammit!" he scolded himself, coming up short of slapping himself around the face. He needed a distraction, a proper distraction, rather than the mundane burglaries and black marketeering he currently had on his hands.

Picking up one of the reports Terry had put on his desk that morning, he managed to stifle a yawn just as his sergeant popped his head around the door. Though they'd only worked together for a short while, they were already developing a strong bond of mutual trust.

"Bet you're glad you took that move from London, eh, boss?"

Lawrence pushed the report aside, stood, and walked over to his kettle. "You read my mind," he told him. "Fancy a brew?"

By now the two had developed a routine, and Lawrence wordlessly took the kettle out and a few minutes later returned with it filled up.

"Anything new on that bloke troubling your girlfriend?" Terry asked whilst they were waiting for the kettle to boil.

Lawrence shook his head. "I wish. Courts are busy, so the bugger only got a ticking off."

Pushing himself off from the door he was leaning against, Terry poured the water into the teapot, stirred, and moments later, they sat either side of Lawrence's desk, enjoying the first brew of the day.

"See this one?" Lawrence pushed a buff folder toward his sergeant. "It's about the only interesting one amongst them.

Terry opened the folder and skip-read the highlights. "Draft-dodging?" He continued reading for a few minutes more, every now and again nodding his head and taking a pull on his tea before finally putting the folder down. "Seems pretty open and shut. Why do you find it so interesting?"

"Let's just say I had a run-in with some of this type of people last year," Lawrence answered. Leaning back in his seat, he took up and finished his tea before informing Terry, "I've been mulling over this for a while. Well, ever since that incident, something has been annoying me. The people we charged with being behind the operation never seemed to me to have the brains for it."

"What do you mean, boss?"

Lawrence shrugged. "Put plainly, they seemed so…self-absorbed? No, not that. Stupid." Lawrence clicked his fingers as if something important had only just occurred to him. He frowned. "Why didn't I think of it before? The couple we charged were simply too stupid to have worked out that scheme. They must have been the front, only trusted enough to look after the bookings for the doctor they had."

Terry pulled the folder back toward him. "If that's the case, who was pulling the strings?"

Lawrence came to a decision. "Get that one up to questioning, Terry. Let's see if we can get some answers."

****

Jane sat outside Penny's room, shooed out by her surgeon. She tried to enjoy the cup of tea she held, but it would give one of Mavis's a run for its money in being undrinkable. As a noise from the other side of the double doors, which led onto the ward gradually got louder and nearer, her sleep-addled mind kept visualizing a herd of wild elephants. When the doors burst open ten seconds later, she thought she hadn't been far off.

Looking around at the clock above the nursing station, her watch having been smashed in the crash, Jane had just about enough sense left to register surprise at finding the time was nearly seven in the evening. Further thought was impossible as she became surrounded by a herd of her friends, all of whom were talking twenty to the dozen at the same time. Jane could feel the headache she'd only got rid of an hour ago begin to make a comeback.

"How are you?" Betty asked, kneeling by her side.

"How's Penny?" Mary wanted to know, taking a position at her other side.

"What the hell happened?" Doris inquired, leaning down to kiss her quickly on the forehead before retreating to lean against Walter, who gave her a slightly shaky smile.

Thelma simply threw her arms around Jane's neck. Then, realizing what she'd done, she hastily stepped back, wringing her hands together whilst keeping her gaze fixed upon Jane.

When she recovered her voice, Jane took in her entourage and said what was uppermost in her mind. "How did you lot get here?"

Doris dangled a bunch of keys before her face. "We borrowed your Jeep!"

Everyone watched Jane silently nod, then shake her head. "But it only seats four!"

No one said anything in return, though they were all thankful Jane didn't bring up the custom-made lock they'd had to destroy to get the vehicle.

"Well, it's just as well you didn't run into any police, isn't it?" Jane declared, actually smiling.

The door flapped open once again, this time admitting Lawrence.

"Apart from myself just now," he stated.

"Lawrence!" Mary began to shout before lowering

her voice as she remembered where she was. She got up and rushed into his arms. "I didn't expect to see you here. In fact, what are you doing here?"

"Ruth called me after Betty phoned her," he explained, hugging her and giving her a quick kiss on the lips. With Mary in his arms, Lawrence looked over his shoulder at Jane and asked, "How are you, Jane? And Penny?"

Jane glanced at the door to the left of where she sat. "The doctor's in there with her now. Well, her surgeon, actually," she amended.

"What happened?' Lawrence asked gently. "All Ruth told me was the two of you had been in a crash. She didn't go into any details."

Jane opened her mouth to speak, but again the door was flung open. Upon seeing who was responsible for the new dramatic entrance, she jumped to her feet, completely forgetting the cup of tea she was holding, which promptly slipped from her fingers and spilled its contents upon the floor. As she took a step forward, her foot slipped in the spreading liquid.

With reflexes born of long, hard, military experience, Tom reached Jane quicker than would have been thought possible, catching her under the arms. The two pirouetted around in a full circle until Tom deposited a rather shaken Jane back into her seat, with Jane keeping hold of Tom's arm, forcing him to his knees so as not to fall over. Once settled in her seat, Jane realized she was shaking.

Betty enveloped her in her arms, resting her friend's head upon her shoulder. "Come on, you're safe," she whispered into her ear, whilst stroking her friend's hair, taking care not to move the bandage circling her head. With her eyes, she urged everyone else to give them some space. Thelma was the first to catch on and proceeded to herd everyone a little way down the corridor.

"Let's give them some room," she said. "I think everything's just hitting her."

"Where's Penny?" Tom asked, looking around.

"Where's my sister? What happened?" Celia demanded, stepping out from behind Tom where no one had noticed her in all the chaos of Tom's entrance.

"I think she's in the room next to where Jane's sitting," Doris answered.

Not troubling themselves with asking anything else, Tom, holding tightly onto Celia's hand, turned and, without preamble and without looking down at Betty still trying to soothe Jane, marched straight into the room Doris had indicated.

"Who are you?" demanded a man in a white coat as he waved the clipboard he held.

"Wing Commander Tom Alsop, and this is Penny's sister, Celia. Who are you?" Tom asked in return.

Upon learning who had just burst into the room, the man tucked the clipboard under his arm and held out a hand. Tom was somehow relieved to find he was smiling. That had to be good, didn't it?

"I'm Dr. Ernest Lilley. I operated on…"

"Tom?"

Brushing aside the offered hand, both Tom and Celia moved swiftly to Penny's bedside.

"Be careful!" the surgeon warned as they both seemed ready to launch themselves onto her.

Lying under crisp white sheets, Penny looked pale and drawn. Her right arm was heavily bandaged and lying upon the counterpane, but she managed a weak smile at seeing the newcomers.

Both Tom and Celia kissed Penny on the forehead, lingering before they took up positions sitting on the bed either side of her.

"How're you feeling, sis?" Celia asked, getting in before Tom.

Penny managed a weak smile. "Like I've been kicked in the guts, and my arm feels like it's going to drop off," she answered.

"A pretty apt description, on both counts, actually," the surgeon replied.

Tom finally looked at him. "So, how's she doing? Will she be all right?" Meanwhile, he held onto her hand as if he'd never let her go. As soon as the man took up his clipboard and began to turn the pages back and forth, Tom knew it wasn't going to be good news. He'd been in the presence of enough doctors lately to know when they were playing for time, not wanting to be the bearer of bad news. He couldn't blame them, but now, when it concerned his wife, he had no patience for any procrastination.

Celia obviously thought the same and actually snapped, "Just tell us. Will my sister be okay?"

"Celia!" Penny dragged up the energy to tell her sister off. "Remember your manners."

"Sorry, sis," Celia apologized, squeezing her hand.

"That's all right. I quite understand." The surgeon smiled. "Let me fill you all in. I was about to tell Penny all this anyway. The local doctor where she crashed did a very good job on her arm, so I only needed to clean up a little. I'm afraid I couldn't do anything about the baby, though."

Both Tom and Celia felt Penny squeeze their hands, and with his free hand, Tom took out a handkerchief and wiped at the tears which had begun to flow.

"You're going to be all right, and I could find nothing wrong with your womb, but…" he qualified, "I cannot assure you that you will be able to have any more children. I'm sorry. If I could give you a certain answer one way or the other, I would, Mrs. Alsop."

"Bloody hell!" Celia swore, not troubling to keep her voice down.

Through her tears, Penny said, "Forgive my sister. I'm sure she's had a hell of a journey to get here."

"You can say that again," Celia mumbled.

Tom didn't appear to have heard. "You're sure she's lost the baby?" Tom demanded, his manner changing and leaning toward the surgeon, not noticing his wife grimacing in pain as he nearly pulled her out of bed.

The surgeon's face was one of intense sympathy. "Quite, I'm afraid."

Suddenly, Tom released Penny's hand, stood, and when he looked down at his stricken wife, his face was a strange mixture of fury and unimaginable sorrow.

"Well, you didn't really want this baby anyway!"

Without saying another word, he stormed out of the room, leaving a distraught and confused Penny behind.

Chapter Thirty-One

As there hadn't been any raised voices, no one waiting in the corridor thought to try and stop Tom as he marched past everyone, head held high and not making eye contact with anyone. Only when Celia didn't follow him out had Mary asked, "What just happened?"

With no one having an answer, everyone shared confused looks before Penny's door opened. Celia stuck her head out and demanded of everyone, "Get in here. Now!" before disappearing back inside.

"Is it just me?" Doris asked, "or did Celia have tears streaming down her face?"

Not waiting for a reply, Doris grabbed Walter's hand and marched into the room, followed by everyone else. What they encountered when they entered was a man in a white coat and Celia both trying to deal with Penny, who appeared confused, angry, and in pain, all at once—not a good combination.

"Penny," Betty began, reaching out to touch her uninjured arm, "what's going on?" However, Penny appeared incapable of speaking, her mouth simply opening and closing without any sound coming out, so she turned her attention to Celia.

In contrast, Celia was simply furious and sat close against her sister, repeating over and over, "I'll bloody kill him! I'll bloody kill him!"

"Doctor?" Lawrence asked, though without a hundred per cent conviction, as the man seemed to be in shock. Lawrence decided now was not the time to pussyfoot around, and when he didn't get an immediate answer, he gripped the poor man by the shoulders and shook him.

The doctor finally focused, and he shrugged himself out of the policeman's grip. "Never in all my time!" he stated.

Doris moved toward him, her hand raised. "Make sense, Doc. What the bloody hell just happened? Where did Tom go?"

"I've never—" When he realized the woman in front of him was about to strike him, he coughed, swallowed, and raised a hand of his own to let her know he wouldn't repeat himself. "I'm sorry," he began, no longer with a squeak in his voice. "He walked out."

"What?" everyone said nearly in unison.

Quickly glancing across to see if either his patient or her sister would care to take over, and seeing that neither appeared so inclined, he elaborated, "As soon as I told them I couldn't be certain if Mrs. Alsop would be able to have more children, he announced something about her never wanting a child, and then he marched out without saying another word."

Shocked silence at both pieces of news pervaded the room, broken only by Penny's quiet sobbing and her sister's repetitive threat. This was broken by an outraged growl from Doris. She tore her hand from her fiancé's grip and rushed for the door, echoing Celia's words, "I'm going to bloody kill him!"

With reflexes born from years of scrapping with the worst criminals London could unearth, Lawrence made a lunge for Doris before she could complete her dramatic exit, managing to wrap both arms around her lower legs. She would have crashed to the ground if Walter and Thelma hadn't been quick on their feet too and stopped them from falling over. Doris struggled briefly against the combined strength of the three of them before slumping into a heap of misery.

"Please, Lawrence?" She looked up at the policeman, who now had a firm hold of one of her wrists. "Just let me have five minutes alone with him?"

A short, sharp laugh startled everyone, including a still mad Doris, and they all looked around for the source. Another snort of laughter was heard, and everyone homed in on the unlikely perpetrator. To the utter amazement of all, Penny had now thrown her head back and was laughing out loud. Even Celia had stopped muttering her threats.

"Penny?" Celia gently shook her sister's uninjured arm.

"Oh, I'd love to see that!" Penny declared. "Tom's got at least half a foot on our Doris, but I know who my money would be on!"

It took thirty-odd seconds before anyone replied.

"Thanks for the vote of confidence." Doris grinned. "Now, how about persuading these guys to let me go?"

Penny shook her head as the laughter left her as quickly as it had come. "No."

This short answer seemed to deflate the American, and at feeling their captive's body relax, Lawrence slowly released his grip. When she didn't try to bolt away, he nodded to Walter and Thelma to also let her go. Walter immediately gathered her into his arms.

"Come on." He led her out of the way into a

corner.

"Can I trust you to handle things in here?" Lawrence asked Betty, who nodded. "Right, I'm going to see if I can catch Tom." As Doris made a move to follow, he stated firmly without actually looking at her, "No! You can't come, Doris. Walter, I'm relying on you to keep her here."

"I was going to say you've got a little color back," Betty told Penny, sitting down where the wayward husband had been, "but maybe that was the laughter."

Still with her working hand in Celia's grip, Penny leaned into Betty's shoulder. "It's very good to see you." She then looked up at the rest of her friends. "It's very good to see you all." She then caught sight of Jane, who was lingering half hidden behind Thelma, near the back of the room. "Jane!" Upon hearing her name, Jane seemed to try to make herself smaller. "Come here, please?"

Before Jane could bring herself to move, Celia asked the doctor, still without moving from her sister's side, "I've got to know, Doctor. What you said before? Penny, my sister, she is going to be all right?"

After first letting his gaze encompass the room, as if in need of assurance that nobody else was going to lose control, he went to the end of the bed and said to Celia, without losing eye contact, as he knew she needed to trust his words, "Yes. Her arm wound isn't serious, though it came close to some big veins. That doctor did a very good job of stopping the bleeding. The bullet went through and barely chipped the bone, so she should be able to start using it again within a day or two and have full, normal movement within a few weeks. It will be quite painful at first, though, I'm afraid."

"And what you said about the baby? About whether she could have any more children?" Celia looked at Penny with eyes wide, making certain she should have asked the question. Penny simply gave her a smile in return and nodded at the doctor to continue.

"That's true as well. It's likely the shock of being shot that caused you to miscarry, Penny." Now she was more awake, the doctor addressed his words to his patient. "There is some heavy bruising on your abdomen, though. Do you recall either being struck or having something strike your stomach?" he asked.

Penny slowly shook her head. "I'm sorry, I really couldn't say. I don't remember anything from when I was shot to waking up in here."

"She struck the control yoke when the plane was hit," Jane said, making her way slowly toward the bed.

As she approached, the doctor nodded his head. "A great piece of metal. Yes, yes, that would certainly account for the bruising."

At seeing her friend up close, Penny extricated her hand on her good side from her sister's and held it out. "Come and sit beside me?"

Jane hesitated, then blurted out, "Are you sure? This is all my fault!"

"Don't be bloody silly," Penny told her, sounding a little more like her old self. "You didn't shoot me. You didn't shove me into the yoke."

Jane ambled around to take a reluctant-to-move Celia's place before telling her, "But if I'd put my foot down and told you to stay—"

"I'd have stowed away," Penny finished for her.

Looking into her friend's bloodshot eyes, Jane

finally nodded and gave her first real smile since the whole situation had begun. "You probably would have too," she agreed. "But you still got hurt. And you lost your baby."

At those words, Penny took Jane's good hand in hers and laid it on her stomach. "I'm still here. *We're* still here!" she amended. "The war tried to get us and failed. We'll survive this. I know we will."

The door opened, and in walked Lawrence, alone. "Sorry," he announced, "I was too late. There's no sign of him."

****

"It's settled, so stop arguing!"

"I'm not arguing," Jane argued. "I just don't like being told what to do," she pouted, settling back into Ruth's sofa.

"Look," the lady of the house said, putting a cup of tea on the side table beside Jane. "It makes complete sense. Yes, we know you like your privacy, and yes, we know you'd be quite happy alone in your room in your billet on base. But we, your *friends*," she emphasized, "have decided to ignore all that. You've been through a crash, broken your arm, seen your friend shot, and there's no way in hell we're allowing you to be on your own for at least a week."

"A week!" Jane couldn't help but shout.

Ruth was unperturbed and merely took a seat and proceeded to drink her own welcome cup of tea before replying, "Yes, a week. Shirley's room is free, so you'll move in there. Mary and Thelma are on base at this moment, packing you a bag."

"How are they going to get into my room?" Jane asked, suspicion dawning.

"Doris took the key out of your jacket pocket," Walter supplied, safe on the other side of the room.

"Mmm," Jane mumbled from between clenched teeth.

"Good to see you agree," Ruth remarked, unable to stop her lips from twitching in amusement.

"Look at it this way," Walter tried. "You've been signed off work for two weeks—but," he hastily added, seeing Jane open her mouth to protest, "knowing you, you'll be back at work in a week. So if you were in your room, you'd only be tempted to try to go back to work even earlier. Am I right?"

Ruth took Jane's silence as agreement. "Look, Jane, you need to allow yourself to recover—and not only your body—and amongst your friends is the best place. You can come to the office with me, if you like," she offered.

"Maybe," Jane allowed, sounding a little brighter at the idea.

****

Jane was woken from where she'd fallen asleep on the sofa by the sound of voices coming from the kitchen. Lifting up her arm to check the time, she was instead greeted by the sight of the cast upon her wrist and the memory that the only present she'd ever received from her late boyfriend Frank was smashed. She had very vague memories of someone at the hospital taking it off her wrist before the cast was applied, but no recollection of what had happened to it. She briefly considered calling the hospital and seeing if anyone could track it down, but dropped the idea as quickly as she'd thought of it. They had better things to do with their time.

The next thing she knew, she became aware of the sofa sagging and someone's arm around her shoulders.

"Here," Thelma said, offering her a handkerchief. "Blow your nose."

Realizing she'd been crying, Jane did as she was told before saying, "Thanks. Sorry, I didn't mean to be a nuisance."

Thelma gave her a squeeze. "Don't be silly. What was it all about?" she asked, using another handkerchief to dry her friend's eyes.

Jane gave a dry laugh. "Now, that was me being silly." She held up her broken arm for Thelma to see. "I lost Frank's watch. The one he bought me before he went back to his squadron the last time."

Thelma hugged her friend even harder. "Oh, I'm so sorry."

After allowing Thelma to nearly hug her to death, Jane decided she'd had enough and gently extricated herself. "What's going on in the kitchen?"

"You could hear that?" Thelma asked. "Sorry. We were trying to keep the conversation down."

"Who's we, and what are you all talking about?" Jane wanted to know.

Thelma got to her feet and offered her hand to Jane.

"I'm not an invalid, you know," Jane told her, not bothering to keep the annoyance from her voice.

"Humor me." Thelma smiled and, a minute later, with an unsmiling, visibly annoyed Jane on her arm, she entered the kitchen. "Make some room for the cripple," she announced, earning herself a scowl from Jane.

"Very funny," Jane muttered, taking a seat besides

Ruth. "Now, what're you all talking about?"

"You sure you're up to this?" Ruth asked.

Everyone watched Jane take in a deep calming breath before replying. She tapped the bandage around her head and held up her plaster-encased arm. "I think I'm in need of something to take my mind off things."

"Fair enough," Doris decreed, pushing a bottle of Guinness toward her boss. "For your health," she added and then, when she saw Jane's gaze had settled upon the bottle set before an understandably quiet Celia, told her, "Doctor's orders."

Not commenting, as surely if anyone deserved a drink it was Celia, she picked up the very welcome bottle and raised it in a quick salute before downing a hefty gulp.

"Right," Ruth said, once Jane had put her bottle down. "Back to business. Before the well, you know, hits the fan."

"Do you think it'd help if I let Tom know I have mafia connections?" Doris suddenly asked, her face so serious, it was a short while before anyone replied.

"I don't think this is the place or time," Lawrence replied, smiling. "Plus, I'd really rather not lock up one of my dearest friends for grievous bodily harm."

Walter placed a hand firmly on his fiancée's. "Leave it be for now, love. Okay?"

Despite her frown, showing she would certainly not be forgetting or forgiving, Doris took her hand and placed it in his but refrained from saying anything further.

"What were you all talking about?" Jane repeated, giving Doris the evil eye, which she ignored.

"You know I went to see my solicitor, the other

day?" Betty asked Jane, who nodded. "Well, on my way back to the train station, I ran into my brother."

"Marcus! How is he?" Mary asked.

"Not the time either," Ruth told her.

"Unfortunately, he had *his*"—everyone could hear the emphasis—"parents with him."

"Bloody hell," Jane exclaimed. Everyone else was quiet, as they'd heard up to here whilst she was in the lounge. "And I thought I'd had a bad day!"

Doris, in the middle of taking a drink from her bottle, promptly sprayed Guinness all over the table as she tried to swallow and laugh at the same time. This set everyone else off, apart from Jane, who just sat back, satisfied to have lightened the mood, albeit temporarily. Jane grabbed a tea towel from behind her and tossed it to Doris, who wiped her mouth and then mopped up the mess she'd made.

"Sorry, Ruth."

"What do you think they wanted?" Thelma asked.

"I didn't hang around to find out," Betty informed them. "I took off as quickly as I could for the train station. However, Marcus ran after me."

"What happened?" Jane asked.

Chapter Thirty-Two

"Betty! Wait up!"

Doing her best to ignore her brother's calls, Betty tried to quicken her pace but only succeeded in nearly tripping herself up, as she didn't spot a gap in the paving stones. Congratulating herself on missing a fall, she didn't see the lamppost looming up in the gathering darkness, and before she could alter her course, she hurtled headfirst into it at near full speed. Wobbling backward, she would have fallen, but a pair of strong hands grabbed her under the arms.

After allowing herself to remain in her rescuer's arms for a minute to recover her wits and allow her head to stop ringing, Betty could stand on her own again. Slowly turning her head, she opened her mouth to speak and was confronted by Marcus. Of course it would be her brother, who else?

"Oh, bloody hell!"

"You didn't have to try to knock yourself out just to avoid me, you know," he said, though there wasn't an accompanying smile.

Gingerly, Betty touched her forehead, wincing as she felt a bump already beginning to form. Turning her attention back to Marcus, she asked, "What do you want?" She looked over his shoulder to see if certain people had also followed her and was glad to see the coast appeared to be clear. "And more to the point, what do *they* want?"

Instead of replying, Marcus took one of Betty's arms and gently put it through the crook of his. Looking around, he spotted exactly what was needed. "Come on, please," he added when Betty appeared reluctant to accompany him. He pointed with his finger and, following it, Betty gave a curt nod.

"We've only rock cakes left, love," the waitress told them as they entered the small café.

"Couple of teas, too, please," Marcus asked as he gently steered his sister to a free table. "Well, if they've only got rock cakes left, it means one of two things," Marcus said as he held out a chair for Betty. He took his own seat. "One, they've a very good baker."

"Or?" Betty asked, unable to stop herself.

"Or they've a bloody awful baker, and the rock cakes are the last things anyone could bear to eat."

Despite the unusual situation, Betty couldn't help but laugh.

"That's better," Marcus said, once she'd stopped.

The tea and rock cakes appeared before them, and Betty waited for the waitress to leave, though not before she noticed how her eyes roamed over her younger brother, who looked rather, she had to admit, resplendent and quite handsome in his officer's uniform. "So, what is it you want?"

Stirring his tea, Marcus took a quick sip prior to answering. "Firstly, I'd like to apologize for *that*," he pointed at her forehead.

"That apology, I accept."

"Thank you." Marcus inclined his head. "As for my parents?" He shrugged. "That's a strange story."

Remembering her brother wouldn't necessarily be

made from the same stuff as his parents, Betty allowed him a small smile. "I've a little time."

"In that case, I apologize for my parents turning up. I'd come up to see Mr. Burrows too and didn't realize they'd followed me."

Betty took up a rock cake and, with obvious effort, sawed it in half, spread on it the tiny amount of jam before her, and took a bite. Hastily, she covered her mouth, pretended to cough while surreptitiously putting the mouthful onto the side of her plate. Washing out her mouth with her tea, she gave Marcus a pointed look. "I think we have an answer to your assessment of this place's cooking abilities," she told him sotto voce.

Without hesitation, Marcus pushed his cake away. "The rock cakes taste like rocks, then."

"Why would they have followed you?"

Marcus ran a finger around his collar. "What do you, ah, know about them?"

"You mean, aside from them not wanting either myself or Eleanor because we were girls?"

Marcus shook his head. "I won't pretend to understand that." He looked up. "Betty, would you believe me if I told you, if I'd have known about you or Eleanor anytime earlier, I'd have looked for you sooner?"

Betty searched his face before slowly nodding her head. "I believe you would have."

"Thank you," Marcus replied, offering her his hands across the table. "Now, back to my parents. Do you know what it is my father does? Or did, I should say."

Betty took a sip of tea. "All I know is that he's a member of parliament, though I'm not sure where."

"Half true. He's no longer sitting, actually." He looked around to see if they could be heard, but the café was only half full, and he'd picked a table against the wall with the specific purpose of making it difficult to be either overlooked or overheard. "The Party asked him to resign." Betty's eyes widened, asking for an explanation. "He's lost everything—money, the house, and probably even more important to him, his social standing."

Betty asked the only question possible. "How?"

"Gambling, mostly," Marcus replied miserably. "That and, though I don't know the full details, hefty involvement in the black market."

****

"Ungrateful bastards!"

"Settle down, George, remember your ulcer," George Palmer's wife tried to soothe him.

"Why should I calm down? Eh? Tell me that!"

Marcus walked into the office for another moving box at that moment and was immediately aware of the tension in the room. Rolling his eyes, he tried to blank out the coming argument. It seemed that whenever he'd been to his parents' house over the last year, they'd done nothing but argue. Growing up, he'd rapidly come to the conclusion his parents barely tolerated each other. Love certainly never even entered the equation. He'd often wondered how he came into existence, and when he'd learned about his sisters, he toyed with the idea he'd been adopted. Unfortunately, his face bore too much resemblance to his father's for that to be a serious possibility.

"Well, it isn't as if you haven't got only yourself to blame, is it!" Darcie Palmer shouted back. "If it wasn't for your greed, we'd still own our house. You would still have a job—an important job, I may add. And we would not have a gang of cutthroats on our tails!"

George made a scoffing noise in the back of his throat. "Cutthroats. Ha!"

"What would you call our every move being tracked by those people you owe money to, then? Boy scouts? Speaking of which, just how do you propose to pay them back? The house has gone, and that doesn't cover half what you owe them. It's not like we've the extra money coming in, either, since your little scheme caved in, and now, what are we going to live on?"

Marcus stopped lifting his refilled box at hearing this. He'd never liked his father—or his mother, come to that—but by the sound of it, a great deal more was going on with them than he'd thought. What on earth had his father been up to? If the man owed money and—Marcus would bet, the irony not lost on him—anything he owned, it was to do with gambling. His father loved cards. However, the cards didn't love him. Even as a teenager Marcus had been able to beat him at any game he was challenged to. Putting the box down, he slowly pretended to add more items, intrigued and hoping to find out more. His mother obliged, not surprisingly, as once she got a bee in her bonnet about something, she didn't let go.

George had backed up against his now-empty desk, his eyes wide as his wife stood before him, hands on her hips, the one person he was afraid of. "It's hardly my fault the doctor was stupid and the group captain and his wife were greedy as well as stupid."

Darcie laughed, out loud, obviously not worried about being overheard, though the same couldn't be said about her husband, as George immediately rushed past her and slammed the door shut.

"Keep your bloody voice down!" he hushed at her. "Do you want everyone to hear what we've been up to?"

"We? Oh, no." His wife shook her head. "There's no 'we' here. I didn't ask you to gamble away your wages, let alone our house. I certainly didn't ask you to take money so some cowards could shirk their responsibilities. They should take their chances, as our Marcus here does."

Marcus juggled a bottle of ink. He hadn't been sure if either of them had been aware of his presence. What his father said next so shocked Marcus that he didn't stop to think before speaking.

"Maybe we should see if—what's her name? Oh, yes—Betty has any money."

"You can't do that! All she's got is a lovely little cottage."

Immediately the words were out of his mouth, he knew he'd said the wrong thing, as both his parents immediately focused attention upon him.

"Has she really?"

Marcus felt a shudder go up his spine. What had he done?

Chapter Thirty-Three

"Well, that at least explains the bump on your head," Celia said, finishing off her Guinness, holding it up and waving it around.

"You can stop all that," Betty told her without looking up. "One's your limit. So don't pull a face or try to play on my sympathies, as it won't work. And," she added, treating Celia to a smile, "if you think Penny would say otherwise, then you're welcome to speak to her about it when she comes home in a couple of days."

"Worth a try," Celia mumbled, going and helping herself to a glass of water and making a point of pulling a face when she sat down and took her first sip.

"I'll say this for your family," Doris remarked. "They make mine sound positively boring."

"Do me a favor?" Betty asked, leaning forward. "When you think of my family, don't include those who actually gave birth to me. I'm not even sure about including Marcus, yet," she ended, her voice trailing off so the others had to strain to hear.

"Have you heard anything from—them?" Ruth asked.

Betty shook her head. "No. And I don't know if I should be more worried that I haven't than if I had."

"What about Marcus? Heard from him yet?" Mary asked.

"No. I had to leave right after he admitted to telling

them about my cottage," she told the group, "or I'd have missed my train back."

"Do you think he told them anything else?" Mary persisted.

Betty opened and closed her mouth, settling back in her seat to think about it. "Truth be told, I don't know."

"What about Eleanor?" Celia then surprised them all. "Do you think he shared with them what he knows about her?"

"That's a good question," Betty agreed, before turning to the girl. "But that's enough for tonight." She looked up at the clock on Ruth's kitchen wall. "Come on home with me." Betty got to her feet and took hold of the back of Celia's seat. "It's very late, you've had a long day, in more ways than one, and I think we could both do with our beds."

"But—" Celia began to protest, but was cut off by a massive yawn. The thing about yawns is that once one person begins, it sets off everyone. "Looks like I'm not the only one," Celia declared when she was able to speak.

As everyone was getting to their feet, Ruth's telephone rang.

"Who on earth's that at this time of night?" Ruth muttered, going into the hallway to answer. A moment later, she called out, "Lawrence! It's a Detective Sergeant Banks for you."

Rushing to take the receiver from his aunt, Lawrence mumbled a brief thanks and took the phone.

"Bit strange, Lawrence getting calls here, isn't it?" Jane asked as Mary helped her through from the kitchen.

That she wasn't complaining, Ruth thought, only reaffirmed her determination to look after her friend for as long as she could. However, she wasn't silly enough to voice this out loud. "Well, he used to live here on and off, so maybe it's someone he knows from London."

Jane placed a hand on Mary's to stop her progress. Her tired eyes looked up at Ruth. "Hold on. Did I hear you say the name Banks? Isn't that the name of Lawrence's second?"

"I think so," Mary began but got no farther, as Lawrence had already put the phone down, having spoken with his hand over the mouthpiece so no one could hear what he was saying.

He'd heard what they were saying, though. "Nothing wrong with your memory," he remarked, and then told Ruth, "Just as well we're calling it a night. I've got to go in to work."

"At this hour?" she replied. "It's nearly half ten!"

Lawrence shrugged, then took down his overcoat and pulled it on. "What can I say? A copper's lot is never done." He leant down and gave Ruth a quick peck on her cheek before saying to Jane, "Do as Ruth says. She only wants what's best." He gave Mary a kiss on the lips. "I'll speak to you all tomorrow, I hope," and he placed his hat on his head and left.

"I'd love to know what that's all about," Thelma commented, joining everyone in the hall.

****

Detective Sergeant Terry Banks had discovered nothing was more likely to make anyone, suspect or not, ill at ease than to perch on the edge of the desk they sat at and stare at them. That was it, simply stare. Of course, it helped if you had a glass eye. Nothing was more unnerving than to look at someone only to find their eyes looking in different directions. He'd lost his right one in the big air raid on Portsmouth back on 10th March 1941, and though it had taken a while, he'd learnt to use it to his advantage. He'd been secretly pleased to discover it had the same effect upon his Inspector as it did on criminal elements.

As soon as he'd taken custody of Percy Dale, he'd picked up the telephone. Lawrence had told him to phone this Ruth Stone woman if their suspect came in whilst he was away. Putting him into their interview room, he'd decided against offering him a beverage and taken up his spot. They'd been there around thirty minutes when the door opened and in strode Lawrence. Seeing the way the suspect was squirming, the newcomer winked at Terry, and the two of them took their seats.

Lawrence picked up the folder. It had been a very long day, and he was in no mood for either messing around or being messed about. "Mr. Dale, you strike me as a man who would do most everything to avoid hard work of any kind. You have family money and family connections, or so you thought," Lawrence read from the documents before him. "However, upon finding those connections couldn't save you from the draft, or conscription, call it what you wish, you decided to find an illegal manner of getting out of serving your country."

Across the desk, Percy Dale squirmed even more, if it were possible, and tried to swallow. Terry took a long sip from his glass of water and poured another, placing it before his boss, ignoring their suspect licking his lips. He had thin lips and very little in the way of a chin. If Lawrence were so inclined, he'd believe there had been some in-breeding going on somewhere in his lineage.

"I shall make this offer only once. Nod if you understand."

Without a moment's beat wasted, Dale nodded.

"Good. First smart thing you've done. Here's the deal. You tell me everything you know, leaving nothing out, about who you were supposed to contact and what happened. In return, I will speak to the judge and do my best to get you a light sentence. If you don't, then it will be years before you see Portsmouth again, if you ever do. You won't be hung for this, but you will serve hard labor and, judging by the lack of meat on your bones, you may not last that long."

Dale tried once again to swallow, now even more nervous. Seeing as they needed him to talk, Lawrence pushed his glass toward him and nodded, showing it would be all right to drink. The suspect drank as if it were nectar, placing the empty glass down with a thud and a small, satisfied sigh.

"Ready to begin?" Lawrence asked. "Good, we're listening. Terry, ready to take this down?"

When Dale began to speak, he kept his eyes down, unwilling to meet their eyes. Seeing as he had the most boring speaking voice Lawrence and Terry had ever heard, this made staying awake a bit of a problem.

"A friend of mine gave me this contact in a London pub…"

"Name of the pub, the contact, and the friend," Lawrence demanded, whilst Terry sat ready, pen poised.

"So, I telephoned the Grand Rover and spoke to the barman who, to stop you asking, did not give me his name. He told me to come up to London the next day, go into the public house at midday exactly, and ask the barman to speak to Stan, and to be prepared to stay in the city for a week."

"A week?" Lawrence asked.

"He warned me it might take up to a week to make the necessary arrangements," Dale hurried to explain. "Anyway, this Stan, who I think was the barman I spoke to on the phone, told me I was out of luck, as the people I needed to see had been arrested last November."

Terry opened his mouth, but Lawrence nudged him in the side, as he didn't want to fill in any gaps in front of Dale.

"Why do you think he left it until you went up? That was…" Lawrence shuffled the papers in the folder until he found what he was looking for. "That was May, this year." He raised an eyebrow in query.

Dale looked, if possible, even more sheepish. "I think he was hoping he'd be able to relieve me of the fee he knew I'd be carrying."

"And did he?" Terry asked.

Bringing up his handcuffed hands, Dale rubbed his cheek. "Rather."

"What was the fee?" Lawrence asked, though he had a fair idea from what he'd learned whilst interviewing the doctor the previous year.

Dale coughed and tried to make it like he'd actually spoken, but when neither policeman reacted, he had to force out the answer more clearly. "A thousand pounds."

Lawrence saw his sergeant's eyes bulge at the figure. Indeed, he himself had to fight hard to hold in any reaction. It did confirm another hunch of his, that the doctor had only been paid a fifth of the fee. Not a bad markup for a few phone calls, he silently mused.

"I can see how that would hurt," Lawrence said, in mock sympathy.

This was lost on Dale, who smiled at him before carrying on with his tale. "I was rather chastened, and as I knew no one else in London who could help, I came back home. None of my friends could help, either, so I began to ask around the more insalubrious public houses."

Lawrence nodded. "Before he cracked you around the head, did this barman say anything else?"

For the first time since Lawrence had come into the room, Dale laughed, though it had a hollow ring about it. "I don't know why," he began, "but as soon as he told me my hopes had gone, he couldn't seem to stop…'bragging' is the only word. Like nobody could do anything else to him."

"We'll see about that," Lawrence told him.

"He pointed out a framed picture behind the bar and told me it was of the fellow who used to own the pub, only he'd lost it in a game of cards. Not the only thing he'd lost, though. The previous owner, someone in the government, he said, but I can't remember the name now, was also the money man behind the whole scheme. He kept in the background, let this group captain and his ex-actress wife hog the glory—you know, be the front, I believe it's called. Mind you, and he went on about this at length, how those two believed they were the brains of the whole thing, he never knew.

Why, the muscle the woman went around with, he may not have looked it, but he was telling this chap everything which was going on."

"And they never caught on?" Lawrence couldn't stop himself from asking.

"I asked the same thing. Apparently, so long as the money kept rolling in, neither of them bothered to query who was providing the backing, paying for the safe houses and everything."

"And he told you this because he was feeling chatty?" Terry asked.

"Perhaps, but I think it was more that he was happy never to have to see any of them again. Or that's the feeling I got. Not only had you lot arrested those three, but this backer, I think he's an MP actually, the chap who used to own the pub, went and lost it in one of the card games, and so he never goes there anymore either."

"It sounds like everything came up roses for this barman," Terry interjected, "or, at least so far, before we got to know about him."

At hearing this, all the blood drained from Dale's face.

"Don't worry." Lawrence dangled a carrot. "We'll make sure he never hears your name. One thing isn't clear," Lawrence added. "From my investigation, you haven't as yet received your call-up papers. So why start looking for an out so early?"

Dale shrugged. "When my friend told me what he'd done, I thought I might as well use the same, ah, service. Think of it as a recommendation, Inspector. Once I'd begun to look, even though it all ended rather badly for me, I decided I might as well see it through."

"Okay, carry on," Lawrence told him.

"I suppose you caught me because I asked around a public house frequented by Royal Navy personnel."

Lawrence couldn't help but laugh. "Let's be honest, Dale. Openly asking around a Navy pub for anyone who could help you avoid the call-up? You were bloody lucky an off-duty copper was able to get you out before you lost more than a couple of teeth."

Unsurprisingly, Dale couldn't do anything but nod in agreement.

"Is that everything?" Lawrence asked.

"I think so." Dale nodded.

"In that case"—Lawrence pushed toward Dale the statement Terry had taken down, along with a pen—"read through and then sign it at the bottom." Dale nodded, again looking rather miserable. "In the morning, we'll have you go through some pictures. See if you can identify this Member of Parliament. Now, Terry here will get you a cup of tea whilst you read."

Leaving Dale in the interview room, the two stepped out, leaving the door slightly ajar.

"What do you reckon, boss, a result?" Terry asked, keeping his voice down so Dale couldn't hear.

Lawrence peeked into the room where Dale was bent over the statement. They'd unlocked the handcuffs to make it easier for him to sign. It wasn't as if he could get away. He turned back to face his sergeant, "Yes, Terry, I believe that's what we have."

Chapter Thirty-Four

"You're sure you should be out?" Doris asked as she pulled the Jeep up outside the Old Lockkeepers Cottage and hopped out.

Penny waited for her friends to come and help her out of the passenger's seat. Not because she couldn't walk but more because she was wrapped up as if she were going on an expedition to the Arctic.

When she'd phoned Hamble late in the afternoon to let Jane know she was being released from hospital, her boss had been all for jumping in her Jeep and going to pick her up there and then, but common sense had prevailed, and she'd called Lawrence to see if he could go and get her, only to be told he was in the middle of an interview and couldn't be interrupted. Reluctantly, she'd had to tell Penny she'd have to wait until they finished deliveries for the day. There had then followed an almighty argument during which Penny tried to persuade her friend she'd be fine taking the bus back home. Eventually, Jane had spoken to a doctor, who'd promised to keep Penny there until she could be picked up later that evening.

Because no one trusted Jane to drive, she'd been in the rear with her arms wrapped around Penny for the whole journey. "A little help here too, please!"

Before extricating Penny, Doris helped Jane unlock her arms and rubbed her friend's arms to get some warmth and life back into them. It took five minutes for Jane to feel able to clamber out and help unwrap Penny. Three wooly hats, four blankets, and two pairs of mittens later, Penny was able to move again.

"To answer your question," she said as Doris, who'd been most insistent, helped her to walk down the path toward the cottage, "yes. I've been lying there for the best part of two days now. My arm's healing, or at least not hurting so much, and, let's be honest as we're all girls here, my body will heal just as well tucked up here as it will anywhere else."

"What about your mind?" Celia asked, popping up from nowhere and wrapping her arms around her sister like she'd never let her go. "You've lost your baby."

Penny hugged Celia back, resting her head upon the top of her sister's head. "I know," she answered softly.

Thirty minutes later, after a quick bath, Penny lay on the sofa, thick socks upon her feet, warm nightdress and dressing gown on, and wrapped in a blanket taken from her bed, since she pointblank refused to be put to bed. "I've spent the last couple of days in bed, and though I know I'm still lying down, this is better than actually being in bed. Besides"—she lifted her feet so Celia could slide underneath—"I'm not going to deprive my sister here of her bed."

"It is yours, sis," Celia stated.

"I know," Penny replied.

Soon everyone had crowded into Betty's lounge, and once Penny had fielded everyone's questions and assured them she'd heal quicker at home than she would taking up a hospital bed, Penny asked the question she'd been waiting to get a chance to ask.

"Has anyone heard from Tom?"

Her anxious look around the room was finally answered by Ruth, whose face betrayed it wasn't good news she had to impart. "I'm sorry. I'd do anything to put a smile on your face."

The only outward sign of Penny's anxiety was the small whimper of pain which escaped Celia's lips as her big sister squeezed the hand she was still holding. "Go on," Penny urged, not noticing what she'd done.

Ruth took a deep breath. "I've spent a lot of the past couple of days, when I've not been helping Walter put together our special edition on the Navy's sinking of the *Scharnhorst*, ringing up RAF Marham, trying to get hold of him. Whenever I did get through to his squadron, I was simply told either that he wouldn't come to the phone or that he was busy. Even when I told them I was calling on your behalf," she added, as Penny had opened her mouth, undoubtedly to ask.

Penny couldn't reply. She'd slumped back, tears pouring down her cheeks, with Celia draped across her, holding her as tightly as she could.

"Come on," Betty said gently. "Let's go out to the kitchen and let them have some privacy." Celia managed to catch her eye and give a quick nod of thanks. Jane alone appeared reluctant to join the exodus and needed a quick prod from Ruth before she joined everyone else in the kitchen.

"Shut the door, would you?" Betty asked Jane, who turned and did so before joining everyone else at the table.

No one seemed to know quite what to say. Betty, Mary, and Doris had all been very busy delivering urgently needed aircraft all over the country since Jane

317

and Penny's escapade and so hadn't been able to do anything about the Tom situation during the day.

"We had the same experience last night," Betty announced, filling in the others.

"Do you think it'd help if we simply, well, dropped in? So to speak," Doris suggested. "They can't very well refuse to let us see him if we're actually there, could they?"

"It wouldn't work," Jane declared. "Penny told me the next time we tried that trick, the Station Commander would throw whoever did it into the cells for the night. He wasn't very pleased with either Penny or Tom the last time she did it."

"Well," Mary asked, "what are we going to do about things?"

The silence which followed was all pervading, as no one had any experience as to how they should proceed to resolve the problems between Penny and her husband. No one had any doubt Penny wanted him back, but if he wouldn't even talk to her, how were they supposed to progress? Nobody voiced it, but everyone was thinking the same thing—one of the problems of whirlwind wartime marriages was the small matter of just how much you really knew about the other person.

A loud knock at the front door made nearly everyone jump. "I'll get it," Mary told the room, jumping to her feet.

A minute later, they heard the front door close, a rapid patter of feet, and Mary burst back into the kitchen, her face looking like she'd seen a ghost.

"My, what's wrong?" Ruth asked, beginning to get to her feet.

"Betty," Mary began to say and then shook her

head. "No, that's not the right way."

"What's not the right way?" Betty asked.

"Sorry," Mary said, coming to stand next to Betty. "I didn't mean that. What I meant to say is…"

A tremendous banging on the door interrupted her.

Betty got to her feet, declaring, "You've left whoever it is on the doorstep?" and before anyone could stop her, swept past Mary and into the hall, where she opened the front door.

Standing there were two of the strangest people she'd ever seen, and once she realized who they were, she fervently regretted opening the door.

The small dumpling on the right, wearing a black pinstriped suit, also wore the typical insincere smile Betty always associated with politicians, whilst the woman next to him, a nightmare in matching tweed, bore a smile of pure greed.

"Hello," said the dumpling, raising a bowler hat. "We didn't get a chance to speak last time."

Betty stepped outside and shut the door behind her. Not, as it turned out, the smartest thing she'd ever done.

****

"Anyone in?" Lawrence shouted. Having looked into Ruth's place and finding no one there, he'd decided to try Betty's, and when nobody answered, he'd tried the door and was surprised to find it open. Going into policeman mode, he dipped his hand into his pocket and brought out a torch, absently wishing he'd signed out a pistol. Some part of his brain was nagging him, prodding him into thinking it would have been a good idea.

Popping his head around the open lounge door, he was presented with a strange sight. Celia appeared to be asleep on top of Penny, her head on her sister's shoulder, her mouth open. Penny herself was awake and stroking her sister's hair as she slept, though her gaze didn't appear to be looking at anything in particular. Not until he waved did she notice his presence, and even then she merely waved back before resting her head back and closing her eyes. Pushing aside his need to find out how she was, he backed up and, as quietly as he could, pulled the door shut.

Moving toward the kitchen, he thought he could hear voices, though he couldn't make out what they were saying. Cursing the old thick door, he carefully took the handle and, gripping his torch a little tighter, yanked the door open in one quick movement, bursting into the kitchen. He immediately felt more than a little silly and said a silent prayer for deciding not to let out a war cry of sorts.

Out of the corner of his right eye, he was immediately aware of something wide and heavy coming down toward his head. Raising his right arm, something heavy did indeed collide painfully with his forearm. Dropping the torch he'd been holding, he yelped in pain and cradled his arm to his chest.

"Lawrence!" Doris cried from his right-hand side, dropping a large frying pan onto the floor.

"Doris! What the hell?" he exclaimed, teeth gritted in pain.

"Why didn't you say it was you?" she asked, reaching out to touch his arm.

He nudged the pan out of her reach with his foot, holding his hurt arm away from her, and sat down next to Walter. Still glaring at Doris and shaking his arm, he leant down and with his left hand picked up the now slightly dented frying pan and placed it on the table. "I did knock and also announced myself," he said through gritted teeth, gratefully accepting the glass of water Thelma placed in front of him. After draining it, he looked around the room, noticing for the first time that everyone seemed to be very ill at ease, which would certainly explain the frying pan, to a certain extent.

Ignoring the pain in his forearm, he scratched his head and asked, "What's going on?" He looked around the gathering again, checking before he asked, "Where's Betty?"

"Exactly what we've been asking ourselves," Jane answered.

****

"I wouldn't bother trying to ask the driver for help," George Palmer told Betty.

Sitting between her mother and father in the back of a taxi, Betty's first thought was that she couldn't have asked for help, as they'd stuffed a none-too-clean handkerchief into her mouth as soon as they'd grabbed her, though why they'd not bothered with a blindfold was both curious and worrying. Furious with herself for not having noticed the giant of a man who'd stepped out of the shadows to wrap a hand the size of a spade around her face, she decided to save her energy for when she might need it. Even if she could somehow have gotten out of the car, she wouldn't have been able to get very far. As well as the gag, they'd also taken the precaution of binding her ankles and wrists. She was going nowhere but wherever they took her.

"Yes," simpered her mother, "we have lots to talk about, lots of catching up to do."

At hearing her parents' voices, really hearing them

for the first time, Betty mused that perhaps being put into the orphanage hadn't been so bad after all, as it meant she hadn't had to grow up listening to this pair. She wondered how Marcus had come out such a nice person. But then she wondered if he was in on this…kidnap. Was it a kidnap? Did such things happen to ordinary people like her? Or was this all the result of reading too much Agatha Christie? Well, whatever it was, she had no intention of cooperating in any way with them. She remembered her dear Elle and jutted out her chin. Yes, they could do their worst. She'd be strong for the both of them.

A little to her surprise, nobody said anything else to her until they turned down a road which she recognized. The lack of signposts didn't bother her, as before her life had been turned upside down by the appearance of the Air Transport Mystery Club in her life, she'd spent many a happy day trekking and cycling around the New Forest. They drove into what she recognized as the village of Lyndhurst, and despite it now being pitch-black outside, she knew she was right. Betty wondered where they were taking her. Not very far, would be her bet. Taxis in the heart of the forest would stick out a mile. She got her answer as they turned into a shingle drive which led behind a low, whitewashed cottage with a thatched roof. A For Sale sign was posted at its front. Under most other circumstances, Betty would have tried to make out if it had a straw finial animal upon its roof.

The car door opened, and her father virtually rolled out and told the driver, "Bring her inside, John."

If she could have talked, Betty would have told them to untie her feet, but before any other thoughts could invade her mind, the huge man merely reached inside the car, took her by the waist, straightened up, and hoisted her over his shoulders as if she were a sack of flour. The wind knocked out of her lungs, Betty endured an uncomfortable ride into a darkened cottage through the back door. Leading them, her mother carried a candle to light the way until they entered a back bedroom.

"On there will do," she told her tame dog, and Betty found herself unceremoniously dropped onto the bed, fortunately not onto her face.

Whilst she was recovering her breath, she heard her father shut the back door and, a moment later, enter the room. Lighting his own candle, he bent down to her. "Now, if I take out this gag, you're not to yell, or anything silly like that. If you do, I'm afraid I'll have to allow Big John to remind you exactly who's in charge. Nod if you understand."

Wriggling her way into a semi-sitting position with her back against the wall, Betty noticed, and heard, this Big John man crack his knuckles—very loudly. She wasn't stupid. She nodded.

"Good." Reaching forward, her father took hold of the gag and none too gently pulled it out, stepping immediately back to stand beside his wife.

"What the hell's going on?" Betty demanded. Just because she'd agreed not to be stupid enough to shout didn't mean she'd be silent. If she could annoy them enough, but not enough to get herself hurt, she'd be quite happy to do so.

Her mother came forward and sat down on the bed next to her, though she appeared loath to actually touch her daughter. "We wanted to talk, and we didn't think you were very keen on the idea."

Betty snorted her disdain. "So you thought you'd resort to kidnap, did you?"

"Kidnap is such an ugly word," George commented. "Don't you agree, Darcie?"

"Well, if you haven't even got the courage to call something by what it actually is, I don't see what we've got to talk about," Betty goaded and was inordinately pleased to see George raise an arm as if to slap her around the face. "Go ahead, *Father*!"

Perhaps the shock of being called "father" stayed his hand. For whatever reason, he lowered it. Even by the candlelight, Betty could see his shock. Maybe by addressing their relationship, no matter how distasteful she found it, she could gain some advantage.

"Yes," George eventually replied, once he'd recovered his composure. "Aren't family reunions lovely. Now, let's discuss how much your beautiful little cottage is worth."

Chapter Thirty-Five

"Boss, is your phone off the hook?" the voice asking the question of Tom came at the same time his office door opened.

Newly promoted to Flight Sergeant, Stan Atkins was one of the few people Tom would allow to burst into his office without knocking. That list didn't include the Station Commander.

Quickly, Tom flattened the picture he'd been looking at, his favorite of Penny. She'd had it taken only a couple of months ago and sent it to him, hoping to cheer him up. Her heart had been in the right place, he'd remembered, only she hadn't thought about it, really—she was sitting on the wing of a Spitfire. The photo was beautiful, but every time he looked at it, it just made him miss flying all the more. Even now, the damn headaches he'd been suffering from since being wounded hadn't gone, and he was still grounded. Every time he looked at the photo, the pain seemed to double.

Hoping his navigator hadn't seen his action, though doubting it, Tom knitted his hands together. "How can I help you, Stan?"

"Firstly, why are you working so late?"

Tom didn't meet his friend's eyes. "I didn't want to go back to my billet."

"You've got another message," Stan told Tom, letting the comment go and laying a piece of paper before his friend.

Tom sighed and looked up with tired eyes. "I don't want it."

Stan sat down, uninvited, and took up the untouched paper. "Can I speak freely?"

After all they'd been through together, it showed how annoyed Stan was with his normal pilot and friend that he felt the need to ask. "Always, you know that," Tom replied.

"Then let me say, Tom, boss, you're being an ass!" Tom raised his eyebrows, but Stan didn't give him a chance to interrupt. "You've got a beautiful, smart, brave wife, and putting aside the question of what on earth she sees in you…"

Tom snorted, but his lips twitched in amusement.

"…you're going to lose her if you go on like this."

"You know what happened?" Tom told him.

Stan rubbed his head. "I don't think I could forget," he muttered, recalling the night Tom got back from Southampton and spent the night in Stan's room, the pair of them talking and arguing over a bottle or two of whiskey.

"I don't want to talk to her," Tom reiterated.

"Yes, you bloody well do," Stan argued back. "You're just too ruddy pigheaded to admit it."

"She lost the baby," Tom stated, pulling open his bottom desk drawer and taking out a bottle of brandy and two glasses. Pouring two shots, he passed one to Stan, who left it untouched whilst Tom knocked his back and immediately refilled his glass.

"How was that her fault?" Stan countered. "It's not like she asked to get shot down, is it."

"She can't have any more children!" Tom told him,

his voice shaking and his picture a painting of misery.

Stan frowned, reached forward, and making certain he'd closed the door so no one could see him, threw back his drink before asking, "You heard the doctor say that? In exactly those words?"

Tom opened and closed his mouth, before casting his gaze around his office, as if the answer would appear in the walls. "Yes—I mean, I'm certain he—I *think* he said that," he finished off, looking totally confused.

"Then why are you being such an ass? All she wants to do is speak to you. That's it. Read it," Stan demanded, pushing the note back to Tom and waiting until he looked back up. "You see? No demands. She's not even calling you an idiot and, sorry to say so, that's the least you deserve."

Tom narrowed his eyes. "She hasn't put you up to this?"

"Calling you an idiot? No. I have spoken to her, and Doris, and Ruth, and at least one other of her friends since you got back, and I know I'm not the only one who's had that pleasure. Once you get this mess sorted out, I think you'll owe a few drinks to quite a number of others as well. I'm the only other who knows the complete story, or what you've told me, anyway, but you're not coming out of this very well, boss. Quite a few people around here know what Penny does and have a great respect for her and her friends. I will advise you not to accept a cup of tea from Sharon, for instance. I've heard her muttering about putting various, shall we say, nasty things in your next cup."

"That good, eh?"

"Bring in a thermos."

Tom opened his top drawer and took out a bunch of notes he'd put away for reading at some point. He scanned through them, and by the time he'd finished, he wore a big frown. They shared another shot of brandy before Tom leaned back in his chair to think, leaving Stan investigating his fingernails.

After Stan thought his boss had thought long enough, he coughed and said, "Well? You going to call her back?"

"I don't think the doctor did actually say she couldn't have any more children, you know."

Stan cleared his throat and then asked, "Do you mind my saying something?"

"As if I could stop you," Tom replied, showing a small part of his long-buried humor.

"Say Penny couldn't have children…"

Tom opened his mouth to interrupt, but his friend didn't give him a chance.

"After all this mess is over, you know there'll be plenty of orphans deserving of a good home. I'm certain the two of you would be able to give them exactly that."

If Tom had been about to blow his top when Stan began to speak, when he'd finished, he was swallowing back his emotions so he could speak. "Since when did you become so enlightened?"

Stan began to blush and had to clear his own throat before answering. "Since I realized how clever Sharon is."

"And how pretty?"

"And how pretty," Stan agreed.

Tom glanced through the various notes before, holding them tightly in his hands, he looked across at his friend. "Do you really think she'll speak to me?"

Stan picked up the telephone receiver and passed it across. "Give her a call and find out."

****

"You're positive it was Betty?" Jane asked.

Lawrence shook his head. "No, half sure, at best." Then, seeing the exasperated look Jane and everyone else around the table was giving him, he added, "Look, I wasn't on the lookout for Betty. I had no idea she was missing when I saw the taxi. The only reason I even looked was because taxis are so rare around here. Are you even sure she's been kidnapped? Couldn't she just have gone for a walk?"

Doris got up and opened the kitchen door wide. "Without telling one of us? Plus, her coat, hat, and gloves are still there." She pointed at the hall table and the coat rack. "In case you hadn't noticed, it's perishing out there."

"Hmm, good point," the policeman allowed, though he also added, "but there's still no proof she's been kidnapped."

"He's got a point," Walter unwisely stated.

Doris opened her mouth, undoubtedly to tell her fiancé off, but she never got the chance as just at that moment the front door burst open, ushering in a very pale Penny being held up by Celia on one side and Nurse Grace Baxter on the other.

"What the hell?" Mary cried, rushing past Doris to give the pair a hand. She pushed the lounge door open with her foot. "What were you two doing outside? I thought you were both on the sofa!" Once she'd made certain a clearly exhausted Penny was tucked up on the sofa again, Mary asked, "Can someone put a couple of bricks in the stove? We need to get both of these idiots warmed up quick."

"I'm on it," Ruth replied and immediately ordered Walter to give her a hand in the kitchen.

By the time Doris helped her to take a tray of tea into the lounge, they found Grace had persuaded Penny, not that she was in any condition to object, to let her look at her wound.

Looking up, Grace pursed her lips. "Looks like life's just as boring for you bunch as ever."

Jane took a seat opposite them, and Grace, being a good judge of people, didn't miss either the cast on her forearm or the concerned look she cast over Penny.

"Let me guess. This was a double deal."

"We had an argument with a Nazi bomber and a British fighter."

Grace raised her eyebrows in surprise. "At the same time? That's got to be some sort of record."

"We haven't checked yet," Mary supplied, passing around the tea.

Grace indicated Mary should put hers on the floor beside her foot. "Thanks. Now, what do we have here?"

"What the hell were you two doing?" Mary demanded, hand planted on one hip, cup of tea in the other. "You could have frozen to death!"

"Hardly," Celia snorted, and immediately quailed under Mary's fierce gaze.

"I'll talk to you later, young lady," Mary promised her.

"We were only trying to help," Penny said wincing under Grace's prodding fingers. "You weren't exactly keeping your voices down, you know."

"So you both decided to go outside and search for

probable nonexistent clues?" Lawrence said.

"Who said we came up empty-handed?" Penny demanded her eyes tight.

This got Lawrence's attention, "Go on."

"Celia's got it."

"Celia," Lawrence addressed the girl.

"Right," Grace stated, reaching down and picking up her tea before turning to the room. "I'm going to pop around morning and evening. I want to make certain Penny, here, stays clear of infection and"—she tapped Penny on her knee until she opened her eyes—"you are to stay inside for the next two weeks. No arguments!" She very nearly yelled those last two words, as Penny opened her mouth to object. "We have to keep that as clean as the cleanest thing you've ever come across, if you don't want to get an infection. Believe me, you don't want that."

Penny was obviously listening to every word. "Yes, right, I'll be good."

"That's what I wanted to hear." Grace smiled. "Now," she said, putting down her empty cup on the side table, "I'd better be getting home. I was only taking a walk along the riverbank when you two interrupted my evening. I'll be along tomorrow to give you a penicillin injection at some time."

"What's penicillin?" Celia asked, concerned for her sister.

"It's a new drug we've only just got at the hospital. It's designed to fight infection. Works wonders, I've been told. Right." She smoothed her skirt and looked around. Only then did she notice everyone was looking at her. "Sorry, did I interrupt something?"

"It's okay," Ruth said, coming back into the lounge

before going over and handing Penny and Celia each a hot brick wrapped in a towel. "Our fault entirely. We keep forgetting you're deaf." Ruth noticed the nurse's head swivel to Lawrence and back to her. "It's all right. He won't say a thing." Ruth looked her nephew right in the eye. "Will he."

Lawrence waited until Grace was looking directly at him before telling her, correctly surmising the girl could lip read, "I promise."

"Oh, I should ask. Penny, did you get an injection at the hospital?" Grace turned back around to ask.

Penny thought before slowly shaking her head. "I'm sorry, I don't remember. I suppose they could have given me one whilst I was out of it."

Grace, however, was looking around the room, a frown forming as she realized someone was missing. "Where's Betty?"

Everyone looked at everyone else. Finally Jane took it upon herself to tell the young nurse they'd all come to like and trust the previous year, when Betty had been stabbed, "She's gone missing."

It took a minute for Grace to process what she'd been told. "Missing? What? How? When?" she asked in staccato fashion.

Lawrence went to stand before her, telling her in a no-nonsense manner, "Missing. I know you're concerned, but you must leave the police to handle this. Understood?"

The expression upon Grace's face clearly showed she was far from happy about this, but also, she knew nothing she could do there and then could help or make a difference. Instead, she fell back on what she'd been doing with Penny. "Tell you what," Grace told her. "I'll phone them in the morning and find out." With a last concerned glance around the room, Grace said her goodbyes and left, Walter seeing her out.

"Celia?" Lawrence reminded Penny's sister.

Someone knocked at the door before Celia could react, and Walter answered it.

" 'Please' wouldn't go amiss," she muttered, nevertheless handing over a handkerchief from her skirt pocket.

Lawrence held it up carefully at the edges between finger and thumbs. Turning it around, he noticed three monogrammed letters in a corner. "G. C. P.," he read.

"George Cecil Palmer," answered a new voice.

Chapter Thirty-Six

"Marcus!" Jane said in surprise.

Lawrence turned his head and jumped to his feet. "This is Betty's brother?"

"That's him," Walter replied, coming in behind Marcus and shutting the lounge door behind him.

"Pilot Officer Palmer." Lawrence held out his hand. "We need to talk." He looked around at the expectant faces. "Preferably, somewhere private."

At those words, Jane moved behind him to block any attempt to leave the room, and she was quickly joined by Mary, Doris, and Thelma. Penny made to move off the sofa but was held back by Celia, who firmly held her down.

"I don't think that's a good idea," Jane told Lawrence. "We're all a part of this, and don't forget, this is someone we consider our sister. So unless you plan on arresting Marcus and taking him off to the cells, we all suggest you hold your *discussion* here."

Lawrence was nothing if not fair in his police work and, after a moment's thought, agreed. "I can't arrest him. So far as I can tell, Marcus hasn't done anything wrong. Have you?" he asked Lawrence directly.

Marcus shook his head and then, shortly afterward, having given it some thought, just as slowly nodded. "But not intentionally."

"I think we all need to sit down," Lawrence stated,

matching action to words and taking a seat.

After a second, Mary came to kneel next to him. "Come on," she told her friends, who still stood guarding the door. "Take a seat. Lawrence and Marcus aren't going anywhere soon, and this may take a while."

Hesitating only a moment, the others sat, although Walter opened the door and left the room, returning a few moments later with a glass of water he handed to Marcus, who'd been glancing around the room rather nervously.

"Thanks," he said, taking a hefty swallow.

As he put the glass down, Lawrence asked, "What do you mean by 'not intentionally'?"

The young pilot officer glanced around the room, very aware he was in the presence of his sister's real family. "I'm sorry, to you all."

"Perhaps you'd better start at the beginning?" Penny suggested. She had a lot more color in her face since being looked at by Grace and was certainly giving him her full attention.

"What happened to you?" Marcus couldn't help but ask. "Sorry, I realize it's none of my business, but you look like you've been shot."

Penny's hand from her other side covered her newly bandaged arm. "How could you tell?"

Marcus's eyes dipped before he answered, "I've seen a few fellows on my squadron in the same state," he told her. "Forgive me for asking."

Jane moved to the sofa, lifted Penny's legs, and sat down, draping them over her lap. She lifted up her broken arm to show him. "We were in the wrong place at the wrong time."

"Can we get back to the subject at hand?" Lawrence asked.

"Yes, sorry," Marcus apologized.

"The beginning," Lawrence prodded.

"I don't know how much you know about my parents, Mister…" Marcus probed.

" 'Inspector' will do," Lawrence supplied, "and for now, assume I don't know anything about them."

After a moment, Marcus nodded, understanding what the policeman meant. Taking a deep, steadying breath, he began.

"My parents aren't what you would call loving, not to anyone, let alone family. As I grew up, I believe I would describe my relationship with them as being one of…convenience. Before I go any farther, please believe me when I tell you that if I'd had any idea I had siblings, I would have gone to any lengths to find them, even then." Marcus sighed as a memory came back. He looked up with, despite the situation, a smile upon his face. "When I first met Eleanor, it was the happiest day of my life. I could immediately see a resemblance between us, and I'm very happy to say she saw the same. I still find it hard to believe she's gone," he added, shaking his head.

Mary fixed him with a steely look. "Make sure you tell Betty that."

Marcus matched her gaze. "You have my word."

Lawrence cleared his throat, and Marcus gave him a quick shrug of apology for digressing. "Anyway, my parents didn't seem to care much for each other. My mother seemed happy only when she was spending money, and my father only when he was making it. However, as I grew up, because they had no interest in me other than my actual existence, I was able to learn what they were really like when they weren't around me, pretending to care. I discovered my father may have been good at making money, as well as self-promotion—I think that was why he became a Member of Parliament—but he was equally adept at losing it." He paused and looked around the room before stating, "Would I be right in saying Betty shared what I told you about the day we met in London? With my parents in Parliament?"

Everyone except Lawrence nodded.

"I'll give you the short version, then, Inspector. My father lost every penny, and his house, in gambling, and his Party found out, so he also lost his seat in the House. There are certain insalubrious people after him for gambling debts. Essentially, he's on the run."

Lawrence got to his feet and began to pace back and forth, but just as he opened his mouth to speak, Jane uttered the words everyone in the room was thinking. "He's a desperate man, then. Do you think it's him?"

"Jane, please," Lawrence asked. "Allow me to conduct the interview."

"Go ahead," she replied, not one bit sorry for speaking.

Lawrence cleared his throat and, unable to avoid sounding a little sheepish, asked, "Well, do you think he took Betty?"

Marcus held out a hand. "Could I take a look at that?"

Lawrence held out the handkerchief but cautioned Marcus to only hold it between one finger and thumb. Nodding, he held it close to his eyes, albeit briefly, before giving it back.

"I've no doubt that's his," Marcus stated.

Stuffing the handkerchief into an inside pocket, Lawrence walked to the window and twitched the blackout curtain slightly aside before turning around. Pausing, he seemed to second guess himself before asking, "What do you think his next move will be? And, would he hurt Betty?"

If he could have taken a step back, Marcus would have, but he did shuffle awkwardly in his seat. "I'll be honest—I don't know."

"Tell Lawrence what you said about Betty," Mary suggested. "Maybe you'll remember something you'd forgotten."

"Not a bad idea," Ruth agreed.

"Can't hurt," Lawrence agreed too, after thinking the suggestion over for a minute. "What did you tell your parents about her?"

"I'll go make some more tea," Doris said. "I think we can all agree Marcus here isn't a suspect..." She waited until Lawrence nodded in agreement, which he did quite quickly, much to Marcus' obvious relief. "Good. Now, don't say anything interesting until I get back."

Jane waited until Doris was banging around in the kitchen before saying, "Ignore her. Carry on, Marcus." Walter got up and went to give Doris a hand. "Ignore them both," Jane added, causing Celia to snort with laughter.

"Well," Marcus began, scratching his head in thought, "I did tell them about this cottage—it slipped out. So I suppose they may think they could persuade her to sign it over to them. Plus, because of this, they probably think she's got a bit of money, too."

"Ha!"

Everyone looked around and found the ironic laugh had come from Penny.

"Sorry," Penny said when she realized everyone was looking at her. "Short of torture, I don't think there's any way in hell Betty would hand over this cottage. She loves the place too much."

"I don't think even torture would work," Celia added.

"Anything else?" Lawrence asked. He snapped his fingers as something occurred to him. "Did you tell them anything about what Eleanor did? Or Betty, for that matter?"

Marcus shook his head. "I hadn't even meant to tell them about Betty, only as soon as it slipped out I'd met Eleanor—and I really hope I never get captured, as I can't keep a secret—even they didn't take long to put two and two together, and I couldn't help mentioning her name."

"But putting aside the fact I want to play you at poker," Doris said as she came into the room, Walter close behind her bearing a tray of tea things, "you're certain you never mentioned what either of them did? Think about it before answering," she cautioned, "as it's just struck me that we don't know if Eleanor left anything in her will."

In deference to Doris's warning, Marcus waited until the tea had been served.

"Positive," he announced, taking a refreshing sip from his cup. "I did make a conscious effort not to. Not because they'd disapprove, but because, well, it was none of their business."

"That's something," Lawrence muttered. "Which would mean they probably do intend trying to extort this cottage out of her, or at least get what money they can."

Whilst everyone was thinking this over, the telephone rang, nearly causing Penny to drop her cup. "Give that here," Celia said, taking the cup from where it was being unwisely held by her sister's bad arm.

"I'll answer," Lawrence surprised everyone by saying, adding, "I left my sergeant dealing with something to do with this case and told him to call this number as soon as he had news." He looked at his watch and said, "Didn't take as long as I thought," before going out into the hall, unfortunately closing the door behind him.

"Don't!" Jane told Celia who'd got up to go and open the door. "I'm sure he'll tell us what we need to know as soon as he comes back."

"But…" Celia began to object, only Penny took her hand in hers and shook her head.

Everyone was on tenterhooks whilst waiting for Lawrence to return, so no one spoke until they heard him put the receiver down.

With the typical impatience of youth, immediately the door opened, Celia asked, "Well?"

Showing he knew the girl quite well, Lawrence replied, "Thanks for your patience, Celia," and then sat back down and finished off his tea. "That was my sergeant," he began and then faced Marcus before saying, his face sympathetic, "I'm sorry, but Terry's confirmed it. We had a suspect look at some photos, and he's made a positive identification. The person who was actually the money, the backing, behind a draft-dodging gang we put away last year was your father."

All eyes turned toward the young pilot, who briefly cast his eyes down before, determination glinting in his eyes, he met Lawrence's interested and concerned gaze, obviously not certain what to expect from him now the news that his father was behind a major criminal enterprise had been revealed.

"You don't look that surprised," Thelma, the latest member of the ATA Mystery Club stated, putting voice to what everyone was thinking.

"I'm not." Marcus nodded. His voice emotionless, he told them, "It goes to prove they really don't care about anyone but themselves. When I told them Eleanor was dead, there was nothing, no reaction at all."

"Bastards," Celia announced and for once, no one told her off.

"What do we do next, Lawrence?" Marcus asked.

Chapter Thirty-Seven

"It's ready," Big John announced and stepped back to once more block the rear bedroom's door.

For what was the umpteenth time since her incarceration, Betty rolled her eyes. Though she wasn't bound, she had no illusions as to her chances if she did try to make a break for it. Even assuming she somehow got past the human behemoth, she still had the small problem of finding help. Despite knowing where she was, it would be quite another thing to be able to get someone to listen to her. Not only would everyone left in the village be asleep, but the noise she'd make trying to wake someone up would give away where she was. If she was lucky, perhaps she'd be able to knock on two or three doors before this thug would catch her up. She was quite a quick runner, but she had no doubt he would turn out to be quicker.

About to open her mouth for the pithy remark she'd been saving up for the last hour, she snapped it shut as George switched on the light. Whoever taught this fool—Betty couldn't bring herself to think of him as her *father*, even inside her head—to interrogate someone, they didn't do a very good job. Pathetic, more like. All he'd done was repeat over and over virtually the same sentence—telling her to sign the document in front of her, or *else*!

After half an hour—she still had her watch, so

could at least keep track of time—she'd grown bored and had begun to count his nose hairs. Looking around, Betty was surprised to see blackout boards had been put in place. With a wry smile, she turned back, thinking she must have been more bored than she thought, if she never noticed those going up.

George got too close for Betty's liking, and she recoiled. Thinking she must have recoiled in fear, rather than as a reaction to his bad breath, he treated her to a grin. "That's better. A little respect never goes amiss."

Betty made a point of looking his person up and down, something which didn't take very long. "In your case, it would only ever be a *little*."

The slap came out of nowhere. Betty's ears rang, and her vision dimmed slightly before coming back into focus. She became aware of something trickling down the side of her face. Bringing up a hand, she touched where he'd slapped her, and her fingers came away covered in bright scarlet blood.

"George!" Darcy cried and made as if to step to Betty's side before she stopped herself. The look on her face could only be described as shock.

Through her throbbing head, Betty wondered if this man had ever been violent toward his wife. She doubted it, as the woman was no actress and couldn't have faked her expression if she'd tried. Looming above them both, Big John also seemed to have been taken by surprise by his employer's action, yet even with the ringing in her ears, she could hear him cracking his knuckles. Interesting. Perhaps he was one of those goons you saw in the movies who thought nothing about cracking a man's head open, yet had a strange code of honor which meant he never laid a hand on a woman's head.

This usually turned out to be a mother-thing, at least in the movies.

"Take her through," George snapped.

Before Betty could get her lips under control to ask where, Big John had taken her by the arm, and she was forced to get to her feet and accompany him, if she didn't wish to be dragged. It may have been her imagination, but he didn't seem to be holding her as roughly as before. Either way, she rapidly found herself deposited on the sofa of a very dark lounge. Coming in behind them, Darcie switched the lights on. With the blackout now fully in place, Betty took a swift look around the room. This yielded no useful information at all, as the only furniture present was the sofa she sat upon and two old tea chests.

She wiped the back of her hand down the side of her face once more and came away with more blood. When no one was polite enough to offer either to clean her up or the use of a handkerchief, she shrugged and wiped her hand on the sofa. Judging by its age, she doubted anyone would notice any difference. From the corner of her eye, though, she did see Darcie's eyes follow her movement and wince. George sat upon the tea chest next to her and was wiping the hand he'd slapped her with. She noticed a glint of light catch something on his finger—a ring. She hoped her cheek had blunted it somewhat.

"Nice place," she said and paused before adding, to see if her guess was correct, "You used to live here."

"Yes," Darcie answered before she could help herself.

"Shut up!" George snapped, causing his wife to nearly fall off her perch. "Now," he said, turning his attention back to Betty, "obviously being nice *isn't* doing anything, so listen closely to what I have to say."

"So this place is up for sale too? Where will you live?" Betty asked, addressing her question to Darcie.

"That's none of your business," George snapped before his wife could answer.

"Because, if you think you're going to get your hands on my cottage, you've another think coming." Betty hoped she'd put enough steel into her voice.

George narrowed his eyes before saying, "What would your friends say if they knew what you and..." He hesitated—actually hesitated as Betty saw him try to recall what her sister's, his other daughter's name, was. "...Eleanor used to do for a living? What would they think of having a thief and a fence in their midst?" He then sat back, his smug smile nearly wiped off as he momentarily overbalanced.

Betty didn't help by bursting out laughing. If he'd expected his threat to leave her quaking in her shoes, she was about to let him down, and enjoy it.

"Go right ahead, George. They already know." At her words, Betty noticed a vein begin to throb upon his forehead. The man was close to losing control. How far should she push him? Deliberately, she dabbed the side of her head and wiped her fingers once more on the sofa. The vein throbbed a little more.

"And what would the police say?"

She couldn't believe the man would actually try that threat, considering the situation. "I can give you the name and telephone number of a detective inspector, if it helps," she bluffed. Lawrence didn't know everything about her, though she knew he had his suspicions. However, going on what he said next, it worked.

"How about I get your name in the newspapers? Wouldn't that look bad? There's no way they'd allow you to keep flying, then."

Betty hoped her face didn't betray the shock she felt. Such a revelation would indeed bring her flying career to a grinding halt, something which would be particularly galling, as it had only just got back on track. However, she wasn't going down without a fight. "Go ahead. I'd be interested to see what they think when I tell them not only about your illegal gambling habits, which caused you to lose not only *this* house"— a lift of an eyebrow from Darcie confirmed what she thought about there being another house—"but also your seat in Parliament. On its own, perhaps even you could wriggle your way out of that," she told him, before going for the jugular, "but I doubt if you'd come out of it smelling of roses if I told them how you'd put your twin daughters into an orphanage when they were born, simply because you wanted only a son."

"And look how you both turned out!" he yelled back, spittle flying. "I knew daughters were a waste of time. Look at the shame you've brought upon the family name!"

"Oh, yes, and you're such a fine figure of a man!" Betty shot back.

At hearing the venom in Betty's words, George sprang to his feet, arm raised again as he made to stride across to her. He never made it, as Darcie surprised everyone. Showing surprising speed, she dashed in front of her irate husband and took hold of his hand as he made to bring it down upon Betty's face.

"No!"

His arm still raised, George peered in amazement

at his wife, whilst Big John took a step toward the pair. None of them were now paying any attention to Betty.

"I've had enough! Do you hear? Enough! I've lost one daughter I never knew, and I will not completely alienate the other whilst there is still a chance of getting to know her."

The pain in the side of Betty's head seemed to dull as the meaning in the woman's words hit home. Whilst an argument raged between them, Betty tried to process the meaning of what she'd just heard. She supposed it all came down to whether she wanted a relationship with this woman. She wasn't given the chance to think further upon the matter, though.

Darcie, taking both her husband and his thug by surprise, dipped her free hand into her husband's jacket pocket. It reappeared with a set of keys. "You're on your own!"

So saying, and displaying the same dexterity, Darcie let go of his hand, ducked under Big John's sweeping arm, and the next thing everyone heard was the bang of the back door closing. A bare few seconds later came the sound of the car engine starting up, and both George and his heavy looked in surprise at each other. Swearing, George took to his heels, closely followed by Big John. The last thing she heard him say was, "I never knew she could drive!"

It took a few moments for Betty's throbbing head to realize she was alone. Heaving herself to her feet, she stuck out a hand, briefly gripping the arm of the sofa as she fought the urge to be sick. Thankfully, her stomach cooperated, and another moment later, she was at the front door, had unbolted it, and was hurrying out of the house.

As she ducked into the shadows provided by a handy hedge, she heard George and his henchman had found out she'd gone too.

"Oh, hell!"

****

"I'm going to have to get back," Thelma reluctantly announced.

It had now turned ten-thirty, and Betty had been gone for around four hours, with nothing heard from or about her. Everyone was assuming her parents were behind it, being the only explanation which made sense, yet apart from money, no one had been able to put forward any other reason for their actions. As Lawrence had rightly pointed out, even if they somehow persuaded Betty to sign anything turning over the cottage to them, no court in the land would make it legally binding. At those words, nobody elaborated as they'd all thought the same thing at the same time. To stand any chance of the scheme working, Betty would have to die. This had ended further conversation.

Jane put aside the same magazine she'd been reading for the last hour. No one had had the heart to tell her it had been upside down. "Come on, I'll walk you to the base. I could do with some exercise."

Doris nudged the slumbering Walter in the ribs. "Hmm, what?"

"Time for your gentleman act, honey," she remarked. "Do me a favor and escort the girls back to camp, and then make sure Jane here doesn't get lost on the way back."

Jane tapped Doris on the top of her head as she passed. "Very funny."

Walter hadn't moved, so Doris dug her elbow into

his side again. "I meant it," she said more firmly.

This got her fiancé moving, and before long, the door shut behind him.

"I should be making a move too," Ruth told everyone, rising and stretching her arms above her head. "Could someone tell Walter, when he gets back, that I've gone home?"

"Of course," Mary answered, escorting their friend to the front door. "If we hear anything, we'll come and get you."

Ruth gave Mary a hug, telling her, "Thanks, that saves me asking. I'll be around in the morning, first thing. I know it'll be New Year's Eve, but it doesn't seem like it, does it?" Mary shook her head and sighed. Before going, she said, "I know what my New Year's wish will be."

As she closed the door behind Ruth, the telephone rang, and Mary picked it up, saying rather absently, her mind on other things, "Hello, the Palmer residence, Mary speaking."

A few second later, Mary burst back into the lounge, startling Penny and Celia, who were dozing on the sofa.

"Christ, where's the fire?" Doris asked, eyes agape.

Ignoring her, Mary went and shook Penny gently by the good shoulder. "Penny! Wake up! It's Tom!"

An alarm clock strapped to her head wouldn't have had the same effect, as Penny's eyes shot open and, obviously forgetting she had Celia's head on her thigh, she swung her legs off the sofa. Celia promptly fell to the floor.

"Hey!"

Ignoring her prostrate and protesting sister, Penny

stepped over her and swept past Mary, who went to close the door.

"Leave it ajar," Doris suggested, and after deliberating for a moment, Mary did so. Doris sat on the edge of her seat.

"We shouldn't really be listening," Celia observed, before joining Doris, nearest the door. Mary bobbed down onto the floor by Celia.

What they heard, albeit one side of the conversation, didn't make happy listening.

"Well, isn't it nice of you to phone me," Penny began. "I've only been trying to speak to you, or contact you in any way, since you walked out on me at the hospital."

Everyone in the lounge could well imagine Tom trying to explain his behavior during the pause which followed Penny's accusation. The question was, would Penny allow him?

They soon got their answer.

"No, I don't want to see you. Why? I should think that's bloody obvious. You accused me of being happy I'd lost the baby!" Penny had got up a head of steam, and by the way everyone in the room was glancing at each other, all felt some degree of sympathy for her husband, though not much. "Of course I want children! I'd told you that. Oh, I can't go through this right now. Just, just leave me alone for a while," she told him.

The next thing they heard was Penny slamming the phone down, and she was in the room before anyone had a chance to pretend they hadn't been listening. Penny stood over them with her hands on her hips. "I guess there's no need for me to repeat what was said."

Celia sprang to her feet and hooked her sister's

good arm through hers. "Come on, let's go up to bed."

Tiredness hit Penny, and she allowed herself to be led out of the room, but not before saying her goodnights.

"I'll make sure to wake you up if we hear anything," Lawrence told them from where he'd been sitting unnoticed by the window.

"At least someone recognizes privacy," Penny said with a gentle laugh before leaving the room.

After helping her sister to change into her pajamas and have a wash, Celia snuggled up onto Penny's good shoulder. "Hope you don't mind my not asking. I would have slept on the sofa, but I imagine Lawrence will be bedding down there."

"And Jane can take Betty's bed," Penny automatically said before stopping.

Celia finished for her. "She'll be back home tomorrow, don't worry. I've this feeling." When she didn't get an answer, Celia asked, "What about you and Tom?"

Her only answer was silence. Choosing to believe her sister was asleep, Celia closed her eyes as well, but sleep eluded her until the small hours of the morning.

Chapter Thirty-Eight

Doris and Mary both burst out of their bedrooms at the same time, rubbing their eyes and exclaiming, "What the hell?"

Standing before them was Jane. In her injured arm she carried a saucepan and was banging the bottom of it with a large wooden spoon. Doris made a grab for the spoon and missed.

"What on earth's going on?" Celia yelled from Penny's open doorway, her hands clamped over her ears. Behind her, Penny had placed a pillow over her face.

"I was making sure you're all up and awake," Jane told them.

Doris rubbed her ears. "Up, I'll give you. Not sure about awake, though. What's the game, boss?"

Jane sat down on the top step of the stairs and flopped back onto the landing. She stared up at the ceiling. "I know it's early…"

"Too right it is," Mary interrupted, looking at her wristwatch. "Six-thirty too early!"

"…I wanted us all awake, so we don't miss— anything."

After exchanging glances, both Doris and Mary squeezed in beside her, and each put an arm around her. Immediately Jane's head flopped down onto Mary's shoulder. Celia came and knelt down behind them, which was just as well, as Jane leant back against her. Steadying herself, Celia unconsciously began to stroke Jane's hair. Then a curious frown came to her face.

"Have you been up all night?"

Eyes closed, Jane managed to say, "Uh-huh."

"Blinkin' hell, Jane!" Doris told her.

"Someone had to." She shrugged.

"What about Lawrence?" Penny asked, as she struggled to put her dressing gown on.

"I sent him off to Ruth's with Walter, along with Marcus," Jane explained.

"Why would you do that?" Mary asked.

Jane opened her eyes and stifled a yawn. "He did volunteer to stay up with me, but I told him he'd serve us best by being fresh and fit for today. We'll be needing him. He said he'd meet us at the station."

Penny finally appeared behind the group. "I assume you didn't hear anything last night, then?"

Jane shook her head, then heaved herself forward and, with a little help from her friends, got to her feet. She picked up her makeshift drum and proceeded back downstairs. "Get washed and dressed, everyone. Doris, Mary, you need to get to work. Penny, remember, Grace is dropping in to inspect your wound and to give you that penicillin inoculation."

Multiple groans greeted her ears as she reached the bottom of the stairs. She turned and looked up at them.

"Don't argue. Despite everything, we've still got planes to deliver!"

Before anyone could say anything to disagree or indeed argue, there came a knock at the door. Jane, all fatigue brushed aside, rushed as quickly as she could to open it.

"Any news?"

Behind Jane, everyone was hanging over the banister. "It's Grace!" Jane shouted. "Better come down, Penny!"

Ushering the nurse into the kitchen, Jane fumbled a little with putting the kettle on, accompanied by the muffled sounds of much rushing about going on upstairs.

"Here, let me do that," Grace offered, pulling out a chair and ushering Jane into it. "You look all done in."

"I did have a long night," Jane agreed.

"By which," Penny said as she came into the kitchen, looking unusual in slacks and a shirt, "she means she was awake all night in case the telephone rang."

"Not all night," Jane protested and then amended, at seeing the look Penny was giving her, "I managed to snatch a few hours' sleep."

"Hmm, looks like a very few," Grace mooted. "Right." She went on, all business. "Take a seat, Penny, and I'll have a look at your arm."

So, with Jane back to tea-making duties, Grace washed her hands, dried them, and was unwrapping Penny's bandage when Doris and Mary made their entrances. Both accepted cups of tea and joined in with Jane to watch Grace's caring ministrations. By the time everyone had finished their drinks, Grace had rewrapped Penny's arm in a clean bandage and was digging into her bag, bringing out a small glass bottle and a hypodermic syringe.

Penny gulped. "I take it this means I didn't have this at the hospital?" Her eyes were bulging, and she sat as far back in her seat as possible.

Grace took a deep swallow from her cup and measured out the dosage before turning her attention back to her patient. "Afraid so." She smiled. "Don't worry, this won't hurt, and it'll help protect you against infections, so…big brave girl time!"

"Do you want me to hold her down?" Celia asked as she suddenly appeared behind her sister.

"I don't think that'll be needed, do you?" Grace faced Penny having put her best evil grin on her face, the needle pointing menacingly toward the ceiling.

Penny lost the power of speech and merely shook her head, though she did hold out a hand, and both Mary and Doris immediately rushed to hold it, joined by Celia.

"I think I'd better hurry up before you lose all feeling in your hand." Grace laughed and quickly matched actions to words, taking Penny by surprise.

****

"Wait up!"

Mary, Doris, and Jane turned their heads at the voice, finding they were being trailed by Lawrence and Marcus, who were jogging to catch them up.

"Heard anything?" Marcus asked virtually the same question as everyone else had that morning. He took up a station on the girls' left, with Lawrence joining them on their right.

At everyone's shake of their heads, Lawrence nudged Jane gently in the ribs. "I thought you were supposed to be on sick leave."

Jane didn't alter her stride as she replied, "My best friend's missing. Nothing's going to stop me from checking that nothing's been heard at Hamble."

"Why would it?" Lawrence asked.

"Why wouldn't it?" Jane shot back before, in a calmer manner, pointing out, "Look, assuming it is those…two…" She quickly amended her language in deference to Marcus, who gave a her a weak smile of thanks. "They know where Betty lives, but the riverbank is only just wide enough for a car to get down, you know that, and unless you know it well, you'd have a hard time either backing up it or turning around so you could make a quick getaway. So why not choose another drop spot?"

As they approached the gate leading onto RAF Hamble, they were greeted by the sight of the guard commander waiting for them. In one hand, he gripped a plain brown envelope. Seeing the group approach, he waved it over his head. "Boss!"

Jane covered the last few yards in a matter of seconds and took the envelope with the briefest of thanks. By the time her companions had caught her up, Jane had turned the envelope over to reveal a roughly scrawled name on the front—Betty.

"Who delivered this?" Jane threw over her shoulder.

"No idea!" he replied, before adding, "The four a.m. guard told me some car came up, threw that out the window, and sped off before he could reach it."

"Betty's taken ill," Jane told him. "I'll take it."

"Do you want to do anything about how it came here?" he asked.

Jane treated him to a rare smile. "It's all in hand, believe me."

Five minutes later, Jane had ordered Mary and Doris to report to Thelma for the day's flying assignments, with instructions to do their duty. Both had walked off, muttering darkly but obeying. Doris had yelled as she departed, "We'll be back as soon as we can!"

When Jane, Marcus, and Lawrence got to the canteen, only Mavis was present, wiping down the surfaces. As the door opened, she let them know, "Tea's off!" without bothering to turn around.

Marcus opened his mouth to complain, but Jane laid a hand on his shoulder, cautioning him, "Believe me, we're better off without."

Picking a table in the corner where they couldn't be overseen or heard, Jane was about to open the envelope when Lawrence held out his hand. Reluctantly, she handed it over.

"Shouldn't it be checked for fingerprints?" asked Marcus.

Lawrence hesitated briefly before deciding, "It's probably too late to get anything off. Chances are, it'll have been passed around the guardroom all night. If need be, I can have a look later."

With no further words, Lawrence slit the envelope open and out tumbled a single piece of paper. Marcus and Jane looked expectantly at Lawrence who, taking it between finger and thumb, turned it the other way up before laying it on the table between them so they could all see what was written. There were only a couple of lines, with no signature:

You will get a telephone call at midday. Persuade Betty to sign my document. Do NOT call the police.

Surprisingly, Marcus let out a bitter laugh. "My God, the arrogance of the man! He even wrote it in his own hand!"

Lawrence's head snapped around. "This was

written by your father?"

Marcus nodded. "No doubt of it."

Nobody spoke for a few minutes. Could there be some hidden message or clue that they needed to figure out? Marcus was the first to crack.

"Well, I can't see anything to do but go back to Betty's cottage and wait. I assume they'll be telephoning there."

Jane picked up the paper, matching how she'd seen Lawrence holding it, turning it this way and that before coming to the same conclusion. "How long are you on leave for?" she asked Marcus, who ran a hand through his hair.

"Officially, until two this afternoon," he answered, "but if you'll let me use a telephone, I'll call my boss, see if I can get a day's extension."

Jane got to her feet, immediately followed by the other two. "Do you think he'll agree?" she asked.

Marcus held the canteen door open for her. "I think so. He's rather close to his sister, so when he hears I need to know mine's safe, I'm pretty certain he'll understand."

They took the short walk to the ops hut, entering just as Thelma was sending the last group of pilots on their way.

"Jane!" Thelma said, surprised to see her. "What are you doing here? Shouldn't you be putting your feet up?"

Jane waved away her friend's protests. "Don't start. Can Marcus here use your phone?" she asked.

"No problem," Thelma agreed, getting out of her chair for him.

The two of them, with Lawrence in tow, went

outside so as to give Marcus some privacy.

"What's that?" Thelma asked, pointing at the envelope in Lawrence's hand.

"Note from the kidnappers," Lawrence said, somewhat off-handed. When Thelma's eyebrows nearly disappeared, he hastened to give her a few more details. "There're no clues to where she is. They're going to telephone Betty's cottage at midday today."

Thelma looked very disappointed. "That's it?"

Lawrence shrugged his shoulders. "Afraid so."

Before Thelma could ask anything further, Marcus joined them, announcing, "All sorted. You can put up with me until the second."

Jane flexed the fingers of her injured arm. "Come on, let's get back, before Thelma here chucks me out."

Waving goodbye to them, Thelma went back to work, only to be startled a few minutes later by the sound of a vehicle going past her hut at speed, accompanied by the tooting of a horn. She stuck her head out of the door in time to see Jane's Jeep, being driven by the lady herself, disappearing at a rate of knots toward the guardroom.

Going back to work, she muttered, "I hope they make it back in one piece."

****

Spot on midday, the telephone rang. By mutual agreement, Marcus picked it up, the idea being if, as they all believed, his parents were behind the kidnapping, then hearing their son's voice might help to throw them off. As expected, it did.

"Yes, of course it's me, Father," Marcus began, not noticing his free hand had begun to shake. Celia did and unbidden, she sidled up next to him and gripped his big hand in hers, tiny by comparison. Surprised at the unexpected touch, he looked down at his hand and then at the girl providing support. He squeezed her hand and smiled briefly down in thanks.

"Now, are you going to be sensible and let Betty go? No. Well, I had to ask, though I can't say I'm surprised." There followed a short pause whilst his father spoke, his voice too low for anyone but Marcus to hear. "Before you go any farther, I want to hear her voice. I want to hear for myself she's okay." Another pause followed before Marcus shook his head and Celia let out a small yip as he gripped her hand a little too tightly.

His father must have put the phone down, as Marcus put the handset to his chest and whispered, "Sorry," to Celia and looked across at Lawrence, who gave him the thumbs up to keep going. Hastily, he put the handset back to his ear.

"Put her on." The next thing, Marcus jerked the handset away from his ear and snarled, "That's not Betty. Put her on!" he demanded. All of a sudden, everyone heard a gruff yelp come out of the phone, and then Marcus was left staring at the handset.

Putting it down, he turned and faced his expectant audience. "I don't think she's there."

Chapter Thirty-Nine

"Lawrence? Good. You need to get back to the station. There's someone you need to speak to, and it can't wait."

Thelma put the telephone down and stared at the woman sitting across from her. It wasn't unusual for the station to get visitors. Often someone would be strolling by the perimeter, and they'd see nothing but female pilots milling around. They'd then sometimes turn up at the guardroom asking questions. Most heeded the friendly warning signs *Mind your own business,* or *This is a military facility. Please go about your business.* The woman before Thelma in the guardroom, eyeing the cup of tea she'd been given with suspicion, didn't fit into that category.

"Mrs. Darcie Palmer," Thelma read from the ID card she'd insisted the woman hand over to her.

"As I've already told you," the tiny woman stated from between clenched teeth, her feet twitching in irritation as they dangled off the end of her seat.

Thelma waved a hand to the guard commander, who'd taken it upon himself to stand beside the exit once he knew something strange was occurring. Together with the letter, the man knew something was going on, and though she would prefer not to have anyone else find out anything about what was happening with Betty, he'd insisted upon remaining.

Thelma was quite confident she could handle a woman who was not only at least twenty years older than she but at least a foot shorter, but to send him away would be to invite suspicion.

"So why are you here?"

The woman let out a sigh of irritation and crossed her arms. "As I've already told *him*"—she jerked her head in the direction of the guard commander, who rolled his eyes—"I'm not saying a thing until I speak to a policeman."

Thelma leant forward in her seat, narrowed her eyes, and locked her gaze upon this woman she'd already taken a rapid dislike to. "Then let me tell you something," she said in a voice low enough Darcie had to lean forward to hear her, so only the two of them would hear. "Betty is a very, very good friend of mine, and if something happens to her, the police will be the least of your worries."

The blood drained from the woman's face, but she stayed haughty and tight-lipped.

Thelma was just deciding if she could accidentally slap the smug expression from her face when the door flew open and Lawrence appeared. Evidently he'd run the whole way there, as he was out of breath.

"Sorry I didn't get here sooner," he gasped out. "I phoned for Terry to meet us here. He'll be along as soon as he can."

Thelma got up from her seat, allowing Lawrence to take her place. He smiled in thanks.

"I gather you would only talk to the police," he began, accepting the ID card from Thelma, who took up a position a little way behind the policeman. "I am Detective Inspector Lawrence. You are"—he made a small show of consulting the card again—"Mrs. Darcie Palmer."

"Betty's mother," she said, raising her head.

"Hmph," Thelma snorted in disdain.

"If you please," Lawrence said over his shoulder before asking the guard commander to wait outside. Once they were alone, Lawrence came straight to the point. "What's so important that you would only speak to me?"

"I won't say a word in front of her," Mrs. Palmer spat out, her true character bursting out.

"Mrs. Palmer," Lawrence said, after taking a few deep, steadying breaths. "I suggest you rein in your temper. You are a strong suspect in the kidnap of your *daughter*." His emphasis was rewarded by the woman snapping back an undoubted retort. "Now, tell me why you brought me here, or I shall, at the very least, lock you up for wasting police time."

Thelma came and leant on Lawrence's shoulder, something he did his best to ignore.

Someone knocked at the door, and before anyone could say anything, in came the willowy frame of Sergeant Terry Banks, who took in the situation at a glance and took up his station beside the door.

"Mrs. Palmer?" Lawrence prodded.

Seeing she had no other choice, she informed them, "I can lead you to Betty, if you agree to set no charges against me."

"Not a chance!" Thelma couldn't stop her mouth from saying.

"First Officer, please keep quiet," Lawrence told her, knowing he'd be in trouble with his girlfriend later for ordering Thelma around. However, the suspect before them didn't need to be aware of that. "No deal," he informed Mrs. Palmer. "You've just admitted to being party to the kidnapping, so you are in no position to be making demands, nor trying to make deals. If you cooperate, and your information proves correct, well, then I'll see what I can do."

Lawrence said no more, giving Mrs. Palmer time to think things over, to make up her mind. After a few minutes, her head dropped and she began to speak.

"We own or, used to own, a small cottage not far from here in the village of Lyndhurst. That's where we—they—are keeping her."

Lawrence passed her a paper and pen. "Write down the address."

"You sure they'll still be there?" Terry asked from the doorway.

"I'd have moved somewhere else as soon as you ran away, if I were them," Thelma couldn't keep from putting in.

"A very good point," Lawrence agreed, earning himself a squeeze on his shoulder from Thelma.

As she wrote, Mrs. Palmer didn't stop, but she did let out a bitter laugh. "I think you give George too much credit." She pushed the paper back to the policeman. "No, it won't have crossed his mind to move her to anywhere else."

Lawrence waved his sergeant over and handed him the address. "Do you know where this is?"

Terry looked at the paper and nodded. "I do. It's only about thirty-odd minutes from here."

"Right." Lawrence got to his feet. "Terry, call in the guard commander, and then lock Mrs. Palmer in one of these cells for now. As acting Commander, First

Officer, with your permission?"

At those words, the little woman hopped off her seat and opened her mouth. "I object! I am not a common criminal! Do you have any idea who my husband is?"

Thelma burst out laughing, and she could see it was only by remembering he was a policeman that Lawrence refrained from joining her. The naïve woman had obviously reverted to default behavior when confronted with a situation not to her liking.

Sergeant Banks placed a hand on the woman's shoulder as the guard commander entered the room. "Would you open a cell for me, please?" Terry asked.

Just before the cell door was closed, Thelma asked the question which had been bothering her. She could no longer keep it in. "Mrs. Palmer, if your husband is cornered, would he…hurt Betty?"

Turning, Darcie answered, "I hope not."

****

Thelma was escorting the two policemen out of the guard room when she became aware of three people running toward the station. Well, three people and a dog, to be precise. "Ruth?" she said under her breath, or so she thought.

Lawrence came and stood beside her, whilst Terry got in the car and started it up. "What do you think they want?"

They all got a clue as the group neared. Ruth was accompanied not only by the station's unofficial mascot, Bobby, the spaniel, but by two men in the khaki uniform of the Home Guard. Not only that, but both Walter and Sergeant Matthew Green, Ruth's new boyfriend, were toting rifles on their backs.

"We thought we could be of help," Mathew announced as they skidded to a halt.

"We came prepared," Walter announced, taking his rifle off his back.

"So I see," Lawrence answered and turned his attention to Ruth. "Would you care to tell me exactly how you knew we were here, aunty dear?"

Ruth directed her gaze over his shoulder, where Thelma was doing her best to merge into the background, from whence she hesitantly said, "Well, er, you know I asked you two to hold on whilst I went back into the guardroom?" The two policemen both nodded, though neither had an expression of appreciation on their faces. "I may have telephoned Ruth and told her what had happened."

"And this?" Terry waved his hands at the rifles.

Walter and Matthew both exchanged glances and then shrugged as Walter told them, "We thought some firepower could persuade them to give up without a fight."

Lawrence looked at his number two. "Did you think to sign out a revolver?" Terry shook his head, and Lawrence twitched aside his coat. "Me either."

"It's not a bad idea, boss," Terry reluctantly suggested.

Knowing time was of the essence, Lawrence came to a decision. "Right, you two. Listen, and listen closely. Until this is over, you are under both my command and Terry's as my second in command. That means you will not do anything unless we tell you. You will certainly not open fire unless we command you to."

The two Home Guards both exchanged looks before nodding in agreement.

"Good. Now get into the car."

"Do you want to take Bobby along?" Ruth asked quickly, looking down at where Bobby sat on her feet to keep warm.

Lawrence smiled. "A nice thought, but no thanks."

Glancing to where Thelma stood, Lawrence blew her a kiss, and then they were gone. They didn't get very far, as Terry slammed on the brakes when they came to the turning which led along the riverbank. "Do you see what I see?"

Shaking his head in disbelief, Lawrence got out of the car, then popped part way back in to say, "Everyone stay where you are. This won't take long," before slamming the door shut. A few paces on, he stopped beside the driver of the vehicle blocking their path. "And what do you think you're doing?"

"Coming along as backup," Jane declared seriously.

Lawrence shook his head again, not believing what he was seeing. Sitting next to Jane in her Jeep was Celia, who had her hand resting on the gear lever. Behind them, shivering yet with a determined expression upon her face, sat Penny.

With every minute possibly vital, Lawrence decided he couldn't waste any more time. "Jane, I know your heart's in the right place, but please, all of you, go home. You shouldn't be out at all, Penny. You know what Grace said about getting an infection."

"She gave me some penicillin," Penny protested. "I'll be all right."

"And we'll take care of each other," Jane put in.

Lawrence ticked off on his fingers, "One, that's a new drug, so don't put all your trust in it. Two, by the

367

way you're cradling your arm, Jane, I'd say you've already over-strained it when you drove this contraption back from the base. And three, what do you two think you're doing involving a youngster like Celia in such a half-baked scheme?"

"I'm fourteen!" Celia protested.

"My point exactly." Lawrence only just stopped himself from snapping. "Now, please, back up a little. We have to get going."

With a sigh, Jane put the Jeep into reverse, unable to hide a wince of pain from Lawrence's searching gaze.

****

Shivering, Betty pulled the tarpaulin tighter around her shoulders and, once again, cursed her luck. She'd spent most of the night and small hours flitting from hiding place to hiding place, Mr. Palmer and the big thug never seeming more than a few steps behind. Knowing she'd soon be caught if she tried to make a run down the road, because of the noise her shoes would make, she'd thought about going through the woods which surrounded the village, but that would have been a surefire way to turn an ankle, and then she'd really be helpless. She hadn't even managed to find a bicycle.

Funny how things turn out, she mused, trying to put her leg at a more comfortable angle. In the act of turning back when she found herself on the edge of the forest, she'd tripped over the handle of a garden roller. Unable to support her own weight on the now-injured foot, she'd lain on the freezing cold grass for some anxious minutes, barely daring to breathe, expecting to be pounced upon at any minute by her would-be captors. Eventually, she'd crawled down the garden to find the back door of the cottage where she'd landed was locked up. Deciding not to risk knocking on the door or windows, she'd tried a shed which had sight of the road, and had some luck.

Now, first light had come and was long gone, and her ankle had blown up like a balloon. Betty didn't know if she'd broken it or if it was a very bad sprain, she didn't even know if it would support her weight, though she knew the time would come when she'd find out. At regular-ish intervals, she risked peeking out of the shed, but she saw no one, neither friend nor foe. The cottage appeared to be deserted.

Her watch was broken, and she had no idea what the time could be. She was cold, hungry, and in pain, with no means of escape. All she could do was wait and hope she was found by friends first.

Chapter Forty

"Have they gone?" Penny asked, standing up in the back of the Jeep.

Celia stood on top of the church wall and nodded, then jumped down and trotted across to join the other two. "I reckon they've got about two minutes lead on us now," she told Jane and Penny as she made to hop back into the passenger seat of the Jeep.

Jane held out her arm to stop her.

"Hey! What's the game?"

"I'm sorry, but Lawrence is right about one thing. You're too young."

Too young or not, Celia had her big sister's stubborn streak and planted herself plum in front of the Jeep and crossed her arms. "Really? Well, he's also right about something else. Neither of you two are fit enough to drive this thing." As Jane opened her mouth to protest, Celia cut her off. "Oh, no, you don't! We all saw you wince just now when you went to put it in gear, and that's nothing compared to what you were like when you got back to Betty's after driving back from the base. That's five minutes, tops. No, there's no way you'll be able to follow them, and don't even think of asking Penny to take the wheel!"

Jane exchanged glances with Penny before folding her arms across the steering wheel. "I wasn't going to. In fact, so long as Penny doesn't object, I was going to ask you to take the wheel."

Celia's head flicked toward her sister, who after a moment's hesitation said, "It's not ideal, but we can't just stay at home and wait. I trust you, sis. Now, what do you say?"

Not needing a second asking, Celia came around to the driver's side of the Jeep. "You'd better shift over, then."

****

It seemed both Mr. Palmer and Big John had given up all pretense of stealth, as for the last ten minutes, Betty had heard both their voices yelling out her name. She hadn't heard any shooting, so that was something, though from her position hunkered down in the shed she couldn't see what was actually going on outside. Whichever way she looked at it, she was in a sticky situation.

"Betty! Where are you?"

There they were again, but were they nearer or farther away? Hiding in the shed under the tarpaulin didn't make it easy to tell.

"Betty Palmer!"

That one could have been farther away, she thought. Moving her head out from under cover a little, she cocked an ear and waited. A few minutes later came another yell.

"Palmer!"

No doubt about it. That one was farther away. "Well, girl," she muttered to herself, "let's see how your luck holds out."

Flinging the tarpaulin all the way off, she put her ear to the door of her shed, and when she was certain she couldn't hear anything, she slowly lowered the latch and pushed the door open an inch, just enough to put an eye to. Slightly cursing herself for having picked a shed with no window to it, Betty pushed the door open just wide enough to allow her to leave. She pushed the door closed and, as quickly as she could, flattened herself against the cottage's wall. Catching her breath and wincing in pain, she tentatively flexed her ankle and had to bite her lip to stop from yelping in pain. Glancing around, she spotted a broom leaning against the wall a few feet away, next to a door she hadn't found last night.

Her fingers nearly frozen, she pulled herself along the wall, reached out for the broom, turned it upside down, and tucked the bristly head under her arm. Looking up and around to check neither of her kidnappers had seen her, she tested her weight. Fortunately, the broom held her weight, and she now had a makeshift crutch. Looking at the door, she reached out with her free hand and turned the handle. It stayed locked. Risking one knock, she listened closely but could hear no sound of any movement inside. Just her luck, she mused, to pick a place probably locked up for the war.

No rest for the wicked, she decided. Carefully, she began to move toward the road, trying to keep as much as possible to what little cover the eaves of the cottage provided. Coming to the end of the building, she looked to her right and couldn't see any movement at all. Was the entire village deserted? Then she looked around the wall to her left and saw something that made her heart beat faster.

Coming down the road was a car she thought she recognized. As it got level to her hiding place, her heart stopped. In the front seat was none other than Lawrence, and she was certain his number two—Terry Banks—was driving. Unfortunately, neither was looking her way. Neither were the two uniformed men they had in the rear. She'd just made up her mind to hobble out as best she could when she heard a yell.

"Palmer! We're coming for you!"

Her body acted before her mind, and she shrank back down onto her haunches, hoping they hadn't actually seen her. As she dipped down, she was dismayed to see that Lawrence's car didn't stop—they hadn't seen her. Was that yell closer than the last? She was cold, hungry, and in pain, and she could no longer tell. Betty never knew if her mind had been affected by the cold, as her body seemed to take control over her good sense. Before she knew it, she was hobbling out of the meager cover provided by the cottage.

Semi-stepping and hopping, she found herself in the middle of the lane and, balancing as best she could on one foot, she started to wave the broom in the air above her head, and her voice shouted out, "Lawrence! Lawrence, stop!"

The police car kept going, and that was when Betty realized the likely reason she'd not found any help was that she was next to a cottage in a cul-de-sac which contained only four cottages—including the one she'd been held in. Unfortunately, one person had seen and heard her and was making rapid tracks in her direction from across the road.

"Oh, hell," Betty swore. Looking swiftly around, she could see no obvious place to hide, so setting her jaw, she took a firm grip on the broom handle and prepared to see how many swipes she could get in.

"There you are!" he spat out, fire dancing in his little piggy eyes as he advanced upon her.

If Betty had ever harbored any hope of some parental connection, then his expression dashed any last expectations. "Come on, then!" she yelled, with more bravado than she really felt, and raised her broom. "I'll bash you on the head and then sweep your remains into the gutter!"

George Palmer stopped a little out of her reach. "Oh, really? Do you actually think I'd be stupid enough to allow you to try?" He reached a hand into his inside pocket and, much to Betty's surprise, brought out a revolver. "Put your hands up and come over here."

In spite of the cold sweat running down her back, Betty didn't obey, though she did tuck the broom back under her arm, turning it back into a crutch. "Can we compromise?" she asked, hoping he'd be stupid enough to allow her to keep her only weapon.

Somewhat to her surprise, he didn't object. With a wave of his hand, he beckoned her forward and, deliberately exaggerating her lack of mobility—not by much, though—she slowly moved toward him. What sounded like an engine being gunned and then a gearbox loudly crunching echoed and, keeping her head looking straight at her captor, she twitched her eyes around, trying to see the source. Could Lawrence be coming back?

As she stopped before him, she had to fight hard to keep the surprise she felt from showing on her face. Coming up the lane that led into the cul-de-sac was a Jeep. Even from her position, roughly a couple of hundred yards away, she could recognize its three occupants. Momentarily, she was caught between shouting for help and keeping quiet and protecting her brave but foolish friends. The Jeep was getting nearer and, despite the racket it made on the road, George Palmer still hadn't looked around.

At a particularly loud crunch, he finally turned. Betty took her chance and, without second guessing herself, swung her crutch above her head and brought it down toward his head. Some sixth sense must have warned him, as at the last second, he began to move, though not quite in time. The broom head dealt him a glancing blow. Not troubling to check if he was knocked out or merely stunned, she tucked her makeshift crutch back under her armpit and hobbled toward the lane and the approaching Jeep.

A beep of its horn told her the Jeep's occupants had seen her, and the driver, she was very relieved to see, was altering its course toward her. It seemed to be using a fuel based on kangaroos, judging by the way it appeared to jump down the lane. Mind you, as it came to a halt, the reason was perhaps obvious—young Celia was driving!

"Betty!" all three occupants shouted at the same time, with Celia hopping out of the driving seat and only just stopping herself from throwing her arms around her. Instead, she put her shoulder under Betty's other arm and helped her toward the Jeep, while Jane got out to give her a helping hand.

All of a sudden, Penny yelled, "Hurry!"

Glancing behind, she saw George Palmer helped to his feet by his henchman. When both straightened up, everyone froze—both men had revolvers out.

"Are you in?" Celia asked, as Betty swung her legs into the Jeep.

Throwing the gears into reverse, Celia stalled it. Before them, the two kidnappers were breaking into a run.

"Hurry!" Penny urged Celia to restart the Jeep.

"Stop yelling at me!" Celia yelled.

"I'm not yelling!" Penny yelled back.

The two villains were now only a few paces away, and as Celia couldn't seem to get the Jeep started, Betty could see no other alternative but to surrender. Things would be infinitely worse now they had other hostages. However, as she was about to open her mouth to tell them so, she could quite clearly see the two men stop dead in their tracks.

From behind the Jeep came the sound of someone slamming a bolt home on a rifle. Turning, Betty went wide-eyed in disbelief. Surely these situations happened only in movies! Standing no more than ten feet behind the Jeep were two men in full Home Guard battle dress, and both had rifles aimed at her two would-be kidnappers.

"Put down the guns!" Sergeant Matthew Green shouted. Next to him, Walter held a steady aim as well. "Now!"

Lawrence's car pulled up behind the two in a squeal of tires, and both the Inspector himself and Terry Banks got out. "I'd do as he says, if I were you, Palmer," Lawrence calmly and clearly said.

Both Walter and Matthew moved a step toward them, still keeping their rifles menacingly pointed at their quarry.

"Put the guns down," Walter said and added, "You won't get another warning."

George Palmer's shoulders dropped, and as

ordered, he stooped and laid his revolver on the ground, Big John following suit a moment later.

Within a few hectic minutes, both were knelt on the road, their hands cuffed behind their backs, with the Home Guard standing over them. Lawrence came up to the Jeep, his face a mixture of relief and annoyance.

"Betty!" He leant in and gave her a quick hug and a kiss on the cheek. "I'm so pleased to find you safe. Are you hurt at all?"

"Just my ankle," Betty informed him, pointing to the appendage. "Probably a sprain."

"Get it looked at, please." He turned his attention to Jane, Celia, and Penny. "Now, I'm going to find a phone to get these two miscreants taken into Portsmouth. As for you lot, get Betty to the hospital and then yourselves back home. I'll be around later to have words with you."

****

"What's the time?" Betty managed to ask as Celia kangarooed down the road toward Hamble.

"Coming up on four o'clock," Penny informed her, making a grab for the side of the Jeep as Celia managed to find yet another pothole.

"Remind me to get another watch," Betty muttered. "I could have sworn it wasn't much past one. Suppose I must have slept more than I thought last night. Look…" She turned to Celia. "To hell with the hospital. Take me home. I'll ask Grace to take a look at my ankle when she comes to look at Penny's shoulder and Jane's arm. I'll say this," Betty announced as she nearly flew out of her seat. "I wouldn't want to be in either of your shoes when our nurse gets hold of you two."

Chapter Forty-One

"You could have waited for us," Doris moaned for what must have been the fifth or sixth time that morning.

"Put a sock in it!" Mary said, throwing a sock at her from the clothes horse to illustrate her point.

"Yes," Betty agreed from where she sat enjoying a very welcome cup of tea with her foot, tightly wrapped, on a kitchen chair. "The next time I'm kidnapped, I'll make certain to wait for rescue until I'm sure you can be involved. Satisfied?"

"Very." Doris beamed, leaning over and kissing Betty on the top of the head before removing the sock from her shoulder.

Nurse Grace put down her finished tea and got to her feet. "Can I trust you to stay off that foot for a week?"

Jane entered at that point and took the seat next to Betty. She took her friend's hand in hers and gave it a squeeze before addressing the kindly nurse. "We'll both take it easy for a week." Grace raised a questioning eyebrow. "Cross my heart," she said, "we both will, this time. I promise neither of us will move from this house until that time is over, and then, we are both on light duties. Sorry, Betty," Jane said. "I know you've only just gone back on flying duties, but there's no way I'm letting you fly again until that sprained ankle is better."

"I know," Betty said, unable to keep the disappointment from her voice.

"Good," Grace said, satisfied. "Now, Jane, any problems with that cast?"

Jane held out her arm for the nurse to take a look. "No harm. Though we barely survived Celia's driving."

"Did I hear my name?" the young girl said, entering the room clad in her best dress that New Year's Day morning.

"I don't think my Jeep will ever be the same again," Jane informed Celia.

"Ha! Very funny."

"No harm done there," Grace informed Jane. "You and Penny are very lucky, you know. For two smart women, you were pretty stupid yesterday." Everyone's jaws dropped at hearing the nurse's harsh words, but as they were well meant, her two present patients simply nodded their agreement.

Betty, however, didn't. "I think you should allow that they may have helped save my life yesterday, Grace."

"I know that," she agreed, before slumping into a free seat. "I was simply worried. Forgive me if I spoke out of line."

Betty held out a hand. "Nothing to forgive. You'll stay for the day? If you're not on duty or have other arrangements, that is?"

"I'd be delighted," Grace said quickly, her face lighting up. "I've the rest of the day free." She looked down at her dress. "I'm not in my finest, though, I'm afraid."

"Nonsense," Doris told her, getting to her feet to show she was in slacks and a blouse. "I didn't feel like dressing up either."

The kitchen door opened, drawing everyone's eyes and admitting Penny, who gave a slight shake of the head, to which Mary replied, "Damn," causing everyone's head to turn toward her.

Betty's eyes darted between the two of them. "Something we should know?"

Mary shrugged her shoulders, and Penny told her, "Go on."

"We were hoping to have a kind of welcome home present for you," Mary began. "Penny's just telephoned Polebrook and spoken to your Major Fredericks." Betty's leg slipped off the chair as she leant forward in interest. "We were hoping he'd be free to come over today. He sends his deepest regrets and best wishes for the New Year, but he's on duty today." Betty couldn't hide her disappointment.

"I'm sorry," Penny assured her friend, giving her an awkward one-armed hug.

A rap at the door interrupted the ensuing silence, and Celia went to answer, coming back with Ruth, Walter, and Lawrence. Both Doris and Mary got up to greet their men.

"Have you seen the time?" Doris smacked Walter lightly on the arm.

Lawrence, his arm around Mary's waist, told her, "Blame me for that. I had him down at the station first thing, giving a statement. The same with Matthew. Sorry, Ruth," he directed over his shoulder. "He said he'd be along later, once he's had the chance to clean up."

"What about me?" Betty asked. "Surely you need my statement too?"

"Of course I do," Lawrence said, pressing a hand to her shoulder. "But I think that's enough work for today. It won't do those three any harm to stew in the cells for a day. They've a lot to think over…"

"Including being responsible for murdering their daughter, my sister," Betty couldn't help but mutter, bitterness lacing her voice.

The back door opened to admit Marcus, in his hands the rabbit he'd gone out to slaughter. "And my sister," he said, but then added, "Let Lawrence do his job, sister. From what I understand, he knows exactly what happened to Eleanor."

Perhaps it was hearing her brother call her *sister*, but Betty looked across and smiled, seeming to relax a little. "Thank you for getting dinner, Marcus. I had no idea you knew how to do that."

Marcus laid the rabbit on the chopping board on the table. "I picked up a few things whilst I was in France," he said, a little reluctantly, but added no further details, and from the way he immediately began to gut and clean the animal, eyes down and fixed upon his work, no one asked him to elaborate.

"Whilst I have you all here," Lawrence said, breaking the silence, "I still have to tell you three"—he pointed at Jane, Penny, and Celia—"off for acting so stupidly yesterday. I'm only going to say this once, as everything worked out for the best. If I ever have to ask any of you"—his eyes made certain to include Mary and Betty in his statement—"to do as I say in a police matter again, you *must* obey. We got lucky yesterday. I hope you agree?"

Lawrence waited until he got an agreeing nod from all the women present before he let out a small chuckle.

"I'm not sure how much faith I should put in you, knowing you all as I do, but I guess I've no choice but to take you at your word."

"So you should," Mary scolded him before grabbing her boyfriend's hand and dragging him toward the lounge.

"Tell me about it," Marcus exclaimed. "I'm still not sure I've forgiven this lot for barricading me in the toilet so they could hare off to rescue this one!"

Betty stifled a laugh before heaving herself to her feet. "Come on, the Saturday Morning Prom's about to begin, and that wireless seems to need longer and longer to warm up these days."

Penny tapped Grace on the shoulder as the nurse seemed frozen to the spot. When she didn't move, Penny tried again. "Are you joining us?"

Grace turned her head back and forth between Penny and where Marcus had now started dividing the rabbit into chunks, eventually turning back to the young pilot officer and holding out a hand. "I'm Grace Baxter."

Quickly noting how the young man hurried to wash his hands, Penny decided her presence wasn't required and joined everyone else in the lounge. Upon entering, it looked like she was in the middle of a Mexican stand-off. On one side of the lounge, Doris was positioned before the windows with her hands upon her hips, and right by the door, so Penny had to awkwardly sidle around him, was Walter.

"What've I walked into?" Penny asked.

"Somebody's dragging their heels," Ruth informed her, not very helpfully.

"I am not dragging my heels," Doris told her from

between gritted teeth.

"I beg to differ," Walter put in.

"We're always so busy!" Doris stated, and Penny saw what was happening.

Moving to the American, she took her by the elbow. "Give us a few minutes, please." She took her through the kitchen, where Grace and Marcus sat at the table, holding hands and looking like they'd known each other for years, and out into the garden.

"Are you mad? It's bloody freezing out here!"

Unable to hold her by both shoulders, Penny put as much force into her hand as possible. "You've no need to be afraid, you know."

"I'm not afraid," Doris pouted.

"Yes, you are," Penny shot back, but gently. "Walter's not going anywhere, you know. He can't be called up, so he can't leave you."

With some difficulty, Doris turned her back on her friend, but Penny merely snuggled up against her friend's back. "I know," Doris finally answered.

"So what's the problem then? Set a date and marry the man."

"What if I die?" Doris cried out.

Slowly, Penny nodded her head. Now she understood. Unhitching herself from her friend, Penny stepped around so she could see Doris's face when she spoke to her. "Is that what's worrying you?"

Doris nodded, wiping her eyes.

"Look, I can't promise that won't happen. You know that. No one can. But isn't that the point of life? Taking a risk? I don't think Donald would want you to live your life alone, would he?"

Dropping her head onto Penny's shoulder, causing

her to wince in pain, Doris mumbled something which could have been taken for a no, and after a few moments, she raised her head and wiped her eyes dry. "You're right, he wouldn't." She sniffed loudly before asking, "What about you?"

"Me?" Penny pretended not to know what her friend meant.

"Tom."

Penny sighed. "We've...talked."

"Since you told him you needed time to think?"

"Maybe not since then." Penny shrugged.

"Are you going to *really* talk?" Doris persisted.

Penny didn't answer straight away, leading Doris to prod her gently in the ribs. "Probably, but not yet."

"Don't throw everything away," Doris pleaded. "Take your own advice and talk to him."

"Come here," Penny said, and Doris wrapped her arms around her, being a little more careful of Penny's wound this time. "When did you become so wise?"

"I think that's a lot to do with you, my best friend." Doris smiled.

"Flatterer. Now, get back in there and set a bloody date," Penny ordered her. "We could all do with a good knees up!"

"What about you?" Doris asked, taking a step back.

Penny looked up at the cloudy sky. "Leave me for a few minutes. I need to think.

With a glance back at her friend, Doris went inside, did her best to ignore Marcus and Grace in an embrace, and proceeded into the lounge. Going across to where Walter was standing with his back to the door, staring out the window, she wrapped her arms around him and told him, so everyone could hear, "February the 14th.

I'll marry you on St. Valentine's Day."

****

After a wonderful dinner of rabbit and fresh vegetables, everyone was sprawled around Betty's lounge either in whatever seat was available or squatted on the floor in whatever spot they could find. Music was playing on the wireless, and there was an atmosphere of sublime happiness pervading the room. Bobby had finally finished chasing his dish around the floor and was lying on his back, having his rather distended stomach rubbed by Lawrence and Mary.

Taking up the conversation where it had left off from the dinner table, Thelma asked Betty, "So you're giving away all of Eleanor's money?"

Marcus looked across, tearing his eyes away from Grace for the first time, it seemed, since they'd met. "So that's what you were doing at the solicitor's. You needed their help to what, make all the arrangements?"

Betty nodded. "Nearly all, anyway. I've kept a certain amount, put it into War Bonds. What?" she asked. "We've got to support the war effort, and it's as good a use for the money as anything."

"And the rest?" Marcus asked.

When she replied, Betty made sure she caught Penny's eye. "The majority has gone to various charities which help war orphans. There's going to be a lot in need of a good home by the time all this is over, don't you agree?"

After much swallowing, Penny replied exactly as Betty hoped. "There certainly will be. I'm so very proud of you, Betty."

"And what were you doing at the solicitor's, Marcus?" Betty asked. "You never did tell me."

"Making a will," he answered after some hesitation. "You may have noticed, I'm in a dangerous occupation."

This admission brought the conversation to an awkward halt before Walter broke the silence by asking Betty, "What about your…Mr. and Mrs. Palmer? Do you want to see them again?"

Marcus came and sat down on the floor beside his sister and took the hand she dangled down.

Betty looked slowly around the room before shaking her head and telling everyone, "This is my family—everyone in this room is my family, in one way or another. We've gone through more together than most people I know, and with the way things seem to happen around us, I can't see that changing. Marcus," she said, looking down at her brother, "you'll always have a home here, whenever you need it."

"Though it may be a sofa," Mary put in, "as I, for one, am not giving up my nice comfy bed."

A word about the author...

Mick spent fifteen-odd years roaming around the world, courtesy of HM Queen Elizabeth II—gawd bless her—before becoming a civilian and realizing what working for a living really was.

He loves traveling, and the music of the Beach Boys, Queen, Muse, and Bon Jovi. Books play a large part in his life, not only writing, but also reading and reviewing, as well as supporting his many author friends.

He's the proud keeper of two Romanian Were-Cats bent on world domination, and enjoys the theatre and humoring his Manchester United-supporting wife. Finally, and most importantly, Mick is a full member of the Romantic Novelists Association. *I'll be Home for Christmas* will be his third novel with The Wild Rose Press.

~*~

Other books by M. W. Arnold
from The Wild Rose Press, Inc.

A Wing and a Prayer
Wild Blue Yonder

CPSIA information can be obtained
at www.ICGtesting.com
Printed in the USA
BVHW041046151021
619016BV00012B/207

9 781509 238781